1/26/2010

To Melly, my favorite niece

FISHSLICE

FISHSLICE

BY

JEREMY HANCOCK

Published by Jeremy Hancock

ISBN 978-0-9813136-0-3

Publisher's note:

This is a work of fiction. Names, characters, places and incidents either are the product of the author's imagination or are used fictitiously and any resemblance to actual persons, living or dead, business establishments, events or locales is entirely coincidental.

To Madam, my love, my wife, my best friend
thank you for making my life complete.

Edited by Jacky Spiers.
Thanks Skin but you still owe me
more that you can ever repay.

ACKNOWLEDGEMENTS.

Nine for all of her help and typing.

Contents

1

The Meteor.

The beginning of the end.

Joseph lay back on the sleeping bag in the golden yellow light of the setting sun. He looked over at his wife admiring the beauty of her naked body lying in the gentle sunlight, she was, to him, the most beautiful thing he had ever seen. They had met a little over a year ago when he had had to rescue her after she had broken her leg while climbing in the park; he was and still is a park ranger. They had been married just yesterday, a white wedding, held in the grounds of the hotel up in the mountains, it had been a small wedding with both of their immediate families present. After the festivities were over he and his new wife, had left for their honeymoon, a camping trip up through the mountains. They had made camp here on the bluff overlooking the magnificent view that was now spread out before them. The surrounding mountains cast ever elongating shadows across the valley making it seem like the slopes below were moving ever so gently as the sun went down.

The breeze caressed his nakedness; he ran his hands over his wife's soft skin, so warm and smooth and kissed her gently on her firm white stomach. She turned and looked at him, thinking to herself how happy she was. She responded to his kiss wanting once again to make love out here in the open with the gentle breeze and the smell of fresh pine trees wafting about them. She reached up and pulled him close and felt his immediate response wanting to become one with her.

It was sometime later that they rolled apart weary and warm from their lovemaking, the breeze making them feel pleasantly chilled as it cooled them. They lay on their backs staring across the valley watching the sun as it disappeared behind the mountaintops and darkness settled. His wife moved closer to him and snuggled in and whispered in his ear "I love you so much, this is a wonderful honeymoon, thank you".

As she was finishing speaking they both noticed a small bright light shooting across the sky. At first it was difficult to gauge how far away it was. As their eyes focused on it they realized that it was descending, it was swooping down and coming up the valley below them. It was very small but very bright and as it passed below them they heard a high pitched whine and could feel the air move on their skins as it disappeared up into the gorge and on into the mountains, they heard the faint echo as it made contact with the forest. Little did they realize they had just witnessed the very beginning of the end.

The only witness to the meteor landing was a lonely skunk standing on a rock not far away from the railway bridge that crossed the valley at its narrowest point. The meteor hissed through a pile of dirt and then slammed into the cement abutment which held up one of the main supports for the old railway bridge on the west side of the valley. The disinterested skunk cleaned its fur, trying to get the last bit of warmth out of the rock, it would be cold soon enough. The meteor's momentum drove the tiny particle deep into the cement and cracks appeared like a spider's web around the entrance point. As it entered and made its way into the cement of the bridge abutment the blackened outer hull shattered and a minuscule white crystal was imbedded into the cement.

The skunk was not far wrong, just five weeks later an icy blast came down from the north, it started pouring with rain, swelling the stream that ran down the valley and saturating the land. The rain ran down the bridge abutment and into the cracks made by the meteor filling them with water and that night the temperature dropped. The rain turned to ice and the world took on the look of a crystal wonderland. Everything was covered, it was a beautiful sight as the sun came up, everything sparkled and glistened and when the wind blew it made the sounds of tingling bells as little pieces of ice tapped against each other and broke off and fell in clear crystals onto the frozen ground. The water that had entered the cracks in the cement froze forcing them open. The crystal had combined with the cement around it taking away all the binding properties that held the cement together. Now, where there had once been only one small crystal, there was a large cavity filled with identical white crystals. Each new crystal combined itself with more of the cement transforming it into even more crystals, which, in their turn, destroyed or combined with more of the cement abutment. The process would be a never ending one until there was no more cement for the crystals to use. Very slowly the huge cement abutment was losing its tensile strength.

Some months later James, an engineer for the railway that ran over the mountains, was really pleased to feel the warmth of the sun as he checked over the controls of his train. It had been a good winter; the snow had come and stayed in the mountains and most of the valleys. He always enjoyed the snow, he was a skier, not one of those that went up in helicopters and skied the fresh powder but he enjoyed going to the ski hills on weekends when he was not working. There had only been one or two days when the mountain passes had been blocked and the trains were unable to run, the blockages had been cleared quickly and now the snow had melted and the world had dried out. He was back into his summer uniform and was looking forward to the run across the mountains to his hometown, he had been driving the trains on this run for twenty seven years and he knew it like the back of his hand. He did not have long to go before he could retire and the thought gave him mixed feelings. He would miss the solitary trips up through the mountains across the valleys overlooking some of the most beautiful countryside in the United States.

Today was no different than any other day, he checked over his train, his passengers were aboard and their luggage was put away, he blew his whistle as he left the station. Humming to himself as the train picked up speed and went up through the mountains, he always wondered what some of the passengers must be thinking as they passed through these magnificent vistas for the first time and looked across the vast land that spread out before them. It was about four hours later that the train swung down around the bend and went across the Humming Bridge, so called because in the winter and fall the air was sucked down into the valley below and sometimes a slight humming could be heard as it passed through the structures of the bridge. As the train thundered across the bridge James didn't feel the very slight tremor as the last carriage crossed back onto the mountainside and continued on its way. Down below the vibrations of the train had caused a huge chunk of one of the cement abutments to fall away releasing a cloud of white crystals, so light that they were wafted up in the air catching the sun and blown gently down the hill settling on anything that they touched.

The brown squirrel had looked up as the train went overhead used to the noises the metal monster made as it flew through the mountains, it was no longer alarmed. But when a great chunk of the cement fell down with a crash the squirrel turned and ran a few feet and then stopped. Looking around he was annoyed to find he was covered in a white powder. This scared him even more so he ran across the valley floor and leapt onto the second cement bridge support where he shook himself vigorously to get rid of the powder, which flew off in all directions. The crystals immediately began combining with the cement.

The squirrel climbed up and sat on the rails above the bridge licking and cleaning himself. The powder was so light that even as he tried to clean himself it sank deeper into his spring coat. After a short while he gave up trying and went on his way, everywhere he ran he left little crystals in his wake. Eventually he came to the logging road that ran along the top of the valley and then down a series of very steep hills and curves into the town below, he sat on the edge of the roadway enjoying the warmth of the sun and the heat of the road surface. He heard the sound of the logging truck coming down from the forest above and ran towards the woods.

The driver of the truck had on his earphones and was singing wildly out the open window, he did not even see the little bundle of fur that ran across the road in front of him. The truck was so heavy, laden with huge tree trunks that he did not even feel the crunch as all seven wheels on the right side of the vehicle ran over the squirrel. The white powder from the squirrel's fur blew up onto the underside of the truck and was deposited with bits and pieces of the dead squirrel into the tires, mudguards and hubs of the truck, the truck continued on down the steep slopes and with each bump a few crystals fell off the underside onto the road.

The Wayward restaurant had been serving the people of the village for over twenty years, it had started off as a small family diner but when they started logging the mountains above it had expanded to accommodate all of the workers and truckers that teemed through the now affluent village. A number of years ago the owners had expanded the parking lot so that they could accommodate not only the truckers but also the large number of tourists that came through the village from early spring to late fall. Today the restaurant was quite busy; there were twenty-five cars and eight trucks in the parking lot. The previous winter had taken its toll on the surface of the parking lot; there were numerous potholes that needed to be filled. The logging truck came down from the mountain and turned into the narrow entrance to the parking lot bouncing on the potholes and with each bump crystals mixed with little bits of squirrel dropped off and crystal powder flew into the air settling on the surface of the lot. As the truck pulled around the building it passed the new carwash facilities and ran through a large puddle, the water splashed up under the vehicle washing off most of the crystals and the remains of the squirrel. The truck driver parked and went into the restaurant to have his lunch not knowing that each vehicle that exited the restaurant parking lot took with it some of the crystals that had dropped off his truck.

Robert was eight years old, a precocious child, who always liked to have his own way. This morning, just as they were finishing breakfast in the restaurant he was taking great delight in kicking his sister Pam under the table. Pam, two years older than him, yelled to her mother to make him stop. Jane, the mother, reached over the table and grabbed hold of Robert's hand giving it a squeeze making sure that he could feel her nails. "Stop that right now Robert or we'll leave you behind when we get to the plane."

Robert just smiled at his mother knowing full well they would never leave him behind; he stopped kicking his sister and ate the last of his toast and peanut butter. Ed, their father, gulped down the last of his coffee and said "Okay, you lot, we'd better get on the road, we have to be at the airport at least one and a half hours before the plane leaves. Jane where are the passports just in case we need them?"

Jane looked worried for a moment and then replied "Oops they're in the outside pocket of the blue suitcase, I left them in there by mistake." Ed shook his head in disbelief. "That blue bag's in the bottom of the trunk, I guess we'd better get them out now before we get to the airport."

The family got up from the table, Ed paid the waitress and left her a two-dollar tip and they went out to the rented car, Ed opened the trunk and pulled out two large black suitcases and put them on the ground beside the vehicle while he pulled out the blue one. As he opened the zipper and put his hand in to get out the passports Robert punched his sister and ran around the car knocking over the two black suitcases, Ed gave Robert a glare and ordered both the children to get into the back seat of the car and to be quiet. He gave his wife the passports, put the blue bag into the trunk and then reached down and put in the other two bags not noticing that they had some white powder on them. He jumped into the car and off they went to the airport. They had no difficulty finding the rental car drop off point and took the vehicle to the airport so that they could unload the luggage before returning it. Ed pulled all the luggage out of the car and placed it beside the curb, left his wife and children to pull the luggage into the airport and wait for him near the ticket counter while he returned the car to the rental office. They pulled the luggage into the airport building, the suitcases were on wheels and they sat on them in the main concourse while he returned the car and got a lift back on the shuttle.

Robert and Pam soon got bored with sitting so they ran around and played musical chairs with the suitcases. When their father returned they only had a short wait in line before they got to the ticket counter, they checked their luggage, got their tickets and went off to go through the security to their boarding gate, number six, where the plane for Chicago would be leaving from. Nobody noticed that everywhere their luggage went it left behind a few white crystals; these were picked up on the shoes and luggage of other travelers.

The family's luggage was put onto the conveyor belts and taken down and loaded onto the little luggage train that took it out to the plane. The white crystals were spread on the conveyor belts, on the luggage train, on the cement around the plane and also deposited in the plane's cargo bay. The plane took off on time to Chicago O'Hara airport.

The crystals immediately started to combine with every piece of cement that they touched, minute pockets of crystals began to form on the cement surfaces while other crystals went into the cracks and crevices.

At first it was mankind that spread the crystals far and wide, the planes, luggage, people, tires, vehicles and then the rats took it into the underground of all the towns, cities and villages, the mice brought it into every house, every farm, every building, every factory, every garage and the insects, the butterflies, the spiders, the beetles and the flies carried the little crystals into every nook and cranny that they went in. In a matter of months every main city in the world had little white crystals destroying the tensile strength of all forms of cement and from there it moved out to the country side. It was in the roadways, the building's, the pylons, in the foundations and even in the underground services, the sewers, the subways, cement conduits, anywhere it could be carried by insects, reptiles, animals, people or some form of machinery, there it found its home and started its relentless insipid destruction and multiplication.

2

Last Chance.

Before the beginning of the end.

Many years earlier before the crystal came.

Judge Matthew Edward Mortimer Jr. sat on the bench of his court looking out over the visitors, clients, police officers, lawyers and the accused, a young man in his early teens accused of robbery and resisting arrest, he thought to himself "There has to be something more that I can do for just a few of these young hardened repeat offenders."

The Judge had sat in the juvenile court in Denver, Colorado for almost five years, he was thirty-seven years old and was quite fit, he worked out at the local health club regularly, he was five feet ten inches tall and he always looked very distinguished. He bore himself as if he had been in the armed forces for years and kept his light brown hair very neatly trimmed. He had seen many types of rehabilitation methods used during those years to try and correct the behavior of the juveniles that came before him. He was very firm but fair in his judgment and he loved his work but many times at home rocking back and forth in his rocking chair overlooking his beautifully landscaped yard he wanted to cry. The correctional methods that were at his disposal worked reasonably well for some but not for all of the repeat juvenile offenders. Though there were not too many of these his heart broke at the thought that most of them would be lost and would eventually be found as prostitutes or become hardened criminals or found dead in an alley somewhere.

For a long while he had searched for a new method of correction to help these few, he had had an idea that had been running around in his head but so far it was totally impractical, otherwise he had come up empty. During the last twelve months he had become aware of a young couple who were making a small impact in the city dealing with the young homeless people on the streets, because they were so passionate about their work, Bella and Joshua, the couple in question, had come to his attention when a friend of a friend had asked the Judge to help find her daughter who had left home a number of weeks before. The Judge had contacted the gentleman that he used for private investigations and asked him to see if he could find the young lady in question and, to his surprise, it was only a few hours before Richard, the investigator, had called back to say that the young lady was living in a home on the outskirts of the city with about six other young people and the home was organized by one Joshua Oberman and his wife, Bella. Richard had nothing but good to say about the home the girl was living in and having investigated the relationship between the girl and her mother a little he recommended to the Judge that she be allowed to stay in this private home for wayward juveniles. The Judge asked for a full background report on Bella and Joshua, something about the investigation report had grabbed his attention, he was not quite sure what it was but he felt there was something here that possibly could help him rehabilitate some of his worst recurring juvenile delinquents.

About two weeks later Richard reported to the Judge in his chambers.

"Hi Judge how you do'en, good to see you again, we don't get together often enough, perhaps you'd like to come to my home for my wife's birthday party in three weeks?"

"Richard that would be lovely, I love your wife's cooking, just send me the time and the date to remind me and I'll be sure to be there, thank you for the invitation. Now what did you find out about this man Joshua and his wife?"

Richard laid a wad of papers in front of the Judge. "It's all there Judge it's interesting reading, if you have any questions get back to me please, you'll have to excuse me, I have to be over in courtroom five in a couple of minutes so if you need me give me a buzz," and with that Richard turned and went out through the heavy oak door of the Judge's quarters. He and the Judge had been friends for many years, he liked the Judge, he knew that the Judge ruled with compassion, fairness and, when needed, firmness.

The Judge pushed his chair backwards, put his feet up on his desk and read the report. As usual it was very concise, direct and to the point, the Judge admired Richard's work. When he had finished reading it he put the report back on his desk, clasped his hands over his tummy and closed his eyes, this was his "thinking mode", he liked to try and pull out the essence of anything that he needed to think about and in this case he wanted to make a summary for himself of what he believed were the pertinent points in the report.

Joshua had been a left baby, he had been found on the steps of the Sisters of Light orphanage in Grand Junction, Colorado, it had been a cool night and the newborn baby had been left wrapped in a warm blanket with a note pinned on it that had read. "His name is Joshua, I can't keep him please find a good home for him". He had spent five years at the orphanage; he had been a very precocious child, very lively and prone to disobey, he tended to put off any potential adoptions because he was difficult to handle and had a mind of his own. Then one day a middle-aged couple had come into the orphanage, they were obviously farmers and hard-working people, the wife had just had her third miscarriage and they wanted a young boy. Much to the Sisters amazement they had fallen in love with Joshua, after all the legal documentation had been completed the last the Sisters had seen of Joshua was his grinning face and waving hand out of the back window of a very old car.

The couple, Janet and Greg Oberman, had a small farm outside Naturita, up in the valley in the mountains, records showed that the farm barely provided enough to feed the family; they lived a very hard life, completely self-sufficient through difficult times. Mr. and Mrs. Oberman died in a fire that burned down the family home while Joshua was visiting a neighbor. Records showed that Joshua was then fifteen years old and he was made a ward of the state, he was put in a foster home from which, after a mere four weeks, he ran away. He spent the next four years living on the streets in Denver, Colorado, he'd run into trouble with the police on numerous occasions for minor infractions. Then he had met a young lady, Bella, who was also living on the streets, they had fallen in love and were married on his twentieth birthday. They had pulled themselves out of the gutter and he had taken a job working in a factory while she worked in a supermarket. After a couple of years they had purchased a big old house on the outskirts of Denver and spent their nonworking time trying to help and rehabilitate street children. They had been quite successful with a number of them.

The Judge decided that he wanted to meet these two young people, they may be just what he was looking for. Two days later Bella and Joshua were sitting on the porch of their home, swinging on the old swing seat enjoying the quiet and solitude of the evening, it was very seldom that they had an evening all to themselves, the six young people who were staying with them at the moment had gone off into town. A big black Lincoln limo pulled up to the curb in front of the house, Bella looked at Joshua who just shrugged his shoulders in answer to the silent query that Bella sent him. They watched as a chauffer, dressed very neatly in a crisp cut suit and wearing a chauffeur's hat, got out and opened the back door to allow a very distinguished gentleman, very neatly dressed in a dark suit, get out. He said something to the chauffer who closed the back door and got into the driver's seat and left the engine running, he was obviously going to wait. The man came up the front path to their home, they saw that he was a very handsome man, he stopped at the bottom of the stairs, looked over to them and said "Bella and Joshua Oberman?"

"Yes," said Joshua "what can we do for you?"

"It's not what you can do for me but what I might be able to do for you. My name is Matthew Edward Mortimer Jr. I'm a Judge serving in the juvenile court, may I come up and speak with you?"

"Come on up your Honor," said Bella with a surprised look on her face, she pointed to a wicker chair that sat to the left of the swing. The Judge undid his coat and made himself comfortable in the chair.

"I hope you don't mind my barging in on you like this but I thought that it would be better if I came and saw you rather than asking you to come and see me." Joshua smiled, the Judge saw that he was a good-looking young man, a very rugged outdoors type but his smile was genuine, it lit him up.

"Yes, not sure I would want to be summoned to court to see you." Bella giggled at the thought.

"Errrr yes quite," smiled the Judge "please don't be offended at what I have to say, everything that I've done has been done for excellent reasons and had to be done before I could come to see you. I've had both of you very thoroughly investigated." The look on both their faces told him what they were thinking and that they were both a little worried.

"No please don't worry, there's nothing wrong and I was very pleased with the reports on both of you." They appeared to relax a bit.

"And what were we investigated for?"

"Let me explain, I think that you're doing a wonderful job here at the home for those teens that are on the streets, giving them somewhere warm and safe to stay for a while. But my reports show you're not having a great deal of success in permanently returning your youths back to their parents or having any real long term effect on their way of life."

Joshua looked grim. "Your reports are right but we do give them a warm and dry home for a while and food in their belly, we can't do any more with what we have to work with."

"Exactly and that's why I'm here, I've been a Judge in the juvenile court for over five years and I'm not satisfied with the results that I'm able to get with some of the really bad repeat juvenile offenders. I've had an idea that's been rocking around in my head for the last one or two years and have been looking for someone who might be able to implement it."

Joshua's eyebrows went up and Bella made an enquiring look at the Judge.

"First let me tell you a little about myself so that you don't think that I'm just spouting off. My father was a very wealthy self made man, he was in the oil business among other interests, he and my mother died in a car crash a number of years ago and, since I was the only child, I inherited a great fortune most of which I've never touched, it just sits there and gets bigger and bigger. I make a very reasonable living as a Judge and live very comfortably as perhaps you can see," he waved his hand towards his limousine, "I tell you all this so that you understand that the idea that I have in mind is very feasible financially."

He saw the interest creep into their faces as he'd hoped it would.

"Joshua I believe that you were brought up on a very rugged farm and can therefore handle all of the responsibilities and work that is attached to such an operation?"

Joshua nodded thinking about those very hard but wonderful years that he had had with his parents. He nodded his answer.

"And Bella was brought up on a farm with eleven siblings, admittedly it was more prosperous than yours Joshua but you and your brothers and sisters still had to do all the work along with your mother and father, is that right?"

Bella smiled thoughtfully remembering all the hard work but all the love and togetherness that had been there during those difficult times.

"My father was a ruthless businessman, a number of years ago he purchased a business from a gentleman out in California. To make a profit he dismembered the business and sold it off in bits and pieces, the one-piece that he kept was a piece of land, a couple of thousand acres or more of wilderness property on the banks of the river Hassayampa. Apparently there was an old Indian gentleman living on the banks of the river in a cabin and through some Indian legislation this gentleman had the rights to live there for the rest of his life. I was aware of this property but had never seen it. Some years ago the old Indian died and I went down to ensure that everything was taken care of, the Indian was returned to his tribal members and received his due death rights. I found, much to my amazement that there were only two ways to get to the cabin where he'd lived, one was a trip up the river; there's a small wooden dock that the Indian used when he canoed up and down the river for his supplies etc., the other was to fly in by helicopter. The cabin is situated on a very large granite shelf that backs onto a cliff formation covered in dense trees and underbrush, not having a great deal of time I was flown in by helicopter. The cabin, a very roomy three-bedroom log cabin is built on the large flat outcrop of rock about twenty feet above the river level. Below the rock shelf there are a large number of acres of fertile soil left as the river cut its way down into the valley, the land drops down in a very gentle slope to the river. Much to my amazement I found that the back of a second smaller cabin was literally attached to the rock wall and was built around the entrance to a cave. The entrance to the cave is about the size of a double doorway and leads its way down, gradually, to a huge cavern, this leads off down to two more very large caverns, the old Indian and some of his predecessors had used this first cave for various Indian rights and the lowest cave as a storage facility because the temperature in the lower cave is permanently just above freezing, they were all dry and clean. In the second cavern is a large icy lake that appears to have no way for the water to enter or exit although the water is always fresh. The old Indian's relations came and took out all his belongings and now the property sits empty as it has done for the last few years. The idea that has formed in my head over the last couple of years is a wish to find someone willing to move into this property and to set up a completely isolated home or a rehabilitation facility for a number of hard-core juvenile delinquents for long term rehabilitation."

The Judge watched Bella and Joshua's reactions, Bella looked a little bewildered and worried and Joshua looked eager and anxious to hear more.

"I've been searching for the right person or people who would be willing to walk away from civilization to start a very difficult life, not only physically but also mentally, coping with bad kids on their own away from any help. The two of you may be an answer to my dreams. What I'm proposing is that I finance the two of you to set up a home for, let's say six to eight boys, who otherwise would be going to spend the rest of their juvenile lives in and out of jail. So what do you think of my idea?"

There was complete silence on the porch for a number of minutes, Bella sat looking over at Joshua a little bewildered, Joshua put his head back and stared at the night sky obviously deep in thought. The Judge sat quietly.

Bella reached out and took Joshua's hand in hers squeezing it gently, Joshua gradually came back to earth and squeezed Bella's hand with a crooked grin on his face. He looked at the Judge and said "I think it's a very hair brained idea, if it had come from anyone else I would say that they're nuts but you obviously are very serious and have thought this out over a long period of time. What you're proposing is quite preposterous; it would cost a great deal of money and commitment, it would mean going back to a life lived by the settlers in the old days, it would be very difficult and very hard. I should just laugh and thank you for the visit and send you back to your limousine Sir but I must admit that my curiosity is piqued. What do you think of this ridiculous idea Bella?"

Bella had gone a little white, she was very tense and was looking Joshua straight in the face.

"My first reaction honey is to say a most definite 'no way Jose' but you have aroused my curiosity too. We've often sat and mused about how we could do more for some of these young people, we've sat and talked and told tales of the hardships that we've been through living on the outskirts of society on our parents' farms but we've always looked back lovingly and remembered how happy we were then and have often said how wonderful it would be to just go back to that simple lifestyle. I think we should have more information, we should let the Judge fill us in with his ideas and then say whether we would be interested or not."

Joshua had a very strange grin on his face as he turned back to the Judge and said "You have our interest Sir please expand on your ideas."

"Okay," said the Judge leaning forward earnestly "let me paint a picture of the area. Through the centuries the river has cut a deep canyon as it meandered around this particular bend, on the inside curve it's left the steep sides of the canyon leading down to this huge flat granite outcrop. The rock has to be at least five hundred feet long on the cliff side by two hundred and twenty feet wide with a curve on the outside edge and the whole thing is almost completely flat and level. Then there's a fairly steep drop, about twenty-five feet, down to this huge extremely fertile plain then a very gentle slope to the edge of the river. The plain below covers many acres, at a rough guess I would estimate about five hundred acres, presently it's covered in wild bush but I believe it could be cleared quite easily. Back up to the granite shelf, at the up stream edge there's a waterfall, quite a large waterfall, which appears to come out of the rock itself, it actually flows down within two or three feet of the edge of the granite crashing down into the plain below and thence into the river. Presently there's, as I've said, a three-bedroom log cabin and a smaller storage log cabin, there's no electricity, there's no running water and the old Indian had a pot that he used to use as a toilet that he would simply empty off of the edge of the granite shelf. What I'm proposing is that I contract a company to come in and do the following, clear a large area of the lower fertile plain and put up some fences and some sheds, these would of course be made of wood logs, these areas you could use for livestock and for growing corn, vegetables etc. The contractor will put up a wood staircase from the lower plain to the granite shelf and also put in a good size floating boat dock. He'll also harness the waterfall with a waterwheel that will turn a generator thus giving you electricity that he'll run into the two log cabins, he'll put in a catcher reservoir on the edge of the waterfall and run water into the cabins. I'll get him to put in a fully modern kitchen with a large hot water tank and refurbish the main cabin for yourselves to live in. He'll build a larger cabin as a dormitory to house the six to eight young men who'll be living there with you, I'll make sure that each young man has his own private area and they'll have electricity, bathing facilities, etc. and a hot water tank put in for their convenience. The contractor will have to have the kitchen and bathrooms raised so that he can put in a waste disposal system from the cabins along the back edge of the granite slab and down to the lower plain at the down stream end and thence into the river, there's no one living downstream of the camp for many miles so I don't believe it'll be any problem to just run the sewage directly into the river. I'll have all the necessary equipment and provisions put into the first cave to maintain you all for the first six months to a year. The plan will be for you to become fully self-sufficient, if it requires any more supplies or materials you just have to say so and I'll get them delivered. You two will have complete cart blanche on how you run the camp, I will, before you leave, go through a number of home educational systems that are available so that you can give the boys a full school education. The young men will be sentenced by myself to the camp until they are twenty years old at which time they'll have the choice of just going out into the big wild world or I'll finance their education to any college or university that they choose to go to and that they can qualify to enter. If you have any need for any funds whatsoever I'll provide them to you, I will, if it's satisfactory with you both, put the sum of seventy five thousand dollars into a bank account in both your names for each year that you remain at the camp."

The two of them just sat there quietly and listened quite intently to what he was saying. He saw their eyes light up at the sum of money that he was prepared to put aside for them, it was, he believed, more than they had ever dreamed of earning.

The Judge continued, "Should any of the young men choose to leave the camp at anytime before they're twenty they are free to do so, however, they will then be in violation of a court order and, should they be caught, they will serve the remainder of their sentence in a prison. The only stipulation that I have is that I remain completely anonymous; I don't want anyone other than the two of you to know who is behind this whole scenario including who will be paying for their education after they leave you. Do I make myself clear on this point?"

Joshua looked over at Bella who nodded to him.

"Yes I think you've made yourself very clear on that point. Now you say that you will give us cart blanche on how we treat and educate these young men, I believe both Bella and myself, through our younger days, have come to realize that perhaps the best education is to let oneself find what one is interested in and what areas of life one wishes to follow. I understand that they must have a full scholarly education but I also believe that each one of these juveniles or street people need freedom to choose their own path. Do you agree with me?"

"I tend to agree with you but it doesn't matter if I agree with you or I don't agree with you, you will be running the camp and how you want to run it is entirely up to you. This is a completely new experiment, if it succeeds it would be wonderful, if we can just get fifty percent of the young men to go on to college or university or to go into a profession it will have succeeded beyond my wildest dreams. I've no idea what to suggest to you to find or what to do to hold onto the interests and the desires and needs of these young people. The legal system has tried numerous different approaches and none of them have been very successful with these repeat offenders. You'll be on your own, the two of you will be the bosses, how you run it will be entirely up to you. If it's a complete failure then at least I've tried, it's better to have tried and failed than never to have tried at all. If it's a failure you come back and whatever money is in the bank is yours. I will, if you have any trouble selling this house, buy it and I will put it on the market after you've left. Let me stress again, what ever this costs I am prepared to pay. I know it will be very expensive but I think, no I believe, that it is a fine way to spend a very small amount of the, and I want to say blood money here but I don't think that's quite the right terminology, that my father has left me."

The Judge sat there looking at the pair of them, he could see, what he imagined, were wheels turning in their brains.

"You've already proven that you're capable of making a home for the street people, this will be a big step up for you but I'm confident that it will be worth our while. Now I'm sure you have a million questions, let's see if I can answer them for you."

It was some two hours later that they said goodnight to the Judge having told him that they would discuss everything and get back to him in the morning, the Judge went back to his limousine with a very happy smile on his face.

Thus had begun "Last Chance", a name that Bella had given the camp, which was a most fitting one. Some nine months later Bella and Joshua moved into the cabin that, to their amazement, proved to be extremely comfortable and was in a beautiful spot. Their only real connection to the outside world, until the introduction of cell phones, was a ham radio through which they kept in constant touch with the Judge. It took them about four months to prepare for their new charges' arrivals; they were capable of looking after up to six boys.

3

Last Chance

The young men arrive.

"**W**elcome gentlemen." Joshua said looking around the table at the questioning and slightly bewildered faces of the six young men who had just arrived by helicopter. He and Bella had met them as they came out of the helicopter laughing inwardly at their remarks of how the camp was so cut off from civilization. They had ushered them all into the main dining room carrying their belongings that were now piled up under the front window. They had managed to put off answering the many questions they had until they were comfortably seated around the big table.

"First let me introduce ourselves, this is my wife Bella," and he took the hand of his wife who was sitting to his right, "and I am Joshua. We are the only people, beside you, who will be living here at Last Chance. As you can see we are quite isolated, the only way to get here is the same way that you got here by helicopter or by the river which is a six or seven hour trip downstream to the nearest town. So as you can surmise the only way that we can stay here and live comfortably is to be totally self-sufficient. We have no idea of your past or why you've been sentenced to come to the camp. As you are aware, you all made the choice to come here rather than spend the time in jail until your twentieth birthday. Neither Bella nor I have any need, nor a desire to know what you've done and what you've been convicted of, these things are your own private business. Now let's go round the table and introduce ourselves, we'll start with you," and he nodded at the young man who was sitting to Bella's right.

"I'm Benjamin Drew and you're right this sure is isolated, it's in the middle of nowhere. People call me Pattern because I very quickly recognize the way things come together and the patterns that they form."

Joshua nodded to the next young man.

"My name's Rob Dunfree."

"Everyone just calls me Indian," said the next young man.

"My name is Wayne Dunsted, we sure are a hell of a long way from anywhere," said the next young man "How the hell can you to stand living here by yourselves?"

"Well Bella and I have been living here for the last four months getting the place ready for all of you and we've really enjoyed ourselves, haven't we honey?" Bella squeezed his hand, "It's been wonderful, we've been very busy but there's a heck of a lot more to be done."

Wayne just nodded.

"I'm Roger Reed, but everybody just calls me Ghost cause at night I can just disappear into the darkness."

Two of them laughed.

"I'm Taffy; they call me that because my father was a Welshman. My real name is Jack Brown," said the last young man.

They all looked expectantly at Joshua.

"Again welcome to you all and as I've already said, because we are so isolated we have to be completely self-sufficient. This is a brand new venture; you're the first group of young people to be sent here. As you saw from the helicopter we have a waterfall close to the edge of this granite slab, it has been harnessed to run a generator and to give us running water. Down below the soil is extremely fertile, some of it has been cleared and there are a few fences and a couple of barns in place. We do have a gasoline powered tractor however there is very little gasoline and this is only kept for emergencies. All the work done here will be done manually or by using the six work horses that you may have seen grazing on your way in. Both Bella and I were brought up on farms which were run similarly to this one, we don't pretend to know everything about everything but we do know how to run a place such as this, it's just like going back to the early pioneering days. To keep this place running smoothly, it must be a team effort, if one person doesn't pull his weight then the others must do his work. For example let's say that today is Pattern's day to look after the chickens and bring in the eggs. If he doesn't do this then someone else will have to do his work or there won't be any eggs for breakfast the next morning, it's as simple as that. I know all this is very new to you and we understand that it's going to take some time for us to get everything running smoothly with you knowing what and when to do all that is required. We understand that this is going to be all new to you and we don't expect you to be able to do everything tomorrow. We do have sufficient supplies to see us through for about five or six months in an emergency but they are only to be used in an emergency. There's no supermarket just around the corner, everything such as milking the cows, churning our own butter, shearing the sheep, slaughtering an animal, clearing land down by the river, ploughing it and sowing and reaping the harvest must all be done by us or we'll just have to do without. Now there's nothing to keep you here, if any of you decide to leave neither Bella nor I will try to stop you, I believe that the judge who sentenced you made it quite clear that you could leave any time you wanted to but you will then be in violation of a court order and when, notice I say when and not if, when you're picked up you'll serve the rest of your sentence in a regular jail. Each of you will be expected to learn to do all the jobs to maintain the camp. If Bella and I decide, after giving any one of you a number of chances, that you cannot or will not fit in and do the farm work that is required of you as well as all the school work then we'll ask to have you removed and again you'll be taken to spend the rest of your sentence in a jail cell. Do I make myself completely understood?"

There was silence for a moment and then a few heads nodded and a couple of them said "Yes".

"Excellent, the large building next to this one is your living quarters, it's divided into six sleeping areas to give you your privacy, there's a common sitting area, a small kitchen and there are showers and toilets. Each of the sleeping areas is numbered." He reached down beside him and brought up a box that he shook vigorously and held it out over the table. "Please will each of you reach in and take out a piece of paper on which is written the number of your sleeping area."

They all did so without saying a word.

Joshua nodded to his wife who said, "Just let me welcome you to the camp, as Joshua mentioned he and I were both brought up on farms a long way from the mainstream but we both look back at those times with very fond memories. Don't get me wrong, it's a lot of hard work but it's very rewarding. I come from a very large family there were a lot of us kids and we were always fighting and arguing and getting into trouble at least once or twice a day someone would be yelling for help or screaming for somebody to stop something or trying to calm down an argument and stop it because it was going to get violent so my mother sat us all down one day and said what we needed was an emergency word, a word that's not normally used in day-to-day speech, a word that when used everyone, and I mean everyone that heard it had to stop what they were doing and go to assist, or stop an argument, stop a fight or do whatever was necessary for the person who had called out that word. A word that would get everybody's attention and could be used to calm people down, to stop violence, to get people to rush to your assistance, a word that we would only ever use in an emergency. She came up with the word "Fishslice", which we all agreed to use as she wished and we went away laughing at silly Mum. We had a very big pond fairly close to the farmhouse which we all played and swam in, we were for ever splashing and fighting and trying to drown each other, there was always someone yelling "stop stop" or "help I'm drowning" which we had got so used to that it was just ignored. Then one day my youngest sister, Trudy, was swimming half way across the pond when she started screaming for help, we just carried on with what we were doing and laughed at her, little did we realize that she had major cramps in both legs and was in serious trouble. Suddenly she screamed out "Fishslice, Fishslice" and much to everyone's surprise we all stopped what we were doing and rushed to her assistance. This brought home to us what our mother had meant so after that we only ever used "Fishslice" in an emergency situation. So I propose that we carry on with this same tradition, yes I know it sounds silly but I'm sure we'll find ourselves in the same situation, hearing the same calls for help or trying to break up an argument or a fight with little success until we say "Fishslice". Are there any questions about this?"

A couple of the young men laughed, the others just nodded their heads. Little did they realize just how important and how many times they would use this word.

"Now have any of you had any experience working on farms or with horses?" Asked Joshua.

Indian raised his hand, "I'm used to being around horses."

"That's excellent Indian, please will you help the others. Now I don't know if anybody explained to you about schoolwork. You are expected to complete your education so that you graduate from high school. We have sufficient home school teaching supplies to take each of you through to that point. There are sufficient funds set aside to pay for all of you, should you decide when you leave here on your twentieth birthday, to go on to a university or to some professional training program. You'll not be expected to repay any of these costs and there is sufficient money to pay for your education, your living expenses and some pocket money."

The young men looked each other, surprise looks coming across their faces. "You mean to tell me," said Pattern, "that I can go on to university and have it all paid for and don't have to pay it back?"

"That's correct," said Joshua "you're going to have to keep up your schoolwork and you're going to have to maintain the work for the camp and you're going to have to qualify and be accepted by a university. It's not going to be easy."

There was silence round the table.

"Okay, I think we've covered the basics, I'll give you a guided tour of this place while Bella gets some supper going. After supper you'll have some time to unpack and sort out your sleeping areas and then we'll all meet back here and talk."

The first four or five months were the hardest; these young men were used to being independent and free to do anything they desired. It was very difficult for them to learn to work together, to have daily tasks that had to be done and done properly. There were many blunders and mistakes made but slowly but surely they started working as a team. Their day started at six thirty in the morning with a large breakfast and then the morning chores had to be completed by noon. There were four hours of solid schoolwork and then the evening chores had to be done before the sun went down. Then, after dark there was a couple of hours where they could relax and then they collapsed exhausted into bed. Gradually they each found the things that they really enjoyed, Indian loved to be around the horses, Ghost liked to helping Bella in the kitchen because he loved to find ways of using different spices and he loved to forage for plants and vegetation that could be used. Rob Dunfree soon earned the nickname of Pug for no apparent reason and he loved to work with the livestock. Wayne, or Jock as he came to be known, turned out to be very mechanical and ended up doing most of the repairs on all the equipment. Jack Brown was the only one that seemed to have difficulty finding a specific area that he was interested in but as the schoolwork progressed his forte was in biology and, after he had to get eyeglasses, he took a great deal of interest in the eyes, ears, nose and throat sections in the school courses.

Once each week everyone took time off for a few hours of recreation, everyone loved to swim naked in the river, when the fish were running everyone enjoyed catching them and having fresh fish for a few days. Once every couple of months everyone went down stream to the nearest village, all the young men were given pocket money and they all eagerly looked forward to these trips to civilization. Joshua and Bella kept a very stern eye on each of them. Slowly but surely they each fitted in. There were only two times when they thought that someone had left on their own accord, both these times it was Indian who just disappeared from the camp, Joshua waited for three days and just as he was about to call judge Mortimer and let him know that Indian had absconded he turned up. He had just wanted some time to himself and had found a way of going up the cliff through the brush and trees and had spent time up on the plateau above the camp.

At first all of them except Pattern had to really work hard in their school work. The home teaching system that Joshua and Bella were using provided a test pamphlet which each one of them took, this showed the areas in their past education that they had missed or were very weak in. They each then had to go into specific lessons to strengthen these areas and could then go at their own pace into new educational areas. At first the schoolwork was very private, each one keeping to themselves a little embarrassed by how much work they had missed but slowly they came to help each other. Pattern was the only one who never had any problems in any of his schoolwork.

After the first year everything became much easier, they were all very adept at taking care of the chores and the scraggly young men who had first come to the camp were now physically strong and very healthy and seemed quite happy to live in the seclusion that the camp provided.

4

A Train Crash.

After the beginning of the end.

Some months after the arrival of the first crystal.

James, the railway engineer, pulled the covers up and snuggled into them enjoying their warmth, he lay there in bed listening to the sounds of the birds singing in the trees just outside his bedroom window. He had not felt too well when he went to bed last night, his stomach was upset and he had taken a Pepcid Plus to try and settle it. He had not slept well and he was loath to get out of his nice warm bed. He looked at the clock, it was seven and he had to be up at the train station for eight. He pulled back the bedcovers and felt the cool of the morning air; he always slept with his window open except in the really cold winter months. As he got up he felt his stomach churn and when he went to the bathroom he found he had the runs. He felt very weak but managed to get dressed and drove up to train station, he went to the ticket gate, said good morning to Barbara the ticket sales lady and went on out to the platform and literally bumped into the stationmaster, Fred MacMurray.

"Good morning James, a beautiful morning, you don't look so good what's the matter?"

"Good morning, I don't feel too good, my stomach's been playing up all night and I have the runs."

"You going to be okay to make the run?"

"I think so, haven't missed a run in years" and just as he finished speaking he had to make a run for the bathroom.

Fred went over to the phone, dialed a number and said "Nicolas are you awake?"

A very sleepy voice came back "I am now what can I do for you?"

"Sorry to disturb you Nicolas but James is sick, he wants to make the morning run but I'm not going to let him. Do you want some overtime?"

"Yes I guess so, I may be a few minutes late but I'll be there."

Fred waited until James came back out of the bathroom. "I called in Nicolas, you won't be doing the run this morning."

James stood there for a moment, Fred expected an argument and then James said "I don't think I'm going to argue with you on that, my head is beginning to spin and I feel awful, I'd better get back home and lay down, thank you, I'm going to make a beeline for my bed."

James didn't even wait for Fred to answer him; he rushed out to his car and made a dash for home before he had to rush to a bathroom again.

By the time Nicolas got into work he was barely five minutes late, he checked over his engine and watched as the last of the passengers got onto the train. Barbara came over to him and handed him a packed lunch, which she did for each train engineer making the run across the mountains. "Thanks Barbara, how many passengers do we have today?"

"You have forty five, among them you have a party of fifteen young school kids with a couple of teachers. I'll see you when you get back."

"Okay" said Nicolas "looks like a beautiful morning, see you."

The train trip through the mountains usually took about six hours, Nicolas got the train up to its regular speed and sat back and relaxed. Eventually the train came round a bend and Nicolas could see down into the valley, it was truly a beautiful sight, he checked the engine speed as he came round the last slight curve and onto the Humming bridge at the very top narrow section of the valley and he heard the sounds of the wheels change as they started across.

Down below on the cement foundation of one of the upright supports of the bridge sat a squirrel, he was busy nibbling on an acorn, he had heard the train coming and felt the slight vibration as it started across the bridge, he was used to this and did not even look up. Suddenly there was a slight change in the vibration and the squirrel heard and felt the cement crack, he leapt off the cement abutment and ran across the leafy ground and up into a tree and turned and watched as the cement base broke up in a cloud of white powder and the upright metal support pillars suddenly broke loose. As the support pillars broke apart, the next support pillars set in the next cement foundation, about one hundred yards away, seemed to bend slightly and then again the cement seemed to just disappear in a cloud of white dust. The squirrel knew that something was wrong and flew from tree to tree as fast as it could followed by the terrible sounds of the bridge collapsing as the train moved across it.

Nicolas felt a shudder and jumped up, he looked at the train's gauges to see if anything was wrong, he felt the train begin to tremble and heard the sounds of the wheels change and then the horrific noise as the metal in the bridge started to twist and bend as the bridge began to collapse into the valley. He realized what was happening and jammed the lever forward putting the engine into full power, the train leapt forward for just a few seconds and then the bridge seemed to lean at a slight angle and he felt the weight of the carriages pull the engine backwards. He could hear the scream of the wheels as they tried to grip but, as if in slow motion, the engine was pulled backward by the weight of the carriages and, as the rest of the bridge collapsed, the engine slid down and crashed into the valley below crushing the passenger carriages beneath it. As James was slammed into the controls of the train his last thought was "Oh shit, I didn't really need the overtime anyway."

The rescue teams found no survivors and a full investigation was commenced immediately.

5

A Plane Crash.

Sometime after the beginning of the end.

A few weeks after the bridge collapsed.

Jeremy Ferguson sat in seat number 46C, he had arrived at Heathrow airport in London, England early to ensure that he could get a window seat by an emergency exit row. This would allow him room to stretch his six foot five, slightly overweight, frame out during the flight but others had beaten him to it, so here he sat in an aisle seat three quarters of the way down the plane. He was forty-one years old and lived in Windsor, Ontario, Canada, he was in fact English, born in London almost within the sounds of Bow Bells, the bells of St Mary-le-Bow church in Cheapside in London, he always thought that if he had been born two miles further south he would have been a cockney. At the ripe old age of eight his parents had sent him off to a boy's boarding school in St. Albans and when he successfully passed his eleven plus examinations they had sent him off to another all boys boarding school in Earls Colne just outside Colchester. Here he had grown up with five other boys, all borders and he had been closer to them than he had been to his own brother.

He left school at the age of seventeen having passed seven of his eight G.C.E. 'O' level subjects and had, since that time, moved around Europe, spent five years in the Royal Air Force and had been stationed in various distant postings throughout the Middle East and Africa. He had ended up immigrating to Canada when he was twenty-seven years old. He never married.

He had lost touch with all the "old boys" in England until one morning around seven o'clock he was woken up by the telephone ringing, half asleep he had picked it up and had heard. "Hello could I speak to James Ferguson please?"

The voice had a broad English accent.

"Yes, this is he, what can I do for you?" He had no idea who was on the other end.

"Tubby, hello this is Bill Brown, you know Willie from school."

"My God you're a voice from the grave," James had said much surprised and sitting up in his bed "how are you? How the hell did you get this phone number?"

"It's good to hear you, I've spent a great deal of time trying to trace you down, you're the last one to get hold of. It seems you've moved all over the world, I had a heck of a time trying to find you, what are you doing? How've you been?"

"Well you're right, I have moved about quite a bit, I'm doing just fine, I own a real estate company here in Windsor and I write a few articles for the local paper when I feel like it. How are you doing? What are you doing? I haven't heard from anybody from school for the last fifteen to twenty years."

"I'm doing fine, married with two children, one boy and one girl, I'm in the financial business and as busy as hell. Listen, the reason I traced you down is because we're having an old school reunion back at Earls Colne, it's going to take place in three weeks, I would have given you a lot more notice but it's taken me so long to find you. We, Welsh, Splash, Rock and myself were hoping you could come but I guess this is a little too short a notice."

All the boarders, that is all the boys who actually lived at the school, had had nicknames.

"You've got to be kidding me, give me the date." James had said as he reached over to the nightstand for a piece of paper and a pencil. Willie gave him the date and he wrote it down.

"If there's any way I can get there I'll make it."

"That would be terrific, I'll book you into the hotel and make sure everything's paid for, if you can't make it let me know within forty eight hours of the reunion and I can get my money back, you can settle up with me when you get here. By the way I have some bad news, I had trouble tracing down Squirrel only to find that he died, quite suddenly while at sea, he was in the merchant Navy and none of us heard about it. We'll hold a short remembrance service at the old village church sometime during the reunion."

"Gee that's a tough one but listen I'll see what I can do and get back to you. What number can I reach you at?"

After a few minutes of idle chat he had hung up the phone.

So here he now sat in the plane returning from his reunion, the reunion had been an incredible experience; Earls Colne was a very small village with just one main street, it had been fun to walk up and down the street looking at all these middle-aged men trying very hard to recognize each other. He had recognized Welsh, Splash, Rock and Willie but some of the others, who were all dayboys, he had had trouble putting names to faces. It had been a wonderful weekend and the last night of his trip he had stayed at Willie's house and they had gone out for Indian food, he had overeaten and they had stayed up the whole night talking.

About half an hour into the flight home he had started getting tummy cramps and he was only to happy that he had ended up with an aisle seat because he had run to the bathroom at the very back of the plane three times so far.

"Ladies and gentlemen we are on the final approach to Chicago O'Hare airport, on behalf of Capt. Douglas and myself we thank you for flying British Airways and hope that you've had a pleasant flight. We look forward to serving you in the future" came over the speaker system.

The head stewardess then said over the speakers, "the Captain has put on the seat belt sign, please return to your seats and put them in the up right position and make sure your seat belts are fastened securely. Personnel please make a final inspection through the cabin and then take up your positions for landing."

The stewardesses walked down the aisles checking everyone's seats and seat belts and then took their seats, two of them sitting in pull down seats at the rear of the plane. James felt the plane starting to drop, all of a sudden he got a terrible stomach cramp, it sent him forward doubling him up in his seat and he had to moan a little.

He undid his seat belt and made a dash for the toilets. One of the stewardesses grabbed him as he tried to pass her. "You can't go now, we're about to land, you must go back to your seat and fasten your seat belt."

"If I don't go right now," he moaned, "you'll be cleaning up a horrible mess under and all over my seat and seat belt."

He pushed her hands aside and dashed into the toilet, he just had time to slam and lock the door, pull down his trousers and pants before he went. He sat there on the toilet with his head in his hands, waiting for the cramps to subside. He reached behind him and pushed the flush button, hearing a loud swoosh as the toilet flushed. He felt a slight bump as the wheels touched down on the runway and then there was a tremendous bang and he was thrown forward against the toilet door. Everything after that seemed to happen in slow motion, he was thrown up in the air until his head struck the ceiling of the small cubicle, he was then twisted around and slammed down till he was jammed between the toilet and the door where he must have passed out.

He came to crammed in that small space between the toilet and the door as he gathered his thoughts. Slowly he pulled himself up and sat on the toilet only to find that everything was leaning at about a forty-five degree angle, he had to push with his hands on the wall to keep himself upright.

"Oh God what the hell happened, we must have crashed, I'd better get out as soon as possible, at least I'm not really hurt" he thought to himself, his left arm and his right leg hurt but he could move them all right. It was eerily quiet. He unlocked the door and pulled it in towards him, it opened about three inches, he pulled again and it gave a little more, he put both of his feet up, one on either side of the door and yanked with all his might, the door flew open and he felt a blast of hot air. He blinked, stood up and pulled up his trousers, then, leaning against the doorframe stepped into the doorway, he was just going to take another step forward when he realized there was nothing to step onto, literally the tail had been completely broken off just one foot in front of the toilet door, he was looking down at the ground about twenty feet below him with the tail section sitting at an angle on the ground. He looked up and there, about two hundred and fifty yards away from him, was a ball of flames, he could barely make out the shape of any of the rest of the plane, the tail must have broken loose and been thrown clear. He backed up and sat on the toilet, pushing his feet against the wall to keep himself upright and covered his face with his hands.

"My God if I hadn't had the shits I'd have been in my seat right in the middle of that fiery mess" he said to himself.

He heard the sirens coming closer as he sat there in a daze oblivious to the fine white powder that was now beginning to coat everything and a silly thought came to him, "thank God I flushed the toilet."

6

Fishslice.

A short time after the plane crash.

Frenchburg, Kentucky.

Rob Dunfree reached out and switched off the alarm, rolled onto his back and stretched out loving the feel of the silken sheets, he rolled over onto his left side and looked at his wife, June. Oh how he loved her, he loved to watch her as she slept and loved to listen to the little noises that she made. They had been married now for three years, had had their wedding anniversary just last week, he reached over and gently caressed her neck and cheek and she moaned deliciously. He kissed her gently on her breast and her hand came over to hold his head to her.

"It's time to wake up my love," he whispered.

There came a moan and a stretch. "Can't we stay in bed for just a little longer?"

"Sorry my love, I would love to but I have to be at the O'Gradie's farm this morning at ten."

"Oh I feel so naughty," she murmured as her hand slipped down and gently played with his manhood, he felt himself reacting to her and laughed.

"You always feel naughty in the mornings," he reached down and held her hand to him squeezing himself gently and then leapt out of bed.

"That's not fair" she moaned and pulled the sheets back so that he could see her laying there naked, offering herself to him with a wicked grin on her face.

"Now who's being fair" he said looked down to see that he was hard and enjoying the sensation. She laughed as he came towards the bed with that 'I want you' look on his face. She rolled out of the bed on the opposite side from him and ran into the bathroom laughing.

He moaned and got his clothes ready to put on.

As they ate their breakfast of toast and half a grapefruit he smiled at her glowing face, they had just found out two days ago that she was expecting, they had wanted a baby for some time and it was a wonderful surprise to find out that she was pregnant at last. Rob would swear that she had taken on a glow of motherhood the moment that they had heard from her Doctor. After they finished breakfast he held her and kissed her longingly and as they got into their respective cars he called to her "We have some unfinished business tonight".

The drive to his office and veterinary clinic took about twenty minutes.

His office was in an old renovated building set at the end of a long driveway with nothing but fields and trees surrounding it, Jessie, his young assistant, had opened up the door and was sweeping the floor and tidying everything up as she did every morning before he arrived. She stood about five feet six inches, slightly on the plump side, short brownish reddish hair that was curly and just seemed to flow anywhere it wanted to, she wore blue jeans and a red blouse over which she wore her customary bright red working apron.

She was a little gem, he did not know what he would do without her, Rob remembered the week, approximately three years ago, that he had opened his practice, this young street girl had come into his office asking for money for lunch, he had offered her a job and she had been with him ever since. She had cleaned herself up and cleaned out the upstairs of the office building and had set herself up a nice little apartment.

"Hi Mr. Boss man, how's the new daddy doing today?" She called to him with a wicked grin on her face as he got out of the car.

"I, no, we, are doing just wonderfully thank you for asking" he sent back to her as he entered the office, "any messages for me?"

"I got a cryptic phone call just a couple of minutes ago, it was a little strange, a man was on the phone and he wouldn't give me his name, he just told me to say to you 'Fishslice, I'll call back in exactly ten minutes'".

Rob stopped in mid stride, a curious look on his face, "Exactly what did he say again?"

"He said, and I quote, 'Fishslice I'll call back in exactly ten minutes'." She saw the expression on his face "Is everything Ok Boss?"

It had been a long time since Rob had heard the term "Fishslice", the surprise look changed to a worried one.

"It's ok Jessie, how long ago did he phone?"

Before she had a chance to answer the phone rang, Rob ran over and grabbed it. "The Dunfree Veterinary Clinic".

"Rob Dunfree please" a gruff voice spoke.

"Speaking, who's this?"

"Hello Rob," the voice drew back memories, it only took a few seconds for Rob to recognize it as the voice of Pattern one of the boys who'd been at Last Chance with him. "Rob I don't want to make this too mysterious, I only have a few seconds on this phone, do you remember Fishslice?"

"Yes, hello this is Pattern isn't it? Yes I remember Fishslice but that was a long time ago."

"Yes your right Rob this is Pattern, now listen very carefully I repeat, Fishslice. There's a plane chartered and paid for in your name, it will be waiting for you at the airport in Frenchburg the day after tomorrow, which is Saturday. It will be waiting for you until half past ten in the morning after which time it will no longer be available. It's booked for you and your wife, it will fly you into Phoenix airport where there'll be a helicopter waiting and paid for which will fly you into Last Chance. It is imperative that you meet me there on Saturday. I can't say anymore, my time is up on this phone, I repeat Fishslice, Fishslice, Fishslice" and the phone was hung up.

Rob stood there for a few minutes holding the phone to his ear not quite believing what he'd heard, he scratched his head with his other hand, a worried look came onto his face, he put down the phone and turned to Jessie who was looking at him with a startled expression.

"Well," he said, "that was the weirdest phone call I've ever had in my life. Hmm I wonder what that was all about."

"Well you look a little green about the gills boss, is everything Ok?"

Rob stood there for little bit longer trying to digest what he'd just heard, he smiled at Jessie and said "Yep everything seems to be Ok, just a voice from the distant past, let's get the office rolling, I have to be out at the O'Gradie's farm in an hour, please get my bag together."

Jessie nodded, turned, and went into the back room to get his visitation bag ready for the O'Gradie's sick horse.

Rob stood there with a puzzled expression on his face for a couple more minutes then called his wife at the hospital where she worked as an emergency room doctor and surgeon. It took a few minutes for the nursing desk to get her on the phone and he smiled as he heard her say "Hello Honey what are you phoning me for at this time of the day?"

"Darling I've just had a very strange phone call, it was from Pattern, you remember Pattern he was one of the boys at Last Chance."

"Oh yes I remember, you haven't heard from him in years, what did he want?"

"He was very mysterious, he quoted an old saying that we had at the home, everyone at the camp agreed, right from the first few weeks we were there that if any one used the word "Fishslice" it meant that who ever heard it had to stop what they were doing and go to the aid of the person who'd uttered it. It was a sign of an emergency. It was only used a few times in all the years that we were at the camp but it really worked when it was used. He was very mysterious, he said he could only speak on the phone for a few seconds, he said that he's hired a plane to take you and I to Last Chance on Saturday, this Saturday, and he said that it was imperative that we meet him there. That was all that he said, I don't quite know what to make of it, he made it sound like something out of a gangster movie. What do you think about it?

"Oh my," he could almost hear her smiling at the other end of the phone, "a mystery, boy I like mysteries, we don't have anything on for this Saturday do we?"

"No I don't think so I was going to spend it doing some of the books for the clinic but that can wait. Are you on duty on Saturday?"

"No Honey this is my weekend off, let's take him up on his offer, let's go down to Last Chance, you haven't been back there for years it'll be a nice trip. You'll enjoy seeing Joshua and Bella again."

"Yes I guess your right and after all Pattern is paying for it, a free trip in our own private plane, okay I agree, let's go down and see what he wants."

"Sounds like a plan to me, I'd better get back to the emergency room, we're not too busy yet but my buzzer just went off. I'll see you at home this evening, love you." She didn't wait to hear his reply, she hung up the phone and dashed back to the emergency room. She was just beginning her fourth year internship at the local hospital, she loved her work, sometimes, Rob thought, just a little bit too much. He had learned to live with the very strange hours and the emergency callouts that went along with the job. They had met in her emergency room; Rob had received a rather nasty bite from a miserable Doberman and had had to go into the emergency for stitches and June had taken care of him and he had fallen in love with her almost immediately. It took him another week to get up the guts to go back to the hospital and ask her out for dinner. They had dated for a little over a year before he asked her to marry him. She was very beautiful, tall and slender, she kept her figure by watching what they ate, she was very health conscious, she had beautiful piercing blue eyes and long blondish hair that hung down to her shoulders but was invariably kept up in a bun. But the thing that Rob found most sensual was her hands, she had very slender hands with long fingers, short nails but she could drive him absolutely wild when she played his body with those slender fingers.

He tried to push the concerns that Pattern's phone call had stirred up as he and Jessie went about their work but every time there was a quiet moment those concerns seemed to creep forward, something about the phone call was really beginning to disturb him.

Unbeknown to Rob, within a few minutes of his strange phone call Joshua, at Last Chance, was interrupted by his cell phone ringing;

he rushed over to his desk and grabbed the phone, opened it and said "Hello Judge."

"Hello Joshua, this isn't the Judge, it's Benjamin Drew, better known as Pattern."

"Well hello Benjamin, God I haven't heard from you in years, where are you? What are you doing these days? Now hang on a second, how did you get this phone number, nobody has this phone number it's for emergencies only."

"Joshua listen I only have a couple of minutes, I must apologize because I've broken promises, rules and regulations. Do you remember "Fishslice?"

"Yes of course I do, we still use it, why?"

"I am invoking "Fishslice", again I say "Fishslice." Before you blow your top you must understand that everything I'm doing is to try and save lives, I know this sounds dramatic but please believe me when I say that this is a life and death situation. I'm about to call Judge Mortimer, I'm setting up a meeting at Last Chance this Saturday. I've contacted Rob and he and his wife hopefully will be arriving there Saturday morning and I'm going to ask the Judge if he too will come to the camp. I'm going to ask him to call you, if necessary, to confirm that I have contacted you and that you are expecting his visit."

"Pattern how could you do this? How did you find out about the Judge? What the hell is going on?"

"Joshua I'll explain everything when I get there on Saturday, please understand this is a dire emergency. I would suggest that you might consider sending the boys away somewhere for the day to ensure the anonymity of the Judge, I must go now I'll see you on Saturday."

Joshua wanted to say more but there was a click on the phone and Pattern was gone. He just stood there scratching his head, "What the hell was that all about" he asked himself as he went into the kitchen to talk this over with his wife. He had a very strange feeling in the pit of his stomach that all of a sudden their lives were about to change.

The Judge was laid back in his big leather armchair with his feet up on his desk completely engrossed in doing research for the case he was hearing in his courtroom that afternoon. The buzzer went on his intercom and he reached over, pushed a button and said, "What is it Jenny I thought I said I didn't want to be disturbed."

"Sorry your Honor, I didn't mean to disturb you but I have a gentleman on your private line who says that it's imperative that he talks to you immediately, he said his name is Benjamin Drew and that you know him."

"Benjamin Drew, hmmmm, we haven't spoken in many years, I wonder what he wants. How the heck did he get this phone number for my private line? Ok Jenny put him through to me please."

The Judge picked up the phone and said "Well hello Benjamin it's been a long time since I spoke to you, what can I do for you today?"

"Hello Judge," came the voice of Benjamin, the Judge could still recognize his gruffly spoken words, "before I start Judge I must explain that I now work and report directly to the President, that is the President of the United States. I can't stay on this line long so please bear with me, I've broken some rules and regulations that were set up at Last Chance and I hope that you'll accept my reasons for doing so after we've met."

"Met, met, why should we meet?" The Judge sat up in his seat, his feet down on the floor and listened more intently to the voice on the phone.

"Judge I'm fully aware that it's you who back everything financially that goes down at Last Chance and have even paid for all the young men's educations for which, believe me, I am eternally grateful and I'm hoping that I am hereby repaying a little of what I owe you."

The Judge's hair on the back of his neck began to stand up.

"It is imperative, it's a matter of life and death, you must and I repeat, you must go to Last Chance on Saturday. I've taken the liberty of booking you a charter flight to Phoenix, you'll find it at the western end of Denver international airport, the name of the charter company is Frank's Charters. Once at Phoenix you'll find a helicopter that will take you to Last Chance, your pilot from Denver will point out where to go. The flights are paid for. There is a situation that is unfolding as we speak that will affect everyone, I repeat this is a matter of life and death."

The Judge felt his stomach tightening up. "How do I know that this isn't some kind of a joke, a very bad joke?"

"I've just spoken to Joshua at Last Chance and I said that I would ask you to phone him to confirm that I am setting up this meeting. Please Judge you must and I repeat you must go to Last Chance on Saturday. My time is up on this phone I dare not stay on any longer I'll see you at Last Chance this weekend."

The Judge sat there, looking at the phone in his hand, trying very hard to understand what he had just heard. He had always been extremely careful to make sure that no one could find out that he was the philanthropist behind Last Chance, Pattern must have access to extremely private individual financial dealings to be able to find this out. He put the phone down and tried to analyze the very brief conversation. He had been extremely proud of the success of the Last Chance experiment, it was more successful than in his wildest imagination. He had secretly followed the successes of all six boys through their university and professional training, there had been some of the most proudest moments of his life when he had sat at the back of the graduation ceremonies at the various universities and had watched his boys graduate. Last Chance had been so successful that he, Joshua and Bella had decided to continue and, after Joshua and Bella had had a six month vacation, they had been only too happy to return to the camp and over the next six months had received another six young men.

Pattern's conversation awoke some very disturbing thoughts, he sat there and decided that he should phone Joshua immediately, he picked up his phone and dialed Joshua's very private cell phone.

"Hello your Honor" said Joshua.

"Joshua I've just had an extremely disturbing phone call from Pattern, it appears that he's found out that I am financially behind Last Chance, he indicated that he has some position close to the President of the United States that might account for his being able to find out about my personal business, he said that he'd just spoken to you, is that correct?"

"Yes your Honor, I too have just received a very strange phone call from him. Pattern told me that he's set up, or he was setting up, a meeting to be held here at the camp this Saturday. He wouldn't tell me what it was about, he said that he could only speak on the phone for a very short time, he said that he had got hold of Rob and he and his wife, hopefully, were going to come down to the camp. He also said that he was going to call you and ask you to come down here this Saturday and that if you were to call me I was to confirm that he had spoken to me. He wouldn't give me any more information other than he indicated that it was imperative that we have this meeting and that it was a matter of life and death."

"Yes," said the Judge "he basically indicated the same thing to me, he wouldn't stay on the line, I didn't have time to ask him any questions. I didn't know that Rob and his wife were invited, he just told me that he had chartered a plane and a helicopter to bring me down there this Saturday. This is all extremely worrying, I wish I knew what was going on but since he didn't leave any phone numbers and I've no way of getting hold of him I guess we'll all just have to wait and see what happens on Saturday."

"I guess that's just about it," said Joshua "I don't see any other way to get any more information."

"I would still like to keep my anonymity if that's possible, is there anyway that you can make sure that the boys at the camp don't see me."

"No problem" said Joshua "I'll make arrangements for them to take a fishing trip downriver for the day, they'll love that and it will leave the camp empty except for Bella and myself and whoever arrives for this meeting."

"That's excellent, well then I guess there's nothing else for us to do at this time. I'll see you on Saturday, if you find out anything else please give me a call right away."

"Okay your Honor, what ever happens it'll be really nice to see you again, it's been a longtime since you've visited the camp, Bella will really enjoy your visit."

"Yes, I guess you're right, time seems to have a way of slipping by, it will be nice to see you both and the camp. Okay see you on Saturday, bye for now." And the Judge hung up the phone, a lump seemed to be forming in his stomach.

7

The meeting at Last Chance.

The Saturday after Pattern's phone calls.

Rob and June were whisked across the tarmac at Phoenix airport in a golf cart and climbed aboard the waiting helicopter, the pilot greeted them with a smile and Rob said "Okay Sir we're all aboard let's go".

"Mr. Dunfree good morning to you and your wife, we have to wait for one more passenger before we take off."

"Another passenger? We didn't know there was anyone else coming with us, you're only making one-stop aren't you?"

"Yes we only have the one destination, that's the Last Chance Camp Sir".

"Who's the other passenger, what's his or her name?"

"I don't have his name Sir, but you'll find out in just a moment, here he comes," said the pilot pointing to another golf cart that was coming in their direction.

An expression of surprise came over Rob's face as he recognized the man as he climbed into the helicopter, it had been many years since he had seen him but he would have recognized him anywhere, it was Judge Mortimer.

June looked at her husband recognizing the facial expression of surprise and amazement. He looked over to her and smiled and gave her a slight shrug of the shoulders. Rob waited until the Judge was settled into a seat and had strapped himself in across from him. He was about to speak when the pilot said, "Hold on folks here we go, sit back and relax and enjoy the flight. Sorry folks we'll not be serving any meals or snacks on this flight but if anybody gets desperate we can always set down at a McDonald's in their parking lot." He smiled as he turned away from them and the noise of the motors increased as they gently rose from the tarmac.

"Well good morning Judge," said Rob holding out his hand and smiling "It's been a long time since I last saw you."

The Judge looked up from checking his seat belt and stared at the young couple before him, he knew that he'd never seen the young lady before but the handsome young man sitting before him was very familiar. His very sharp mind started snapping through its memory banks, it only took a few seconds for him to put a name to the face.

"Well if it isn't Rob Dunfree, yes indeed it has been many years since we met. How are you doing young man?"

"I'm doing just fine Sir, please let me introduce my wife, Judge my wife June, June this is Judge Mortimer."

"I'm very pleased to meet you," said June as she lent forward and held out her hand that was instantly held tightly yet gently and was shaken as the Judge smiled at her "I've heard a little about you from my husband."

"Well I hope it wasn't all bad," grinned the Judge as he relaxed back in his seat, a stern expression came over his face as he turned to Rob and said, "Rob can you please tell me what's going on, I got this very strange phone call from Benjamin Drew, I checked with Joshua at Last Chance who confirmed that he too had received a very similar call, Joshua could tell me nothing more than that Pattern had insisted that I be at the camp today. Both of them used the phrase, "it is a matter of life and death", now what's going on, please shed some light on all this for me?"

"I'm afraid Judge I can't tell you anymore than you already know, I too got a phone call from Benjamin Drew in which he said basically the same thing that he told you. June and I both thought that we'd better come to Last Chance as he requested, our flights were booked and paid for so here we are."

"Well that doesn't help much does it? I guess we'll just have to wait and see what happens."

For the rest of the trip the three of them chatted amiably with Rob doing most of the talking, bringing the Judge up to date with what had happened in his life since he'd sentenced him to Last Chance, unbeknown to him the Judge was well aware of a lot of those happenings.

The three of them had talked so much that they did not realize how fast the time had flown by until they heard the pilot say "Okay folks we're just a few minutes out, we're going to drop-down into the river valley heading downstream until we land at the camp. I've been instructed to drop you off and be back to pick you up at about nine tonight, is that all right with you?"

The Judge looked at Rob and June who shrugged their shoulders and nodded, he said "I guess that's all right, this whole trip has been a surprise for us so we'll just go along with what ever has been arranged."

They all looked out the windows as the helicopter swooped over the edge of the plateau and dropped down to within only a few feet above the river, it was beautiful as they followed the water down the valley. The pilot held the helicopter for just a few moments away from the camp till he found the X painted on the granite ledge where he was supposed to land.

From the air the passengers found the camp to look very similar to the way they remembered it, all except June who'd never seen it before and who was now amazed how beautiful and quiet it all seemed.

The landing was very smooth and they waved goodbye to the pilot. They moved quickly away from the helicopter and once they were clear it took off flying on down the valley.

They were greeted with a loud and cheerful "Hello you all" from Joshua and Belle as they came forward to greet them warmly. They shook hands with the Judge and then Rob was lost in hugs and kisses from both Bella and Joshua, as he broke loose he introduced June to them and she too was hugged and kissed.

That was all the time they had before they heard the whine of another helicopter swooping down onto the X mark, it was much smaller than the one that they'd arrived in, it looked like a little bubble with a rotor on top and obviously it could only hold a maximum of two people but all they could see was a pilot. As the rotors stopped the pilot stepped out and they recognized him as Pattern.

He strode quickly over to them carrying a large brief case and was lost in hugs and kisses for a moment by Bella and Joshua before he turned to the Judge. Firmly shaking his hand he said to everyone, "I apologize for being so mysterious and thank you for coming," and then he was hugging Rob, "God it's been a long time, I'm so glad to see you and you must be his beautiful bride" Pattern said as he turned to June, "I've heard a little about you and all of it was good." He took her hand and he pulled her into him giving her a very warm and friendly hug.

"I'm very glad to meet you, I too have heard many things about you," she said with a grin, "most of which were good."

He grinned at her and she realized that she already liked him.

When all the greetings were finished Pattern looked at the expressions on their faces, he saw anxiety, questions and a little annoyance. "Let's go into the main cabin and I'll try and explain my very strange behavior to you. By the way Judge everyone here knows me by my nick name "Pattern" in fact everyone at work, including the President, calls me Pattern."

"I have a nice pot of tea brewing and have just made a fresh batch of cookies, come on lets all get settled down around the table and we can listen to what Pattern has to say," said Bella.

"Okay," said the Judge, "I've a million questions to ask him," the annoyed expression on his face changed a little to wonderment as he looked around the camp. He hadn't been here since it had been renovated originally; he'd made a point of leaving this end of the experiment completely up to Joshua and Bella, he was surprised at the changes that had happened. He remembered it had had just two cabins sitting on this massive outcrop of granite, now he could see that there were two more buildings, all of them made from logs, set against the cliff face. The huge waterfall that came out of the rock, way above the ledge, now served to drive a generator set in another log cabin way to the left at the end of the ledge. He was even more surprised as they entered the main cabin; it was beautifully furnished and it felt warm and welcoming. The main room was very large and served as the meeting room, schoolroom and playroom and of course the huge table surrounded by eight chairs in the middle of the room served as the dining table, work table, meeting table and everything else table as required. Everything was immaculately clean and he immediately felt comfortable.

"Okay" said Bella "sit down, come on sit down, I'll get the tea and cookies, June would you give me a hand please?"

"Sure, what can I do?" Asked June as she moved over into the kitchen, which was just up some stairs off the large dining room. The men sat down at the table.

"If it's okay I'll sit up at the head of the table right here," said Pattern looking around to see if there were any objections as he pulled out the chair at the head of the table. The Judge and Rob sat to his right and Joshua sat down to his left. As the ladies put out steaming cups of tea and a big plate of cookies and some sugar and milk, Pattern put his big brief case on the table in front of him, pulled out a large three-ring binder and a plastic container which looked like it held some sort of powder. As the ladies sat down and everyone helped themselves to the milk, sugar and cookies, he put the briefcase down on the floor and opened the binder showing a large sheath of papers.

"What I'm about to say must be held in the strictest confidence. I know as I go through this you'll have lots of questions to ask me. Please let me go right through this and answer your questions at the end, as I go through I hope to answer your questions before you ask them. First let me tell you a little about myself." He stood up and pushed his chair back a little.

"Please forgive me standing I like to walk a little bit and move when I'm speaking for any length of time." He looked up at the ceiling gathering his thoughts. "About four years ago I was consigned to work directly for the President, that is the President of the United States, I was asked to head up a very small specialized team, there are only three of us as permanent members of the team, we are to investigate any thing that the President requests of us. We have at our disposal some of the best minds in the United States, they have of course got full-time positions but it's arranged that as soon as I call upon them they will drop everything that they're doing and assist my team in our investigations. I get the incidents or situations to be investigated directly from the President and I report our findings directly back to him." He looked at the very surprised faces sitting around the table.

"What you see in this binder is a completed report that has yet to be presented to the President, no one knows what's in this report except myself. Specialists in their own field have verified all of the data. So you can understand why, what I am about to tell you, must stay in this room, at least until I have presented these finding to the President tomorrow morning and he's decided to inform the public which he must surely do sometime in the very near future. I am still officially taking a final report from a scientist in Phoenix at this time and I have taken a very big chance in getting here for this meeting, I have to leave here in two hours to cover my trail. I had to make sure that my phone calls to you were very short and I couldn't give you any information over the phone, I'm going to break my "Need to Know" clearances since I believe that there are certain steps that you all can take to save yourselves and maybe some others."

He saw a look of interest and a touch of fear in their eyes.

"About four months ago we were asked to investigate an incident, may be you remember or read something about the train wreck, the one where a bridge collapsed up in the valley that killed a group of school children? My team and I went up there and found that one of the cement abutments supporting the bridge had almost completely turned into powder and a second abutment was almost two thirds broken down," he picked up the plastic container and shook it. "This is some of that powder, I'll show it to you a little later. The official reason for the train crash was that one of the steel supports had collapsed, this was, in a way, correct but it was only part of the truth. The cement had lost all its adhesive qualities and had some how been broken down and transformed into these powder crystals. We were still investigating this occurrence when we were rushed over to the Chicago airport, you must remember the horrific plane crash where two hundred and fifty people were killed, they are still officially investigating the accident, pointing fingers and strongly suggesting that the undercarriage of the plane collapsed on landing. The real cause of the tragedy was that a section of the cement runway collapsed as the plane touched down causing the undercarriage to collapse and the plane to roll over, break apart and burn. My team found that the cement had turned into the same crystals as the bridge abutments. Upon examination we found pockets of the crystals in various places on all of the runways and through out the airport buildings, that's why the airport has been closed down, not because of the threat from terrorists as has been put out by the media. How long this can be kept a secret I don't know but they're feverishly trying to replace the damaged cement. I've had this powder analyzed by no fewer than six different laboratories throughout the States." He flipped over the pages in the binder. "They all came to exactly the same conclusion. The crystals in this plastic container are a brand new substance, it's never been seen before. We went back to the scene of the train wreck and, after further investigation, came to the conclusion that some months earlier a meteor was seen to land somewhere in that valley. We have concluded that possibly the meteor introduced a brand new substance into the bridge abutments and that had broken down the cement. We've found that it's a complex crystal that, when it comes into contact with cement or mortar or any substance in that category, will combine with those materials, break down their adhesive properties and form new crystals exactly the same as the original crystal, these new crystals then combine again with the cement forming even more of the new found crystals. This is a never-ending cycle. Thus anything made at all of cement, mortar etc. that comes into contact with even so much as one of these minute crystals will eventually break down and collapse."

He paused to watch their faces and it only took a very short time for each one of them to comprehend what he was saying.

"Do you mean that this crystal can, no is, breaking down all the cement that it comes in contact with?"

"Yes, I mean that this crystal is in fact breaking down cement and mortar throughout the entire world. I've traced this crystal to every main city throughout the world. It's so light that it can be carried in the wind, carried by birds, insects, rats, mice, people. Any thing that's made of cement and comes in contact with it will eventually break down and the resulting powder will then be picked up and carried to new areas where it will start its horrific damage all over again. It has been carried by insects, birds and rats into every nook and cranny that they get into, the rats have taken it down into the underground waste and water systems; the birds have taken it up into dams and the bases of electricity pylons. Anything that's made with or uses cement etc. either has been or will be infected, I use that term deliberately, and will somehow, sometime, break down into this new crystal."

"Oh my God" stuttered Joshua "airports, bridge, roads, shipping docks, high rises, basements, my God civilization relies on and has built itself on cement. It's in every single home, hotel, shopping plaza, if this is true and it's happening, you're talking about the break down of modern civilization."

The faces showed the seriousness of the situation, fear, worry and shock.

"Yes," said Pattern "you're grasping the horrific situation that this little crystal has put us in, let me assure you this is the truth and nothing that we know of will "kill" or stop this crystal. The only thing that may halt it for a while are extremely high temperatures, I mean temperatures that you would find in a blast furnace, even then after a few weeks it seems to start up again. The way the crystal works doesn't seem to follow any exact same paths, sometimes it will just react with the surface of the cement and make it flaky, some times it will eat it's way down into the very center of the cement and then break it down from the inside. There's no way to foretell its speed, nothing, rain, cold or heat seems to effect it the same way every time therefore we can't even guess when a particular cement host will break down and collapse."

The tea was getting cold and the cookies lay partly eaten as everyone sat and took in what Pattern was telling them.

"Okay, let's take this one step further. Since we can't foretell how fast things will break down there's no way that the President can prepare or make arrangements to protect the general public. What we have to recognize is that the following will occur, there will be a complete break down of the electrical power supply, dams will burst, pylons carrying the wiring will collapse, generating stations will cease to operate and of course the most immediate worry, nuclear generating plants will have to be closed down immediately. The transportation systems will no longer be functional, all roads made of cement will no longer be traversable and all bridges and culverts will collapse, this will mean there will be no movement of goods and services. All air traffic throughout the world will come to a standstill, about the only thing that will be able to fly will be vertical take off planes and small private planes that can land on grass airstrips or on water and since these are few and far between they'll be of little use in delivering goods and services. Water and gas supplies will cease to function as parts of their piping and pumping stations break down. Waste systems will break down as the pipes collapse and pumping stations cease. I'm guessing that the first thing to fall in the cities and in the towns will be the façades of some of the buildings, then the very buildings themselves will begin to crumble and collapse, it may start at any point in a high-rise building, from the basement, underground parking facilities or some supporting member within the building itself but they will eventually fall. This will of course make the cities and towns a very unsafe place to live, the population will flee by whatever means they have from the cities and towns into the countryside. Food and supplies will run out, there'll be a complete break down of our present way of life, we'll go back to the law of the gun, there'll be a complete break down of law and order, there'll be marauding gangs of thugs and people trying to obtain the things that they need to survive. The Armed Forces will be of little use because of the vast area of our continent, they'll be better equipped to move around but their supply lines must eventually dry up. There'll be nothing coming in by boat because all the docks will cease to exist and there'll be no way to load or unload. People will set up their own bastions to survive in and they must learn very quickly how to provide for themselves. It will be a dog eat dog world."

His audience sat back in their seats, their faces a little white with almost an expression of disbelief, he realized that they understood what he was saying and were making their own judgments.

"Now I come to the main reason for calling this meeting. I understand that while here at Last Chance it was agreed by all of us boys that we would never try to find out who was financially backing and paying for the camp and for each of us to complete our education and Judge I apologize for breaking this promise, with all the services that I have available to me it took me about one-half hour to find out that it was you. I also took the liberty to investigate you and your finances."

The Judge now looked at him with a curious expression on his face. Rob turned and looked at the Judge, the expression on his face turned from worry to wonder, he had always wondered how there were always funds available to pay for all the boys educations and who paid to keep Last Chance going, never in his wildest imagination had he ever considered that it was Judge Mortimer.

"Forgive me but with the understanding that what ever is said in this room will be kept confidential, I found, Judge, that through the death of your parents you became an extremely wealthy man. Other than to pay the costs of Last Chance and your "boys" education, you've not touched any of that wealth. I say this because of what I am going to propose to you all. Within the next few weeks this country and indeed the whole world population will break down into anarchy, the number of dead will be horrific, the number of people who survive will be very small, only those that can provide for themselves and that can defend what they have against marauding gangs will make it. I believe that one of the best places that will be able to survive will be here at Last Chance provided that we immediately start preparing for the holocaust that is about to begin. Judge, I would suggest that you immediately transpose all of your wealth into ready cash, I would suggest that you recall all the other boys and their families back here as soon as possible, I've calculated that we'll need a minimum of fifteen couples, preferably each person with a trade or profession that will help the community at large. We'll need defenses against attacks, we'll need accommodations, supplies and goods and chattels to sustain us until we can provide for ourselves. I've calculated that the plain below us, if properly cultivated can provide enough food and sustain enough livestock to keep up to fifty people very comfortably. Judge, all this will cost a small fortune and only you are capable of financing all this and through your contacts you may be in a position to make all this happen extremely fast. I believe that it may only be a matter of two or three weeks before this crystal becomes public knowledge and then Lord only knows what will happen."

The Judge was nodding his head, Pattern new that he was absorbing all this information, analyzing it and making decisions, he was a very analytical person.

"Let me just say in closing, I have to make this report to the President tomorrow, I've no idea what his and the government's reactions will be. Believe me when I say that all avenues to stop or prevent these catastrophic things from happening have been thoroughly investigated, tested and analyzed, the crystals are spread out so far throughout the world that even if we were to come up with some way of stopping them from spreading anymore we're already too late. There is nothing that the President or anyone else can do to stop this horrific break down of civilization, as we know it. I, personally, plan to stay working for the President investigating further the ramifications from this report until such time as I find that I can do no more good for the population and will then look to the safety of myself and my partner. I realize that what I've told you is an awful lot to absorb and understand."

He picked up the plastic container and removed the lid; he saw them all visibly pull back a little.

"This is the crystal, it is perfectly harmless, you could ingest it, breath some of it in, although it wouldn't do your lungs any good, it wouldn't do any deliberate harm to them. The only things that this will hurt or destroy are compounds like cement or mortar, so it's perfectly safe to handle and look at if you wish. I'll leave a copy of this report here; I know that you'll all want to read it, I must insist that it's not discussed or shown to anyone outside of our group. I'll now sit down and open this up for questions and discussions."

He closed the three-ring binder, sat down and pushed the open plastic container and the binder into the center of the table in front of all the others.

They didn't realize how much time had passed; there were questions and discussions about all the different aspects that Pattern had put before them when he looked at his watch and said, "It's time that I left, I must get back before anybody misses me, I leave this in your hands folks. Rob if you wouldn't mind being my contact point, I'll stay in touch and let you know how to get hold of the other boys when I find out. I wish to God all this had never happened but believe me when I say that if we can prepare Last Chance and get the right people here it will be one of the best and most likely places to withstand the ravages that are to come." Pattern said as he shook hands with the men and gave the ladies a big hug.

"I'll be in touch shortly Rob," and with that they saw him off to the helicopter and watched him fly off down the river.

As Pattern was following the river away from Last Chance he thought to himself, "now I've just one more person to speak to" and, as his helicopter climbed out of the canyon and rose to his flying height, he checked his watch, England was eight hours ahead so he knew that he had to leave it until after midnight.

The others returned to the dining area.

"I can put together some sandwiches and pickles etc., everyone must be hungry by now" said Bella.

By the time they heard their helicopter coming up the valley they had reviewed the report and discussed everything that they could think of over and over again. They had all come up to the same conclusions that Pattern had, Last Chance was going to be the best chance they all had of weathering the terrible storms that were coming. The Judge had agreed that he would make finances available. It was decided that Joshua and Bella would, of course, stay and look after Last Chance, they would have to put the situation before the six boys that were living there, most of them were just finishing their sentences and it was agreed that, should any of them want to leave Last Chance, then it would be acceptable with no repercussions. Joshua and Bella said that they would also be responsible for clearing off the huge granite shelf ready to construct some form of living quarters for all those that would arrive, they would also be responsible for getting everything organized as it was delivered.

Rob and his wife would be responsible for contacting the other old boys, putting together anything that they thought they would need and to organize housing for everyone that would be living there. They all agreed that the Judge should have the final decision should there be any discord, he would also be responsible, since he was going to finance everything, in deciding who was and who was not going to come to live at Last Chance. It was agreed that the primary residents, along with those already living at Last Chance, would be the old boys and their families and then those that the Judge felt would be the best asset to the community. The Judge confirmed that he would make funds available as soon as he could. Even though there was a very somber mood over everyone, as the helicopter left, Joshua could not help but notice there was an underlying current of excitement.

Later on that evening Joshua and Bella sat on the swinging couch looking out over the river, Bella snuggled up to her husband who put his arm around her and sat watching the evening sun go down and disappear over the canyon walls. As it started to go down the fading light changed the colors of the canyon walls and the ever-lengthening shadows made it almost look as if they were moving, they heard the sound of the boat's motor before it came round the bend in the river. As the boat came into view they could hear the chatter of the boys clearly in the still evening air. As soon as the boys saw them they waved and yelled and Joshua and Bella waved back. They moored the boat at the dock and raced to see who could be the first one to get to Joshua and Belle. The first one was of course Sage, although he was the youngest he was the most athletic, then came Alex, he was the oldest one; he was the one that would be leaving the camp first in three months time. Jay and Slade made it together, they always were an inseparable pair, then came Kyle and the last one was Walt who always seemed to be last, kept plodding along which hid the fact that he was the cleverest one of the bunch.

Joshua and Bella sat and listened to their tales of what had happened at their favourite fishing hole, the boys had had a good time and they'd all brought home some fish that Bella went and put into the fridge in the kitchen. Joshua let them let off steam and waited for them to quiet down.

"Gentlemen," said Joshua "we have to have a meeting some things have come up which I need to discuss with you. Let's all go into the cabin, perhaps we could persuade Bella to make us all a hot cup of chocolate."

The boys all rushed into the cabin and sat around the table expectantly waiting for Joshua to speak.

"Okay, since you boys all got back here on time we'll have a treat, while you're talking I'll make some chocolate," said Bella from the kitchen door.

"Gentlemen there was a meeting here this afternoon, one of the old boys, who used to be here, now works very closely with the President of the United States, he showed us a copy of a report that he's about to present to the President. This report contains the following," and he proceeded to explain to them everything that had been said and what had been decided at the earlier meeting.

The young men sat and listened intently, by the time Joshua had finished speaking they were full of questions. It took Joshua another hour to try to answer all their concerns about what was going to happen, eventually they grew quiet and then Walt said "Alright Joshua, let's say that all that's in that report is true, let's suppose that the catastrophes that it says are going to happen actually happen. Let's accept that a lot of other people are going to come and live here somehow, what are we supposed to do?" And he waved his arms at all the other boys

"That's an excellent question," said Joshua "I've already had discussions with Judge Mortimer who sent you here in the first place, Sage I know that your time here will be finished in three months and that you're going to go on to university, you others have time before you must leave the camp, the Judge has agreed that as of this evening you're all free to leave here any time you wish. The sentences that the Judge gave each one of you are herewith completed, if you wish to leave you may do so and there won't be any repercussions, however I hope you realize exactly what is going to happen out there, it most certainly won't be a safe place to be and there won't be any universities or colleges for you to go to. All those at the meeting this afternoon have asked that you all stay here and help us to try and weather the coming storms. It's entirely up to each one of you to choose what you wish to do, what ever you decide will be accepted. Just on a personal note, Bella and I want you all to stay here, we realize that all this is going to take away your dreams of going on to university and college but there's nothing we can do about that."

There was complete silence at the table, Joshua watched their faces, they showed worry, anger, sorrow, and disappointment. Jay looked over the table at Slade, they always seemed to have some way of silently communicating, Slade nodded and so did Jay. "Jay and I will stay," said Slade.

"It's very hard to believe what's in that report" said Walt, "but if it is correct then the logical thing to do is to remain here, if we do so and the report is rubbish we'll have lost nothing but some time, if we leave here and that report is right then we could find ourselves in a terrible mess, therefore the only logical conclusion is for us to stay and see what happens, I will stay here too."

"That young man is so damned logical," thought Joshua.

It took a few more minutes before Kyle said, "I agree with you Walt I'm going to stay."

"Me too" was all that Alex said.

"Well then," said Sage "I guess if you all are going to stay someone had better stay to look after you so that means I stay too."

The others all grinned and then looked at Joshua, "That's wonderful, I'm sure that you've all made the right decision, tomorrow everything will begin to change, we have to get this place ready for all the people who'll be coming and the stuff that's going to be delivered." He looked over at Bella and noticed a couple of happy tears in her eyes.

8

Report to the President.

At the White House

The morning after Pattern's meeting at Last Chance.

Julian Taylor, the President of the United States, stood in the shower, the hot water beating down on his back, his wife Mary watched him through the glass door as she came into the bathroom. He was a tall man, stood six foot four, lean in build but beginning to show his age, he had just turned sixty, he was a striking man, very charismatic and always had an air of authority, Mary grinned to herself as she watched the water bounce off his salt and pepper curly and almost uncontrollable hair. Mary herself was now fifty-eight years old, she had dark brown hair that she wore in a bun most of the time, she was a little plump but people always found her very attractive and very easy to talk to. They had been married for thirty-five years; they had met and were married while in law school. Julian was now in the third year of his presidency, they fitted very well together. Some people whispered that perhaps the President's wife had a little too much influence on his policies and decisions. This morning the President had meetings in the White House and Mary had to go and open a new University wing. They had two children, one boy and one girl, both of whom were married and, much to their joy, and pleasure, they had three grandchildren, with whom they loved to spend time.

"Julian my love," called out Mary "you'd better hurry up, you have an early morning meeting and I have to get out of town."

Julian turned around to face her through the glass door, blew her a wet kiss and said "I'll be right out, I still have time to have some breakfast with you before the day begins."

Pattern arrived at the White House an hour and a half early, he passed through security and picked up an armed security agent that followed him around the outside of the building watching as he, with his little hammer, tapped here and there listening very carefully. The security guard showed no surprise at his strange antics and then Pattern headed indoors to see the President.

The President stood up and leaned over his desk as Pattern was ushered into the Oval Office right at his appointed time. Pattern shook hands with the President and then with the Vice President who was seated to Pattern's right in front of the desk.

"Well good day Pattern," said the President "as you can see the Vice President is here for your meeting as you requested, it's an unusual request for you, normally you give me a lot more notice when you want to meet with me," he looked down at his desk "I don't have a lot of time, so please go ahead."

"Gentlemen," began Pattern "you may want to cancel all your meetings for this morning and possibly for this afternoon."

The President looked at him very carefully, he could read people very easily, in fact that was one of the prime attributes that had got him to be where he was today. He realized that Pattern was serious and a feeling of dread came over him.

"Well that's a tall order, let's see what you have for us before we make any rash decisions."

Pattern reached down into his briefcase and pulled out three thick files, he pushed one to the President and one to the Vice President.

"Sir you instructed me to look into the train derailment when the bridge collapsed, do you remember?"

"Yes indeed I do."

"As I was doing that investigation you asked me to follow it up with a look into the air crash in Chicago, these are the results of my investigations." He opened the file in front of him.

"Pattern must we go right through this file, can't you just give me the bottom line of the report?"

"No Sir, this time there is no bottom line, this is extremely important, I might suggest that this is the most important document that you will ever see, in fact I would go so far as to say that it is the most important report ever made to a President of the United States. Please gentlemen if you'll follow through with me please?"

The President realized just how serious Pattern was and opened the folder in front of him, he nodded to the Vice President who did the same.

"Go ahead Pattern" he said and Pattern proceeded to go through his report in much more detail than he had done at Last Chance. As he progressed towards the end, about one hour later, he saw that both the gentlemen were looking a little green around the gills.

"Gentlemen I assure you that everything possible has been done to prove these findings correct and accurate," he said as he came to the end of the file, he reached down into his briefcase and put a small jar of white powder on the desk in front of the President.

"That is the sample of the white powder that I got from both the train wreck and the plane crash."

He reached into his briefcase again and put a slightly smaller jar of white powder in front of him.

"Gentlemen just before I came to this meeting I took the liberty of checking around the White House, at the base of one pillar in the front of the building a small piece of the cement broke off and I found this white powder in the pillar, of course I haven't had it analyzed but I believe it to be identical to what is in the other jar. This would go to show just how far and wide this problem has spread." He sat back in his chair studying the other two men.

"Are you telling me that the White House is all ready infected by this crystal?"

"Yes Mr. President it is, I don't know how badly or where else it's infected other than the base of that pillar but very shortly this building will be unsafe to live or work in."

The President leaned forward and pressed a button on the consul to his right. "Beth please cancel all my appointments for today and if you wouldn't mind ordering in a lunch and please stay available."

"Yes Sir but you know you have that meeting with the Ambassador from Kuwait."

"Yes Beth, you'll just have to cancel, give him my apologies and reschedule."

"Yes Mr. President I'll cancel all your appointments, reschedule the Ambassador, take my lunch here at my desk and I'll take the liberty of ordering you a lunch to be delivered when you request it."

"Thank you Beth," he said and broke off the connection. He sat back in his chair and looked straight at Pattern. "Now let me see if I have this correct, what you're telling me is that there's some new substance, introduced theoretically by a meteor, that has been spread throughout the world, this crystal is somehow combining with any and all cement, concrete or mortar that it comes in contact with and is breaking down the tensile strength of the cement and turning it into the same white powder that we started with, is that correct?"

"Yes sir that is basically correct." Pattern sat still allowing them to digest his report.

"And you've traced this powder or crystal to nearly every major airport around the globe and, here and there, it's destroying the cement. You are telling me that there's no way of stopping this from spreading."

"Yes sir that is what I'm saying." There was silence in the room, Pattern could see their minds working.

"My God," said the Vice President "just about every structure in this country is supported in some way by cement. You're telling us that in time everything will collapse, is that in fact what you're saying?"

"Yes gentlemen there's no doubt that in time anything that is made of, or contains, concrete, cement or mortar will turn into a pile of white crystals and there's nothing that we can do to stop it at this time."

"Are you certain that there's nothing we can do to prevent it?"

"As you can see from my report, we've had this crystal tested by the best laboratories and minds in the country, I've had a team of people rush around the world checking out all the major international airports, in that report you'll find that approximately ninety percent of all the airports had some form of infestation. I'm basing a lot of my conclusions on that information. Needless to say I've not had the time or the manpower to go any further than the major airports, I've therefore concluded that if the country has at least one infestation at an airport then the crystals have spread further into that country."

The President sat there staring up at the ceiling, Pattern could see the muscles in his jaw twitching and the Vice President sat fiddling with his pencil, their initial shock was turning into concern and worry.

"Well Pattern I gave you the position in this investigation team because you had an uncanny way of putting things together when only little bits where available, please give me your opinion of where we should go from here."

"Mr. President I don't see any possible way of stopping or even slowing down the spread of this crystal. I can't see any proactive steps that you can take to fight its destructive path, therefore the only immediate action that can be taken, to my mind, is to try and reduce the number of catastrophic incidents that may occur. I would suggest that the public should not be informed until such time as they find out for themselves, which will be soon. As soon as they become aware of what's going to happen there'll be panic and without a doubt you'll lose control in the streets. I believe that the very first thing you should do, in fact if it were up to me I would give the orders this afternoon to shut down all nuclear power stations immediately."

"Oh God yes," moaned the Vice President, "that never occurred to me, God help us if we were to have a meltdown or an incident like Chernobyl."

"Exactly," carried on Pattern "you could possibly use the threat of an imminent terrorist attack to justify this without upsetting the public too much. I would suggest that you have a competent team sent out to all airports throughout the country to find out the present state of their structures. I believe that in three or four weeks or sooner you'll have to close all airports and restrict all flights to those aircraft that can land on grass strips, take off vertically, or land and take off from water. If you get to this point then the news will have been broken to everybody and you'll have a state of chaos. I would suggest that you bring home all American forces immediately along with diplomats and families. It would be extremely difficult to have service people overseas when their homes, families and friends are facing the catastrophic situation at home. I would in fact give immediate leave to all but the most important people otherwise you might be faced with mass desertions.

As far as possible the immediate families of those serving on ships should be moved to those vessels. The ships could help to maintain some semblance of order and you would still have control over some of your forces. I would move yourselves and your families to one of the Navy vessels and set up a Com center there. You'll have to decide what you can do to ensure the safety of the government officials and their families, it will probably be best to move them to a naval vessel also."

There was silence and then the President looked at Pattern, he suddenly looked much older and it seemed to Pattern that dark shadows had formed below his eyes. "This is an horrific situation that you're suggesting, have you had any contact with anyone in other countries to find out if they're aware of this new crystal?"

"Sir I didn't think that it was in our best interests for me to do so but I do have a fairly close contact in MI five and he indicated to me that they were doing some investigations because of an incident somewhere in England. I think that it would be prudent for you to speak to the other heads of state since this is a global situation, especially if you're considering bringing home all the U.S. troops."

"Yes I see what you mean, what sort of time frame are we looking at?"

"This is where things get very hazy, the tests that I've had done gave us no indication of the speed that an infection works. There seems to be no explanation as to why a crystal infests a particular place or depth. We could find nothing that would speed up or slowdown an infestation, it all seems to be totally random. How this will occur is probably based on how a crystal entered the location. For example let's say you have a block of cement holding up a light standard, if a crystal comes in contact with it from the air then it would probably give you a surface infection, if it were carried by an insect and there was a crack then it might be a deeper infection, if it rained or water splashed on it then it might carry a crystal further into a fissure and it may commence really deep in the cement. However this is all conjecture since we've found, especially in the runways, that there are no cracks or breaks in the surface yet an infection was found deep down inside the cement. Sir I would estimate that you have possibly three or four weeks before the airports become too dangerous to use, however during that time you are wide open to major crashes."

"Pattern you have not advised me wrongly to date but I hope to God you're wrong about this. You realize that I have to get your findings checked and double checked before I make any major decisions."

"Yes Sir of course I do, I hope that I am wrong but I fear that I'm not."

"What scenario do you foresee happening?" Asked the Vice President.

"Sir I believe the following will happen, not in any particular order and not in the same order from one area to another. All electrical power supplies will cease as the pylons carrying the cables fall and the supply stations break down. All your dams will collapse causing major flooding. All your water supplies will fail. The sewer systems will collapse, as will your gas supplies. Any transportation system that has cement structures such as bridges, overpasses, tunnels etc. will no longer be passable. All your boat docks and shipping yards will collapse. Your oil supplies will cease. Most of your land defense systems will no longer be functional, communication systems will break down. Buildings will collapse; any structure that has a cement foundation including cement blocks will fall, there'll be virtually nowhere safe to live in the cities and towns. There'll be no supply of the necessities of modern life available anywhere. I believe what will hit the people the worst is the realization that there'll be no possibility of help or rescue for them from anywhere. Millions of people will die, only those that can find a place to live and become totally self-sufficient will have a chance to survive and even those will have to defend themselves against marauding gangs of desperate people. There'll be no law and order and what little military personnel that are available will be of little or no use. The very worst and bottom scenario is the complete collapse of civilization as we know it, in fact third world countries will come off better than the quote "civilized" ones."

The Vice President looked like he was about to pass out, he had stopped fiddling with his pencil and just sat there staring at Pattern. There was complete silence, Pattern noticed that he could hear a bird chirping somewhere outside the window.

"Decisions, decisions, decisions," whispered the President "we're facing a catastrophic mess, I must make some decisions."

He reached over, pressed a button and spoke to his secretary, "Betty please would you contact the Secretary of Homeland Security, I believe that he's in the country somewhere, tell him there's a meeting here at the White House at four o'clock this afternoon, this is an emergency meeting and I want him here in person, is that understood Betty?"

"Yes sir I'll get right on it."

A little later Pattern left a very disturbed and worried President in the White House and rushed over to LaGuardia Airport.

9

Lord Bradistock.

London, England.

The day after Pattern's meeting at Last Chance.

The morning after the meeting at Last Chance Lord Bradistock was in a business meeting at quarter past eight in his offices in London, England, there were three gentlemen and three ladies in the meeting with him all of whom were top executives in their own right, two of them had places in the House of Lords and they were having a heated discussion about the upcoming parliamentary elections.

Outside the meeting room, Paula, the Lord's personal secretary was sorting papers on her desk. This was the central office and clearinghouse of all the businesses in the conglomerate that Lord Bradistock owned and ran all around the world. Everything from diamond mines in Africa, gold mines in South America, farmlands in Australia, the lists went on and on, the Bradistock family was old money and between the present young Lord Bradistock, his father and his grandfather, they had managed the family businesses to new heights. Unlike many of the other British Aristocracy Lord Bradistock was very much a 'hands on' businessman. He was also recognized, mainly in the news tabloids, as being one of the most eligible bachelors in the United Kingdom. He was a very handsome man, he was thirty two years old and had never been married, he stood six foot four in his bare feet, he weighed approximately two hundred and forty pounds and was extremely fit, he had a full head of thick curly brown hair which always seemed to be a little bit uncontrollable. He had graduated from Oxford University with honors in business administration and English. He had been brought up in the lifestyles of the rich and famous and he was one of the few of the British Aristocracy that expended a great deal of effort and energy to helping others. He took great care of his employees. He was well respected by rich and poor and was a frequent guest of Royalty.

The Bradistock family had a very large estate in Devon, they owned approximately two thousand acres of beautiful countryside from the rolling grounds down to the rocky coast, included in this was what the family and everybody else jokingly called the "castle". It was in actual fact the family home and had been so since 1452 when the then King of England decreed all the lands the property of Nigel Bradistock in recognition of his help and support of the King in war. He had installed Nigel Bradistock and his rather homely wife as the first Lord and Lady of Bradistock. The present day estate consisted not of a castle but a magnificent stately home that the family had, all through the years, been very careful to maintain. They had saved most of the articles that the family had accumulated through the passing years, dating right back to those first days after the King's decree. His great great great grandfather had been a pack rat and, being a very wealthy man, had managed to accumulate a collection of all sorts of weird and wonderful things from teapots to crossbows and everything in between, all of which were now arrayed and displayed throughout the house.

The house consisted of fifteen bedrooms, fifteen bathrooms and other rooms that made up small suites for visitors. The center of the house was the grand ballroom, this was a magnificent room with thirty two foot ceilings that was used for entertaining. The present young Lord often put on lavish dinners and entertainment not only for his friends, but also to raise money for his charities. Some were for his employees and since he was a philanthropist, it was often used to put on meals for the poor. Nobody, except Paula his secretary, knew how much Lord Bradistock gave away to the needy not only in England but also abroad.

The phone rang in Paula's desk, it was a phone, a private phone whose number Lord Bradistock only gave out to very few people. That phone had not rung in the last eight months, Paula was quite startled by it.

She lifted the receiver and said "Lord Bradistock's secretary, may I help you?"

"Paula?"

"This is Paula, to whom am I speaking?"

"Paula, hello, this is Pattern, how are you?"

"Pattern, sir, hello."

Paula was surprised to hear Pattern's voice although they had often spoken through the years. The Lord had spoken of Pattern and had told her of the circumstances of how they had met and that he was on the special list of friends that he would speak to whenever they called.

"What can I do for you Sir?"

"Paula it's extremely, and I repeat, extremely urgent, that I speak to Lord B is he available?" The young Lord preferred to be referred to by his friends and acquaintances as Lord B rather than the Lord.

"I'm very sorry Sir but he is not available at the moment, he's in a meeting, if you give me your number I'll get him to get back to you as soon as possible."

"It is imperative that I speak to him now, I have a situation that he must hear about immediately, it is that urgent, would you please interrupt him, wherever he is, and give him a message while I stay on the phone. Would you please just tell him that Pattern wants to repay his debt and it needs to be done now?"

"Yes Sir if you just hold on I'll go in and see if he'll speak to you." She didn't wait for his reply she pushed the button and put him on hold, got up from behind her beautiful antique cherry wood desk and went over to the old oak carved door to the meeting room. The building was in the center of London and it was very old, it had been in very bad condition when Lord B bought it some ten years ago. He had refurbished it at great expense changing it from an almost derelict building to a magnificent office structure putting it back to its original days of Victorian glory. She tapped on the door and heard a very gruff voice say. "Come in."

She slipped quietly into the room, the Lord looked up very surprised to see her. When he said that he didn't want to be disturbed in a meeting that is exactly what he meant, he realized something very important must have come up for Paula to interrupt his meeting.

"Excuse me ladies and gentlemen just for a moment, it appears that my secretary needs me."

The room went quiet as Paula went over to him and said quietly in his ear. "I apologize for disturbing you Sir but I was asked to, it appears that here is an emergency. I have Pattern on the phone and he needs to talk to you immediately."

His eyebrows went up, an expression of surprise on his face.

"Pattern," Lord B whispered "what on earth does he want, he never phones me here at the business office, he only contacts me when we're going to go hunting together. Did he say what he wants Paula?"

"He told me to give you a message Sir and I repeat, "Pattern wishes to repay his debt to you and it needs to be done immediately", he's waiting on the phone for you Sir."

Lord B's face showed astonishment and everybody around the business table gazed at him questioningly.

He turned back to the table in front of him, "If you'll excuse me for a moment please Ladies and Gentlemen, it appears I have a very urgent message, it shouldn't take too long. Please help yourself to coffee from the sideboard and if you require anything else my secretary here will take care of you. Thank you." He got up and went into his secretary's office and sat in her chair, picked up the phone, pushed the button and said, "Well hello Pattern it's wonderful to hear from you, this is most unusual. How are you doing and what's so urgent?"

"Your Lordship," said Pattern, "I apologize for interrupting you but something has come up that is extremely urgent and I need to discuss it with you. I don't want to sound too mysterious but I can only stay on this phone for a short while, I have to see you in person immediately."

"This is most unusual Pattern, where are you?"

"I'm in the States."

"Can you come over here, is that possible, how about you come over this weekend?"

"Sir it's impossible for me to come over to England at this time and this can't wait until the weekend, is there anyway that you could meet me in New York?"

"Now Pattern you're asking an awful lot, I have business to attend to and right now I'm in the middle of a meeting discussing election plans. How urgent is this?"

"Sir I can't tell you too much on the phone but let me put it this way, there may not be any election in England in five months, there may never be another election in England at all or in the States or in any other country for that matter ever again, it's that urgent."

The Lord's face went white, he looked a little shocked, he knew the position that Pattern held with the President of the United States. After their initial meeting where he had been asked, by a representative of the Government, to give Pattern a lift to Northern Canada in his private plane he had become curious and he had had a private detective do a full investigation of Pattern and had been extremely surprised to find out that he worked directly for the President on very special investigations. If this was as urgent as Pattern said it was then he needed to meet him as soon as possible.

He spoke back into the phone, "If you're sure that it's that urgent and you can't come over here then I guess I'd better come over to LaGuardia Airport and meet you," he looked at his watch and figured out how long it would take to get to his private jet ready and how long the flight would take, "I could be there in approximately ten hours, where would you like to meet, some restaurant in New York or in my office?"

"Sir the timing will be fine but, if you don't mind, please stay on your plane, I'll meet you there, we need a very private place to have this discussion and I really shouldn't be seen with you at this time."

"That's Ok, if you want to check with the flight control at LaGuardia airport to find out where the plane will be held, I'll make sure that we have a meal and drinks setup for you in the plane, see you in approximately ten hours."

"Thank you very much Sir I assure you you won't regret this," and there was a click and the phone went dead.

Lord B hung up his phone and sat there staring at the beautifully carved and painted ceiling, he felt his pulse rate going up and his skin began to crawl with goose bumps as he recalled Pattern's voice and the emphasis he had put on secrecy. "There may not be any election in England in five months, there may never be another election in England at all or in the States or in any other country for that matter ever again" rang in his mind. A dull feeling of fear started to form in the pit of his stomach, he dreaded what he was going to find out in New York.

He went back into his meeting room, everyone's saw that he was a little shaken. The Duchess of Northward looked at him, "Are you all right Lord Bradistock, you look a little shaken?"

Lord B sat down in his seat at the head of the huge conference table, Paula was fussing over a pot of coffee on the sideboard, "Yes I'm fine, just a little shaken, I've had some fairly bad personal news. I hate to break up this meeting but it's imperative that I leave immediately. Can we put this meeting off to let's say," he looked at the calendar on his computer in front of him, "Let's say we reschedule the meeting for next Thursday at eight o'clock, is that convenient with everyone?"

The others looked a little shocked, they realized it must be something extremely urgent to tear the Lord away from this meeting, it had been in the works for a long time and in itself was quite urgent. Each one of them checked their own computers and one by one they nodded. "Why don't we get the secretaries to set up a place and a time for the next meeting?" Suggested Sir William Balsam, there were nodding heads all the way around.

"Thank you thank you very much, that's settled then, if you'll excuse me, I must be about this urgent business." He turned to Paula who had a very strange expression on her face. "Paula please, I need you in my office immediately."

He got up and left the room leaving everything on the table, he moved to his office that was directly next door to the meeting room. Paula put down the coffee pot that she was holding and followed him. His office reflected his way of life; it was decorated with beautiful antiques, it was a man's office and he was very comfortable in it, he sank down into the overstuffed Victorian desk chair and waited as Paula came in and closed the door behind her.

"Well Paula that phone call sure messed up my schedule. I can't tell you what it's all about, I wish I could, but I've no idea what it's all about myself but it looks like I have to go to New York immediately and I mean right away. Please change all my appointments for the next, let's say, twenty four hours, it's going to take me a good ten hours to get to New York and then another ten hours to get back, I hate that damn flight, and to make the trip there and back straightaway will be exhausting."

Paula smiled, she knew the Lord really did not like flying and only put up with it because there was no other way to cover the great distances he had to travel throughout the year.

"Call the plane and tell them to get ready immediately. Please contact home and explain that I won't be home this evening, explain to George where I've gone on urgent business and that I'll contact him on my way back. Would you pack a bag for me please Paula, nothing dressy, very casual and comfortable, it may turn out that I might not even get off the plane, we'll most probably have the meeting right there on the airport tarmac. Ask the pilot to make sure there's a nice meal prepared by the chef for when we arrive in New York, a meal for two please. I should get away from here in the next twenty minutes to half an hour and I'll head straight to the airport. Do you have all that Paula?"

George was the butler and in charge of every thing at Lord B's stately home.

"Yes Sir I have all that, I'll have your stuff packed up and ready to go in twenty minutes and make sure the plane is ready to leave when you get there."

Paula turned and left the office, Lord B sat there for a minute gathering his thoughts, he picked up the phone and pushed the button on his speed dial, the phone rang twice before it was picked up.

"Hello to whom am I speaking?"

"Patrick, this is Lord Bradistock."

"Well hello your Lordship, haven't heard from you for a while," the voice became much more familiar in tone, "how are you? What can I do for you today?"

"Patrick," Patrick was head of MI5, the top intelligence unit in the United Kingdom, he was a personal acquaintance and somewhat of a friend of the Lord, they had gone through University together. "I've just had a very disturbing phone call, I can't tell you what it's about because I haven't the faintest idea other than there's something very big and very immediate in the wind. Have you heard anything?"

There was complete silence on the phone for a moment. "Can you be any more specific?" Patrick said, "There's an awful lot going on in the world, I'm not quite sure what you're trying to get at."

"This may be something that might interrupt or cause the upcoming elections to be canceled here and possibly even in the United States."

Again there was silence, Lord B knew that Patrick was sifting through his photographic memory. He could run through his brain as you or I run through a filing cabinet.

"Sir I don't believe there's anything that I know of that could interrupt the elections here yet alone in the United States."

Lord Bradistock new that there would never be any specific information given out over the telephone and, in Patrick's position, he knew that very little information would ever be given out at all even in a private meeting.

"Thank you Patrick, I appreciate your candor, I'm going to have a meeting shortly, if I find out anything that I think you should know about I'll be in touch."

"Thank you very much, I'm sorry I couldn't be of any more help, I would appreciate any information you could give me, in the meantime I'll put out some feelers to see what I can find out about anything that might disrupt the elections."

"Thank you, I'll be in touch."

Lord B hung up his telephone.

Paula arranged to have the plane ready, the pilot said that he would be prepared to leave within an hour and asked if she knew where they were going since he had to file a flight plan. Paula told him that he would be flying to LaGuardia airport and it would possibly be an immediate return flight since it looked like there was going to be a meeting on the plane at the airport and that he was to make sure that there was a nice meal for two people to be served when it landed. She then phoned George at the Bradistock estate.

About nine hours later Lord Bradistock and Pattern were seated in the big overstuffed leather chairs in the private jet, the jet was parked on the cement apron set aside for private aircraft at LaGuardia airport in New York. Lord Bradistock had only had to wait twenty minutes after his plane came to a complete standstill before Pattern's helicopter swooped down and landed close beside the jet. Lord B just had time to tell his chef aboard the plane to lay out the food and drinks so that he and Pattern could sit back and eat while they were talking before Pattern came up into the plane carrying a briefcase. Lord B noticed that Pattern seemed to be very edgy, looking around as if to make sure that nobody was watching him. The two men greeted each other warmly, they were very good friends and only saw each other once or twice a year. On the table between them the chef laid out a plowman's lunch, fresh lettuce, sliced tomatoes, Branston pickles, a thick slice of smoked ham and a variety of cheeses, there was some thick slices of fresh baked crusty bread with extra salted butter and to wash it down glasses of lager and lime served in chilled glasses. Pattern visibly relaxed as the main door to the jet was closed.

"Well it's really nice to see you again" the Lord said taking a sip from his lager and lime, "I must say all this cloak and dagger stuff has me totally confused, what on earth is so important as to make me rush over here? I noticed that you seem a little edgy, what the hell's going on?"

"Your right, I really didn't want anyone to see me meeting with you, officially I'm not even here, this is what you might call, in the movies, a clandestine meeting," he smiled enjoying the flavor of his ice cold drink, "it really is good to see you and, unfortunately, I don't have a lot of time so we'll have to catch up with all our latest news at another time."

The Lord nodded and waited for him to carry on.

"Okay, you know my position, you know what I do and you know who I do it for since you had me thoroughly investigated after our first meeting, that saves me a lot of time, I don't have to try to prove where my information comes from and goes to."

"That was supposed to be a secret investigation," smiled the Lord.

"I'm very fortunate," said Pattern "in my position there are very very few things that are a secret from me."

Pattern reached into his briefcase and laid a thick folder on the table and turned it so that Lord B could read it. "That's a report that I've just presented to the President this morning, it's highly classified, its contents are known by only a small group of people. I'll let you read through it and then we can discuss it."

Pattern watched Lord B's face as he read, he knew he was able to put pieces of information together and add up all the facts in short order. Watching Lord B's face he knew that he understood the seriousness of the report.

His Lordship sat back in his chair, very little of the food had been eaten, staring blankly at the roof of the plane, Pattern could almost see the cogs turning behind those staring eyes.

"I see why you dragged me over here so swiftly," his Lordship said coming back to the present, "that's one hell of a report, I won't even ask you if everything has been checked, I know in your position that everything has been authenticated, my God, the consequences are horrific, is there nothing that can be done to stop this?"

"No, I've had our best scientists working on that, they've come up with a blank. It's a really strange animal, there doesn't seem to be any rhyme or reason to where it strikes first or how fast it reacts, the only thing that seems to slow down its rapid growth is exposure to extremely high temperatures, as in a blast furnace. These don't totally stop it, they just slow it down. There's absolutely no doubt that where ever this crystal comes into contact with any cement or mortar it will eventually break it down and form more crystals."

"The consequences are catastrophic," said Lord B "what's your best estimate, what sort of time do we have before this becomes public knowledge, what is the President going to do?"

"At this time, my best estimate would be that we have, at the very most, four to five weeks before the news breaks, I would only really guarantee two weeks for safety sake. I have no way of knowing what the President will do, he's going to have meetings this afternoon, he doesn't know what to do himself, I left him a little shell shocked. Whenever the news leaks or the President makes it public there'll be instant panic and chaos everywhere. We are of course continuing to study the crystal and may soon be able to formulate a better estimation of the time that we have left but, as I've just said, my best estimate at the moment is a maximum of four to five weeks but I would say only two weeks to be on the safe side."

His Lordship sat looking out of the aircraft window for a moment and then said "Pattern I really appreciate this information at least it gives me some time to make some preparations. What are you going to do?"

"I've already set things in motion, a group of us are setting up a camp, more like a community, in a remote location. As we speak preparations are being made. We'll be moving to this location before any knowledge of the crystal gets out to the public, we're going to try and have everything set up in the next two weeks. We're preparing to be self sufficient for a minimum of five years, I firmly believe that the instant that the public realizes what is happening the law of the gun will take over. There won't be any police and the army will be of very little use, it will be every one for themselves. I think, possibly, that your camp in Canada might be the best bet for you Sir but of course that will have to be your decision."

"Yes I see what you mean, right off the top of my head I can't think of a better place to try and weather this out, I think you're correct, I'll have to move extremely fast."

Pattern looked at his watch, "I must be out of here, needless to say I was never here, we never had this meeting."

The Lord nodded and they both stood up, they shook hands and his Lordship said "Thank you for entrusting this to me, you've no idea how much I appreciate it. I hope this isn't the last time we see each other."

"I've no way of knowing what will happen in the future but rest assured that I know where you'll be in Canada, if that's where you decide to go. I'll keep in touch, I know you have an amateur radio station setup and I know your emergency frequency."

"Excellent, an excellent idea my friend, I thank you again and hope that all goes well with you" Lord B said as Pattern started down the steps of the plane."

Pattern looked back over his shoulder and waved, "Good hunting my friend good hunting," and he turned and started back to his helicopter as Lord B disappeared back into his plane and the steps started to retract.

Fifteen minutes later the Lord's plane was taxiing to take off as he sat back and closed his eyes letting his mind mull over the terrifying report he had just read. His mind worked its way from page to page pulling out and noting a specific point here and there. There was only one logical conclusion, that being that civilization was about to face a most terrifying and horrific trial. He realized that he was very short of time, he should really make all his arrangements within the next two weeks to be assured that he was prepared before the public found out what was going to happen. He ran through a list of places throughout the world trying to figure out what would be the best move for him and his household, he quickly came to the conclusion, as had Pattern, that his camp in Canada was the best and safest place.

He thought about his camp, it was his favorite place in the whole world. In 1882 an extremely wealthy railway Baron had met two old hunters in a bar who, after they had all imbibed in many drinks, had invited him to go hunting with them in the Rocky Mountains in Canada, North of Fort James in what today is British Columbia. Two weeks later, much to the chagrin of the two hunters they found themselves leading a very large entourage, led by the Baron, up into the Canadian wilderness. The only way into the area at that time was by canoe, it was a long trip, the two hunters had two cabins set on a magnificent lake surrounded by snowcapped mountains and miles and miles of treed wilderness, it was truly a wonderful setting. It was a very successful hunt but more importantly the Baron had fallen in love with the wilderness. Upon returning to civilization he purchased twenty five thousand acres surrounding the area from the British government.

The following year his young wife fell ill and became quite frail, the doctors said that she needed to move out of the city, somewhere where the air was fresh. He commissioned a well-known architect to design and build a massive log hunting lodge right on the spot where he'd camped with the two hunters. The hunters were livid with the intrusion into their solitude and ended up moving off further into the mountains. His wife loved the lodge and moved in permanently, this meant that the Baron had to leave her for long periods of time to look after his business ventures. His wife spared no expense in setting herself up and ensuring her comforts, she had some alterations made to accommodate large groups of her friends who would come up during the summer months. On the main floor of the Lodge was a very large dining room with huge windows overlooking the lake, there was a very well appointed kitchen, a very large living room with windows overlooking the bushes, trees and the mountains to the back of the building. Right across the front of the structure was a huge room called the grand room with towering ceilings and a massive stone fireplace. One side, overlooking the lake, was made completely of glass that could be opened onto a porch that ran the whole length of the building. This was the entertainment room where everybody spent most of the time. There were four bathrooms and four bedrooms on the main floor and on the upper floor there were the eight bedrooms and six bathrooms, every room had its own fireplace. She had had the servants quarters built to the right of the lodge which consisted of seven bedrooms, four bathrooms, their own kitchen and eating area and a living room, this was connected to the main building by a covered walkway.

His wife named the lodge "Victoria's Retreat". The second year that she lived there gold was discovered in a stream that came down one of the mountains into a valley about five miles from the lodge, since this was on the Baron's property the gold was his.

For the next four years there was a lot of coming and going and miners digging for gold, then the gold ran out. The small amount of gold left was not worth their while and the mine closed down.

In the fall of her eighth year at the lodge his wife fell seriously ill and died, the Baron was broken hearted and closed up the lodge, he never went back to it. It sat fully furnished, exactly the way that his wife had left it, for the next three years during which time the Baron lost a lot of his wealth.

The Baron met the Lord of Bradistock, Lord B's great great grandfather, on a hunting trip from England, they became friends and one evening, after a few drinks they were playing poker. The Baron lost a considerable amount of money to Lord Bradistock and on the final hand he had three aces, he put up Victoria's retreat as his bet. Lord Bradistock won the hand with a running flush, the Baron walked away furious and Lord Bradistock walked away owning twenty five thousand acres of Canadian wilderness which he had never seen.

When the gold mine had been productive the Baron had put in two wooden bridges across the precipitous valleys, this had allowed transportation to come up and go and down the rugged road through the mountains from his mine to Fort James. At the base of the mountain a small town sprang up and between the town and Victoria's Retreat was a vast marsh that, most of the time, was impassible. The town consisted of approximately fifteen houses and stores that became vacant when the miners left.

The following summer Lord Bradistock went up to the retreat by canoe and instantly fell in love with the charm of the place. He was a very shrewd businessman and recognized the possibilities for a hunting and fishing camp, a commercial venture. He commissioned the same architect who had built the original lodge to build twenty separate three bedroom log cabins in the woods surrounding the main lodge for hunting parties. Water would be brought in from a waterfall back a short way into the woods on the side of the mountain. This could be heated as needed. He put a young local hunter in charge of running the business and the property was soon widely known as one of the best hunting and fishing camps in the Rocky Mountains, it was a very successful venture.

The mining town, which had been abandoned, slowly became home to an odd assortment of people. The Lord Bradistock that had won the camp past it on to Lord B's great grandfather and then on to his grandfather who had the whole camp modernized, had electricity supplied by a generator powered by the nearby waterfall and septic waste systems put in for each of the buildings.

The town had slowly expanded because, during the summer months, tourists came and stopped at a small inn at the foot of the mountain where the gold mine was located. The visitors came to pan for gold, though the mine was not viable as a commercial venture the visitors paid to pan and hunt for gold, anything that they found they could keep. Many of the visitors left finding quite a lot of gold, some of them came back year after year and so the village had grown to accommodate the tourists.

Among the permanent residents in the village were a doctor and his wife. They had been a surgeon and a nurse at one of the major hospitals in Vancouver, he had become quite ill and they had moved into the Valley for rest and relaxation and had never left. The present Lord had set up a complete surgery and clinic for the doctor and his wife to look after the residents and all the visitors that came through. There was a well equipped hardware store to accommodate the hunters and fishermen and gold seekers. There was a small auto repair garage run by a very strange young couple, a post office and a wonderful restaurant run by two sisters. A white water rafting company had built a small commercial venture just outside the village on one of the many rivers.

Lord B had put in a road from the village through the marsh to the lodge but this could only be used when there had been a long dry spell. He looked forward to spending a month in the camp relaxing each year, he was a hunter and fisherman. A very outlandish character called Wild Willy ran the present lodge, he was very efficient in promoting and running the business. There had been many changes to the Lodge, today there were twenty five cabins, four very large barns for storage, the servants quarters had been expanded and now had fourteen bedrooms, the main lodge had been expanded to include a huge recreational area which housed pool tables, a stage and dance area, a television and video room and yes even a few one armed bandits. During the summer months only the very wealthy could afford to stay at the camp, no amount of money was spared to keep them extremely comfortable. During the winter months it was a lot less expensive to stay there and it was usually at least half full of hunters and people that love to live and play in the snow.

For the first couple of hours of his return flight Lord Bradistock sat gathering his thoughts, he could feel the hairs on the back of his neck rising and that strange butterfly feeling forming in the pit of his stomach, the feelings he always got when he realized he had to rise to a difficult challenge. He headed up one of the biggest corporate conglomerates in the world, he had inherited the vast financial empire when his mother and father had been killed in a car crash in the south of France a little over ten years ago, being the only child he now had sole control.

His pride and joy was the family home, Bradistock stately home, it had been in his family now for over two hundred years and it was today a living museum of all the things that his family had collected throughout the years from all over the world. The home had been modernized with each progressive generation and though it was a massive stone structure today it was extremely comfortable to live in. It had eight hundred acres of beautifully manicured grounds, with lakes and ponds with magnificent fountains and beautiful flower gardens and even a very large maze. To keep up the grounds and the home he employed forty-eight full-time workers from the local community. Most of his employees were second or third generations of the same family and he looked after his employees extremely well. Positions were kept for a lifetime due to exceptional benefits and pension plans, his employees were extremely loyal.

He realized that now he faced most probably the biggest challenge of his life, the hardest part of any decisions that he was about to make would be the closing down and leaving behind of his beloved Bradistock castle.

He suddenly realized that he had accepted Pattern's report as true and that the consequences were unavoidable, with this realization his mind clicked over to plan his next moves. Time was of the essence; time would be his major adversary. He had to make one more check, one more attempt to verify Pattern's report, he picked up the phone and dialed a number and the phone at the other end rang twice.

"Bill Morgan here, what can I do for you?" A very gruff voice with a very posh accent answered the phone.

"Hello Bill, Bradistock here, long time no see." He and Bill had attended University together and had remained very good friends all through the years, Bill now headed up the most important and largest forensic laboratory for the British government.

"Well hello there Bradistock, nice to hear from you, what can I do for you?"

Just like Bill, always straight to business thought Lord Bradistock "Bill I want to ask you some questions, I realize, in your position, you can't give out certain top secret information and I'm not asking you to do so. However when I ask you a question, if you remain silent I'll be able to read into your silence what ever I wish."

"This sounds very serious and I thank you for recognizing the fact that I may not be able to answer your questions, fire away."

"First question, have you been involved in or have you heard of any tests or investigations into a brand-new substance in the form of a white crystal?"

There was a humph at the other end of the line, he could hear Bill's breathing quicken but there was absolute silence.

There was a long pause to make sure that there was no answer, "second question, if there were such a white crystal is there any way of preventing it from spreading?"

Again there was silence from the other end.

"Last question, is there anything that can be done to prevent the terrible damage that such a white crystal could cause?"

Again there was that terrible silence. "I see, thank you for listening to me."

"I'm sorry that I couldn't be of any further assistance to you," said Bill, Lord B thought he detected a slight worry in his voice. "There's really nothing else I can say at this time."

"Again I thank you very much you have been a great help to me, I hope to see you and your family soon, goodbye Bill," and he hung up the phone.

He sat back in his chair, he now had confirmation of the truth of Pattern's report, now he could move ahead to try and make the best use of the time available to him.

He picked up the phone again and dialed.

"Bradistock castle, George the Butler here what can I do for you?"

George had been the Lord's right-hand man for over the last twenty five years, the Lord had grown up with George in control of the whole household and grounds, he was very competent, very loyal and a very dear friend.

"Hello George, something's come up and it needs our immediate, I repeat our immediate attention, I can't explain over the phone but I'll do so as soon as we meet. It means that we must close down Bradistock estate as fast as possible and I mean close it down completely and move it lock stock and barrel to the hunting lodge in Canada. I realize this is a shock but it's unavoidable and it must be done as fast as possible."

George replied in his usual very matter of fact voice, "That is a shock Sir, I take it that you mean that you wish to move all the office and paperwork etc. to the lodge?"

"No George, I mean we remove everything out of castle to the lodge, we'll be at the lodge for an indefinite period, everything that can be moved out of the castle is to be moved."

"I see," said George in a very surprised voice, "that's quite a move."

Nothing usually disturbed George, he seemed to take everything in his stride.

"We're going to have to move very fast, we have to establish residence completely in Canada within the next two weeks, I don't care what it costs, we must be moved within two weeks."

"I see Sir, then I shall have to proceed immediately, with your permission, I'll look around for a moving company to come in to pack up the belongings, how do you intend to transport everything?"

"George don't fuss about getting the lowest bid, get as many people in as you need and I mean that, I'll contact the company airline and commandeer a plane or planes as required."

"I see Sir, the timeline is very short but I'm sure that it can be accomplished. What would you like me to tell the employees?"

"I'm on my way back in the corporate jet, I should get back home in approximately six hours, set up a meeting with all the employees and I mean all the employees, anybody that's off duty have them come in for the meeting, you can explain that it's very urgent and imperative that they're at that meeting, in the meantime start organizing the company to come in and pack up the belongings."

"Yes Sir, I'll see that everyone is in attendance, if someone can't be available I'll have someone from their family in attendance, I'll see you in approximately six hours."

"Thank you George see you then" and the Lord hung up his phone.

The whisper went through the castle like wild fire, never, in all the history that anyone could remember, had a Lord called all his employees to a meeting, something serious must be up, everyone started to speculate. Phone calls were made, people were called back in and George contacted one of the biggest moving companies in southern England, Behemoth Moving and Storage who, after he had agreed to pay them almost twice their usual fee had promised to send in a platoon of people to have the entire house packed up in one week.

Lord B was growing calm, the war was on, his mind was racing, he was in action, he had two weeks and by God he'd make the most of those two weeks. The next phone call he placed was to Amsterdam. The diamonds that were produced in South Africa were sent through to the diamond exchange in Amsterdam, he owned one of the largest cutting company's in the diamond district. A phone rang and a voice came through with a heavy accent. "This is the McWilliams Diamond Merchant, where may I direct your call?

"Yes, this is Lord Bradistock, please put me through to Jorgen Weiss?"

"Yes, Sir," the voice sharpened up "I'll put you through to him right away." He was put on hold for a few seconds and then a voice came on the line.

"Lord Bradistock, Sir" he had an accent but his English was impeccable "pleasure to hear from you, what can I do for you?"

"Jorgen, how much diamond stock do we have in Amsterdam?"

"I beg your pardon Sir?"

"I need to know, in monetary value, how much stock do we have in Amsterdam."

There was silence for a minute.

"I could look it up exactly for you Sir but as you know we maintain quite a vast stock, as do all the other diamond merchants. The release of diamonds is rigidly controlled."

"Yes, yes, I know all about that Jorgen, on your estimate, what is the value of the diamonds we have at your disposal?"

"Sir, the rough estimate… The rough estimate, is twenty to thirty million pounds worth in cut diamonds and about the same in uncut diamonds." There was silence.

"Jorgen, I'm going to ask you to do something, I'll follow it up in writing, I want you to transport all of your cut and uncut diamonds to a bank in Canada. Unless I'm very much mistaken we have outlets throughout Canada, so we shouldn't have any problem sending that large an amount but if you do have problems take care of them. I'll phone you back and give you the exact address where I want them transported and I want you to do it quietly. I don't want any problems and if you have any, take care of them. I don't want any fuss or bother, I don't want anyone to know, I want you to keep doing business as usual but I want that forty to sixty million moved within the next three working days."

There was again silence on the phone.

"Sir, this is unheard of, may I ask why?'

"I have to make some very serious financial decisions in the next few days and I may need a great deal of leverage and since the prime interests will be in Canada, I need those collaterals in place."

"I understand Sir, it must be one hell of a deal. I will, of course, do as you say, if you can call me back with the address they'll be there lock, stock and barrel within the next three days."

"Thank you Jorgen I appreciate that, I'll be in touch shortly." He hung up the phone and picked it up again. The phone rang in the office of the gold mine in northern British Columbia.

"Hello, Ferguson's Mining can I help you?" came the pretty voice of a secretary.

"Yes you may, would you please put me through to William McDeigh please?"

"Who may I say is calling?" asked the voice politely.

"This is Lord Bradistock."

"Oh yes Sir, I'll see if he's available."

"If you don't mind, make him available."

"Yes Sir." There was a moment and then a very gruff voice with a slight Scottish accent came on the line. "Yes Lord Bradistock, what can I do for you?"

"Um, how's everything going?"

"That's a strange question Sir, very seldom do we ever hear from you, business is going very well, we keep up our full quota and production is excellent."

"That's very good," Lord B said "how much bullion to do you have on hand?"

"I beg your pardon Sir, can you repeat that please?"

"I want to know how much gold bullion you have on hand."

"Would you hold on a minute Sir?

The Lord could hear the rustling of paper.

"Do you want it in weight or in value?"

"Give me the monetary value in Canadian dollars," more rustling of papers and clicking of calculator keys.

"Well Sir this is getting toward the end of the week so we have one complete load ready to be shipped. Um, the estimated value of the shipment is, ah let me see here, is about forty-five million dollars and then we have our reserve, uh, in case of a rush on the market we have a reserve of about twelve million dollars worth."

"Tell me, what happens if we cancel that shipment and redirect it?"

"I beg your pardon?

"I said what would happen if we redirected that shipment?"

"Well, um, um, well Sir, I've never heard of such a thing, let me think for a minute, let me think. It would mean that we would lose some market value and some confidence in our ability to fulfill our commitments, the shares in the company would most likely go down quite drastically, people would assume that the mine was not producing sufficient to fulfill our obligations. I definitely wouldn't recommend it."

"Alright, listen to me, find some excuse, the best one you can possible come up with, put it out on the newswire that this month we can't fulfill our obligations. I understand that the shares will go down and there'll be a bit of a hue and cry but I want that gold bullion redirected and I want it redirected in the next two to three days and I don't want you to let anybody know where it's going or why. Am I clear?"

"Um, yes Sir but I'd like you to put that in writing for me to cover my arse."

"I have your fax number, I'll have something faxed to you in the next two or three hours and I'll get back to you with the address of where I want it sent. Do we have it all clear?

"Yes, Sir. You know you've just ruined my day."

Lord B laughed. "Yes I understand completely, trust me when I say that I really need this bullion to leverage some very big financial moves within Canada, you'll hear about it in the next three or four weeks," and he hung up the phone.

The next phone call was put through to his hunting lodge, the phone rang and rang and rang until the answering machine picked up and he heard Wild Willy's voice. "Bert here, I'm not available but leave a message and I'll get back to you" and then a buzzer.

"Bert, Lord Bradistock here, I need to talk to you, I need to talk to you as soon as possible, you have my number, call me please," and he hung up the phone. He sat back in his seat and relaxed thinking of other things that he had to do as fast as possible

Five hours later he was driving into the Bradistock estate in his Land Rover. When at home he preferred to drive himself around. If he was going any distance he was chauffeured in his limousine. George greeted him at the main door.

"Good evening Sir, welcome home," he said as he took the Lord's jacket and hat, "I trust we've had a successful and comfortable trip?"

"George it was a very insightful trip and one that's going to change our lives forever. I need to talk to you briefly, is everyone here for the meeting?"

"Yes Sir, everyone's in the Grand Hall, I took the liberty of serving some refreshments and coffee while they waited for you."

"Excellent George, thank you. Come into the library for a moment, we need to talk." They moved into the library, a magnificent room finished in white carved oak and bookshelves around the huge fireplace, the Lord sat down in a comfortable armchair, George stood in front of him.

"Sit down George, please." George sat down opposite his employer and waited expectantly.

"There are some things that I can't tell you at present," began Lord Bradistock choosing his words carefully. "It's necessary for us to move lock, stock and barrel to Victoria's Camp; it will be for an indefinite length of time. As of yet I can't tell you the reason why but enough to say, we must complete the move in two weeks. At the meeting I intend to let everybody know of this and will offer everyone the opportunity to come with us, this will include any of their immediate family and anyone who they have to look after on a permanent basis at the present time. Everyone will have a choice of coming with us or staying at home and I will provide him or her with a comfortable retirement package. I need to know George, what you'll do before I go into the meeting."

There was silence in the room for a moment and then George spoke, "Sir I and my wife have served your family for many years, we'll come with you to Canada, in fact, the idea quite excites me. It'll be a major change and quite a challenge and you know I do so enjoy a good challenge," a wicked grin on his face.

"Thank you George, I appreciate your loyalty, now do you think anyone will be willing to come over to Canada?"

"I should think the majority would be willing to come."

The Lord nodded. "I hate disturbing families and possibly breaking up homes but it can't be avoided. Ok, George, let's go and see the rest of the staff."

They walked down to the Great Hall, everyone was talking and whispering and wondering what the hell was going on, a meeting like this was unheard of, in fact the Lord hardly ever saw some of his employees except in passing.

"Ladies and gentlemen, please be seated."

Down the center of the hall was a massive cherry wood table that was used for banquets and could seat fifty people comfortably. There was almost silence in the room as people found seats and saw that Lord Bradistock was going to the head of the table. Quietly they all sat down. Lord B stood at the head of the table and looked around, "Ladies and gentlemen, friends, something has come up which entails a major change for Bradistock Castle, it means a complete change in all of our lives, I have had to make a major decision that must be carried out with the utmost speed, I can't tell you the exact reasons behind my decision but suffice to say that there is no alternative. I don't know if you all know that part of our estate is a property known as Victoria's Camp, it consists of a grand lodge, twenty-five cabins, and other out buildings set in the heart of twenty-five thousand acres of wilderness just to the northeast of Fort James in British Columbia, Canada."

Everyone was looking at each other with faces of expectation and worry.

"I have decided that I must close Bradistock Castle."

Moans and whispers ran around the table, they were all obviously anxious to ask questions.

"Please, let me finish and afterwards I'll answer your questions if they haven't been answered by the time I'm done. I intend to move everything to Victoria's Camp, this includes all my business and office requirements and everything here at Bradistock Castle. The camp is extremely modern, it has all modern facilities and it's been rented out to some of the wealthiest people in the world, it will now become my home, our home. I am asking each and every one of you to come with us," he nodded to George, "to come with us for an indefinite period of time to live and work at the camp. Needless to say, I'll pay for all expenses for anybody who will make the trip; if you have houses to sell I'm quite prepared to purchase the homes at fair market value. Not only am I inviting you to come, I am inviting and am willing to pay for all of your immediate family and for any persons that you are presently looking after, this will be restricted to husbands and wives, children, mothers and fathers and any grandchildren that are living with you and, as I said, anyone who you've been looking after or who lives with you. These persons aren't carved in stone, exceptions can be made depending on the circumstances." The faces cheered up a bit with expressions of wonder and curiosity. "Now for the catch, the move to Canada must be completed within two weeks."

There were sounds of breath being let out, a couple of moans and a few wows.

"I recognize that at first things may be a little crowded but I assure you that we will immediately start building to be sure everybody has a comfortable home to live in. I know I'm rushing you but I don't have any time or any other alternatives. Please think this over, talk it over with your family, I can give you twenty-four hours to make a decision after which time I will make arrangements for passports, travel documents and transportation for all those that wish to come. Anyone that chooses not to come I am prepared to give you a generous severance package. I will need everybody, and I mean everybody, to work here for the next two weeks to ensure that Bradistock Castle is packed up and moved. Termination packages will be paid on the last day and since we're moving for an indefinite period of time I can't promise you'll be rehired at any time in the future. I wish to say that I thank you all for the work that you've done and the way you've looked after Bradistock Castle and my family. I appreciate every one of you and I hope that every one of you will join me in this endeavor. Now, if there are any questions I'll take them."

A dozen hands flew up in the air.

10

The Cabins.

Frenchburg, Kentucky.

Just after the meeting at Last Chance.

Saturday night, after coming home from Last Chance, Rob and June went to bed but couldn't sleep, they mulled over everything that had happened over and over again. The bottom line they came to realize was that Pattern was right, there were no alternatives, they must move to Last Chance as soon as possible. They made love slowly and very gently needing that closeness and togetherness that can only be found in making love, eventually they fell asleep in each other's arms.

June was on duty at the emergency room at the hospital on Sunday, Rob saw her off to work and then jumped into his car and went out to his clinic, today was his day off but he had better start things rolling for the move to Last Chance and he had to talk to Jesse.

As he pulled up to the clinic he saw Jesse coming running round the corner of the building with a bag of dog food, she must have been feeding the two dogs that they were boarding for a couple of days.

"Well hello there Boss" came her happy greeting "what are you doing here on your day off, you should be home in bed with your beautiful wife." She grinned and winked at him.

"Good morning to you too Jesse, my wife has to work today and I have some things I need to talk to you about, can you break loose for a while?"

"Sure Boss, you look really serious, anything wrong?"

"Well that depends, let's go sit down in the office, okay?"

"Okay I'll follow you in" she said as he went into his office and sat down behind his desk and, after she'd put the dogs into their cages, she came and sat down opposite him.

"Let's have it, what's worrying you?"

"Jesse I got some really startling information yesterday and it's going to change everything," he said and then proceeded to tell her all that had been discussed at Last Chance; she hung on his every word listening intently.

After he had finished she sat there for a few minutes looking a little weird. "Wow!!!! If that's all true, we're really in the shit, what are we going to do?"

"Well," said Rob "we're all going to move to this camp that is about to become a community at Last Chance. Do your remember me telling you about my teen age years growing up in a camp stuck out in the middle of nowhere?"

She nodded at him.

"Well a group of us have decided to try and make that camp into a sort of sanctuary for us all to try and get through the tough times" he carried on " Now the question is do you want to come with us? June and I really want you to come but it is, of course, up to you. You're free to make up your own mind. It'll be pretty rough till we get everything at the camp set up and running"

"I don't need to think about it, not even for a second, if you two are going then so am I. I don't have anyone else, you two are all that I have, you can't get rid of me that easy" she said with a quick laugh.

"That's wonderful," he said and she could see that a worry had been taken off his shoulders "I was worried a little in case you wouldn't want to go."

"Well what do we have to do first Boss since it looks as if we are going to be in a big hurry?"

"We have to do two things as fast as possible, we need to make a list of everything that we could possibly need to take with us from the clinic here. It's been suggested that we should be prepared to be isolated for up to five years, so we need to stock up and purchase everything that we can possibly think of that we'll need to set up a full veterinary clinic to handle every kind of animal from small to big for that length of time."

"Wow, isolation for five years, what no men for me?" she burst into nervous laughter.

"Oh yes there are some fine young men already living there and I've no doubt more will be joining us, so you should be just fine."

"Now that's a relief. Well making the list shouldn't be too difficult thanks to the computer world, how soon do we have to get things delivered here?"

"As soon as possible," said Rob "it would be best if we could be to Last Chance within the next two weeks; that should give us plenty of time to get in what we want. We've all that is necessary for the operating room we just need to order some pharmaceuticals and some more instruments. We'd better make sure that we take lots of books covering everything to do with veterinary science, if you could look after that, most probably the best place to start would be the University."

"Sure Boss, I'll get right on that, what was the other thing that we should do?"

"I've been put in charge of finding some sort of living quarters that we can get to Last Chance for everyone. The only thing I can come up with is something like a log cabin."

Jesse sat there for a moment and Rob could almost see the wheels turning in her head, she looked worried for a moment and then it seemed as if a light bulb had just been turned on and she grinned,

"A number of years ago I was sent to spend a few months at a correctional camp, it was very rustic, we had to sleep in A frame cabins. They were really simple, just two walls set about twenty feet apart at the bottom and leaning inwards, coming together as a point at the top, with a floor across the bottom, they were quite spacious and quite comfortable. The camp was about a hundred miles north of here and I remember one of the guards saying that everything in the camp had been made locally, perhaps something like that might work?"

"I'd forgotten about A frames, that might be ideal, I wonder where they were made."

"Well it should be easy to find out, all we have to do is to go onto the Web."

She moved over to her corner desk and started typing on the computer, within ten minutes she had a list of three manufacturers of preformed homes or cabins in their area. Rob phoned the first one on the list, it turned out they only made prefabricated houses. The second one made prefabricated log cabins, these could be made to any specifications that you wanted, put together at the factory and then disassemble and shipped wherever you wanted them, all of the main supporting walls were made of solid logs, this made the shipping very costly. The third manufacturer must have been the one that Jesse had been told about because they made A frame cabins to your specifications. They mainly supplied wilderness camps where the cabins needed to be simple yet functional.

To his delight, Rob found out that they were only fifty miles away and that they were open on Sundays, this was a busy time of the year for them and they had quite a few orders to fill, he could if he wished come to see them that afternoon.

The rest of the morning Rob and Jesse spent making a list of things to take with them and started to pack stuff up, they left at noon, stopped on the away at a McDonald's and grabbed a quick burger and fries which they ate as they drove. They had no trouble finding the manufacturer, it was well signed and they pulled into the parking lot and went into the office.

"Good afternoon can I help you folks?"

"I certainly hope so," said Rob "I spoke to someone on the phone this morning he said that we could come around and have look at your A frames."

"Certainly," said the jovial gentleman stepping forward and shaking their hands.

"My name is Bert and I'm the owner, pleased to meet you. What exactly was is it that you wanted to look at?"

"I'm Rob and this Jesse, we want to look at some smallish A frames, we are setting up a camp" said Rob, thinking to himself that he wasn't really lying, after all Last Chance was really a camp.

"Well okay follow me, you're in the right place, we've all sorts and we can make anything that you want," said Bert leading them back through the factory.

"This is where we actually cut everything to size. Our camp A frames are very simple, the basic model has just the two outside walls leaning up against one another, these walls are made of two by six wood frames covered with wood sheathing which is covered with a waterproof barrier and then finished off with roofing shingles. The two end walls are again made up of two by six frames and then finished off with wood sheathing and a waterproof barrier that's overlaid with waterproof wood or aluminum slats, we can put in windows and doors where ever you would like them. All the windows are basically the same size and shape, if you want special ones they cost a little more to make. The inside of the walls are merely finished off with an acrylic varnish, we don't put in any heat barriers unless specially requested. The floor is made up of a frame of two by twelves covered with a wood sheath and finished off with thick industrial linoleum. At one end of the structure is the kitchen, we supply the cabinets and the sink etc, the center section is the living room and dining area and at the other end we put in a bathroom, completely enclosed of course. Over the bathroom there's a loft which you get to by way of a spiral metal staircase. You can get, at very little extra cost, a loft put in at the other end above the kitchen. Once everything's been cut we put it altogether out the back of this building, making sure that everything fits and then we take it to pieces and ship it out. When we ship it we ship out everything that is required to put it together right down to the nuts and bolts, nails, varnish, etc. The purchaser doesn't have to buy anything, we supply it all. Now we can get much more complicated and we can make all year-round residences, it's completely up to you."

"We'd be interested in your basic model, preferably ones with a loft at both ends. Now what about the plumbing and the electrical?"

"We do provide everything for all of your electric needs right up to and including the outside stack and the fuse box and all of your plumbing needs to connect everything together terminating outside the front or the rear of the cabin."

"Do you have one of these assembled that we could look at?"

Bert took them out the back of the building into a very large yard and immediately they could see four A frames in various stages of construction each with the piles of yet to be used materials sitting beside them. The last one was almost complete and this is the one that he led them to.

"As you can see this one is almost exactly as you've mentioned, it's almost complete, all that's left to do is put in the linoleum which we don't fit here, we ship it out in one complete roll. We don't put in the electrical stuff or the plumbing connections here, we just supply everything that you would need and you can put in the plugs and fixtures where you want them, you can specify how many plugs etc. you will need and we'll include them in the package."

They walked around the building, it did not look very large from the outside but when they got in it was really quite spacious and bright. The kitchen looked quite functional, the bathroom did not have a bathtub but had an ample shower, sink and toilet. What really surprised Rob was that there was quite a lot of space in both of the lofts, plenty of room to put in two single beds with a dresser and bedside table. He was really pleased with them.

"What are the outside dimensions of the base and what do you have to put the whole thing on?"

"The standard dimensions are twenty by forty feet. You can place it on a basement, cement piles or a cement slab, basically anything that gives it a level support, the floor supports are designed so that you could, if you wanted to, just support the whole thing at the four corners."

"Now how do you ship these?" Asked Rob as they were standing in the living room area.

"Well there are two ways, we can prefab the walls in movable sections and the same with the floor or we can completely disassemble everything and then ship it in bundles of pieces, it depends on where it has to go to and how it'll be transported."

"How much are you asking for these?" Asked Rob as they all went back into the office.

"Well," said Bert as he sat down at his desk and pulled out some papers "there are a few variables, the standard model that you saw out there, without the second loft sells for thirty thousand dollars, with the second loft they'll cost you thirty three thousand dollars. How many are you looking for?"

"I'm not sure but we need at least fifteen." Rob saw Bert's eyebrows go up.

"Now that's a fairly big order, we usually only get orders for four or five at the most, I can give you a bit of a discount for that number. I tell you what I'll do, I'll sell you them with the second loft at thirty thousand dollars each provided you order at least fifteen. How does that sound?"

"Okay, now what's the soonest you can let me have them?"

"Well, I'll have to order in the lumber and the kitchen cabinets usually take a while, if we really push it we could have them ready for you in about two months, how does that sound?"

Rob looked at Jesse who just shook her head, "that's no good, I need them much sooner than that."

"How soon do you need them?"

"Well let me see, today's Sunday I'd like them ready to be shipped by next Sunday or the following Sunday at the very latest."

Bert looked at them to see if they were serious, then he grinned and tipped his chair backwards.

"You've got to be kidding, nobody could get them made in that time, no one builds these on spec and stores them hoping a buyer will come along, everything's built to order."

"I'll pay you more than you're asking for them if we can get them within that time frame" said Rob "and no, I'm not kidding."

Bert looked at them and realized they were serious.

"It doesn't matter how much you're prepared to pay, it's impossible within that short a time."

Jesse looked at Rob and said, "Boss I guess we'll just have to look around for something else, there must be something somewhere that we can get in the next two weeks."

"You're right Jesse," said Rob turning back to Bert, "well I thank you for your time but our time limits are pretty well set in concrete," "no pun intended" he thought to himself, "this all came to us very suddenly, we are in fact purchasing them for someone else and they are adamant that we must have them delivered in two weeks, we'll just have to look for something else. I thank you again." he shook Bert's hand and he and Jesse turned to leave.

Just as they were going out the door Bert called out to them, "hang on a minute, how much are you prepared to pay?"

Rob turned back to him and said, "It doesn't really matter if you can't get them ready by the time we want them does it?"

"Hang on a sec, listen, I'm in litigation with a company out of Texas, a little over a year ago they ordered some special cabins, they wanted them just a little bigger than our standard model so we made them an upside down "U" shape, we put in a section between the top of the "A" frame to widen the upper floor. This made the lofts much bigger, they insisted in putting the kitchen with an eating area and the bathroom with one bedroom in the upper lofts and the other bedroom on the lower floor, it made for a hell of a lot more space for almost the same basic floor space, they insisted that they be made completely out of cedar wood which, as you probably know, is more expensive. We manufactured them, they ordered twenty-five, it's the biggest and most expensive order we've ever produced. We shipped them five cabins, they were extremely pleased with them and said they would give us a delivery date for the other twenty. They never came back for the remaining cabins and, other than the deposit, they refused or were unable, to pay the total amount owing. We're suing them and it's dragged through the courts for almost a year. The remaining twenty cabins are stored, indoors, in three old barns on the back of this property, if you're prepared to pay their outstanding bill I could let you have them immediately and that would also save me any more time and money for the litigation."

Rob and Jesse moved back in front of his desk. "How much do you want?"

Bert ruffled through some folders and pulled out a sheet of paper and passed it to Rob, Jesse looked over his shoulder as he read the bottom line, she looked really surprised and shook her head. Rob stared at the figure for a moment, "is that one million dollars?" He said looking up at Bert.

"Yes that's right, these are, without a doubt, the best cabins we've ever made, cedar will never rot and it doesn't twist or warp, they have the two extended lofts and the quality of the kitchen cabinets was upgraded. If we were to sell them separately we would have to get fifty five thousand dollars each, but I can't sell them while we're in litigation unless we sell them as a job lot and cancel the lawsuit. You can understand why we're taking legal action, manufacturing them and not being paid for them almost finished off the company financially."

"Yes I can see the predicament you're in, are they still in good condition?"

"Yep, they've been stored indoors and are as good as the day they were made, would you be interested in them, it's a lot of money."

Jesse stepped back and looked at Rob in surprise realizing that he was considering the proposition.

"Oh come on Boss that's way too much."

"Let me make a phone call," he said to Bert taking out his cell phone "we'll just step outside for a moment," and he pulled Jesse outside as Bert sat with a look of surprise and bewilderment on his face.

As they got outside Jesse turned Rob around to face her, "come on, you can't possibly be considering them, that's one million dollars, how can we get that sort of money?"

"The Judge, who is financially backing all this, said that money would be no problem, the most important thing is time, these we can get immediately, they may be the only housing that can be purchased and delivered at such short notice, let's find out if the money is available." And he dialed the Judge's cell phone.

"Judge Mortimer here."

"Hello Judge, Rob here."

"Hello what can I do for you?"

"I'm looking for housing for Last Chance, it'll have to be some kind of preformed cabins and as we discussed we'll need a minimum of fifteen cabins. It would seem that nobody has these things in stock, they're all built to order. I've found one manufacturing company here who has twenty cabins stored away because the purchaser refused to pay for them and they're in litigation, he's prepared to sell us the remaining twenty cabins for the amount that's owed against them. They are, however, much more expensive than the standard model but they're available immediately."

"Yes I can understand that, these aren't the type of thing that are built on spec. How much are they are asking for them?"

Rob took a deep breath and looked at Jesse, paused for a moment and then said, "they want one million dollars."

There was silence on the phone for a second, "have you seen these cabins?"

"I've only seen the standard model which would definitely be ideal, Bert, the owner of the company, assures me that these others are much better than those very basic ones."

"Accept his offer, we can't nit pick, we have very little time so if those are available immediately and he's prepared to load them into transportation containers this week then buy them."

Jesse saw a look of surprise come over his face. "Are you sure Judge, that's an awful lot of money?"

"Rob in a few weeks money will be worthless, get this Bert to fax me a bill of sale and the bank account that he'd like the money put into on Tuesday, the money won't be available until then. I'll sign the order and have the million dollars transferred that day. Tell him I'll have containers to him by the end of the week. With the paperwork that he faxes to me tell him to put down the number of containers that will be required to ship everything. Is all that okay?"

"Sure," said Rob with a little wobble in his voice "I'll take care of it right away. Thank you Judge, I'll be in touch."

"Well, when the Judge said that money would be no problem he really meant it. Let's go in and spend a million dollars." He said in wonderment to Jesse as he hung up his phone and led her back into the office.

"Bert you have a deal, one million for those twenty cabins."

Bert almost fell out of his chair, his face lit up not quite believing what he was hearing.

"Err, are you sure? That's fantastic, now how are we going to do all this?" He said with a grin on his face as Rob explained how it was all going to happen.

Rob and Jesse went back to the clinic. The first thing that Rob did while Jesse continued to pack everything up was to try and call Wayne Dunstan, Jack Brown and Roger Reed, the other three old boys from Last Chance, he had not been able to find a number to contact Indian. He was concerned because he'd been phoning them quite regularly and all he ever got was an answering service. He shrugged his shoulders disappointed that he could not get hold of any of them. He called up all his suppliers ordering vast quantities of everything that Jesse had printed out for him. He had to explain to most of them that he was in the throws of opening two more veterinary clinics, he had to pay extra to ensure that everything would be delivered within the next three to four days. Jesse canceled all of his appointments explaining that the clinic would be closed for personal reasons until further notice. He could feel the excitement rising inside of him, he called Pattern and asked if he could find any other way of contacting the other four old boys, Pattern said that he would look into it and told him that he knew that Wayne was a mechanic, Roger Reed was a chemical engineer doing some sort of pharmaceutical research for an international company and was married to a lady who was into animal husbandry. Jack Brown was an eye specialist married to a Doctor Anna Reed who was a dentist and he would have a phone number for getting hold of Indian very soon and would call him back.

That evening when June came home she told him that she had arranged to go on vacation from the hospital starting in two days time, much to the administrator's disgust and annoyance. She had done some checking around and found out that one could, if one had the money, buy one of the Army's surplus mobile operating rooms that came complete with everything that one could possibly need for field doctoring and operations. Rob called the Judge and asked if he would find out where to purchase one, the Judge said, "No problem," he knew who to contact and would purchase one and have it shipped.

Two days later Rob and Jesse, with June's assistance in the evenings, had the clinic and the house packed up and ready to leave for Last Chance. The morning after June's vacation from work started they said a very sorrowful good bye to their old lives and left to drive down to Last Chance with all their belongings packed into a U Haul truck. They stayed in touch with the Judge by cell phone and they arrived at the container transfer station two days after the Judge and his party had arrived.

On the second day of their journey Rob had made contact with Indian but he still hadn't got in touch with the other "old boys," he continued trying to do so via his cell phone.

11

The Water Tower.

Las Cruces, New Mexico

Two days after the meeting at Last Chance.

Maxine had been married to William Beaumont for thirty-five years, they had just celebrated their thirty fifth anniversary last week. She had managed to get William to go to the Royal Steak House for supper, it had been very difficult for him but they had had an excellent meal. Other than work William very seldom left his home. They lived in a small adobe house in a valley just outside Las Cruces, New Mexico. They had met when they were in university. Maxine was three years older than William. He was only fifteen when he started university and had been a child prodigy, categorized as a genius and had been diagnosed, later in life, with an obsessive-compulsive disorder.

Maxine had always had a very mothering nature, she had looked after her aging parents until their deaths and when she met William and saw the problems that he was having socially and at the University it felt natural for her to fall in love and move in with him. Even today she wasn't sure if William was in love with her. Was he able, did he understand what being in love really meant? She only knew that she loved him and that he desperately needed her. They had been happily married for thirty-five years.

William was a professor at the New Mexico State University in Las Cruces, he taught Astro-physics and had remained at the University after finishing his doctorate. Maxine, extremely brilliant in her own right, had never worked, she spent her whole life looking after her parents and then William.

They say that genius is borderline to madness, that there is an extremely fine line between the two, this was never more evident than in William's life. It was extremely difficult for anyone to have a conversation with him, everything that he had ever heard or read was stored in his memory, if you asked him a simple question he was liable to fly off into a long dissertation in answer. Maxine had to "translate" most of his dialogue and had to run interference for him when meeting others. His mind became fixed on a particular thought or problem to the point that nothing else mattered. Many times she had had to rush out of the house and rescue him as he would be about to leave the house on his way to work, his mind so engrossed in a specific problem that he would forget to get properly dressed or have breakfast. He was socially unacceptable.

He was in fact very well known by the police, they were in touch with Maxine all the time and kept an eye on William because he tended to get lost and do some very strange things. The hardest thing that Maxine had had to live with was his obsessive-compulsive disorder, this is what kept them from doing much outside of their home. William had to have everything in exactly the same position day in and day out, if anything was out of place it would drive him nuts until he put it back in exactly, in his view, the right place. This was the only house they had lived in and Maxine had quickly learned that symmetry was the key to keeping William happy. She had arranged the household with that in mind. Every stick of furniture lined up with the walls, windows and fireplace, everything remained in exactly the same place and then William was content.

This morning William rolled out of bed, Maxine laid there snuggled in the sheets and pillows enjoying the warmth and comfort, he stood there naked for a moment and she noticed that he was beginning to look a little old, things were beginning to sag but then he is fifty nine years old she thought to herself. He reached out and pulled the cord that twisted open the vertical blinds on the window then pulled on the other cord that opened them to the sunlight. Even though she couldn't see his face, she knew exactly what he was doing. Up on the hill, just a short way away was the water tower, it was a huge circular reservoir standing on a vertical support and it supplied the water for the whole of the town, William, as he did every morning, stood in exactly the same spot and lined the edge of the vertical blind up with the edge of the tower. This morning he stood there and fidgeted with the blind, he reached out and shook it a little, he then held it still, again he nudged it and shook it gently, standing back in exactly the same position, he was becoming agitated. He shook his head, and again he fidgeted with the blind.

"That's enough William," she said gently "what's the matter?"

"It won't line up." He said annoyed.

"What won't line up?"

"The blind, it won't hang straight," she could almost hear his mind working. He said "It is logical that the blind must be hanging straight now I have tried three times to allow it to hang and find it's own place, gravitation dictates that when an object is hung straight down from the same pivotal point, if allowed to hang free, it will always come back to the same spot. Yet it will not line up with the edge of the support of the water tower, therefore the only logical conclusion is that the water tower is now no longer sitting vertical. There can be no other answer and that does not make sense, I must investigate this," and he turned to leave the room.

Maxine recognized his fixation on the problem before him and knowing him as she did she knew that he was about to leave the house naked and drive up to the water tower to investigate. She jumped out of bed and gently grabbed his hand as he was about to leave the bedroom.

"Come on my love let's get you dressed and then we'll have some breakfast, this is not your problem, I will call the authorities."

He stood there while she pulled his vest over his head and as she handed him his underwear and told him to put them on he began to come back from his problem.

"Yes," he said turning to his wife "you're correct this is not my problem but it is extremely aggravating not to be able to line up my window blind."

"Yes," said his wife "it is aggravating and I'll take care of it, I'll call and get them to check the water tower, you must go to work this morning you are teaching a class at nine."

Dazedly he said, "Yes, you're right, I must go to school."

Maxine thought to herself "Thank goodness for that, I've got him back on track."

They went through their morning ritual; it was exactly the same every morning. As she got him off to school she said quietly to herself. "I'd better sort out the problem with the blind so that it's right for tomorrow morning."

She went into the bedroom and stood in exactly the same spot as he did, she knew exactly where it was, he was one foot from the edge of the bed and she could see the indentations in the deep pile carpet, she stood and closed her left eye and tried to line up the blind with the water tower, the blind was ever so slightly out of line. She shook the blind and let it hang back down on its own only to find exactly the same thing, there was a fraction out between edge of the blind and the edge of the water tower.

"That's very odd" she said to nobody in particular and thinking to herself "William is never wrong in these things, if the blind is hanging vertically and it won't line up to the water tower then the water tower can no longer be standing vertical. That's an impossibility but it's the only logical conclusion."

"I'll call up the authorities," she said out loud to herself as she went into the living room and picked up the phone "they'll think that I'm stark raving mad, they already think that William is mad and now they'll think that I've gone off my rocker too but here goes anyway" and she dialed the number of the Las Cruces water department.

"Three one three, three one three, base to three one three, come in please," came over Trevor's truck radio. He reached forward and picked up the mike. "Base this is three one three what can I do for you?"

"What's your location?"

"I'm on the Outer Drive heading out to that problem on Margarita I'm just going into the bowl beneath the water tower." The water tower was on the highest point above the town, directly below it the land formed a natural bowl with the road running right down through it.

"This may sound a little funny, it was reported by Mrs. Beaumont, she says that there's something wrong with the water tower, it's leaning."

"What!!!!" Said Trevor, "That's garbage, how can the water tower be leaning? I suppose you want me to check it out?"

"You know what the policy is, we must check out all complaints, anyway you're right there and it'll only take you a minute."

"Okay if you say so, I'll check it out and put it on my report sheet."

He shook his head as he was coming up out of the bowl and turned left onto the dirt driveway up to the water tower. Everything looked okay. He pulled up and got out of the truck, looking up at the water tower and slowly started to walk around it, something did look a little odd he thought to himself, it was not until he was halfway around that he realized that the whole damned tower was in fact leaning. He stopped and rubbed his eyes, sure enough it looked like it was leaning. He walked around a little further and stopped dead in his tracks, his eyes widened as he looked at the base of the tower, it was made of cement blocks and he could now see that the lower three or four blocks had started to crumble and looked like piles of white powder. Even as he started to move back to his truck there was an audible creaking sound, he ran as fast as he could to his truck, grabbed his microphone and yelled into it "Base, base three one three here, do you read me?"

"Base here."

He didn't realize that he was almost screaming, "Listen, the damned water tower is falling over, the base is collapsing, the whole thing is leaning over, it's going to collapse."

"Slow down Trevor, what are you talking about, how can the water tower be falling down."

"It's collapsing I tell you, the base, the cement base, it's collapsing, it's falling down towards the road. My God, the traffic is bumper to bumper down there in the bowl, it's rush hour and it's hardly moving. You've got to get someone out here to clear that traffic."

"You've got to be kidding. Are you sure? I'd better......."

The rest of what she said was lost in the noise as the base of the tower came crashing down, tipping the millions of gallons of water out of the reservoir and pouring it down the hill side. Trevor ran out of his truck and looked down the hill, the massive wave of water tore up trees and huge rocks as it crashed down the hillside. He dropped to his knees, impervious to the cloud of sparkling white powder that was blowing around in the gentle breeze, as the wall of water washed away the first vehicle, a transport truck, in the long jam of cars and trucks as if it were made of cardboard.

12

Funds and Quarter Master.

Denver

The Monday after the meeting at Last Chance.

Janice got up from her desk and went over to the large heavy oak doors leading into the conference room; she paused with her hand on the silver knob and grinned to herself. She knew what she would see as she entered the other room; it was always the same every morning between the hours of seven and nine. She would open the door and she would see three pug dogs sitting at the head of a very large conference table. She smiled as she thought to herself "I think I've been working here just a little bit too long."

She forced the smile from her face and opened the door and stepped into the room, it was a very large room, well lit from the huge windows on two sides, all overlooking different views of the city below. Around the walls were numerous small working tables with computers on them. The focus of the room was an enormous polished cherry wood conference table, capable of seating at least forty people but her attention was directed to the head of the table and there, just a she imagined it, sat her three pug dogs. The head pug dog was in fact George Giovanni who was the owner and President of Giovanni Property and Financial Management Inc., a short fat little man with a bald head and wearing trifocal glasses, he was, as usual, immaculately dressed in a dark suit and a white shirt with a maroon tie. To his right sat his eldest son Peter Giovanni, the second pug dog, built very much like his father, only just starting to go bald on the top and wearing reading glasses. To his left sat the youngest son, Paul, the third pug dog, who was two years younger than Peter but looked much older, his face was more wrinkled and he was already wearing bifocals and was completely bald. They always reminded Janice of the picture of the dogs sitting around a table gambling. They all looked up from the piles of folders and papers on the desk in front of them with a bit of surprise on their faces as she stepped through the door.

"Excuse me Mr. Giovanni I know that you don't like to be disturbed in your morning meetings but I have a Judge Mortimer on the line. He is quite emphatic that he speak to you immediately, he said it is extremely important and requested that I see if you would take his call. What would you like me to tell him Sir?" she said addressing the elder Mr. Giovanni.

The old man looked surprised. "Judge Mortimer, now what on earth could he want?" He looked at his two sons "have either of you had any dealings with him recently?"

Both Peter and Paul shook their heads. "No" said Peter "we only ever see or hear from him when we're filing his income tax papers so we haven't heard from him in months."

"Hmmmm, thank you Janice, perhaps you'd better put him through to me."

Janice stepped back into her office and closed the door behind her, she had worked for the Giovanni Property and Financial Management Company for the last thirty-five years. Old man George Giovanni lived upstairs by himself in an enormous penthouse suite on the fortieth floor of his towering office building. It was rumored that his great grandfather had been a loan shark with close ties to the Mafia and that it was his father who had taken the company legitimate. It was now a very reputable property and financial management company, scrupulously honest and aboveboard. The Giovanni family was exceedingly wealthy and managed estates and portfolios for a number of the richest families in the state. Old George was now eighty six years old, his wife had died about twenty years ago as he was building this high-rise office complex so he had sold his beautiful estate just outside the city and built himself his penthouse suite. To Janice's knowledge he very seldom left the building. The only people who were allowed into his suite were his gentleman's gentleman, his oriental chef and the cleaning staff, even his immediate family had to make an appointment before they could enter his abode. Peter, the youngest son, was now fifty-eight years old, had a wife, three grown married children and four grandchildren. Paul was sixty, married with two married children and three grandchildren, both sons owned very large homes on the outskirts of the city. All in all it was an excellent company to work for, Janice could have retired about five years ago but she enjoyed her work and old man Giovanni paid her very well and she had a soft spot for him.

She walked over to her desk and pressed a button and spoke into the phone. "Judge Mortimer Sir, I apologize for the delay I'll put you through to the President immediately". She did not wait for a reply but pressed a couple more buttons and then sat down and continued with her work.

As the red button flashed on the consul in front of him George Giovanni pushed a button and put the Judge's call onto the speaker. "Well good morning your Honor it's nice to hear from you and most unusual, what can I do for you, by the way you are on the speaker phone and my two sons are present."

"Good morning to you Sir and to your sons, I thank you for taking my call, I know that every morning you have a meeting from seven and that you don't like to be disturbed and I apologize for that. I have a very unusual request, at least for me it is unusual, I'd like to have a meeting with all three of you this morning at twelve noon if that is possible?"

An expression of surprise came over the three faces of the men sitting at the conference table.

"Well let me just check our schedules, Peter would you check on the computer please?"

There was a moment's silence and then the Judge could hear the clicking of computer keys in the background "Yes father I think it would be okay, perhaps we could order in some lunch instead of going out".

"Yes your Honor that would be fine, we can expect you here in the conference room at twelve."

"Thank you" said the Judge "I would appreciate it if, at that time, you could have a complete list of all the assets, companies, stocks and bonds etc. that my father's trust fund now owns. They, along with their present worth on today's market and if you could just briefly outline what each company's functions are and do the same with my own portfolio, is that possible?"

George Giovanni's face showed the shock and surprise that he felt at this request. He had in fact managed the Judge's father's trust fund since it had been set up some fifteen years ago. He had been a very close friend of the Judge's father, they had in fact been partners in a couple of financial ventures. His father had been a very honest businessman but had been quite ruthless in his dealings, he had hurt and actually destroyed quite a few people and families in his quest to amass his fortune. At the time of his father's death the Judge was just completing his university courses. He swore that he would never use any of the trust for himself and in his will it was left to a large number of charitable organizations. This was the first time that the Judge had ever requested any information on the trust and its worth, so this was all very surprising.

"That won't be a problem," said George "Everything's in the computer and we can print it out for you. Now when you say the present worth of each of your assets do you mean what they would be worth on the open market today or what we estimate they could be worth at sometime in the future?"

"What they are worth on the open market today please."

"I see," said George Giovanni "We'll have that information ready for you at twelve noon Sir, we'll see you then." And he hung up the phone. George turned to his sons and said; "Now I wonder what all that's about? Peter please do a printout of his trust fund and his personal portfolio ready for the meeting."

Exactly at twelve noon the Judge stood in front of Janice's desk, he could not but help admire the decor of this office and indeed the whole office tower, no penny pinching in its construction, he found himself wondering how long it would be and what would happen when it all collapsed. He shrugged off that dark feeling as Janice looked up and said "Good morning Judge, they are expecting you but I'll just let them know that you're here."

She pushed a button and spoke into the phone "Mr. Giovanni, the Judge is here."

"Send him straight in please Janice."

She motioned for him to go into the conference room and, as he stepped into the room, George and his two sons stood up and welcomed him and shook his hand.

"Please sit down your Honor," said George, motioning for him to take a chair to his left.

Having all sat down the Judge said. "First let me thank you for seeing me at such short notice, I realize that you are very busy people. I'll make this meeting as short as I can. Do you have the information that I asked for?"

George realized that there were to be no niceties so he nodded and looked at Peter who pushed a folder across to the Judge and one to his brother and one to his father.

"Gentlemen," said the Judge "I've very recently received some very startling news, it turns out that I have very little time left to be of service to this community." He had worded this statement very carefully so they could come to any conclusion that they wanted to, "and since I've had very little time to myself I intend to do exactly what I want while I am still able and so I intend to resign my judicial position immediately."

A look of shock, understanding and what he read as sympathy came across their faces as he finished his statement. He knew that they had interpreted his words to mean that he was ill and had a very little time left, which was exactly what he had hoped for.

"We're very sorry to hear that," said George "what can we do for you Sir? What is wrong?"

"I would rather not discuss my problem if you don't mind and if you would give me a moment to run through your report I'll let you know."

He turned over the papers in the folder as they looked at one another and nodded slightly, his own portfolio was on top, he had a reasonably good idea what was in it, mostly stocks and bonds. He ran his finger down the list nodding to himself. On the third and final page he saw that his net worth was approximately one million four hundred and fifty thousand dollars. He then turned to the next page which was his father's trust fund, again he ran his fingers down the list, here and there recognizing some of the stocks and bonds but most of the individual items did not mean a great deal to him. On the bottom of the third page he saw a company called the Bean's Container and Transportation Company worth approximately one million dollars, he reached for a pen on the desk and made a mark next to that company's name and then he continued on down the list. On the sixth page the last item was "liquid assets, approximately ten million dollars." He was shocked to see the trust's final worth was two hundred and forty eight million dollars, he sat back in his seat, a very surprised look on his face, it was worth a great deal more than he ever imagined.

"I had no idea that the trust fund had grown to that amount," he said to George.

"Well Judge, it hasn't been touched, I mean, no money has been taken out of the trust since your father set it up for you except for the small amounts that you have directed us to transfer to your personal bank account through out the years for your charity donations, so it has grown exponentially. We did our best to manage your funds."

The Judge smiled, knowing that the small amounts that he spoke of were in fact what he had paid out for the upkeep of Last Chance and for the boys' educations. "You have done very well and I thank you. Now let's deal with the trust first, you say that it's worth two hundred and forty eight million dollars on the market today is that correct?"

"Yes sir that is our best estimation".

"I see that there's approximately ten million in liquid assets, I would like this to be transferred to my personal banking account immediately, this afternoon."

The gentlemen sitting across from him looked very surprised.

"That leaves the value of the trust at two hundred and thirty eight million," continued the Judge "I also see that you have a company called Beans Container and Transportation Company that has an estimated value of one million dollars, I presume that the trust owns that company outright am I correct?"

There was a moment's silence while Paul brought up some information on the computer behind him.

"Yes," said Paul as he turned back to the conference table "it's owned outright, we manage it through a local management company in San Diego. It owns approximately one hundred and fifty containers and forty five trucks and owns or leases a number of container facilities throughout the country"

"I would like the ownership of that company to be transferred directly to myself immediately, that leaves the value of the trust at approximately two hundred and thirty seven million dollars." He sat back in his chair and looked across the table, he knew that what he was about to say next would really surprise them and he also knew that they would accept his offer. "Gentlemen, I propose to sell to you the entire trust fund less the ten million and the one million dollars for the Beans Container and Transportation Company, valued by yourselves at approximately two hundred and thirty seven million dollars for two hundred and seven million cash. The one caveat is that the sum of two hundred and seven million must be deposited in my bank account by the end of banking hours on Friday, that is Friday of this week."

George and his sons looked shocked.

"You mean," sputtered George clearly trying to grasp the meaning of his offer, "you want to terminate the trust, you want to remove the liquid assets and take control of the Beans Container and Transportation Company and you want us to deposit, by Friday, the sum of two hundred and seven million dollars into your personal banking account and you will transfer the total of the remaining trust over to us?"

"That is correct," said the Judge.

George looked at his two sons, the Judge could almost see the numbers flying around in their heads, he could see the greed in their eyes and knew that somehow they would accept his offer.

"Father that is a very acceptable offer, the question is can we come up with that sum of money at such short notice?" said Peter.

George was very busy crunching numbers on the paper in front of him, a smile came to his face, "I believe we can, it will take some arranging but our immediate potential profit would be well worth it."

George turned to the Judge. "Are you sure that this is what you want? Ethically I must point out that given some time we can get a lot more for you than you want from us, it may take a few weeks or months but it would be well worth it."

"I've given this a lot of thought, my time is very limited, this will give me more money than I will ever need, this is exactly what I want and it's an excellent business move for yourselves."

"Then we have a deal," said George "we'll get all the appropriate paperwork out to you by the end of work today. We'll have the ten million deposited into your personal banking account this afternoon and we'll send you all the information about the Beans Container and Transportation Company. Now what would you like to do about your personal portfolio?"

The Judge flicked back the papers in front of him to his personal portfolio.

"I see that it's worth approximately one million four hundred and fifty thousand dollars, are you prepared to purchase the entire portfolio for one million dollars and add to it to the other two hundred and seven million, depositing it by the end of banking on Friday?"

George hesitated for a moment and then nodded, "that sounds fair, so be it."

There was an awkward silence for a few seconds and then the Judge stood up and shook their hands as he said, "thank you gentlemen it goes without saying that everything that has been said in this room remains in this room, I don't want anyone knowing about my personal problems. I guess this meeting is now concluded, I will await your papers."

As they asserted very strongly that nothing would ever be said to any one else he briskly walked out of the conference room leaving behind him a very befuzzled three people who were smirking, very happy and satisfied with the profit they had just made.

The Judge returned to his chambers in the judicial building, he sat down in his chair and put his feet up on the desk. He had enjoyed his work here but he had to admit to himself for the last couple of years he seemed to be getting into a rut, well he was being pulled out of that rut now wasn't he? He pulled out a writing pad and began writing his resignation which he made effect as of Friday noon, he knew it would take a couple of days for all the paperwork to go through and made it quite clear that he would not be sitting on the bench as of the end of work this day. It was strange to think that all this and what it meant would soon disappear, he wondered what would rise from the ashes; he hoped he could be a part of that.

He slipped the paper into a draw and thought about his secretary Jenny.

"I've loved her ever since the first time I saw her," he thought to himself, she was about ten years younger than him, he had first seen her when she came before him on a misdemeanor charge. She had a long rap sheet of misdemeanors but it was her impish impertinent look and attitude that caught his eye and as he gave his sentence and ordered her to do community service he saw her expression harden and her jaw muscles clinched down tight. He knew at that moment that she would complete her sentence even though she would hate every second of it. She was not very tall, slightly built with beautiful curly light brown hair but what really caught his attention were the cheeky green eyes. About six months later he saw that she was again going to come before him on yet another misdemeanor charge so he had had Richard thoroughly research her background finding out that she had been living on the streets after her parents had kicked her out of the house. But what really stood out was the fact that a lot of her brushes with the law were the results of her being dared or challenged by someone to do something and he wondered if perhaps here was a way to help her.

After he had heard her case he looked her straight in the eye and said "I could order you to do more community service or I could send you to jail for a period of time but I believe that you can still make something of yourself so I've suspended your sentence and I've set it up with the local community college for you to live on campus, complete your high school diploma and proceed on to a legal secretarial course. There will be no cost to yourself, I've found a benefactor who will pay for your clothes and other incidentals. I'm not ordering you to go to this college, I'm going to dare you, no, I challenge you to make something out of yourself by choosing to take up my challenge."

He saw her face muscles harden for a second and then they relaxed, her beautiful green eyes sparkled and she thought to herself "A Judge, a God damn Judge has found my one weakness." All her life she had never walked away from a dare or failed to take up a challenge and now this Judge had laid one out before her, she knew that he had found her main weakness and she smiled. She looked closely at the Judge realizing that for some reason she was attracted to him, he was a handsome man, not because of his facial appearance but because of his whole demeanor, he was small in stature yet seemed a bit bigger than life. She would like to know him better.

She had, as he had predicted, taken up his challenge and went back to school, the benefactor was, of course, himself and he followed her successes. She was indeed a very intelligent young lady and had passed all the courses with ease. Much to his surprise she had applied for a job at his judicial establishment and, without any help from him, she was accepted and started out in the typing pool. He watched her progression from one job to another until she applied to be his secretary when his old one, Ann, had retired. He was very pleased when she got the job. She had now been working for him for almost three years and because of his position and her past history they'd never had anything but a professional working relationship. She was excellent at her job and seemed to enjoy the position. He thought that she liked him but he had had very little experience with the ladies so he could not be too sure, he really looked forward to seeing her each morning and made excuses for her to come into his office. Now that he was about to resign he realized how much he would miss her and perhaps now was the time to see if she had any interest in him. He gathered his courage up and pushed the button "Jenny please come in here for a moment."

"Yes your Honor I'll be right in."

He got up and sat on the corner of his desk, something that he never did and fidgeted uncomfortably as she came into the room.

"Please sit down Jenny."

Jenny thought to herself "this is most unusual he never sits on the edge of his desk."

"Jenny I've received some news and I have to make some hard decisions and I wanted to discuss some things with you but not here. I wondered if you would have dinner with me this evening at say about six?"

Jenny could not help herself and she grinned like a schoolgirl. What was all this about? It obviously had nothing to do with her work or he would have brought it up right then and there, if only he knew how long she had yearned for him to ask her out, knowing full well that, because of their respective positions and her past brushes with the law, he could not do so even if he had wanted to.

"Well err um yes that would be wonderful" she managed to blurt out "I have to work late tonight but I can get off at six. Where would you like me to meet you?"

"I'll pick you up here at the courthouse if that's okay?" He said slightly over enthusiastically.

"Okay I'll see you then."

"Okay then that is all thank you for coming in." He managed to say blushing as she got up and left his office.

He sat thinking about taking her to dinner hoping that he would find out that she had some feelings for him, he would find out this evening. He pushed these thoughts aside, spoke into his intercom and got Jenny to ring him through to his bank manager.

"Well hello your Honor" came the cheerful voice of Dennis Holmes the bank manager, "what can I do for you today?"

"Dennis I need to talk to you, can I come round to see you?"

"Let me just check my calendar," there was silence on the phone for a moment, "I'm free for the next hour and a half would you like to pop round?"

"I'll be there in five minutes," said the Judge hanging up the phone, his bank was literally just around the corner, he jumped up and went out through the back entrance and walked to the bank. As he walked up to the bank manager's secretary she nodded and said, "Your Honor he's waiting for you please go on in."

Dennis had been the bank manager of this particular branch for the last three years and he and the Judge were on good terms.

"Sit down your Honor," said Dennis pointing to a chair opposite his desk "what can I do for you today?"

"Dennis I have some rather large sums of money being deposited into my checking account this week and I have a slight problem."

"What sort of problem, we can usually take care of everything. How large are the sums being deposited?"

"Well," said the Judge watching Dennis's face "this afternoon or tomorrow at the latest ten million should be deposited and by the end of banking hours this Friday a further sum of two hundred and eight million will be deposited." He saw Dennis's jaw drop, he quickly recovered..

"Now that's an awful lot of money to have in a checking account, you should put it somewhere where it can make a lot more interest."

"I understand that but for the time being I need it readily available, in fact this is where I have a problem. I want a number of people to be able to withdraw funds from that account, I don't want to have to sign or cosign each time someone wants some money, how do I accomplish this?"

"This is most unusual," said the bank manager "with so much money in the account it leaves you wide open to theft. Are you sure that this is what you want? How much are these people going to be able to take out?"

"Yes this is the way it has to be, some will just take out a few thousand at a time and others may be spending a few million. How do I do it?"

"Well this is most unusual, are you sure that you want them to be able to just sign, say a check and spend millions of dollars without you knowing or cosigning? If that's what you want then the fastest and easiest way would be to have their names added to the account. That would mean that we would have to have a form filled out by each person with their signature and your signature authorizing them to be added to that account."

The Judge sat there thinking for a moment, "some of these people are out of town, can we do all this by fax?"

Dennis thought for a moment, "yes I think that would be all right provided that there was a note from you authorizing us to accept each facsimile. I'll give you some forms, how many will you need?"

"Let me think" said the Judge "you'd better give me ten forms, I don't think I'll need anywhere near that number but I'll have them ready if I need them."

"That's an awful lot of people to have access to all that money, I must, in my position, advise you very strongly not to do this, that is my advice as your bank manager. You should have at least two people signing for each sum of money taken out and we should notify you and get your personal authorizing for each withdrawal that doesn't bear your signature, somehow we must protect you from fraud."

"Thank you for that advice, I appreciate it and I will take it under advisement but I don't want to be informed when money is spent and the funds will be required very quickly without any delay so, in the meantime, we'll set things up that way."

Dennis shook his head and reached into a draw in his desk and slid some forms across to the Judge saying, "I'll set it up as you request much against my better judgment. I'll also put a note in your file stating that I have very strongly advised you against these actions so that, should any funds go astray, the bank will not be liable."

"That's fine and if you wish I'll happily sign that note stating that you've advised me forthwith and that I've not taken your advice and will not hold the bank liable for any missing funds. As these names are added to the account I want them to be able to charge and sign for purchases on an accompanying credit card, is that Ok?

"Yes that can be arranged as well."

"Now I have an even stranger request," said the Judge watching Dennis's face change to shock and amazement as he laid out his request.

As the Judge left the bank he called home to speak to his gentleman's gentleman, who was also his chauffeur, who was also his right hand man, who was married to his housekeeper/cook, both of whom lived with him in his home. Brad and Cassey had been with him for the last twelve years, they had both been in the U.S. Air Force and both had been injured in a helicopter crash in Iraq. They were both helicopter pilots and because of the injuries, which left Brad with a slight limp and Cassey with a slight loss of strength in her left hand, they had left the forces and, while on vacation just after they resigned their commissions, had met the Judge at a formal dinner. In a discussion over glasses of brandy the Judge had jokingly asked them if they wanted to come and look after him because he had just had to fire his housekeeper for stealing and, much to his surprise, his gentleman's gentleman had left with her. Brad and Cassey had thought about and discussed his offer, even though he had only made it in jest and, as the gathering ended, they had informed the Judge that they would be interested in coming to work for him. Two weeks later they had moved in and now the Judge did not know what he would do without them. They had never had any children and their one passion in life was, whenever they could afford it, to rent and fly a helicopter, Cassey's only other interest was a love for all things that ran on steam. She would spend most of her spare time working, repairing, renovating and running anything that ran on steam, they were both accomplished mechanics.

"Judge Mortimer's residence may I help you?" came Brad's familiar voice.

"It's me Brad," said the Judge "question for you, are you and Cassey doing anything this evening?"

He heard Brad saying something to Cassey who was on her way into the kitchen and then, "no your Honor we were planning a quiet evening at home why?"

"I'm going to book a table at Adelaide's restaurant for supper and I wondered if the two of you would like to join me?"

"Well yes we'd love to," came a very surprised retort "may I ask you what the occasion is?" This came as a complete surprise to Brad; the Judge had never asked them out for supper before.

"I have some things to talk to you about and it would be best to do it over a nice meal."

"I hope it's nothing that we have or haven't done."

"Oh no, it's nothing like that, this is nothing to do with your work."

"That's a relief, what time would you like us to meet you or would you like us to pick you up Sir?"

"I'll meet you there at around seven Ok?"

"That will be fine, see you then Sir," and a very confused Brad hung up the phone and he went through to the kitchen to find his wife peeling potatoes for the evening meal.

"Well my love," said Brad wrapping his arms around his wife's waist and kissing her gently on the back of her neck "we have been invited out for dinner."

"Oh that will be very nice and who has invited us out for dinner?"

"Are you ready for this, the Judge has invited us out to join him for dinner at the Adelaide restaurant."

He released his wife and she turned round in his arms.

"What's that? The Judge has invited us out for dinner, come on now you're joking?"

"No honest, we've to join him at the restaurant at seven."

"Oh I wonder what's going on, that's not like him at all. It's not something that we've done is it?"

"No, he assured me that it has nothing to do with work, he didn't want to discuss it on the telephone so we'll just have to wait and see what he wants till tonight."

"Well I was just finishing off these potatoes so I'll put them away for tomorrow. You'd better finish up your work because it's not much time before we have to leave."

Brad pulled her closer to him and she wriggled in his arms pulling back a little.

"Now come on Brad," she said smiling wistfully "you have that "I want you now" look on your face."

"Well what's wrong with that?" Said Brad, his voice a little softer.

"You dirty old man, I swear, the older you get the hornier you get." She said moving against him. "We've too much work to do right now." She reached down and gently patted his crotch, "But keep that thought in mind until tonight and perhaps then, if you're good boy, we'll look after you" and she pushed him away with a wicked grin on her face.

"You're evil my love," he said as she moved away "but I love you anyway, I'll look forward to tonight."

She watched him move away rubbing his swollen crotch and mumbling something to himself, she laughed and turned around to finish peeling her potatoes.

The Judge decided not to return to his office, he phoned the Adelaide restaurant and made the reservations for six fifteen and then he went shopping. At exactly six a taxi, with the Judge in it, pulled up at the steps in front of the judicial building and as he got out Jenny came bounding down the steps with a big smile on her face, the wind blew her hair back gently and he thought to himself "She is beautiful, I hope she has some feelings for me." He held open the door of the taxi for her and as she got in he felt like a schoolboy on his first date. The restaurant was only ten minutes away, she thanked him for inviting her out to dinner and told him how work had gone that afternoon with him away. She realized that she was blubbering on a bit but she was so nervous now that she was going out with him, she wanted to cover it up so she talked. The Judge just sat there equally as nervous and put in the right "yeses" and "nos" at the appropriate times, or at least he hoped they were put in at the appropriate times. All he could think about was that he wanted to reach out and hold her, he had trouble keeping himself in check.

He paid the taxi as they got out and went into the restaurant, it was quite an expensive restaurant but one of his favorites. The Maitre D greeted them as they entered the dining area. "Well good evening your Honor, we have your table waiting, I believe you made a reservation for four, this way please."

Jenny gave the Judge a questioning look and he saw she was a little disappointed. He waited until they were seated, he insisted that she sat on his right close to him.

"There'll be two people joining us in about an hour, would it be alright if we just ordered a coffee for now and waited for them to join us?" he asked Jenny.

"Of course, no problem" she said but her eyebrows rose.

The Judge called over the waiter and ordered two coffees and explained that they would not be ordering a meal until after his other guests had arrived.

The Judge turned to Jenny and said, "Jenny I have some things to say to you but first I want you to read something."

He reached into his pocket and pulled out the rough draft of his resignation and passed it to her. She picked it up and read it; a look of shock and possibly anger came over her face, she looked at him and he saw that she was visibly shaken.

"Before you get all flustered and upset let me explain."

She put the paper on the table because her hand was shaking.

"This is it," thought the Judge "God I hope I don't blow it".

"Just this past weekend I received some extremely important information, I don't want to go into that particular area until the other guests arrive, suffice to say that it means that I must immediately resign my position."

He saw a look of worry come over her face.

"No it has nothing to do with my health, I think that is what you were thinking isn't it?"

"Yes that's what I was thinking, if it's not that what else can it be, you really don't have to resign I'm sure you can work this out, I really don't want you to resign."

He saw tears come into her eyes.

"Please don't cry there's nothing to cry about, let me explain," and he reached into his pocket and gave her a clean white handkerchief, she wiped her eyes and nodded at him to continue.

"Because of this news there's no other way than for me to resign, it has nothing to do with my reputation or my work, it's something that's beyond my control. In a very short time, possibly within two weeks I must move to the West Coast."

She held the handkerchief to her eyes and he realized that he had better hurry up and explain the situation because she was getting more and more upset.

"Jenny, I want you to come with me," he blurted out before he even realized what he had said and now that he had started it came out of him like a flood. "I've always had very strong feelings towards you, no that's not right, you have to forgive my blundering I'm so nervous, you make me so nervous."

She looked up, a look of surprise on her face, "what do you mean?"

He reached out and held her hand in his, he sat there awkwardly for a moment. "Jenny I love you Jenny, I know it sounds so silly but I do love you, I've loved you since you came into my court all those years ago. I haven't been able to do anything about this through the years but now that I'm resigning I can do anything that I want. I believe you have some feelings for me, I need to know if you do or not." He sat looking at her, watching her face pass from sadness to surprise and then to what he hoped was happiness.

"I really don't know how to say this, to put this into words and I'm so God damned nervous, you see what you do to me. Do you have any feelings towards me or am I barking up the wrong tree?"

She sat looking at him for a moment and then he felt her hand grip his more tightly. "You've always been full of surprises but this is the biggest one." She put down the handkerchief and took hold of his hand with her other hand. "I have no idea what this is all about and it seems that it will have to remain a mystery until a little later but" she looked him right in his eyes and gripped his hands tighter "I have very strong feelings towards you, I always have had. You are the reason why I've stayed working for you, I love to just be near you." She felt a pleasant calmness come over her, her nervousness and disappointment passed away. "I've loved you since that silly time when you challenged me to go back to school."

The Judge relaxed, he was euphoric, he listened to her speak and realized that he had never been so happy as he was at this moment. He was pulled back to earth as he realized that she had stopped speaking and was looking at him puzzled.

"I apologize," he said "what was that last question?"

"I was asking for a little more detail in your plans" she grinned at him.

"I was so happy in the moment, all I wanted to do was to sit here and hold onto you, I lost track of what you were saying."

He looks like a flustered young man on his very first date she thought to herself. "I understand," she said "I really do."

"Thank God you have feelings for me" he said "I was so terrified that I might loose you even before I found you, this makes things so much easier. The other guests should be here very soon and I can explain everything. But, as I said before, I must move out to the West Coast, there are things that have to be done. I know this is such short notice and I realize that I'm really rushing everything, but I have no choice. Jenny will you come with me?"

She looked at him and realized he was deadly serious. Her whole world was being turned upside down, she had never felt so happy, she realized that every thing was changing extremely fast. All her dreams and desires were suddenly being realized, she knew that she could trust this man with her very life and so she just sat there and said gleefully, "I have no idea what this is all about but yes I will come with you."

She saw an expression of wonderment and happiness come over him and before she had time to be embarrassed and in front of all the other patrons in the restaurant, he had moved over to her and they were lost in a long sensual kiss and embrace.

A discrete clearing of a throat and the Maitre D. saying, "Excuse me your Honor, your guests have arrived" interrupted them as he seated Brad and Cassey.

"Err we seem to be interrupting something," said Brad very surprised at what they had just seen. As the Judge and Jenny separated embarrassed and blushing, he thought to himself "What on earth is happening, I've never seen the Judge behave like this before, perhaps this is what he wanted to talk to them about."

"Good evening," said the Judge to the two of them, a little flustered, "Thank you for coming, Brad I believe you know Jenny, Cassey this is Jenny, Jenny may I present Cassey." The two ladies smiled at each other and nodded.

"Alright, I owe you all an explanation, if it's all right with you I suggest that we leave ordering the food till later, this may take some time. Perhaps you would like to order a drink and we can get down to business."

They all ordered a drink and when the drinks had arrived the Judge started to speak. "Just this last Saturday I was informed......." and he went on to explain everything that was in Pattern's report to the President and what they were planning on doing; going to Last

Chance. They sat and listened in amazement, which turned to shock at the end of his explanations as they realized what this meant and what the consequences were going to be for everyone.

It took almost an hour for the Judge to complete his report and they had exhausted their many questions but at last they sat there in silence looking at each other deep in their own thoughts.

"Now you understand the reason for this meeting and if you don't have any more questions I would like to put forward some proposals." He reached over and held Jenny's hand, "Jenny has agreed, unless this has changed her mind, to come with me to Last Chance."

He looked over at Jenny.

"I haven't changed my mind, this only goes to make it even more certain," she said holding his hand tightly.

"Cassey and Brad, I would like to invite you two to join us and move with us to Last Chance, I will understand if you don't want to."

Cassey looked over at Brad, they both realized that their lives were about to be completely changed yet again, they were being swept up and pulled along.

"Honey what do you think, this is all so sudden and so horrific, do we need more time to think about it?"

"Right off the top of my head I don't see any alternative for our survival," replied Brad quietly, still reeling from the shock of it all "Right now I would say yes we will come to Last Chance and I can't thank you enough for telling us this and inviting us to come with you. But I must reserve the right to change our minds after we've had time to digest all this and discuss it between ourselves."

"Yes of course," said the Judge "that goes without saying. Now then, with the supposition that you will come, there are some things that we need to do as fast as possible. Jenny I need you to collect any books, legal books and documentations that you think we should take, I'll help you with this and we need to pack them up in boxes ready to transport them."

Jenny nodded.

"Let me just say that there are no financial limitations on what we can spend, I've arranged for funds. I, apparently, own a transportation and container company, I've yet to contact them but this is what I am planning; I'll arrange for containers to be made available wherever we need them for the transportation of anything that we want to take to Last Chance. I'm hoping that there's a container depot that this company owns somewhere down close to Last Chance, if there isn't one then we'll find one and lease it. While the roads are passable I'll have the filled containers delivered and stored there. I need to know if it's possible and if you and your wife can air lift those containers by helicopter to Last Chance."

Cassey and Brad looked at each other and nodded and Cassey said, "it is possible, we would have to know the size and weight of the containers but it is possible. It would probably take a special helicopter, probably a big Sikorsky, that's one of the largest made, it would cost a hell of a lot but it would be possible."

"Can you two fly one of these helicopters?"

"Yes of course" said Brad without hesitation "but to rent one, the cost would be prohibitive."

"Would you two, that's if you don't change your minds about coming with us, take on the responsibility of making all the arrangements down there in California and move the containers by air to Last Chance. Let me know the actual costs and I'll arrange to have the funds available to you."

Again Brad and Cassey looked at each other.

"Yes," said Cassey "we'll do that. Can you tell us exactly what Last Chance is like?"

As they ordered their dinners the Judge went on to tell them about Last Chance in great detail.

While they ate they talked about all the possibilities of what could happen, the more they talked about things the closer Brad and Cassey came to making up their minds that the best chance for them was with the Judge and his friends.

As they were finishing their desserts the Judge said that he was in charge of purchasing and ensuring that they had everything that would be needed to maintain their community for five years. He said he had no idea how to even begin.

"Now Judge" said Cassey "we may be able to help you there, we have a couple of very dear friends that are visiting us from San Diego, they're staying at a hotel here in town and we're supposed to spend the day with them tomorrow. They're old friends, we served in the forces together for years, he was a Master Chief Petty Officer at the naval base in San Diego. He worked his way up through the ranks and ended up as the chief Quarter Master, which is the equivalent to the head-purchasing officer in civil life of some big firm or corporation. He retired just three years ago, surely he would be able to give you some pointers."

"Now that would be a start" said the Judge "can you set up a meeting?"

"Hang on a second," said Brad reaching into his pocket for his cell phone, "let's see if they have the phone on."

He dialed a number and put the phone to his ear, the phone rang twice and Brad heard, "Roger Metson here."

"Hello Roger, Brad here, got a minute?"

"Sure have, go head."

"Roger something extremely important has come up and I think you might be able to help us, I know we're going to spend the day with you to tomorrow but would you mind if we had a meeting, let's say at eight thirty," said Brad looking at the Judge who nodded his approval and whispered, "tell him we'll treat them to breakfast at Diaglo's."

Diaglo's had a fantastic reputation for breakfasts.

"We'll treat you both for breakfast at Diaglo's."

"Oh that would be fine they have quite a reputation, we'll meet you there at eight thirty, okay?"

"See you then," said Brad closing his cell phone and putting it back in his pocket.

"There you go Judge I think he'll be a great help, they're a wonderful couple, they're around our ages, he retired with thirty years of service and they've been a little lost since then. His wife, Jill, is a fantastic seamstress, she used to do all the alterations and repairs for a lot of the noncommissioned officers."

"Well let's see if he can help us, at least it'll be a start," said the Judge.

They made small talk for a little longer and then Cassey nudged Brad and grabbing his hand under the table she gave it a squeeze and said "well come on Brad, I'm really tired, we'd better get going home."

Brad got the message and yawned and said, "if you two will excuse us, it's time for us to go home. Judge we thank you for the delicious meal but even more for telling us about the report. I think," he looked at his wife and squeezed her hand, "we're now certain that we'd like to accompany you to Last Chance. We'll see you in the morning, I take it that we'll all be traveling down to Diaglo's together in the morning?"

"Yes it would be easier, well goodnight to you, we'll see you in the morning."

Brad and Cassey left and as they were going out of the door of the restaurant she whispered in his ear, "They need some time alone."

"You've been very quiet, is everything okay Jenny?" asked the Judge.

"Oh yes," she said reaching across to hold his hands "everything is wonderful, I just needed some time to adsorb everything."

"Well I guess we'd better get out of here," he said signaling to the waiter to bring them the bill. As it arrived he gave the waiter his charge card and while they were waiting for him to return he said "Jenny I'm so happy to be with you, if only we could have done this before."

"Everything had to fit into place and now is the right time. Tomorrow morning, while you're having your meeting, I'll go into the office and submit both our resignations and pack up our personal belongings and the legal books. It shouldn't take me long, I should be finished around lunchtime."

"That would be excellent," said the Judge as he paid the bill and got his credit card back, "Okay let's go."

The got up and as they were leaving Jenny slipped her hand into his, her hand felt good in his. They hailed a cab and got into the back seat.

"Where to folks?" Asked the cab driver.

The Judge looked a little embarrassed at Jenny, she kissed him gently on the lips, "Let's go to your place for tonight," she whispered in his ear with a twinkle in her eyes.

He pulled back a little and looked at her, he loved her, he smiled, squeezed her hand and gave the cabbie his home address.

The following morning as the Judge lay holding Jenny, he gently kissed the back of her neck and watched goose bumps rise on her back, her hand slipped back and smuggled down between his legs.

"Oh my!! Judge," she whispered "I feel that you're ready to make love again," she giggled and wiggled her bottom at him, "wasn't last night enough?" She moaned at the thought.

"I love you, I've always loved you, I just want to lay here and hold you for ever" the Judge whispered in her ear "but I fear we must rise, it's seven fifteen and I have the breakfast meeting at eight thirty."

"Oh dear, not even time for a quickie," she laughed and threw back the sheets tantalizing him wickedly with her naked body.

"I didn't realize you were such a brazen hussy," he laughed at her as she pulled out of his arms and walked cheekily into the bathroom.

They got dressed and went downstairs meeting Brad and Cassey in the kitchen. The coffee was ready and Cassey poured them a cup and with a smile on her face she said, "did you both sleep well?"

The Judge saw Jenny blush a little and laughed saying "yes we slept very well thank you."

Jenny and Cassey saw the two men off for their meeting then Jenny left for the office and Cassey started to pack up their belongings.

When Jenny got to the office she found the returned faxes from Rob and Pattern with their signatures on them to put them on the Judge's bank account. She immediately faxed them over to the bank along with the same form with her signature on it. Then she started packing up everything in boxes that were brought up for her from the basement.

On the way over to the breakfast meeting Judge phoned the Bean's Container and Transportation Co.

"Bean's, what can I do for you?" Came a cheerful voice.

"Judge Mortimer here, to whom am I speaking?"

"This is Mr. Halloway's Secretary how may I help you?"

"Please can you tell me who is the head of the company?"

"That would be Mr. Halloway."

"What's Mr. Halloway's first name and is he available?"

"His name is Ernest and he's in the office would you like to speak to him?"

"Yes please and thank you."

There was a couple of clicks and then a gentleman's voice said "Ernest Halloway here what can I do for you?"

"Ernest, this is Judge Mortimer, we've never met but apparently I own the Bean's Container and Transportation Co. as of this last weekend."

"Yes Sir," said Ernest with a question in his voice, "I have been informed that you are the new owner."

"That's excellent, I don't plan to make any changes; I'd like things to run just as they've always done, I want to assure you that I have no intentions of actually coming up there to run the company, I want you to carry on as usual."

"That is excellent news." The Judge could hear the relief in his voice.

"I do however need to have some materials moved for myself, I'm in the process of establishing a camp down near Phoenix, Arizona. I'm under an extremely tight time schedule and I need to move very fast, what's the closest depot that we have on the west side of Phoenix?"

"Give me a second," there was silence on the phone for a minute then, "we have a staging depot on Highway 10 at the town called Turnopah, we don't actually own it, it's leased."

"What exactly do we have there?"

"It's a staging depot, we bring the containers in, they have mobile container lifts to take the containers off the trucks and then they store them until the next truck comes in to move them on."

"That's exactly what I need, I'll be contacting you in the very near future to have containers delivered to specific locations to be loaded and then to be taken to this depot. I must emphasize that this must be done as fast as possible, if this means diverting trucks and or containers from other duties then this must be done without question. I will, of course, pay all of the regular prices and if any overtime is required I'll pay double-time for Saturdays and triple time for Sundays and any expenses such as meals and accommodations for the drivers."

"I understand Judge, since you're prepared to pay the overtime and all the other expenses I can assure you that you'll have no problem finding drivers."

"That's excellent," said the Judge "please would you have twelve empty containers delivered to that depot and left there for me?"

Judge could hear the rattle of paper.

"That's no problem, I can have six delivered by tomorrow evening and the other six delivered the next day."

"That's excellent then I'll be in touch very shortly, thank you for your assistance and I hope to meet you very soon."

"Okay then good bye for now," and Ernest hung up the phone.

Roger and Jill Metson were already at the restaurant when the Judge and Brad arrived, Roger was a short stocky man with a mop of fair curly hair, he was, obviously by his bearing, an ex military man. His wife, Jill, was about the same height as her husband, a jovial lady, she wore no makeup and was very attractive. The Judge, who prided himself in being able to read people, immediately liked them.

They all sat down and after a little polite conversation they ordered breakfast and then Roger said, "now what's all this about?"

"I believe that you were a Quarter Master in the Navy, is that correct?" asked the Judge.

"Yes that is correct I was the Quarter Master in charge for the entire naval station and all the ships that came and went at the San Diego naval base."

"Please bear with me for a moment, what exactly did that entail?"

Roger looked a little surprised, "I had to ensure that everything that was necessary to keep the base running was available in stock or was purchased and delivered as required. The only items that had to be specially ordered by specific individuals were the weapons and ammunitions and any pharmaceuticals. I had a basic stock itemization for things such as toothpaste, clothing, food, beer, etc. If anyone wanted special items then they had to request them through me. Everything would be put out for tender, I would have the final decision on which proposal we were to accept, I would then place the order, we took delivery and made sure that the order was filled correctly then it was paid for. Is that sufficient?"

The Judge liked them, he realized what a tremendous asset they could be.

"How did you go about ensuring the number or quantities of your basic items were always in stock?"

"I developed my own computer programs, there were equations for each item. For example let's take toothpaste, all I'd have to do was punch in the word toothpaste into my computer program, it would ask for how many personnel, it would ask the size of the toothpaste required and what period of time the stock was to last for, then it would automatically work out, based on an already established length of time that a tube of toothpaste of the required size was expected to last the average person. It would then tell me how many tubes of toothpaste I would be required to purchase and to whom to send out a tender. This type of formula can be applied to just about anything for the basic needs and wants of the base once one has the computer programmed for each specific item."

"I see" said the Judge "we're setting up a community of approximately fifty people, would your system work for this number?"

"Certainly, it would work for any number of personnel. Just in case you're wondering, when I retired I, of course, kept copies of my computer programs, contacts, forms and places that we purchased from. We weren't sure, in fact we still aren't sure, whether or not I'll remain retired. I'm seriously thinking about trying to find a job in a purchasing department in the private sector, retirement doesn't suit me very well, I'm just too young."

The Judge sat there looking at the couple, he decided then and there that he would invite them to join them at Last Chance, Roger would be invaluable in setting up the community.

"I have something I need to explain to you both" and he laid out before them Pattern's report and what they were proposing to do at Last Chance.

Roger and Jill sat there listening with dumb founded expressions on their faces, by the time the Judge was finished they had turned to a look of shock. They sat there for a moment trying to understand the ramifications of what they'd just heard.

"Judge I would normally tell you that you were out of your mind and needed to be locked up, that is the wildest story I've ever heard but" said Roger as he reached over to his wife's large shopping bag and took out a newspaper, "I've read about the train wreck and I've read about the aircraft crash, both of which would appear to be within the realms of normality, have you read today's paper?" And he slid the paper across the table in front of the Judge and Brad.

The Judge looked at the headlines, they read, "Water tower collapses. Fifteen people die." It continued on to say that a massive water tower just outside of Las Cruces, New Mexico had fallen over pouring millions of gallons of water onto rush-hour traffic in a gully just below it. It appeared that the cement base holding up the water tank had collapsed on one side, a team was being sent down to investigate. The Judge sat back in his seat and Brad looked at him and said "it's started, there'll be a lot more reports like this and then the population will panic."

"So now," said Roger tapping the newspaper, "I must err on the side of caution and I tend to believe your tall tale."

"So now what is it that you want from us?" Asked Jill.

"We estimate that there'll possibly be up to fifty people living at Last Chance. Pattern suggested that we should be prepared to live basically in solitude, trying to remain undetected at the camp for up to five years. So we've, again this is only an estimate, about two weeks to completely equip the camp with everything that we need and I've been designated to find and purchase all that is necessary. I wondered if you both would join us at Last Chance, if so, would you aid us in working out what we need to buy and where to buy it?"

Roger and Jill sat there for a moment, he turned to her and said "Wow Honey this is really heavy stuff, my head is swimming trying to take it all in. What do you think?"

"Well," said Jill "if we are to believe that this report is true and accurate then it would only make sense for us to join them. Later on, if the report is proven to be true, then we would have made an excellent decision." Roger knew that Jill was always a very logical person, he had relied on her advice for many years, she was very seldom wrong. "If we just suppose or we even just think that the report might be correct and we help them and we move to Last Chance and then the report is proven to be incorrect what have we lost? You've said that you wanted to look for something to do, that you're not sure if retirement is what you want at this time so even if the report is wrong we would have helped them, it would have given you something very interesting to do, we would have met some very interesting people so we wouldn't have lost anything. I would say that the most logical thing for us to do would be to jump in with both feet and move to Last Chance." Jill had a small grin on her face as she said this to her husband.

"My love you're always so damned logical, I love you and you make a great deal of sense." He said as he turned back to the Judge and said, "I guess Judge, you have two new recruits, what would you like us to do?"

"That's wonderful, I know you won't regret it. Alright how do I go about working out what we need to buy?"

"First of all, how are you going to pay for all this?"

"I had a trust fund, a very large trust fund, that is, as we speak, being cashed out and the funds deposited into my checking account, there are sufficient funds to cover anything that we need."

"Well then" said Roger "that's the hardest part over and done with. I have all the computer programs that we need at home, I also have contacts of where to purchase everything, it would only take me a day or two at home in San Diego to place orders for everything."

The Judge looked over at Brad with a surprise to look on his face.

"I told you he'd be extremely useful, didn't I?" Said Brad grinning broadly, "how long do you intend to stay here, when will you be going home?"

"Well we had intended to stay here for the rest of the week and then move on to Seattle for a while but this can be cut short, if we can find a flight we can go home this evening."

"This is wonderful," said the Judge "Brad how soon can we be ready to go down to the area near Last Chance?"

"Well the ladies are packing up now, we should be able to leave tomorrow morning but how are we going to get down there?"

"Okay," said the Judge "I have to go over to the bank, if you'll come with me, I can put you all onto my bank account, that way you'll all have access to any funds that you might need. Apparently I own a container moving company and there's a transfer the station fairly close to Last Chance, I suggest that we all move down there and establish our headquarters there. There must be a motel there somewhere especially since quite a few truckers must be passing through the area. Brad how fast can you charter a helicopter, one big enough to take all of us and our luggage?"

"Well if I charter one for a month I can get one tomorrow morning, I may have to grease a few palms but I'm sure I can get one."

"Well then let's do that, where are you staying tonight?" The Judge asked Roger and Jill.

"We're staying at the Hampton Inn."

The Judge sat thinking for a moment.

"Let's do this, let's all go over to the bank, Brad you then go home and pack up everything and make arrangements for the helicopter. Roger, you and Jill, check out of the hotel and come and spend the night at my place, we've plenty of room. I'll go back over to the courthouse and finish packing up everything there and move it all back home. Tomorrow we can just close up the house and you can fly us down to the container yard, once we get there you can drop Jenny and myself off and then fly them on to San Diego. Then Brad you must, with your wife, find us a helicopter to move the containers that last leg of their journey to Last Chance. How does that sound?"

They all looked at one another and nodded.

"Good then that's settled, now let me just stress right now, money is no object, time is of the essence, we have to cut corners to save time, if we have to pay double or triple the normal costs then that's what we'll do to get what we want as fast as possible, is that clear?"

"Sure is," said Jill as they all nodded in agreement.

"Okay, let's pay the bill and go over to the bank."

They all went over to the bank, the Judge made sure that the ten million dollars had been deposited, they all signed onto his account and went their own separate ways. The Judge wired the one million dollars to pay for the cabins and made sure that Rob, Jenny and Pattern had also been signed on as cosigners onto the account. He prepaid two million dollars onto his visa card and got the bank to inform their visa branch that he would be spending large sums of money all over the country and to honor all the purchases.

The Judge then went to his office building and was thrilled to bits when, as he stepped into his secretary's office, Jenny came rushing out of his office and leapt into his arms kissing him madly.

"Oh my," he said smiling and pushing her gently away from him, "that is most inappropriate behavior for a secretary in the judicial system, this calls for instant dismissal, you're fired, pack your bags and leave immediately." They both roared with laughter.

"How're you doing?"

"Just fine, all our personal items are in those two boxes," she said pointing to two large brown cardboard boxes by the door, "I'm presently packing up your library; I think you have all the judicial books that you'll require. There'll be another three or four boxes and then we'll be done."

He kissed her one more time and then whispered in her ear, "we'd better get going then."

That evening the six of them ordered in dinner at the Judge's home and Jenny went to help the Judge pack up his personal belongings.

"Matthew is this all of your clothes?"

"Yes Honey why what's the matter?"

Jenny roared with laughter, "none of these outfits are really very suitable for camping." She pointed to the rows of suits and dress shirts. "Don't you have any T-shirts and shorts?"

The Judge stared at her for a moment, "you know I never thought of that, I've lived in suits most of my life, it'll be really strange not to wear a shirt and tie. Hmmm! I don't think I have anything other than one pair of shorts that I use when I mess around in the garden."

Jenny looked at him and smiled, "I think you need some help, we really don't need any suits anymore, tomorrow on the way to the heliport we'll stop and buy you a new suitable wardrobe."

"Okay if you say so, I guess I really do have to change."

They finished packing up everything else in the house and put everything into a rented U-Haul. They sat around talking and vocalizing their worries and thoughts, it was quite late when they all went to bed. In the morning Brad and Cassey went ahead with the U-Haul to make sure that the helicopter was ready for them and the others made a diversion to find the Judge some suitable clothes, by noon they were in the air and going to the transfer depot.

13

Finding Indian.

Frenchburg, Kentucky.

Just before Rob and June left for the transfer station.

Before they left for the transfer station Rob sat at the small desk that he used for business in his home trying to put together a list of things that they would need when they moved to Last Chance, the phone ringing startled him, he picked it up. "Hello, Rob here, how can I help you?"

"Hello Rob, Pattern here, got some information for you."

Rob wondered if he was always so efficient, he never seemed to waste any words.

"What do you have for me?"

"I've a contact number for Jack Brown, Roger Reed and Indian. As I said before Jack is an optician and he's based in Miami, he's married to a lady called Anna who is a dentist and also has a practice in Miami, I've found out that they belong to 'Doctors without Borders' and are presently somewhere in the Sudan, in the Dafur region. The people in the main base they're operating from in Khartoum are a little worried because they haven't been in contact for the last few days, this isn't unusual but they are a little concerned, they're both due to come back to the States in ten weeks, I'll continue to try and get hold of them through some of my contacts. Apparently Roger is on an assignment somewhere down in South America and can only be reached by GPS. Indian and his partner Quiet Sunshine run a Do Joe in New York City. Indian joined the military after he left Last Chance, he quickly went up through the ranks in special ops, he was so good that they put him in a training position, that's when he met Quiet Sunshine who is a full-blooded Navajo Indian lady and they became a team, on and off the field so to speak. They were all set to make a full career out of the military when Quiet Sunshine's sister and her husband were killed in a car crash, they left behind two children, two young girls. Quiet Sunshine and Indian resigned from the military, took in the two young girls and moved to New York where they opened a successful Do Joe. The Do Joe is really just a front for their main business, one or either of them or both can be hired to train Special Forces personnel anywhere in the world. I'm not saying that they're mercenaries, everything is very legitimate and even the U.S. military calls them in for certain special training. Right now Indian is somewhere overseas but you can reach Quiet Sunshine at the following number. Do you have a pencil handy, I'll give you both numbers?"

"Yes I'm ready," said Rob and Pattern gave him the phone numbers.

"I'll keep in touch if I have any further information for you" said Pattern "until then goodbye." The phone was hung up.

"Always brief and to the point aren't you," thought Rob, he looked at his watch, it wasn't too late, "Well okay let's see if we can contact Indian."

He quickly dialed the number, the phone at the other end only rang once and then it was answered, "Hello darling hello, didn't expect your phone call till tomorrow, how you doing?"

"Err, excuse me, I'd like to speak to Quiet Sunshine please."

"I beg your pardon, who is this and how did you get this number?"

"Quiet Sunshine is that you?"

"Yes this is Quiet Sunshine, who are you and how did you get this number?"

Rob could hear the annoyance in her voice.

"Quiet Sunshine this is Rob, I grew up with Indian at Last Chance perhaps he's mentioned my name, he probably called me by my nickname Pug. I got this phone number from another gentleman named Pattern who also grew up at Last Chance."

There was a pause at the other end and then a little more amiably.

"Yes Pug, I mean Rob, Indian has mentioned both you and Pattern with some fondness, you'll have to excuse my abruptness this phone number is strictly private, I wonder how Pattern got hold of it?"

"Pattern has some position in the intelligence community. Quiet Sunshine it is imperative that I speak to Indian as soon as possible. Is he there?"

"No he's overseas at the moment, needless to say I thought that this phone call was from him since he's the only one, or used to be the only one, that uses this phone number. I don't expect him home for some weeks."

"Do you have a phone number I can reach him at?"

"I'm afraid not," said Quiet Sunshine "it's our policy when we're working overseas that all contacts must be made through the home office here, if you like I can get a message to him."

"I understand," said Rob, a little frustrated, "please if you could get a message to him as fast as possible, if you have a pencil handy I'll give you the message."

"Go ahead give me the message I don't need a pencil, my memory is excellent, trust me."

"Okay, please give him the message exactly as I give it to you, even though it sounds a little strange. 'Fishslice, I repeat Fishslice. Indian this is Pug, it is imperative, a matter of life and death that I speak with you as soon as possible, here is my home phone number and cell number if you call this evening and here is my office number should you call during working hours tomorrow'," and he gave her the numbers.

"Yes Rob that message is a little strange but I'll give it to him just as you've given it to me. I'll try and get hold of him as soon as I put down the phone."

"Thank you Quiet Sunshine I hope we meet in person very soon."

"Yes that would be very nice. Goodbye for now" and she hung up the phone.

It was less than half an hour later that the phone rang, Rob picked it up. "Well hello there Pug, Indian here, longtime no hear, how you doing? Got a message from Quiet Sunshine, what's all this about, what's all this Fishslice stuff about?"

"Hello Indian," Rob grinned to himself, Indian was always very quiet spoken usually very serious but he was always a very happy go lucky individual. "It's nice to hear your voice at last, you're right it has been too long. I hear you're overseas, guess you're really busy?"

"Well I'm not too busy at the moment, I'm stuck here in this God damn hospital half way up a volcanic mountain and I'm not allowed to get out of bed."

"What happened for Pete's sake? How bad are you?"

"Well I'm in Aden, you know in South Yemen, had a bit of an accident and broke my left leg quite badly. Was doing some training for Yemen Special Forces; they'd opened up the old British hospital half way up this mountain. It was being used for training purposes as well as an emergency field hospital for the British troops that are involved in the training exercises. I have, I guess, what they call a halo, on my leg holding the bones in place, I've been on my back for four weeks and they won't let me out of bed for at least another two weeks."

"Oh dear, I'm sorry to hear about it, what happened?"

"Well I was parking my Hummer in an old three-story parking garage here in little Aden when the whole god damned thing collapsed. Thank goodness my Hummer had some armor plating around it or I might have been much worse off, two people on the ground floor were killed unfortunately."

Rob paused for a moment then said "Hang on a moment, let me guess what you saw, the parking garage appeared to just collapse and afterwards you saw a cloud of crystal white powder everywhere which seemed to float in the air and then proceeded to cover everything in a fine white covering, am I correct?"

"How the hell did you know that?" replied Indian "that's exactly as it was, even as I sat in the messed up Hummer I had to admire the crystalline beauty of that fine powder, you must have read it in the newspapers or something."

"Indian I presume you're on a cellular phone, am I correct?"

"Yes of course, what has that got to do with it?"

"I have to talk to you about that white powder, I wish we were over a landline it would be much less likely that anyone could overhear our conversation but I guess I'll just have to take the chance."

"Gee if it's like that I can get us a secure connection through this cell phone going via Quiet Sunshine would your rather do that?"

"That would be excellent, didn't know that you had that capability. What would you like me to do?"

"Just hang up and wait for a phone call from Quiet Sunshine, as soon as you answer she'll put you through to me on a secure line, talk to you in a moment."

The phone went dead. He hung his up, waited for about five minutes and when it rang again he picked it up.

"Hello."

"Hello," came Quiet Sunshine's voice "I'm putting you through right now."

There were a couple of loud clicks and then he heard Indian say "Hello are you there?"

"Yes Indian I'm here, are we now secure?"

"Yes, now what's this all about?"

"Now about that white powder," began Rob, who then proceeded to explain to Indian everything in Pattern's report for the President.

When he was finished there was silence on the phone, Rob could almost here Indian thinking.

"So that's how you knew about the white powder."

"Well yes, I really just took a guess but I was right."

"How sure are we that everything that you just told me is true?"

"Pattern assures me that everything possible has been done to ensure its accuracy, the fact that your parking garage collapsed would confirm everything that he said. Indian there will be total chaos and anarchy once things start to collapse in a few weeks or months, it would seem that Last Chance is our best bet and I'm trying to get hold of all the boys to see if they want to come back to Last Chance. It turns out that Judge Mortimer is and was our financial benefactor, he was at the meeting we had at Last Chance, seems that he's quite wealthy and has agreed to finance everything that we need to take to Last Chance for our survival. You, Quiet Sunshine and your two girls are of course invited to join us."

"My God, what a hell of a mess, the whole modern world is built around cement and concrete, it's the structural basis for just about everything, I should say when that breaks down so will civilization, you're right in that scenario, Last Chance will be our best bet. You realize of course, that at some time in the future we'll have to defend our lives."

"Yes Indian we have thought of that, God forbid, we are hoping that, with your expertise, you could take over the responsibility for the defenses for Last Chance if you decide to come and join us?"

"It's vulnerable by air and by the river, it'll be very expensive to purchase and have delivered the right armament, how much can we spend on this?"

"The Judge said there's almost unlimited funds available to us, I take it by your response that you're going to come and join us?"

"Yes of course," said Indian "it would seem the only logical thing for us to do, however I'm stuck here in bed for at least two more weeks. I'll discuss all this with Quiet Sunshine, we'll put together a detailed list of the armaments that we'll need and she'll be in contact with you."

"That's excellent," replied Rob "now listen, God knows what sort of condition the airports around the world are going to be in, you'd better be very careful when coming home, I know it would take longer but it may be better if you came back by boat or at the least take small planes that land on grass runways."

"I understand and will take that under advisement, you realize that you've just changed all our lives?"

"Yes, nothing will ever be the same again. You have my phone numbers please stay in touch and let me know what's happening, I'll be moving down to Last Chance very shortly but you can get hold of me on my cell phone."

"Will do that, talk to you soon, Quiet Sunshine will be in touch very shortly. Bye for now." And the phone connection was broken.

Indian hadn't hung up the phone; Quiet Sunshine had only broken the connection to Rob.

"Are you still there honey?"

"Yes I'm still here," Indian could hear the anxiety in her voice.

"Did you hear all that?"

"Yes I did but I wish to God I hadn't."

"What do you make of it all?"

"It's unbelievable, can you visualize what's going to happen when the public realize that they have to evacuate the cities and towns and there's nowhere to go, what will everyone do? Only the fittest and those that are willing to fight will survive, there'll be no food or water supplies, no electricity and no gas, it'll be a mess."

"So you agree with me that we should go to Last Chance, it seems to make a great deal of sense and if things turn out to be not as bad as we think we'll only have lost some time. You've never seen the camp, it's totally isolated and it's on a bend in the river on a huge granite slab some twenty feet above the river level with a large number of acres of very fertile land that make up the river level plateau. It's almost impossible to get to it from the plains, some two hundred feet above, so it's only really vulnerable from the river and the air."

"We really don't have any alternative, how long before you come home?"

"I should be able to leave the hospital in two weeks but I'll certainly try and get out sooner now. I'll try and get an airlift by the Royal Air Force to England, from there I'm not quite sure what I'll have to do it'll depend on world circumstances. You realize this is going to be one heck of a shock for the girls." One of the girls, Dianne, was now sixteen years old, the other, Paula, was fifteen years old, they were both city girls, they had been brought up in New York and even though they were of Native Indian descent the most they had seen of life outside of New York were the visits to the cabin that Indian and

Quiet Sunshine owned up in the Catskill Mountains where, after just one or two days, they very easily got bored.

"Yes they're going to have to grow up in a hurry. Will you write up a list of the armaments or shall I?" asked Quiet Sunshine.

"Well I guess I'm sitting here doing nothing but twiddling my thumbs so I'll put a list together and fax it to you. I think the best place to buy them, although it won't be the cheapest, would be from old Schwabs in San Diego, you want to see if he's got them and how fast he can deliver them and what it's going to cost?"

"Okay you fax that to me and I'll get right on it, as soon as I have an answer from Schwabs I'll contact Rob. Now in the meantime New York is no longer a safe place to live, I'll pull the girls out of school immediately, I'll close the Do Joe and we'll pack up and move up to the cabin and wait for you there."

"Yes you're right of course, as soon as the infrastructure starts to decay all hell will break loose, it'll be everyone for themselves, the gangs will take over, the police, if there are any, won't be able to control the situation, so it sounds like a good idea to me," said Indian "you'd better make sure that we're prepared for all eventualities, I think by the time I get to you it may be best to go overland to Last Chance. Perhaps it would be better if you and the girls left immediately for Last Chance then you wouldn't have to make the arduous journey with me."

"There's no way that we're leaving you behind, we'll leave for the cabin immediately and wait for you there, better that we're all together than to get separated, don't even think about it, you know what I'm like when I've made up my mind."

"I knew that's what you'd say," said Indian "but I had to say it anyway, I know that when you've made up your mind nothing can change it, okay so we'll meet at the cabin. You take your Hummer to get to the cabin and then we'll take mine from there, mine's fully equipped and we'll tow the horses behind just in case we can't go all the way on wheels."

Indian heard a little laugh on the telephone. "Now what's that for?"

"I was just thinking, we may be going back to the old ways and the old saying of 'go west young man go west' now takes on a whole new meaning."

A smile came on Indian's face, "I see what you mean, you'd better make sure that we have all the very best equipment to really go back to the old ways."

"I understand what you're saying, be assured we'll be very well equipped by the time you get home, as devastating as this seems to be, the idea of what we must do is quite exciting, I know it's wrong to feel this way but all the same we've always risen and worked well when challenged, this may be our greatest challenge ever."

"I know how you feel, I'm getting that little knot in my tummy that I always get when we're preparing to face something new in combat or training. Don't worry my love we'll be fine as long as we have each other. I'll be home as fast as possible. I love you, talk to you soon."

"I wish you were home right now," said Quiet Sunshine.

"So do I," said Indian hearing the ache in her voice.

"I'll take care of everything at this end, you just get home as fast as possible."

"I will my love, I will, I'll get that fax off to you right away, I'll phone you as soon as I've sent it off. I love you, be careful don't take any chances."

"Love you to, talk to you soon," and Quiet Sunshine hung up the phone.

As Indian put down the phone on the small table beside the bed, Joan, the British nurse, came walking down the room towards him. She was a beautiful redhead who loved to tease the patients, swinging her hips as she walked and grinning wickedly. There were only two other patients in this small emergency hospital room beside Indian, and every time she came into the room all eyes were turned to her.

"Joan, sweetie pie, could you please pull back the blinds on my windows, it's almost sunset."

He caught a whiff of her perfume and admired the lines of her bottom as she lent over his bedside table and pulled open the blinds.

She turned her head to him giving him a smile as she straightened up. "Is that a better view?"

"Oh yes, I could look at that all day long," he smiled back at her. Joan liked to flirt with the patients but Indian seemed a little different to most, he lay in the bed naked except for a little bit of the sheet pulled up between his legs, there was no air conditioning and the temperature, even at this time of day, was around ninety five degrees, the other patients were uncomfortable in the heat but this one, he seemed quite content. His light brown skin seemed to glow a little and with his jet-black hair braided into a single braid that hung down over his shoulder to just below his left nipple, he was a very handsome man. Joan guessed that he must be at least six feet four inches tall, thick in the chest with little or no fat on his frame. As she pulled back to stand beside his bed she let her fingers rundown his arm knowing that she was deliberately teasing him. She knew that the military men that came under her care were nearly always a long way from home and loved ones and from past experience she knew that it brightened their day and helped them heal when she teased them and made them laugh. That was one of the reasons why she was such an excellent nurse.

"Thank you Joan," said Indian "you know how I love to watch the sunset and the sunrise."

"You're welcome," said Joan turning around and wiggling her bottom at him as she left the room. Indian had had his bed moved to this spot, from here he could look out over the harbor way below him. Aden harbor was a huge horseshoe, the side that he was on was made up of volcanic hills that led down to little Aden, a small town that flourished from the sale of goods to passengers on visiting luxury liners and commercial ships that came into the harbor to refuel from the many oil pipelines that terminated at the harbor. On the far side of the horseshoe the brown desert sand came almost right down to the water, on that side he could see some of the oil refineries, their ever-burning waste gas chimneys nestled between the ocean and the sand; this had been and still was a very strategic harbor. From way up here on one of the volcanic mountains he had an excellent view of the sunset, there was very seldom a cloud in the sky and he thought to himself that each sunset was probably the most beautiful that he had ever seen. He laid back and enjoyed the changing colors and lengthening shadows letting his mind absorb all the latest news. Life would never be the same again.

He took out a pad of paper and, as the room turned blood red from the sunset, he wrote out a list of the armaments and weapons that he thought they would need for Last Chance. As he wrote out the list he realized that it would be almost impossible to get replacement ammunition or parts so he made sure that he ordered enough to allow for usage and breakage. He also wrote out a second list for Quiet Sunshine, things that could be used to replace modern weapons, some of his most favorite weapons, hunting bows, special arrows, hunting knives, etc. He felt a strange calm come over him, it was a feeling that he always got as he planned a military maneuver, it was sinking in; he began to realize what they would be facing.

About a half hour later, just as the sun disappeared below the sand dunes, he had got Joan to fax off the two lists to Quiet Sunshine and had spoken to her briefly on the phone to confirm that she had received them. He relaxed in his bed, "Now I just have to heal and plan how to get home," he thought to himself.

Quiet Sunshine read through the lists and smiled to herself, all the items on the lists were the same things that she would have put down, it was uncanny at times the way that the two of them thought so alike and yet they were so different. She looked at the clock and knowing the difference in time between New York and California she decided she would try and get hold of Schwabs immediately. She looked up his phone number on the computer and dialed.

"Yer, hello Schwabs meat market here what can I do for you?"

Quiet Sunshine knew that there really was a Schwabs meat market, it was in actual fact, a very successful meat specialty shop in San Diego still it was a front for the semi legitimate arms dealings that went on behind the meat warehouse.

"I would like to speak to old man Schwabs please, tell him that this is Quiet Sunshine."

Everyone called him old man Schwabs, he was in actual fact only sixty two years old and extremely overweight but he had fifteen children so everyone called him old man Schwabs.

"Well hello Quiet Sunshine," the voice was like a metal rasp being slowly pulled over the edge of a tin can, Quiet Sunshine easily recognized Schwabs's voice.

"Hello Schwabs how are you, how are your one hundred children?"

"Cheeky as always" laughed Schwabs "my small family is well and how is my friend Indian?"

"He is well, out of the country at the moment. I would like to make a purchase."

"Do I bill a client or is this purchase for yourself?"

"This is a purchase for ourselves, do you have a pencil and paper handy?"

"This conversation is being recorded, I don't need to take notes."

Quiet Sunshine knew that he had an excellent memory and really did not need to take notes or refer back to a taped recording, she read off the list of weapons and ammunition that she wanted.

"What's it going to cost me?"

There was silence on the phone for a few minutes, she could see in her mind's eye Schwabs's big fat chubby fingers playing across the calculator while he grinned to himself.

"Total cost will be five hundred and ninety thousand dollars. Okay?"

"When can you ship them?"

"Well, I can get them to you in about fifteen days."

"That's not good enough, I need them in three days."

"That's not possible, I need at least ten days."

"What will it take to get them delivered in three days?"

Again there was silence, Quiet Sunshine smiled to herself, she knew old man Schwabs was thinking how much he could do her for.

"Well, I'll have to take some of these goods out of the other people's orders, it would mean that I would have to grease some palms, it would cost a great deal of money."

"Just what's it going to cost?"

"Now let me see, if you really have to have them delivered in three days it will cost you seven hundred and fifty thousand dollars."

"Too much, I'll give you six hundred thousand."

There was a laugh at the other end, more like the sound of a sick hyena than of a man. "Come now, you don't expect me to lose money do you? My best offer is seven hundred thousand."

"You're a hard man to make a deal with, I'll give you six hundred and fifty thousand not a penny more."

"You make me cry Quiet Sunshine, if it was anybody else I wouldn't do it but for you and for my old friend Indian I'll lose money and I'll sell them to you for that price, I'll be losing money but you two have sent me a lot of good clients. You're a very hard lady to bargain with."

"That's a deal, I'll make arrangements for the payment and call you back shortly. Thank you" and she hung up the phone.

She called up Rob. "Hello Rob, Quiet Sunshine here, I need to make a purchase six hundred and fifty thousand dollars, how do you want to do it and where would you like the goods delivered to?"

"Oh hello Quiet Sunshine, I'm not quite sure can I call you right back?"

"Sure I'll wait for your phone call" and she hung up.

Rob called the Judge who gave him his Visa card number and information and the address of the container transfer station, he called Quiet Sunshine and asked if they would take a credit card. She said she was not sure, that she would call him back if she had a problem, so he gave her the credit card information and the address of where to send the goods. She called back to Schwabs who laughed and said that it was his first sale using a credit card, she gave him the information and after a short pause while he got the sale authorized, he said that it was acceptable and she gave him the address for delivery and he said that they, the goods, would be there in the allotted time of three days.

14

Consequences.

Seattle.

One week after the meeting at Last Chance.

Ronald Stanton was a very wealthy man, he had made his fortune in real estate. He was sixty five years old, very fit, he worked out every day and loved to swim over a hundred lengths of his swimming pool which was located on the thirty fourth floor in his office tower. He had built his office tower ten years ago in downtown Seattle, it was his pride and joy and on the top floor, the thirty eighth floor, he had his offices of which he had had one section made into a beautifully decorated bedroom and bathroom with a huge jacuzzi bathtub. He always prided himself in remembering where he had come from; his father had been a city worker so, to remind himself, he had had all the walls of his office floor made of glass. The glass was leaning out at the top at such an angle that he could, when he lent against the glass, look down and see the people way down below in the street, he loved to lean on this imagining that he was flying and watching the goings on in the city below. The glass had been fortified and was set in metal frames that were buried into the cement of the building. He was married and had three children. He had married a very beautiful young lady ten years his junior and his children were attending university, two at Harvard and one at Yale. His family lived in a magnificent estate just outside of Seattle, to everyone that knew them theirs was a perfect marriage.

Very early in his marriage he had found out that his wife did not enjoy any sexual activities, she always attempted to satisfy his needs but she never really got any enjoyment for herself and so they had come to a mutual understanding, she knew that he loved her dearly and had agreed to allow him to fulfill his sexual needs outside of the marriage provided it was done extremely discreetly. Through the years he had found that he was a voyeur and loved watching young people make love.

This evening he finished up his work in the office and went through to his bedroom, he had a hot bath and then ate some supper that his secretary had ordered for him. He put on his favorite music, dimmed the lights and made himself comfortable in his big overstuffed armchair wearing only a silk bathrobe and watched a beautiful sunset over the city. As it got dark he heard the buzzer of his intercom, he pressed a button.

"Visitors for you Mr. Stanton would you like me to send them up?"

"Yes please Fredrick thank you."

A few minutes later the doors to his private elevator opened and a young man and a young lady entered his bedroom, they stepped forward and greeted him warmly. He had arranged through an agency for them to come this evening, he had purchased their services before and had always enjoyed himself.

"Would you like a drink George?" Ronald asked.

"Just a fruit juice please."

"And what about you Angie?"

"I'll have the same please, possibly something stronger later," she answered with a grin.

He poured them the drinks and they sat and chatted for a few minutes and then Angie lent over and snuggled with George. They hugged and kissed and started petting each other, Ronald moved out of the way as they moved over to his bed that was quite close to the outside wall of glass.

George slowly removed her blouse, she wasn't wearing a bra. She undid his shirt and he shrugged it off, she reached down and undid his trousers and slowly she pulled them off, he wasn't wearing any underwear, he was slim and quite muscular, Ronald could see his muscles rippling as she played with him. George reached down and pulled off her remaining clothing and Ronald got up from his chair and slid off his silk robe.

"God it was beautiful to see two gorgeous young people making love," Ronald thought to himself as he moved over by the windows next to the bed. He liked to look over the city and play with himself and watch the lovers on the bed. Ronald watched as the two of them made love, time seemed to stand still. About an hour later he lent back against the glass windows, this is what he really enjoyed, the feel of the cold glass pressing against his back pushing on his buttocks as he watching the two making love on the bed.

As the two on the bed started to climax Ronald came off the glass a little and then as he listened to the sounds the two lovers made he threw himself back against the windows knowing that he was just about to reach his own climax. He didn't see the puff of white powder that came out around the top of the window frame, he hardly heard the grinding sound as the metal frame came out of the cement as the cement turned into a snow white powder all around the window. For a few seconds Ronald imagined that he was flying and then he realized that he was lying on the glass as it flew away from the building and he screamed. He seemed to just ride the glass as it flew, swaying this way and that from side to side like some giant leaf in the night breeze, he threw his hands out flat trying to hold onto the glass. The glass made a sudden rush and hit the building shattering into thousands of razor-sharp shards and Ronald was cut to pieces and went crashing down into the crowded street below. Nine people were killed and dozens were cut by the falling glass.

On the bed the young couple screamed with pleasure as they felt the blast of the cool evening air on their naked bodies. Then their screams of pleasure turned to screams of horror as they jerked apart hearing Ronald's screams as he disappeared into the street below.

15

Consequences.

Allegheny Mountains.

Seven days after the meeting at Last Chance.

U.S.P. Allenwood is situated in the foothills of the northern Allegheny Mountains, it is located two miles north of Allenwood on U.S. Route 15, eleven miles south of Williamsport and one hundred and nineteen miles north of Washington, DC. It has a section that is a high security penitentiary for men. This houses some of the worst convicts in the United States. On the lower floor of the east wing, in the very last cell on the left hand side were three inmates, Spike Pixon was a giant of a man, he stood six feet seven inches tall and weighed three hundred and sixty eight pounds and all of it was solid muscle, he was the kingpin in this section of the prison, a title that he had attained through sheer brutality. He had been in this prison for the last eighteen years and was serving a double life sentence for killing three young ladies and two police officers. Nick Sayre, one of the other two men in the cell, was a big man in his own right but was dwarfed by Spike; he was serving a life sentence for killing a bank manager and a bank security guard during a foiled bank robbery and had been in prison for the last ten years, he was owned by Spike and was his first in command. Lance Laver, the third man in the cell was much smaller, a handsome younger man and was the sexual plaything for both Spike and Nick, he too was serving a life sentence for murdering his wife and his girlfriend and had been in this prison for the last five years. Spike and Lance were the most feared people in the whole prison.

They had learned through the grapevine that they would be getting a new person in their cell this evening since each cell held four convicts. They had a vacancy in their cell because Roger the Rat, who had been living there, had been found murdered out in the yard one week ago, everyone knew that Spike had killed him but there was no proof. They heard a commotion as the sound of the metal gates at the entrance to their wing opened and then there were cat calls, whistles and jeers and they knew that the guards were bringing their new cellmate down the center walkway, the noises were coming from the convicts sealed in their cells on either side as they passed. It only took a minute or so before four guards appeared in front of their cell with a very handsome younger convict.

Dick Anderson, the head guard, said briskly "Gentlemen move to the back of the cell please."

Spike, Nick and Lance moved leisurely back and lined up along the back wall beside the toilet that was in the corner. The only other things beside the toilet in the room were four bunk beds, two on either side of the cell close up to the bars at the front and four small metal chests of drawers for their clothing. Normally the cells were designed to hold two convicts per cell but because of the over crowding they were forced to house four inmates into each one.

Dick Anderson spoke into his lapel mike, "Open the gate to cell one hundred please."

There was a loud clang as the electronic locks opened and then a slight screeching sound of metal moving on metal as the barred gate to the cell slid open.

Dick Anderson stepped slightly to one side and two of the other guards pushed the young man into the cell, "This is your new cellmate, his name is Rodney Dicks, looks like you have some fresh meat tonight Spike." He then spoke into his lapel mike again and the cell gate crashed shut and locked and the guards moved back down the hallway amongst cheers and catcalls from some of the other prisoners.

The young man took one step forward into the cell and then froze as the mountainous Spike stepped forward in front of him and the other two men in the cell moved around behind him, all three were looking at him as if he were a piece of meat that they were considering buying.

"Well what do we have here?" Said Spike.

"Nice fresh young pussy, it looks like to me," said Nick reaching out and running his hand down the bare shoulder of the new man.

"Errrr my name is Rodney Dicks," stuttered the young man with a look of terror on his face, "I'm errrr here I mean errrr I mean How Do."

Spike just looked down at him, "Turn around slowly" he said.

Rodney was terrified, he knew that there would be no help from anyone, he was on his own, there was absolutely no chance of fighting or disobeying these three men, he knew that Spike alone could tear him limb from limb if he so desired. He lowered his head and slowly turned around, he was twenty-eight years old but looked much younger, he had jet-black hair and was quite well built with a slim waist and wide shoulders.

"Well lookey here" said Lance ogling the young man "he knows how to do as he's told, ain't that nice?"

"Maybe he'll be a good pussy, he does have a nice arse," Lance said as he reached out and stroked Dick's butt.

Dick was shaking all over, he was new to jail life, he had been brought here to serve out his sentence of twenty years for murdering his girlfriend and her new lover, this was his first hard core prison time. He stopped turning as he was facing Spike.

"I'm Spike and I own this fucking prison wing, I control every fucking thing that goes on with the convicts, that means that I own you boy, is that fucking clear?"

Dick could hardly speak but he managed to stutter " yes Spike, errrr yes sir errrr yes I understand."

Spike stepped back and nodded to Lance who stepped in front of Dick and started to unbutton his shirt. Dick stepped back pushing Lance away.

"What the fuck" said Lance reaching forward and grabbing Dick by the shirt, "what the fuck do you think you're doing, standstill you young bitch."

Dick struggled with Lance and pushed him away, the next thing that he knew he was being held up in the air with his face one inch away from Spike's.

"So you don't know what it's like to do as you're told, well you're going to find out, I like things a little bit rough, I like my pussy soft and well beaten," and Dick almost lost consciousness as Spike's ham like fist hit him on the side of his head. He was tossed about like a rag doll between Spike and Nick, he moaned and groaned and begged for his life. The shirt was torn off him and then Spike held him in midair as Nick and Lance pulled off his trousers and his underpants.

"Well just look at that pussy," said Nick as Spike forced Dick to bend over and Lance pulled his arse cheeks apart, "I can't wait to get myself a bit of that arse."

"No oh please no don't please no don't please oh please don't" screamed Dick as Lance reached between his legs and grabbed his balls "oh God that hurts, please please oh please don't."

Spike lifted the man in the air.

"You make too much fucking noise, the screws will come and they'll spoil my fun, you've got to learn to do as you're told when you're told" and he literally threw the young man across the cell splattering him against the back wall. The three inmates stood stock still in shock, their mouths open, their eyes wide as the young man seemed to disappear or seemed to break up into a great cloud of white dust, they stepped back so that their backs were against the cell door to avoid the dust.

"What the hell did you do?" Whispered Lance.

"Mother fucker, you sure hit him hard against that wall, you smashed him into dust. Oh shit." Nick mumbled.

"What the hell's all that about?" said Spike as he pulled the shirt out of his pants and held it across his mouth so that he didn't breath in the white powder. "What the fuck happened to him, what the fucks going on, Lance see what happened to him."

Lance pulled the shirt out of his pants and covered his nose and mouth, he looked at Spike and then moved forward into the cloud of white dust that was already beginning to settle on everything in the cell. He got to the rear wall just in time to hear a moan and a groan coming from a hole in the cement, he reached in and grabbed a hand and pulled Dick out of the hole. Dick was coughing and splattering and spitting out blood and white muck as he fell to the floor and lay there wrenching and coughing.

"Be quiet" said Spike "shut up, shut the fuck up, you don't want to draw to much attention."

Nick grabbed a sheet off the bed and threw it over his head.

"Don't kill him just cover his head so he can breath, so he won't make so much damn noise that the screws will come" said Spike.

They stood there for a minute or two as the dust settled and then Spike cautiously moved to investigate the hole in the wall. He stepped right up to where the wall had been and reached in, almost at full arms reach he felt the surface of the inner wall but it was not hard like cement is meant to be, he seemed to be able to grab handfuls of it and it turned to powder and fell through his fingers. He stepped back, removed the shirt from his face and with a big grin said, "I don't know what the fuck's going on but it feels like the wall's just collapsing into this white dust. Nick you know the layout of the prison, what's on the other side of this wall?"

Nick stood there thinking for a couple of minutes and then said, "The way that the prison is built, the end of each of these wings is the outside perimeter of the prison. There's no more prison outside that wall, if memory serves me right, there should be a grass verge and then that road that runs down beside the prison and on the other side of the road is a field and then the woods."

Lance went to say something but Spike told him to shush.

Dick under the sheet had stopped all the noise and was just sobbing and crying.

"Now let me get this correct" said Spike walking back and forth across the cell "If this cement wall crumbles like it's fucking crumbling here and we can get out there is nothing out there to stop us from getting free, is that what you're saying?" He stopped moving and looked at Nick

"That's what I think," said Nick "I can't be one hundred percent but I'd bet my life on it."

"You just did, you just bet your fucking life on it," said Spike and Nick knew that he meant it. Spike tore a piece of the sheet off and tied it round his nose and mouth and moved back into the hole in the wall. He began clawing at the back, feeling what should have been cement just breaking up beneath his fingers. The other two watched as the man seemed to move into the cement, he had almost disappeared when there was a slight yell. Spike moved back into the cell, he looked like a white giant, covered head to foot in the white powder.

"Well I pushed my hand right through that fucking wall," Spike said "The last couple of inches is cement, I think I busted my knuckles." Nick saw a little bit of blood washing the white dust off Spike's right hand.

"What the fuck's going on," said Lance "I can't believe this is happening, cement just doesn't break up into white powder. What the fuck's going on?"

"Who knows," said Spike "I don't give a fuck, I just know that we might be able to get out of this place. Now listen, the screws have just shut us up for the night, there won't be any more checks until tomorrow morning, if we can break out through the remainder of the wall now, we'll have six hours before they discover that we're gone."

"Shit, I'm with you Spike," said Nick "let's get out of this shit hole."

"Me to" said Lance "but if that outside layer is still cement what we going to use to break through?"

Spike looked around the cell and then pointed at the young man under the sheet. The other two got his meaning and the three of them grabbed hold of Dick, Spike hit him square in his face under the sheet and he went limp. The three of them wrapped his unconscious body in the sheet and then they picked him up like a battering ram. Spike stepped into the hole in the wall and they started swinging Dick back and forth, the head of the sheet began to look bloodier each time Dick's head smashed into the remaining cement. If he had been conscious, Dick would have then felt the rain on his bleeding head. It only took about fifteen minutes of crashing the body through the outer layer of cement before there was a hole big enough for them to get through. They threw what was left of Dick onto one of the bunks and Spike stuck his head out through the hole.

"Your fucking right, there's a drop-off then I can see the road and a bit of a field on the other side but it's raining pretty hard, shit it feels so good," said Spike.

Lance and Nick could see where the rain was washing off some of the white powder from the side of his face.

"Okay" said Spike "Lance you go first, just get out of the hole and jump down then you Nick and I'll come last, when I get down we'll make a run for it across the road through the fields and into the woods. Complete fucking silence, is that understood?"

Nick and Lance nodded.

"Once we get into the woods if you can to keep up with me then Ok, if you can't keep up with me you go your own fucking way, do I make myself clear?"

The other two nodded.

"Let's go," said Spike and pushed Lance into the hole. Lance climbed through the hole in the outside wall, hesitated just for a moment and then jumped down.

Nick was watching and saw him just disappear, there was a thump and a whisper came up "it's further down than we thought, there's a drop of about ten feet but it's only grass when you land."

Nick climbed through the hole second and then jumped down, Spike followed him almost immediately and almost landed on top of him. The three of them stood up and looked around, there was nothing to see, the rain felt really good as it washed the white powder from them. Spike looked at the other two and then all three of them ran across the road, through the field and disappeared into the thick woods.

16

Quiet Sunshine moves to the cabin.

New York.

The second day of Rob and June's journey to the Transfer Station.

After Quiet Sunshine had finished arranging the purchases from old man Schwabs she moved swiftly around their apartment, very efficiently packing everything for herself, the two girls and Indian. She was used to packing, sometimes when working overseas the packing had to be done extremely fast. She moved into the girl's room, it was a mess, it did not seem to matter how much they nagged at the two girls their room always seemed to be a mess, she swiftly went through all of their things packing up all of their essentials. Diane had a favourite teddy bear, she had had it since she was three years old, it was old and raggedy and had no eyes, every night she took it to bed with her and Paula had a fluffy yellow duck that used to speak when you squeezed its beak but most of the words had, through time, disappeared and now when you squeezed the beak you just got a series of grunts. Every night Paula would put it on the bedside table and squeeze the beak before she went to bed, both of these she packed up in their bags.

She went into the Dojo, there were special bags for some of the accoutrements that were used there and these she swiftly sorted and packed, putting the bags that she wanted to take with her over by the door to the garage. She went down into the basement and went over to the work bench, she reached just under the metal vice and pushed a hidden button and pulled the whole bench and the shelving above it forward, it moved very easily and very quietly on hidden casters, behind were two heavy metal doors. She unlocked and opened them;

on the wall at the back were a number of different firearms with their ammunition, all of which were legal and had been registered, she quickly wrapped them in oilcloths and waterproof bags and put them by the garage door. She went back down to the basement and on the back, where the armaments had been hanging, she pulled hard on one of the hangers and the back of the cupboard opened up to reveal more weapons, these were the ones that had not been registered along with their favorite toys, these were a variety of bows along with a variety of different arrows and knives, these she swiftly packed and placed with the others ready to go with her.

She opened the garage door and there in the garage was her hummer, it was bright yellow and was polished and shining, this was her hummer, Indian kept his hummer up at the cabin; his was fitted out for rough terrain. She loaded all of the bags into the back and then opened the back door to the yard and whistled, around the corner came what looked like a brown shaggy bear, it was in fact their dog Iggy, he was massive, he stood about four feet tall and could stand beside the kitchen table and without raising his head he could lay his jaws on the table. Three years ago they had been visiting some friends who bred Bouviers, one of them had got out and had mated with a Rottweiler down the road, the friends had been disgusted. She'd had five puppies and their friends asked them to take one, they picked the runt of the litter who had now grown into this enormous brute. Iggy proved to be very bright, they had taken him through basic dog training and then through police training and then had trained him to not only obey verbal commands but also hand signals. She opened the back door of her hummer and he flopped onto the back seat taking up the whole thing. She went to the back of the garage and made sure that the Harley Davidson motorcycle there was covered and put a black bag underneath it.

She got into the hummer, pressed a button to open the garage door and drove out and as she pressed the button to close the door behind her she said to herself as much as to the dog, "Well Iggy, this may be the last time we see this place, let's go down and pick up the girls, you know that they won't want to go up to the cabin don't you?"

Iggy just looked at her and put his enormous head down on his paws.

The girls had just started university, Diane was very bright and had skipped a year in school and Paula was bordering on genius and had skipped two years of school so they had started university together. The university was an hour's drive from home, each day Indian, herself or one of the neighbors who went that way to work, gave them a lift and brought them home. At the cabin they had learned to ride and they enjoyed it but they had never been on a long trek on a horse.

"They're in for a rude awakening," she thought to herself.

She parked by the university's main entrance, in a few moments she saw the two girls come out, they were laughing and talking with a couple of young men. They were both very attractive young ladies. Diane was only slightly taller than Paula, they both had long black hair, their features were from their forefathers, both being full blooded Indians. Quiet Sunshine loved them dearly and was very proud of them. She hooted the horn to get their attention and they ran over to the hummer carrying their schoolbags. They saw everything packed in the back, Paula got into the front seat and Diane moaned as she pushed Iggy to one side, climbed in and he flopped his head back in her lap nuzzling her happily.

"What's all that in the back?" Asked Paula as they pulled away.

"Okay you two I have to tell you something." Quiet Sunshine said as she pulled the hummer into the fast lane. "I want you to just sit and listened to me, save your questions till I've finished. Do you understand?"

"You sound serious" said Diane as she stroked Iggy's head. "What's up?"

"First of all let me tell you that we're not going home, we're heading straight out to the cabin."

The girls groaned and Paula said "Come on, that's ridiculous, we have school tomorrow, I can't miss it, we're coming up to exams. What's going on?"

Diane leaned forward almost squashing Iggy to hear better.

"I said please let me finish before you ask any more questions. Suffice to say right now that I've packed up everything that I think we will need to live at the cabin until Indian comes home."

Quiet Sunshine heard them both groan this time, they were both bursting with questions so, accelerating down the highway, she continued quickly explaining all about Pattern's report and what the crystals were going to cause. By the time she had finished speaking they were heading down the motorway that led to the cabin. The girls sat there stunned.

Paula was the first to speak. "That's just not possible, it can't be true. What are they going to do about it?"

"That's right," said Diane "the government will stop it and get rid of it, won't they?"

"There's nothing, at this time that anyone can do to prevent the collapse of everything that's made out of concrete or cement. It's inevitable that there's going to be chaos, people will be fleeing the cities for safety, we just have to be very thankful that we've been forewarned and can get a head start. So you see, you won't be going back to the university, in a short while there won't be any safe university buildings. As soon as Indian gets home we'll be heading down to Last Chance. You remember Indian talking about it; it's the camp where he grew up down in Arizona and it's quite isolated, there'll be a bunch of us living there until we know that it's safe to move around the country again, that may be quite a long time but we should be safe down there."

The girls sat back quietly trying to understand what they had just been told, then the questions started as they realized that their lives had just totally changed.

The trip to the cottage usually took about three hours, by the time they were half way there the girls had exhausted all their questions and they just sat there looking glumly out of the windows.

Quiet Sunshine and Indian had bought the cabin ten years ago, they used it as a getaway when they needed to just be by themselves. It was in the hills well away from any road. The driveway, which was more like a cart track, wound through a couple of fields, through a wood and then up a steep slope to the top. The cabin was concealed by a small wood and was very hard to see from the surrounding countryside. As one sat on the long porch that ran the whole length of the front of the cabin one could see right down the valley, it was a beautiful sight. The cabin was made of wood logs; there were two bedrooms and a large living room come kitchen. Originally there had been no running water only a hand pump but when the girls joined them they had had the water piped in and a hot water tank and then a septic tank and drainage system put in, so, tucked in between the bedrooms where the closets had been, there was now a bathroom. They had had electricity run in over the top of the hill from the closest farm so they now had all the modern conveniences. They had put in a television for the girls but even with all the modern conveniences the girls really had no interest in staying there.

To the left of the cabin was a barn setup for horses complete with a large paddock. They owned five horses, they were good solid riding horses, there was a thoroughbred horse farm about five miles down the road and, for an outlandish fee, they looked after and kept the horses down there until Quiet Sunshine and Indian needed them. The owners of the horse farm frowned on their five horses; the farm was for beautiful thoroughbred racing horses whereas their horses were really wiry overland riding and working horses however they liked the extra cash. To the right of the cabin was a two-car garage and again it was made out of logs with a large storage and work area at the back.

Quiet Sunshine pulled the hummer up in front of the cabin and jumped out, she opened the back door and Iggy climbed out over the cussing Diane and disappeared feverishly into the woods. Diane knew that the dog would not go far, he loved to run but he was always within earshot. The girls got out and helped her unload the hummer and took everything into the cabin.

"As soon as Indian gets here we'll be leaving, is that clear?"

"Yes" said the girls taking their bags into their bedroom.

Quiet Sunshine always kept the cabin fully stocked, there was nothing perishable but they always kept it so they could move in and have food and drink immediately on hand.

"I'll have to get some more supplies if we stay here more than a week" thought Quiet Sunshine as she hustled around the kitchen to get supper ready. After supper they all went for a walk through the woods with Iggy leaping and bounding happy to be in the wilderness. They then went back to the cabin and sat talking till late into the night and finally went to bed.

Next morning Quiet Sunshine was up early, the rising sun had awakened her as it streamed through the bedroom window. It took a lot to get the girls up, they just grumbled and groaned and wanted to sleep, Quiet Sunshine told them they had things to do. After they had eaten breakfast and cleaned up they went out to the garage and Quiet Sunshine pulled out Indian's hummer. It was shiny black; there was a very powerful winch on the front bumper and a slightly smaller one to the left on the rear bumper, the exhaust came up above the top of the vehicle and the whole engine was waterproofed so that it could go through three or four feet of water. Above the windshield was an extra anti roll bar with five powerful spot lights mounted on it, it was fully equipped for going cross country and rough terrain. This was Indian's pride and joy, he loved to take it out through the woods and fields and across the rivers and streams, this was his form of relaxation and then, much to Quiet Sunshine's annoyance, he would spend hours cleaning and polishing it from top to bottom in every nook and cranny. They all got into the hummer and drove down to the horse farm, Iggy was told to stay behind at the cabin and as they drove away they looked back and he was sitting on the front porch at the top of the steps looking around as if he was the Lord of the Manor.

They drove into the immaculately kept acres of the horse farm; there were magnificent horses in the fields that were surrounded by white wood fences.

"It's like something out of a movie," said Quiet Sunshine and the girls agreed as they pulled up in front of one of the very large barns, a beautiful black lady came over to greet them with the biggest smile on her face, she was dressed in a white flowered blouse and wearing jodhpurs and riding boots.

"Well hello you all," Jherika said happily hugging each one of them "haven't seen you lot for a while." Jherika was the youngest daughter of the owners of the farm, her parents were getting up in years and of their three children she was the only one that was interested in running the farm. She had been through university and was very competent and Quiet Sunshine really liked her.

"What are you doing up here during school time? Is Indian with you?"

"Hello" said Quiet Sunshine as she managed to break loose from a big friendly hug, "Indian should be coming up here shortly, he was overseas and broke his leg, he should be on his way back as we speak. We decided that we would come up here while his leg heals." She looked at the girls to make sure that they understood to be careful what they said.

"Oh, I hope it isn't too bad. You girls are really growing up fast, we'll have to get together and catch up on everything real soon, unfortunately, at the moment, I'm getting ready to make a delivery, we have a plane to catch, we have a foal that's been purchased by the royal family in Saudi Arabia and we have to take her to the airport. Did you want to get your horses?"

"Yes please," said Quiet Sunshine nodding "we'll take all five of them, is our horse trailer still in the same place?"

"Yes it is, please just go ahead and help yourself, I'm really sorry that I can't stop and chat, we really will have to get together real soon."

"Thank you," said Quiet Sunshine as Jherika turned and ran back to the barn. They backed the hummer around behind a large storage shed and hitched a six-horse trailer up to it. They then drove further into the farm to the very back section where they found their five horses grazing in a field well apart from all the thoroughbreds. The girls rushed forward and were greeted with wet floppy muzzles. There was no problem in getting the horses into the trailer and taking them back to the cabin, Iggy was thrilled to see the horses, they all got on very well and Iggy knew that having the horses at the cabin meant that they were going to go out riding and he loved to follow them.

They put the horses in the paddock, cleaned and rubbed them down, then spent the rest of the day tidying up around the buildings and cleaning all the tack. That evening they drove into town and had supper at the small restaurant and picked up some more supplies.

The next morning Quiet Sunshine woke the girls up at the crack of dawn and, much to their dismay, she said "We're taking the horses out for a run today, get dressed ready to ride." She closed the bedroom door so as not to hear their usual complaining. She cooked them all a good breakfast and then afterwards they saddled up three of the horses and rode into the woods.

About an hour later Diane said, "Okay, okay, that's about enough, let's head for home my butt is getting sore."

"Sorry Diane we've got a long way to go yet, I don't think you quite understand what will probably happen when Indian gets here. We're going to try to drive down to Last Chance, if we're extremely lucky we will be able to drive all the way there but we're going to have to be prepared to ride a lot of the way. Don't forget that some of the bridges and overpasses will have become impassible and there will be horrendous traffic jams, we may not get too far before we have to rely on the horses, it may mean that we have a long ride ahead of us, I mean possibly three or four or more days on the horses. Therefore today we're going to ride until the sun sets, we should just be home in time to see the sun go down. So cheer up, we have a long way to go."

"You've got to be kidding," yelled out Paula "my butt is getting sore already. We don't know that we won't be able to drive all the way down there so we might as well just wait and see."

"That's right," moaned Diane "let's just wait and see, things may not be anywhere near as bad as you think they'll be, let's just go home."

"Sorry ladies," Quiet Sunshine said smiling to herself "this is the way it has to be, we can't up and wait and see, we must be prepared for all eventualities. Come on, you know how to cure a sore butt; you just take the weight off it with your legs. I have lunch and drinks in my saddlebags," she tapped the bags hanging across the rump of the horse, "we'll stop for a break in a couple of hours and have something to eat."

Quiet Sunshine tried to block her ears to keep out all the noise and whining that the two young ladies made, she watched Iggy happily running around the horses and then shooting off in one direction or another.

By the time they got home that night the two girls were worn out. They got back to the cabin and fell off the horses and headed for the cabin.

"Hey where you do you think you're going?"

"Oh God, I've had it, I'm going to bed," said Diane.

"Me too" said Paula "that was just insane, my butt is so sore and so are my legs."

"Oh no you don't" said Quiet Sunshine "you've yet to look after your horses, you must learn that they're your most prized possessions, they come before your comforts. You have to cool them down and brush them down and make sure they're fed and watered. Then you check your tack and if everything is all right then, and only then, can you look after yourselves."

"You've got to be kidding" moaned Diane "I can hardly stand, can't we do that in the morning?"

"Oh no you have to do that tonight to make sure that the horses don't get sick, come on the pair of you, you've got to learn," and Quiet Sunshine led the bedraggled pair to the barn to look after the horses. Iggy looked at them as if they were all a little nutty and flopped his tired body on the front porch resting his head on his paws.

The next morning Quiet Sunshine woke the girls up at sunrise and threw a set of saddlebags onto each of their beds.

"Now what are they for?" Mumbled Paula as she tried to cover her head up in the blankets.

"Okay get up you lazy bums, today we're going to learn to camp, I want you to pack up your clothing and essentials in these saddlebags. If we have to leave the Hummer this may be all that we'll have to carry our stuff in, pack it carefully, put in some waterproof clothing, some warm clothing, your toothbrush and toothpaste and any other essentials and only pack essentials. We'll be camping for the night."

Both the girls shot up in bed. "Oh come on this is getting a little bit too ridiculous, you know we've been camping before. Mother and father used to take us out at weekends sometimes, they would rent a big motor home that we'd have to rough it in, we got pretty good at that, so we know what camping's all about."

Quiet Sunshine roared with laughter, "that's not camping that's not roughing it, I mean camping out in the woods, no fridges or stoves, you'll be sleeping on the ground and...."

"Don't be so ridiculous," interrupted Diane "this is all totally unnecessary, we'll just drive down to Arizona besides why can't we just take a plane, you're just trying to punish us, what have we done wrong?"

Quiet Sunshine could hardly control her merriment.

"There probably won't be any planes flying and even if there were it would be extremely risky, I've told you before that it may not be possible to even take the Hummer all the way so we'll be on horseback, we'll have to camp out, you'll have to sleep on the ground, you'll have to cook over an open fire. I don't want to have to try and teach you everything about camping when it becomes necessary to do it so you'll have to learn this week, now come on jump out of bed and let's go."

She left the girl's bedroom and laughing to herself made breakfast. A short while later the girls came out of the bedroom carrying their saddlebags, each one was bursting with clothing hanging out of them and stuff tied around the top of them. Quiet Sunshine just sat down and laughed till she cried.

"Well what's wrong with you? What's so funny?" Asked Diane.

"You can't pack saddlebags like that, things will fall out, it will fall off the horse."

She threw her neatly packed saddlebag onto the table.

"That is what a packed saddlebag should look like."

"That's all right for you" said Paula "but we need to take more than you do."

"Let's see what you have in yours," said Quiet Sunshine going over to Paula's. She started to unpack one side of the saddlebags she pulled out a game boy and an electric hairdryer.

"Where do you expect to plug this in at?" Asked Quiet Sunshine "you know that trees don't grow with electric plugs in them. Okay I guess I'll have to show you how to pack saddlebags but before we repack your bags, over there on the table you'll find a bedroll ready for each of you. I'll show you how to make it up and how to roll it and tie it onto your horses."

The girls went over and looked at the bedrolls.

"Well what do we put them on?" Said Diane.

"Where are the air mattresses?" Spat out Paula.

"There aren't going to be any air mattresses, you don't have room for anything like that, the bedrolls go directly onto the ground, it's really quite comfortable if you know the right way to do things. Let's eat breakfast while it's hot and then we'll get you packed up and we'll head out, this is going to be a lot of fun."

"Shit, it may be fun for you but it's going to be sheer hell for us," moaned Paula as she sat down for breakfast.

When they had cleared off the breakfast dishes Quiet Sunshine showed them how to pack up their saddlebags. When she had finished packing Diane's Paula said, "oh come on, that's absolutely ridiculous, there's not enough clothes in there for even two days use, we have to take more than that."

"That's all the room that you have, you can only pack what will go into the saddlebags, there's no trunk on the back of a horse. If you want clean clothes then you'll have to wash them in a stream or something."

Diane's face squeezed up in a grimace and through clenched teeth she said, "I'm not washing my good clothes in a filthy dirty stream."

Quiet Sunshine burst into laughter, "well if you don't want to wash them in a filthy dirty stream then you'll just have to wear them dirty, there are no laundromats out there in the woods."

At that the girls became quiet and finished packing their clothes and their bedrolls. Quiet Sunshine thought to herself "I'm really beginning to enjoy this but I wish Indian was here."

It took all of Quiet Sunshine's patience to show them how to set up camp that night, she ended up laughing herself to sleep listening to the girls bitch trying to get comfortable in their bedrolls.

The morning after they got home from the first campout, much to the girls dismay, Quiet Sunshine had them back up again at daybreak to do another trek and another campout, this she did every day until the girls could sit in their saddles quite comfortably all day, could make a very rudimentary camp, could actually get a reasonable night's sleep and still had lots of energy left to look after the horses and to laugh and joke in the evenings. Quiet Sunshine was very pleased with their progress.

The morning after Indian called Quiet Sunshine she gently woke the girls and told them that they could sleep in that morning, she was going to take Iggy and go into town to buy some last minute supplies.

The girls were delighted and, as Quiet Sunshine closed the bedroom door, they rolled over and went back to sleep. Quiet Sunshine put Indian's Hummer in the garage and shut the doors, put the back seat of her Hummer down flat, whistled to Iggy who happily jumped in and flopped down, always ready for a car ride, and off they went to town.

Half an hour after Quiet Sunshine had left the cabin a big black Lincoln, covered in mud, came to the top of the last rise of the driveway to the cabin, it pulled up sharply as Spike, the driver, saw the cabin a hundred yards away. The Lincoln rolled back a few yards and then Spike drove it off the track and into the bushes, only its back end was visible from the driveway. The three men got out and walked through the brush up to the cabin. Paula and Diane were startled out of their sleep by a loud banging on the front door, Diane jumped out of bed and went to open the door, Paula grabbed a blanket and wrapped it around her shoulders and followed close behind. Diane opened the door a crack and was then thrown backwards across the front room knocking Paula over as the door flew open and the biggest man the girls had ever seen crashed into the living room accompanied by two other men.

"Who the hell are you? What the hell do you want? Get out of our cabin," shrieked Paula as she tried to get up off the floor. Spike strode over to her, grabbed her by her hair and literally lifted her off her feet, Paula screamed in pain, tears started to run down her face. Spike put his face within two inches of her's and said, "I'm Spike and you'll do exactly as you're told, do you understand?"

Paula could barely speak, the pain from her hair was so intense, "Yes, yes I understand, please put me down, please put me down."

Spike gave her one last shake and then let her feet touch the floor but he still held onto her hair.

Diane was shaken by her fall, she got to her knees as she heard her sister screaming, she watched as Spike lifted her off the ground and shook her like a rag doll. The next thing she felt was her own hair being grabbed and she was pulled up to stand on her feet. A gruff voice, whose breath stunk, said quietly in her ear "You better do as you're told you pretty little thing."

Lance held onto Diane's hair, he slipped his other hand around her waist and pulled her back against him, he could feel her shaking and loved the smell of her, "My but don't you smell good," he said and licked the side of her neck. Diane shook as she said "Let me go, please let me go, don't do that, what do you want?"

Spike looked around the cabin. "Are you two alone?" He asked giving Paula a little shake.

"Yes," said Paula "but our aunt will be back very shortly."

"Well isn't that nice, then there'll be three of you pussies won't there?" He laughed, "I guess we'll just have to wait for Auntie to come home won't we?"

He pushed Paula over to Nick who wrapped his hand in her hair and held her still.

"Hold these two for a minute while I have a look around," Spike said looking into both of the bedrooms and throwing the bathroom door open, he then strode out.

He was only gone for a couple of minutes and as he came back in the front door he said, "Doesn't look like there's anyone else around but guess what, there's a big beautiful Hummer in the garage, it'll make a good ride for us."

"Spike I'm awfully hungry," said Nick "can we get the girls to cook us up a meal?"

Spike strode over in front of Diane and ran his hands over her breasts, Diane shrank away from him only to be held in place by Lance behind her. Spike laughed, "Okay you two cook us up something we're hungry, we haven't eaten any real food in the last twenty-four hours, cook us up something good. Let's go."

They let the two girls go and they ran over and held onto each other.

"What do you want to eat?" Stammered Paula.

"Well what've you got, how about some eggs, bacon, sausages and toast, potatoes if you got some and coffee, lots of coffee, how does that sound?" Said Nick as he sat down at the table.

The girls moved into the kitchen area and as they did so Diane whispered into Paula's ear, "Take your time, be as slow as you can,

Sunshine should be back shortly." And she turned on the burners of the oven.

It only took Quiet Sunshine twenty minutes to pick up the last few things that she thought they might need on the trip to Last Chance, Iggy stayed in the Hummer while she was in the shop and watched the people go by. She threw the shopping bags into the back hatch of the vehicle and drove back to the cabin. As she came up the last slope of the driveway she spotted the back end of the black Lincoln in the bushes, she stopped, quietly got out of the vehicle and went over and looked at the car, the seats were full of old drink containers and bags of old food.

"Something's really wrong here," she thought to herself. She very quietly moved through the underbrush so that she could see the cabin, the front door was open, it should not have been she always made sure that the girls kept it shut to keep out any bugs. Then she saw that the doors of the garage were open and now she knew that something was terribly wrong, the girls would never leave the garage doors open. She went back through the brush to the Hummer, quietly opened the back door and whispered into Iggy's ear and pointed to the woods. Iggy moved silently into the brush, it was amazing that such a large animal could move so quietly.

Quiet Sunshine shut the back door of the vehicle and got into the driver's seat. She drove on and parked a little ways away from the front door of the cabin, she peeped the horn and got out of the vehicle and limped around the back and opened the hatch. She reached down under the carpet and pulled out a walking cane then she called out, "Hey girls come on and help your Auntie in with these groceries. Come on girls."

She picked up one of the bags and moved very slowly around the vehicle towards the cabin, her head was down a little bit, her shoulders were rounded and she was leaning very heavily on the cane.

"Come on you two lazy things come out, goddamn it I can't carry these in by myself hurry up, get out here you lazy pair."

All of a sudden Spike came rushing out the front door and jumped down the steps, he was followed by Lance who held Diane in front of him by her hair with his one hand and in his other hand he held a large kitchen knife up against her throat, they stopped to Spike's left. Lance was immediately followed by Nick who had Paula by her hair and was half lifting her and half dragging her with a knife in his other hand, he half dragged her to Spike's right. They both forced the girls down to their knees, pulled their heads back and rested their knives against the girls' throats.

Quiet Sunshine stopped and dropped her bag, "Who are you? What are you doing with my girls? What do you want?" She stammered in a very frightened voice. She saw Iggy start to move out of the forest on the other side of the clearing to the back of the men who could not see him, she made a hand gesture that only Iggy could understand and he hunkered down on the ground and watched her.

"Well Auntie," said Spike with a big grin on his face "we were just visiting your girls and they just fixed us a nice breakfast. Welcome to the party." He could obviously see that the crippled lady in front of him was terrified of him, the only thing that was holding her up was her cane.

"Oh please please sir, don't hurt my girls, we'll do anything you ask, just don't hurt us," whined Quiet Sunshine. She saw that Nick and Lance were relaxing as they recognized that she was not going to be a threat. "What do you want with us? What can we do for you?" She begged.

Spike threw his head back and roared with laughter, "Well you have two such sweet young nieces, I think maybe we should just all go back into the cabin don't you?"

Nick and Lance laughed with Spike, Quiet Sunshine saw that they had lowered their knives to their sides, her left hand made a strange motion in the air that only Iggy recognized and then she seemed to fall forward slightly and grabbed the cane with both hands.

There was a deep throated growl and the sound of a large body crashing through the brush, Nick's head turned to his left just in time to see this great huge brown beast leaping at him, he tried to bring up his knife hand, but too late, Iggy's massive jaws closed down on the forearm holding the knife and Nick screamed as he felt the bones being crushed, he let go of the knife in sheer agony as he was pulled down to the ground pulling Paula with him.

Lance turned his head to the left to see what was going on but out of the corner of his eye he saw the crippled lady suddenly straighten up and there was a blur as her right hand flashed down and up again. He caught the briefest flash of light on metal but could not move in time, he felt the knife go in through the front of his throat cutting his carotid artery, severing his windpipe and then slicing through the back of his neck. His hands let go of his knife and Diane's hair as he tried to raise them but could not get them up to his neck. He slipped to his knees as Diane looked around, she could see the blood pouring out from his neck drenching the front of his chest and could hear the gurgles as the air came out of his lungs and he tried to suck some back in only to be filled with bubbling bright red blood. Everything seemed to happen in slow motion, Lance just sank to one side and died right in front of her eyes.

Iggy let go of Nick's arm as he pulled him down, Nick screamed again as he felt those powerful jaws close on his neck, he could feel the teeth breaking into his skin and then they stopped, Iggy looked over at Quiet Sunshine. Again her hand made a strange motion and Iggy closed his jaws, Nick heard the crack as his neck was broken, that was the last sound he ever heard.

Spike swung his head back to face Quiet Sunshine, he growled like a wounded animal and she saw a look of sheer hatred on his face, he just charged at her with his arms stretched wide, she just stood there as if too scared to move. His look of hatred changed to that of triumph as she was almost within his grasp then, suddenly, with fantastic speed, the old lady slipped to his right, the cane, now in her right hand, seemed to break in two and as Spike moved past her, out of the corner of his eye he saw the glint of steel as the two and a half foot razor-sharp stiletto blade that had been in the cane, pierced his side just under his right arm between two of his ribs. It passed right through his right lung and through his heart as his momentum carried him forward. Quiet Sunshine held onto the handle of the blade, as he passed her the blade sliced across between his ribs while the other end neatly cut his heart almost in two, as he fell forward the blade slid out. He never made a sound; he was dead before he hit the ground.

Paula sat up as Iggy came round and laid his head on her lap a little blood on his jowls, she burst into tears and sat there crying and hugging him. Quiet Sunshine stood there watching the two girls, she dropped the blade on the ground as Diane, tears running down her face, got slowly to her feet and started kicking Lance's body as hard as she could and screaming profanities at him, calling him every name under the sun until she was almost too exhausted to carry on. Quiet Sunshine moved over to her and held her as she buried her head against her neck and cried. They moved over slowly and helped Paula up and the three of them stood hugging each other for a long while, Iggy just sat and watched.

Quiet Sunshine took them into the cabin; she sat them down at the table and got a wet cloth for them to clean themselves up.

"Are either of you hurt?" She asked.

"No," said Diane shakily "no they didn't hurt us but who in hell were they?"

"I don't know," said Quiet Sunshine "they could have been anybody, this is the sort of thing that I thought was going to happen much later on, I don't know why this happened now but it did. We're all okay, that's the main thing. Perhaps now you'll understand how serious this whole situation really is."

Both the girls nodded, Quiet Sunshine realized that they had both just grown-up. A short while after they had pulled themselves together, they went outside and, using the winch on the front of Indian's hummer and a length of rope, they dragged the three bodies off into the brush. Quiet Sunshine rummaged through the men's pockets and came up with a brown wallet and a lady's coin purse, the wallet belonged to a William Balla and the purse belonged to his wife Catherine.

"Well somehow," said quiet Sunshine "I don't think that these gentlemen are Mr. and Mrs. Balla, I think we'd better go and checkout the Lincoln a bit more thoroughly."

They went over to the car in the woods, Diane opened the back door and retched at the smell of old food and drink beginning to rot, disgustedly she started pulling it out throwing it onto the ground. Paula went round to the front passenger door and started going through the glove box. Quiet Sunshine slipped into the driver's seat and felt underneath it and then found that the keys had been left in the ignition, she pulled them out.

"Did you find anything girls?"

"No," said Paula and Diane in unison.

"Well I guess we'd better checkout the trunk," said Quiet Sunshine as she got out of the car and went round to the back and slipped the keys into the lock of the trunk, she was just opening the trunk as the girls came round to join her. The trunk lid flew up and there was an old piece of canvas that much to their surprise suddenly moved. The three of them leapt back and when nothing came out of the trunk they moved back so they could see into it. Quiet Sunshine reached in, grabbed hold of the canvas and pulled it out to find a young man, who could not have been more than eighteen years old, tied up with his mouth taped shut wriggling in the bottom of the trunk, when he saw the three of them he started to moan and cry.

"Okay, okay" said Quiet Sunshine soothingly, "it's all right all three of the men are dead, they can't hurt you anymore, please just lay still while I cut you lose. Do you understand?"

The young man's head nodded vigorously.

Quiet Sunshine reached under her top and her hand came out with a short knife, she cut through the young man's ropes that held his legs together and then cut his hands loose and the three of them helped him get out of the car. He stood there wobbling a little as Quiet Sunshine slammed the lid of the trunk down so that he could lean against it.

"Now hold still," she said, "this may hurt a bit, I'm going to pull off your gag."

She worked the corner of the sticky tape loose so that she could hold it tightly between her fingers, she put her other hand in the young man's head to hold it steady and with a swift jerk pulled off the gag, the young man gasped as its came off, it must have been quite painful.

"Thank you, thank you very much, who are you and where are we?"

"I'm Quiet Sunshine, this is Diane and this is Paula, right now you're at our cabin in the Catskill Mountains. The three men that were in this car attacked us and fortunately they are now all quite dead. Who are you and what happened?"

"Wow, how did you ever kill them? My name is Kerry, my mother and father and I were driving back to California from New York, we stopped at a roadside rest area to stretch our legs when those three men attacked us. They made me watch as they killed my mother and father and hid their bodies in the bushes then they tied me up and threw me in the trunk telling me that they would see that I was well looked after later on. I've no idea how long I've been in there, it seems like an eternity." The young man hung his head down and started to sob.

Quiet Sunshine moved next to him and held him in her arms and just let him cry. The girls, a little embarrassed to see a young man cry, went around the car and threw all the garbage back into it and then led Quiet Sunshine and the young man back to the cabin."

Quiet Sunshine set the three young people around the kitchen table and made some hot tea, she heard the three of them beginning to talk, which is exactly what she had hoped for.

"Do you have any family or friends in the area?" Asked Paula.

"No" said Kerry, "we don't know anyone we live in San Diego, there's only the three of us," his head went down and his eyes glazed over a little, "I mean" he stammered "there were only the three of us but now I guess it's just me."

Diane could see the tears beginning to well up in his eyes; she reached across the table and held his hands. "Come on now, you have us we'll make sure you get home safely, won't we?" She said looking up at Quiet Sunshine who was putting large mugs of hot tea and some cookies on the table in front of them.

"Well we are going somewhat in that direction, we'll have to wait until Indian gets here and then we'll decide what we can do for this young man. Indian will be here within the next twenty four hours at which time we'll have to immediately leave the cabin and head west, let's see what he has to say."

17

The Transfer Station.

Turnopah, Arizona.

Wednesday after the meeting at Last Chance.

"There it is, over there, to your right," said Jill Metson pointing out of the window of the helicopter.

"I see it," said Brad as he veered the helicopter over towards the transfer station. They'd all spent the time during the flight talking about what might or might not happen once everybody knew about the white crystals.

"It's much larger than I thought," said the Judge peering out of the window "can you land down there Brad?"

"Sure can, everybody get ready for landing, make sure your seat belts are connected and tight, there's plenty of room down there I'll land just behind the buildings."

As they were coming down the Judge saw a lady come out of the building looking up at them wondering what they were up to. Brad made an excellent landing, they all waited until he'd switched off the rotors and then they got out of the helicopter.

The lady came across to meet them. "Well what do we have here? Who are you? What gives you the right to land a helicopter in my transfer station?"

The Judge stepped forward with his hand outstretched and smiled at her, as she took his hand and shook it he asked, "And who may you be please?"

"I'm Ethel, Ethel Madison, I'm in charge of this place, I run it and who are you lot?"

"My name is Mortimer, Judge Mortimer, these are my friends, let me introduce you they are Brad and Cassey, Roger and Jill and Jenny. I don't know whether you've been informed or not but I'm the new owner of the Bean's Container Company."

"Oh yes, I just got a fax in this morning, welcome to the Turnopah Transfer Station, we've never had a helicopter land here before, noisy things aren't they?" she grinned at the Judge. The Judge saw that she was really surprised by their visit. Ethel stood about five feet five inches high, was rather over weight with auburn curly hair that hung down to her shoulders, she was quite attractive and when she smiled her whole face lit up.

"Well come on into the office and tell me what this is all about," she said as she turned around and led them into the building.

"Okay, now what's going on?" Asked Ethel as they entered a surprisingly large office.

"Well," said the Judge sitting on the corner of one of the two large desks "I'm afraid that we're going to commandeer your transfer station, or at least a portion of it, for two or three weeks. We're in the process of establishing a new camp not far from here and the only way to get anything delivered there is by air. We intend to have all our requirements trucked here to the transfer station and then we'll take them over to the campsite. There'll be quite a lot of activity, if you have any regular business it can carry on as usual, I don't foresee any problems if we work together. None of us are familiar with how this transfer station works so I would ask if you would please cooperate with us and we will help you in any way that we can."

"Well" said Ethel as she sat down in a chair behind what was obviously her desk "This is all a very big surprise, I wish someone had forewarned me, anyway I don't see any problems, we're not all that busy yet. If you'd come in the middle of next month it would have been a different story because we're really busy at that time of the year. How this station works is very simple, trucks come in with containers on them that are destined for different areas of the country where that particular truck, for some reason, doesn't go. We have a container lift here, actually we have two container lifts, they're mobile so that we can drive them over the container on the back of a truck, the container is released from the chassis of the truck and we lift the container up. The truck is then free to drive away and we move the container to a storage area, we have the capability of stacking one container above the other. When the truck that's going to do the pick up comes into the yard that particular container is carried over and put on the truck, firmly attached to the frame and the truck can then drive away. At the moment we have six contains waiting to be picked up, they're stored over to the right, you may have seen them as you were landing." She punched a few keys on the computer on the desk in front of her and then carried on "There are three trucks due in tomorrow to pick up containers and there should be four vehicles in to drop off containers but the last time I heard one of them had been delayed. The station is manned at all times, twenty four hours a day and seven days a week, the only time we're closed is two days over Christmas. There are two of us that work during the week, myself and an older gentleman called Harry and then we have a lady called Alice who comes in and works weekends. As you can see we've a fairly large office, through there" and she pointed over to the right, "is a bedroom and a full bathroom. Over there to my left there's a storage room and a well-stocked kitchen. All three of us take care of all the paperwork and we also operate the container lifts. That's about it, we've two telephone lines and we have a high-speed Internet connection by cable which is where most of our business comes from."

"If we have a high-speed Internet connection then I'll be all set," said Roger Metson "I can do all my ordering and business very quickly by computer."

"That's excellent," said the Judge "thank you Ethel, to compensate you three for the inconvenience and the extra work that we'll be causing you, starting immediately, you'll all be paid double-time, hopefully that will help. If you could explain the situation to the other two, Harry and Alice, I would be grateful. If we could set our main station over here at this desk and use this computer we would be a little more out of your way."

"That would be excellent," said Ethel, she was obviously very happy at the thought of all the extra dollars they would be making. "I'll tell the others as soon as I get a moment, that desk will be ideal for you and I'll be pleased to assist you in any way that I can."

"Okay," said the Judge "well folks we have arrived, what do we have to do next?"

"Jill honey," said Roger "did we leave the computers on at home when we left?"

Jill thought from moment and then said, "Yes I believe we did, we were going to switch them off and then you said you might have to get into them for some reason or other so we didn't."

"If we left them on I should be able to get into our computers using this one on the desk and if I can do that then we've no reason to go back home, everything that I need is on one or other of our computers. I can check it out in a few moments once I get onto the computer here," said Roger as the others moved out of his way and he sat down at the desk and started working.

"Well" said Cassey, "I guess Brad and I had better get on down to San Diego and get us a Sikorsky helicopter, we've all the funds in place, it's going to be very expensive but somehow we'll get one and bring it back here. How does that sound?"

"Good," said the Judge "I guess we'd better get our stuff off the helicopter. Is there a hotel or motel close by?" he said turning back to Ethel.

"There's a small motel about two miles down the road," Ethel said "it's clean, the truck drivers use it if they have to stay overnight and they've quite a good little restaurant."

"That sounds ideal," said Jenny "I'll go ahead and use a phone and book us in, I guess we'll need three rooms."

The Judge thought for a moment, "better make it four rooms Jenny, you never know who's going to be here and who isn't and see if you can rent two vans from somewhere."

"Ethel can I use your telephone for a moment and do you have a telephone book, I'll look up the closest car rental agency and see what we can get."

Ethel handed Jenny a telephone book and watched as they all swung into action. Jill, Brad and Cassey went out to get their belongings out of the helicopter. The Judge pulled out a cell phone and dialed a number.

"Hello Joshua this is Mortimer, how's everything at the camp?"

"Oh hello there Judge, everything's fine, what's happening?"

"Just thought we'd better let you know, we've just arrived in Arizona and are setting up headquarters here at a container transfer station on Highway 10 at a place called Turnopah. We're going to be operating from here, have all the containers and everything delivered here then we're going to transport them to you via helicopter. Brad and Cassey, you don't know them yet but you will do soon, are helicopter pilots and they're going on to San Diego to get a large Sikorsky chopper. Depending on how much time that takes we should be starting to bring the first of the containers to you within the next day or two. How's everything at your end?"

"Everything's fine here, all six young men have decided to stay here so we have cleaned off most of the upper ledge. Is there anything special that you think we should do before things start arriving?"

"The only concern that I have," said the Judge "is with the livestock. We don't really have anyone, at present, who knows anything about the numbers of animals that we need. We're just going to have to take a wild guess, what do you think about us just letting them all run loose on the plateau at the camp"

"I don't see anything wrong with that, they can't go anywhere, they have the river on one side and the steep cliffs on the other so they should be just fine. Eventually we'll have to build some pens and build some fences but for now I think we'll just let them run loose. What livestock are you going to buy?"

"Well," said the Judge "not having anyone here to advise us, we're going to purchase two hundred milk cows, two bulls, ten riding horses, five hundred chickens with cockerels, about fifty sheep and rams, about fifty pigs, a couple of hog, a few geese, some ducks and a dozen goats. Roger Reed's wife, Mary, is into animal husbandry but I haven't been able to contact them yet so we're just going to have to hope those animals will be sufficient, how does that sound?"

"Sounds fine to me, we have enough land to accommodate a lot more than that. Don't forget to buy some crop seeds."

"We have them on the list, if all goes well we should start shipping stuff to you in the next couple of days. Anything that has to stay on the granite ledge we'll have the helicopter drop off there everything else can go down at river level. Hopefully, in the first delivery, there'll be a couple of heavy-duty rechargeable electric forklifts so that you can empty the containers and we can bring them back here as we go along if necessary, is there anything special that you want?"

"No," said Joshua, "I think your man the quarter master knows a hell of a lot more about this than I do, we'll go along with whatever he wants to purchase. We'll be waiting here for your delivery, let the fun begin."

"Okay then, I'll be in touch shortly," said the Judge hanging up the phone.

"Hey we're in luck," said Roger happily looking up from his computer, "we left the computers on at home, this means that we won't have to go to San Diego, we can do it all from here. I'll get started on ordering stuff immediately, is there anything special that you want me to get?"

"Well, as we discussed on the helicopter coming down," said the Judge "we'd better get the forklifts as fast as possible, the animals and their feed we should be able to buy locally, other than that your free to buy anything that you think we can possibly and I repeat possibly need, you have a freehand."

"I got you Judge, I'm about to spend a lot of your money, you know it feels really good to be back at work again," said Roger happily as he turned his attention back to the computer.

"Honey," said Jenny wrapping her arms around the Judge from behind, "Enterprise rent a car will have someone here in about twenty minutes to pick us up and take us to their agency where we can pick up two full-size vans, okay?"

"Well done," said the Judge turning round in her arms and kissing her gently "Well it's all begun."

They heard the helicopter taking off and disappearing into the distance as Jill came back into the office. "Cassey and Brad are off to get the big helicopter, all our stuff is stacked up just outside the front door, what's next?"

While Roger started ordering everything, Jill, Jenny and the Judge picked up the vans and rented the rooms at the local motel that proved to be old but clean and well kept with an adequate restaurant. Just before it was getting dark Brad and Cassey returned with an enormous Sikorsky sky crane S-64 helicopter. It was a very ugly looking thing but Brad assured them that it was capable of lifting anything that they would need. They'd also ordered two tankers of fuel for the monster that was now en route to the transfer station. That evening they met Harry when he came on duty, he was thrilled to hear about the extra money that he would be making and said that he was very willing to cooperate with them in any way that he could.

Roger stayed at his computer placing orders until late in the evening and then they all went back to the motel exhausted but very pleased with all that they had accomplished that day. Tomorrow was another day and hopefully things would start to be delivered.

The next morning they were up bright and early, had breakfast at the motel restaurant and headed out to the transfer station, only to find that during the night three empty contains had been delivered and as they were pulling up at the gate three trucks were coming into the compound with three more empty containers. Things started to get a lot livelier as the day went on, deliveries started coming in from all directions, luckily four forklifts arrived from a local distributor in Phoenix just before lunch and were immediately put to use unloading transport trucks and transferring their goods into the empty containers. Just as they were about to leave for supper the first of the containers holding the cabins arrived and were unloaded from the trucks, the aircraft fuel arrived and was safely stowed away from the compound in the flat dessert area at the back of the station. The next day they started transporting the containers to Last Chance and late that evening Rob, June and Jesse drove in.

18

The White House

The President's second meeting.

It was exactly one week to the day from his last meeting with Pattern that the President sat in his chair in the Oval Office and saw the very worried expression on the man's face sitting opposite him.

"Well good morning, you look a little glum this morning, let's get right down to business. What did you find Hugh?" He said to the Secretary of Homeland Security, Hubert Cunningham or Hugh as he was known to just about everybody. He was a large overweight gentleman who wore thick reading glasses and was completely bald on the top of his head, if you met him in the street you would pass him by without a second glance but he was in fact a brilliant man. His forte was in organization and setting up command structures, he had worked with the President for many years in one capacity or another, they were quite close friends.

"Well Mr. President let me first say that you didn't give us very much time, so this is a very preliminary report. I must also say that I was extremely skeptical about the report that you presented to me at our last meeting. However, in the last few days, I've had teams of people across the country examining the cement at all of the airports. We managed to do this without arousing any fears by blaming it on a report of possible terrorist activities. Not all of the people doing the examinations were well qualified so some of the results may not be too accurate," said Hugh Cunningham as he pulled out a report from his briefcase and pushed it across the desk to the President, "The bottom line is that at every airport at least one area of the cement was suspicious. The teams were asked to concentrate mainly on the runways and if you run down the list of airports you can see those where the cement was, without a doubt, decaying. We recovered eight vials of the suspicious white powder, from eight different airports, which I sent to the top laboratories in the country. The next eight pages of the report show the results of their investigations, they all reported the same thing, the crystals were a completely new entity, they didn't fit in with any known mineral or substance that had ever been seen before. It was confirmed by all of the laboratories that the crystals, when introduced into some concrete or cement, somehow combine with the elements in them to replicate themselves thereby causing the concrete to break down. Six of those laboratories have sent back preliminary notes saying that to date they have been unable to find a way to stop the crystals from reforming. As I said before, I was very skeptical of your original report but now I must confirm everything that is in it including the possible outcomes."

Hugh looked at the President and saw for the first time that he looked haggard and tired and very worried.

"Thank you Hugh," he said as he looked down at the report "How soon, in your opinion before these airports become unusable?"

"Well Sir I would suggest that we get a team of engineers into each airport and get them to concentrate on only one runway with the intention of maintaining the integrity of that runaway for as long as possible. It may be possible to break out bad patches of concrete and replace them with fast drying cement but the way this crystal works, I would estimate that at the most you have another two or possibly three weeks and then it will be too dangerous to land any aircraft at any of these airports."

"I see," said the President leaning back in his chair staring up at the ceiling "Pattern was right, I was so hoping that he was wrong but deep down I felt that his report would be accurate." He looked down at Hugh, "God help us, it seems that we can't stop this tragedy from unfolding."

He pushed a button on his consul and said to his secretary "Please ask the Vice President to join me immediately and who do we have out there waiting?"

The speaker went quiet for a moment and then his secretary said "Sir the Vice President will be with you in a moment. You have the

Secretary of the Interior, the Secretary of State, the Secretary of Defense, the Attorney General, the Secretary of Energy, the Secretary of Transportation and the White House Chief of Staff as you requested."

"Please send them all in," said the President, he sat back in his chair and watched these seven people come into the room thinking to himself that they made up the majority of the most influential and important people in the government. He motioned for them all to be seated and they did so just as the Vice President came in through the side door to the office. Julian said good morning and shook the Vice President's hand and then he sat down in the chair beside him at the large cherry wood desk.

"Good morning ladies and gentlemen I have requested this unusual meeting to address one problem and one problem only. A few days ago I received a report which I would like you to read," the President said as he handed out a copy of Pattern's report to each person. "Today I have received another report that has been completed by the Secretary of Homeland Security after the allegations in the first report were investigated," and he handed each person a copy of Hubert Cunningham's report. "I would like each of you to read these reports and then we'll open it up discussions."

The President sat back in his chair and watched as the others read the reports, "it has begun," he thought to himself.

Four days later the President sat down at his desk in the Oval Office with his head in his hands. The light on his phone started to blink, he pushed a button.

"Yes Beth what is it?"

"Sir the Secretary of Homeland Security is here to see you."

"Yes that's right, please send him in."

The door opened and in walked Hubert Cunningham.

"Good morning Hugh," said the President indicating for him to take a seat. The President got out of his chair behind his desk and went round and sat opposite Hugh in one of the comfortable armchairs.

"Good morning Mr. President."

"Please tell me you have some good news for me."

"No Sir I don't, without a doubt this damn crystal has spread out everywhere, it's having effects far faster than we thought. My greatest immediate worry is for air travel, we must ensure that flying is safe. Further to my previous report I now must recommend that you immediately take action to ensure the safety of the traveling public. Having got back the reports of the runways that we were having scrutinized I have to now recommend to you that we immediately reduce the capabilities of all the airports throughout the country to one single runway each, if we concentrate all of our efforts into maintaining those single runways so they are safe for landings and takeoffs we may have a few more days of fairly safe flights. We just dare not take any chances, I have to recommend to you that you make a public announcement restricting the use of the airports."

"You know what this means, if we have to reduce the number of flights across the country, we'll have to go public with everything to do with this fucking crystal. We'll lose control of everything, there'll be riots in the streets, law enforcement will break down, people are going to start to exodus the cities only to find that there's really nowhere for them to go. I was hoping to leave this until the very last minute, is there no way that we can hold off on these flights for a little while longer?"

"I suppose you could put out some cockeyed story about terrorists or terrorism or something to control the reduction in flights and runways but you're going to have to close down those runways soon. Besides, Sir, you're going to have to give all the Americans overseas a chance to return home before flying becomes an impossibility. You have to think about our embassies and government personnel and serviceman abroad, they have to be able to get home to their families, you have to give these people time to come home."

The President rested his head in his hands.

"This is a terrible mess, you're right of course people must have some warning and be given some time to return home."

His phone ringing interrupted him.

"Yes Beth what is it?"

"Sir I have an urgent telephone call from the British Prime Minister."

"Put him through please."

The President pushed a button on the telephone to put it on the speaker.

"Good morning Mr. President, how are you today?" came the broad British accent.

"Good morning, I've had better days."

"We have had reports of a major nuclear accident in the Northwest of Russia, we've just started getting reports in, have you heard anything about it yet?" Asked the Prime Minister, he was a very forceful man in his second term in office, and he and the President had an excellent rapport.

"I have the Secretary of Homeland Security with me, you are on the speaker."

"Good morning Hugh, do you have any reports of the accident in Russia?"

The President looked across at Hugh who just shook his head and shrugged his shoulders.

"No, as of this moment we've heard nothing, this is completely new to us but no doubt if there's something going on we'll find out about it very fast."

"Mr. President, we've had an aircraft drop through the runway at Heathrow airport overnight, we've had a number of other smaller issues where concrete has broken down. I presume that you are aware of this new problem that has been introduced into the structural components of concrete, cement and mortar, we've had a number of deaths due to this, I can no longer ensure the safety of our airports. I intended to make a public announcement the day after tomorrow to the British public, I feel I have an obligation to let them know exactly what's going on and give them the full ramifications of the consequences. I thought you should be the first to know of my intentions to announce it over all our broadcasting stations here and abroad. Where exactly do you stand on this problem?"

"Mr. Prime Minister we're going through the same things that you are, we are almost completely certain that this whole mess was started out by a meteor, a minute meteor I might add, that finished up in a cement abutment. From there it appears to have spread like wildfire not only throughout the United States but as you know, throughout the world. We've had our best minds working to find a way to stop this catastrophe, to no avail. I am presently in a meeting with Hugh and we were, as you called, discussing when to inform the American public. Rest assured that on completion of this meeting I was going to call you and ask you what your intentions were and if you had any resources to stop or slow this mess down. I appreciate you letting me know your situation, this confirms my decision, I too must make a public announcement and let this horrific cat out of the bag. God help us when this becomes public."

"We've also had everybody working on this, to date we've come up with nothing that can help. The worldwide incidences are increasing rapidly, I believe that it's my duty to inform the British people of the situation as it stands at present."

"I understand completely, I've been wrestling with this decision myself, when exactly do you intend to break the news?"

"I've started putting things in place with our broadcasting companies, it will be in approximately forty eight hours, we should try and coordinate our speeches. With the five hours difference in times, if you schedule your speech at five p.m. when most of your people are on their way home from work, I'll schedule mine for ten p.m. when most of our people will be home getting ready for bed, I think that will probably work out the best for us."

"So be it, I'll schedule my broadcasting to the American people at that time. If any changes come up within that time you will be the first to know. God help us, I hope to God someone can come up with a solution to this thing."

"Then it's decided, I'll be in touch with you if there's any change." And the phone went dead.

The President pushed the appropriate button and turned to Hugh.

"Well there it is, our decision has been made for us, we go to the American people in forty eight hours at five p.m. and then we'll watch the shit hit the fan. I'll lay out all the facts as we know them to the people, I won't sugarcoat anything. I'll start things in motion immediately, I want to broadcast on every possible network throughout the United States and also to reach our people abroad, we have to make sure that nothing is leaked before I make my presentation, it's best that everybody hears at the same time. I'll announce the closing down of the airports, down to one operational runway wherever possible, I'll recall all of our diplomatic personnel from all of our Embassies and the immediate withdrawal of all our military personnel and their evacuation back here to the United States I'll advise all of our citizens who are abroad to get back immediately. The government will bear the cost of all and any emergency flights."

The Secretary of Homeland Security nodded and the President noticed that his face was quite white.

"We'd better make some decisions about what to do with the government and their families, I'll get in touch with the appropriate people, I think the only sensible decision is to move everyone to one of our aircraft carriers at San Diego. Hugh, your job is to find me an answer to this fucking crystal before I go to air."

Hugh stood up, picked up some papers, looked at the President and just nodded as he left the room.

The President sat at his desk with his head in his hands, within thirty minutes reports started coming in regarding the nuclear accident in Russia, apparently one of their nuclear reactors had collapsed and there had been a meltdown, there was a fairly large radioactive field of dust being blown, at present, across the Russian wasteland. It appeared that the building that housed the reactor had imploded.

The President put in a call to the Russian President and gave him his condolences, he then went on to explain about the discussion that he had just had with the British Prime Minister and about the speeches that they were going to give and when they were going to give them. The Russian President agreed to speak to the Russian people soon after the British Prime Minister and he, the American President, had informed their people.

The President went into his private quarters and found his wife getting ready to go out to open up a brand spanking new state of the art childcare center. She looked at him and saw the expressions on his face. "My love, is it that bad?" she said.

"Yes," he answered "it is that bad, the British Prime Minister and the Russian President are going to inform their people in approximately forty eight hours, I too must make the same kind of horrific speech. It's time we prepared to move to a safer place."

"I understand, are there no other alternatives?"

"No I'm afraid there aren't, I'm going to make arrangements for us to move to one of the aircraft carriers, the John F. Kennedy, at San Diego, it's always been prepared to function as an emergency Presidential command unit. I must set things in motion immediately."

Mary moved over and they held each other tightly for a few moments, "we have to do what we have to do," she whispered in his ear "I'll carry on as usual today so as not to alarm anybody. You make whatever arrangements you deem necessary and I'll work my way around them."

He nodded, they parted and he went out to put the wheels in motion.

19

Breakfast at Last Chance.

Bella brought two great big steaming platters piled high with pancakes from the kitchen and dropped them in the middle of the table.

"Ok gentlemen," she said grinning down the length of the table "that's the last of the breakfast, you're gonna eat us out of house and home."

"What! Is that all we're gonna get?" grinned Sage taking another big pancake "we're gonna starve, Ah, gee whiz, you don't give us enough food to keep us going all day. What are we gonna have for lunch?" The others just laughed at him and the plate of pancakes was handed round the table.

"All right gentlemen," said Joshua from the head of the table as he watched the two big piles of pancakes disappear onto individual plates and as he passed a huge pot of syrup to Jay on his left, "Gentlemen I have received an update, Judge Mortimer and some of the others are settled in approximately thirty miles from here, as the crow flies, at a container transfer station. They have a very large helicopter with which to lift the containers and drop them down here. The first container that comes in will have a couple of large forklifts among other things, these we can use to move stuff around. The pilot of the helicopter assures us that he should be able to drop a container anywhere you wish except too close to the canyon wall, he can actually drop them up here on the upper edge of the granite. I have no idea as yet what's going to be dropped or when. As they get the supplies at the transfer station they will bring them to us, we need to be prepared to accept them and stash them to the right place. So gentlemen, we're going to divide you into teams of two. Jay, you and

Sage take the down river side of the plateau where, at the very far end, we're going to put any fuel. They will be bringing in tankers of gasoline and fuel for the helicopters. These must go at the very, very far edge so if anything happens they will be well away from everything else. Then next we're going to have the animals, they're buying all the livestock locally, these will be picked up and dropped off as they become available, we're just going to let everything run free, don't try and pen anything up. Don't try to stop the chickens from getting out of pens, there will be just too many, just let everything run free, eventually we'll build fences, pens and places to keep all of the animals. The containers that the animals come in need to be kept so get the helicopter to drop them as close as you can, in a line, to the back of the plateau. There is enough wild food, foliage and grass to feed any livestock that they bring. Kyle, you and Alex stay up here with Bella and me and we'll guide in the containers that have the cabins in them and anything else that belongs up here in the living quarters or on the shelf. We're going to be in constant communication with the pilot and with those working up at the transfer station so we'll know what's in each container and each one will be labeled with the contents marked clearly on the doors. Some of them we'll need to empty as fast as possible; for example, beds, once we get the container delivered up here with the beds and bedding we'll need to get them out and set them up in the second cave, every one will be bunking in the caves until we get the cabins up. Walt, you and Slade take the upstream end, anything that doesn't belong on the upper deck and is not livestock will be directed down to you, you can stack these containers two high, any higher than that and it may be difficult for us to unload them so only stack them two high. You're going to have to guide the containers down, they're going to attach ropes that hang underneath the container at each corner so, if necessary, you can move them a little bit as they come down by pulling on the ropes to make sure they get exactly into the right spot. These containers are very, very heavy so don't strain yourself, let the helicopter do the work, the pilot assures us they'll have no problem dropping these down on a dime. If you have any slack time between loads coming down to you you can go into the containers and start unloading those that you think we need right away. Walt and Slade, will be getting containers filled with various sizes of plastic pipes, one of the very first things we have to do as we put up the cabins is to put in a new sewage system, our existing one can't handle the increase and for that we're going to use eight inch piping, so anything that has to do with eight inch piping, couplings, diverters, tees, Ys etc. you can unload ready for use. Sage and Jay, you make sure that the animals are ok, let them out as soon as they arrive and check them on a regular basis, some of these animals have never been allowed to run free so keep an eye on them. Ok so far?"

"How are we going to keep in touch with the pilot?" asked Walt.

"Here you go," Joshua said as he turned around behind him and handed each one of them a radio from a box behind his chair. "They're set up on the right frequency, we've set it up so that everybody can hear everybody. If there's an emergency or anybody wants help, everyone is to respond as necessary. Ok, we're going to have to get all this stuff here in two weeks, there's a hell of a lot of it coming. They have a gentleman up there that's experienced in supply and demand for military camps and he's ordering, or has ordered, every possible piece of equipment that he can think of. God only knows how many containers we're going have but we're just going to have to cope. They estimate that it'll take approximately one hour to deliver a container and for the helicopter to get back and pick up another one. The weather, as usual is clear," he said with a grin. The weather was always nice at Last Chance, often a little too hot but there was always a breeze coming down the canyon following the river, "That means that every hour we should be getting a container. The time now is five past six, the first container should be coming at six thirty, this container will have the forklifts and other equipment, it will have a backhoe, front-end loader, tractor, posthole diggers, etc. Since most of this equipment is going to be needed on the lower level we'll drop it down on the plateau to you Walt and Slade and you need to unload it. Apparently it also contains a supply of gasoline. If you have any spare time this is how we're going to lay out the lower level as far as the livestock and the driveways are concerned," and, as Bella removed the dishes from his end of the table, he laid out the plans for the new Last Chance. "As you can see, eventually, we're going to need quite a few fences and we're going to have to open some new pathways and roadways down into the lower section. Now these specifications don't have to be stuck to rigidly, we've basically planned to have roadways running end to the end so that we can get to the fuel. If you have any spare time you can get the front-end loader or one of the other pieces of equipment and start clearing a path through the underbrush trying very hard not to frighten or scare the animals. I know, I know," he looked at the worried faces of the young men in front of him around the table, "I know you haven't driven, you haven't had a chance to learn to drive or use the equipment, well now's your opportunity."

There were big grins all around the table. Walt rubbed his hands with glee, their eyes lit up.

"Ya mean we can drive this equipment? Wow! I've got dibs on the front-end loader," said Jay.

"Gentlemen, gentlemen, this equipment can't be replaced, this is all brand new stuff, as I understand it's all set up and ready to run, there are papers and instructions with each piece of equipment. We don't want any accidents, we don't want any breakages, read the directions carefully and make sure that they stay with that piece of equipment so the next person can read them. It's very easy to have an accident, it's extremely easy for people to get hurt, take your time, learn the piece of equipment and start slowly and be careful. Bella and I are as green as you all are with this kind of equipment so we're all going to have to learn. Remember that in two or three weeks it will be impossible to replace any of this machinery. Any questions?"

There was silence around the table.

"Excellent. Ok, let's test these radios and make sure that everything's working. I see the pancakes are gone. Bella and I will help anywhere we're needed but our main concern will be to stay up here to get the cabins and things landed. It's going to be an extremely busy, exhausting time. Bella, if you don't mind, about twelve if you can start having lunches ready, we'll just take them on the run as one pair gets free they can come up and get their food and then get back to work again. Gentlemen remember, the most important thing is to be ready for each and every delivery."

They all pushed their chairs back from the table.

"I would like turkey, roast potatoes, greens and macaroni and cheese for lunch please," said Sage grinning as he stood up.

"You're gonna get cold sandwiches, pickles, and homemade ginger beer," said Bella giving him a swift stern look, they all roared with laughter. You could feel the nervous tension and Joshua realized that they were all as excited as he was. All the phones squawked at the same time.

"Base here, Joshua speaking."

"Well good morning, Joshua," came the Judge's voice "are you ready for us at your end?"

"Yes Sir, we've just finished breakfast and divided up the teams, everyone has their radio and we're all going to get into place, there'll be someone to direct each container as you bring it. How're you set up at your end?"

"We're all ready, they're just hooking up the first container. Some of the cabins have arrived and some of the livestock is on its way, it seems like we have supplies coming in from all directions, it's going to be a busy few days. Hang on a second." The radios went quiet for a moment.

"Ok, I've just been informed that they're lifting the first container right now. It's loaded so that your front-end loaders, no, I apologize, I meant your forklifts are the first things to come off, I suggest you keep these up on the granite. The pilot assures me that he can hold the container on your granite while you take off the two forklifts and then he can lift it and drop it where you want him to down on the plateau."

The radio squawked.

"That's excellent," said Joshua standing up "I was a little concerned with how we were going to get those forklifts up here because we're gonna need them for the cabins. Once we have them unloaded we'll have him drop off the container down below. I think the best idea is for each of our teams to wear a different color, that way your pilot can easily identify where the containers are going to go to and who they're dealing with."

"An excellent idea."

"Ok, let's have green for down river, red will be up river and yellow will be on the granite. We're ready for you."

"Here we go then, talk to you in a bit," and the radios went quiet.

"All right," Joshua said turning to Bella "Bella, make sure they have the colors right. T-shirts, anything green, anything red, anything yellow, just put it on. Let's go, the first load is taking off as we speak, this one will probably be the trickiest one since he's gonna drop off the forklifts up here and then deliver the rest down below. Let's go gentlemen, let's go, they should be here in twenty minutes."

20

Secrets.

The Transfer Station.

"Good morning," said Harry as he watched the group come into the office at the transit station. "Oh boy, am I glad to see you lot. I don't know what you've been buying but stuffs been roaring in here, I've had the busiest night I've had in years."

Roger grinned and sat down at the desk in front of his computer.

"Harry, you haven't seen anything yet, there's a helluva lot more coming in."

"Well I'm glad I'm not working on the day shift, looks like you're gonna be real busy and the sun's only just come up." Harry said as he put on his coat. "Ethel's in the bathroom, she'll be out in a minute. I'm on my way home, I need to get some well deserved sleep" and he waved to everyone as he went out the front door.

"Good morning everybody," Ethel said as she came into the office drying her hands on some paper towels "Looks like Harry's been busy during the night, we've got a whole pile of containers in. Don't know how you're doing it but boy are you moving fast."

"That's all due to our friend Roger here, he seems to be getting things moving really quickly, just what we want. All right Roger, tell us what we've got and what we need to get done today," said Jenny.

Roger shuffled through a pile of papers as the others went over to the coffee pot and poured some coffee, Jenny handed a cup to the Judge.

"Better put a couple of fresh pots of coffee on," said Brad "I think we're going to be needing it. Ok Roger, when do you want us to start hooking up and moving stuff to the camp?"

Roger looked up, "Well, it looks like all the cabins are here and the machinery, the forklifts, backhoe, tractor and bits and pieces are here. I suggest you take the machinery first, they'll need it at the camp to move things around." Brad nodded.

"I'll head out and get the chopper ready," said Cassey "we should be able to take off in about half an hour. It's pretty easy moving these containers, they've all got eyeholes on the top of them so they can be lifted by chains if necessary, we can just hook on to those and lift them up and then we can lower them with a winch. We should be able to put them down anywhere they want them put down as long as they're not too close to the canyon wall." Her husband nodded.

" Hang on just a second Cassey" the Judge said as he took out his cell phone.

"Good morning, Joshua," and he stood there talking on his cell phone for a few minutes, then turned to the rest of them. "They're ready, they've split into teams, two people per team, one upriver, one downriver, the rest on the granite slab, they're color coded and they've all got radios tuned to the same frequency so Cassey, if you and Brad can tune in to that frequency on the chopper, everyone should be able to hear everyone else. How does that sound?"

"Sounds good to me," said Jenny "If Cassey and Brad are up in the chopper do you need anybody else up there with you?"

Brad looked over at his wife. "I think we can handle it, everything can be handled from the cockpit. The two of us should be fine up in the air."

His wife nodded.

"Ok, now Roger, what do you want us to buy locally?"

Roger again shuffled through a pile of papers, took out his pencil and started ticking things off a very long list.

"Judge, we need livestock, we need feed and seed locally. I've ordered a whole pile of all the necessary crops and seeds but I think we should get a few locally. I can't buy the livestock over the computer, you're going to have to go out and buy them. There's a local market or auction house about halfway between here and Phoenix however they won't be having another auction for about two weeks but they should be able to put you in touch with anyone who wants to sell livestock."

"Ok, well I guess Jenny and I can go out and do that, we're just going to have to take potluck because neither of us have the faintest idea of what we're looking at regarding livestock, do you have a list of the animals we need?"

Roger nodded handing the Judge a sheet of paper.

"Holy, molly! Cows, chickens, bulls, sheep, what the hell's this one here Llamas or alpacas?"

The rest of them started to laugh.

"Well, you just never know, they're good for transporting stuff and their coats are good for making things and they're no problem whatsoever, they'll eat just about anything, very much like the goats I believe, better to have them than find out that we want them but don't have any," said Roger grinning widely.

"Ok, ok, if you say so," said the Judge grinning back at him "Is there anything else that we need while we're on the road?"

Roger looked up and down his list.

"There may be a few more things along the way but I suggest you concentrate on the animals, it's imperative that we have a sufficient quantity of all of them. It will be far better to buy more and find that we don't need them than to buy less and find we don't have enough. If you come across any other strange animals that you think we might need, buy them."

Jenny just looked at him and shook her head. "Two weeks ago if someone would have told me that I was going to go out into the countryside to buy up vast quantities of animals I would have laughed at them, laughed until I rolled onto the floor. Now look at me, I'm going out to buy farm animals and I don't know what I'm going to buy so anything that catches my eye I'm going to purchase, you may be very surprised at what you get in the end." Everybody burst into laughter.

"Ok, I think we can handle it down here at the transit station can't we Ethel?" asked Roger.

"Sure can," said Ethel trying to catch her breath from laughing so hard "There's not really much to do here, we've just got to make sure that we move the containers out to a position where they can be picked up by the chopper as they require them and make sure that there's room to bring even more containers into the yard. Where would you like them placed for air mail pick up?" she asked looking at Brad and Cassey.

Cassey sat there thinking for a minute.

"You know what might be best, it may be best if we took them out of the compound and put them over close to where the chopper is right now, that land is pretty flat and it's solid and then we won't have to worry about the rotors blowing too much dirt up all over the compound. You could bring it out, drop it off, we could pick it up and while we are delivering it you could bring another one out. It means you'll have to take them out the front gate and get them around to the back."

"No problem," said Ethel with a wicked grin on her face "It would be much easier if we cut down a section of the wire fence at the back, it'll only take a couple of minutes, we've got bolt cutters. We can just cut out a panel and drop one of the poles and we've got a clear space out to the back, when you're all finished we can put it back up again. How's that sound?"

"An excellent idea Ethel, you're brilliant. Ok, let's do it."

"Can anybody use a cutting torch?" asked Ethel moving over to a big tool chest. "We've got the torch in here in this chest, the tanks are out the back, they're here for an emergency in case we've got to cut off locks or doors or something, we've never used them before. Can anybody use it?"

Roger nodded. "No problem," he said "I'm quite proficient with them, it'll only take us a few seconds to cut down the fence. Let's go Ethel, show me where everything is."

"Ok folks, let's go, we have begun," said the Judge.

They all moved off and as they did so another truck pulled into the yard with a big trailer on the back.

And so their days went by, supplies came in almost every hour, the chopper took off on a regular pick up and drop, everything seemed to be going very smoothly. The livestock came in as the Judge and Jenny paid top dollar for them. It was a question of how they were going to airfreight the animals from the trucks they came in to the transfer station then on to the camp. It was solved very easily by Brad, they just took the truck they came in through the hole in the back fence, disconnected the cab and literally picked the trailer portion up with the chopper and dropped it off on the grassy plateau at Last Chance. Those at Last Chance let the animals out to range free and on the next run Brad and Cassey picked it up and brought it back, it was hooked back up to the truck and off it went. They worked from dawn to dusk each day, having meals brought into the station and eating them on the go and then collapsing into their beds at the motel after the sun had gone down.

On the fourth day a truck pulling a half container on the back pulled into the transit station, an innocuous black Cadillac SUV followed it. As it pulled to a halt two men got out of the front of cab and one stood by each of the front wheels, four more got out of the Cadillac, one man stood by each of rear wheels while the other two began to approach the building. Roger and Ethel had come out hearing another truck come in and stood watching.

"What the hell's all this about?" said Ethel.

"God only knows. What the hell are all these men doing here? I hope to God we're not in trouble, I know we're not supposed to be lifting some of these animals and things in the original trucks but they don't look like law enforcement officials, I guess we'll just have to wait and see."

The two men from the Cadillac walked over to them, one of them carrying what looked like the automatic reading machine similar to the kind that the people who read gas and water meters carried with them.

"We're looking for," he looked down at his machine "for a Judge Mortimer, is that you Sir?" he said looking at Roger.

"No I'm afraid I'm not, the Judge is out the back. Can I sign that for you?"

"No sir, you can not, please would someone go and get him?"

Roger looked at Ethel who nodded and walked back through the office. The Judge was out the back writing with a huge black felt marker on the doors of one of the containers, making sure that the people at the camp would know what was in it before they opened it.

"Hey Judge," called Ethel "some men here need to see you, they say you've gotta sign for this one, it looks very strange, there are six men delivering it, it looks like they're standing guard on the container. Big men, they look like they're security staff or police or somebody. The one that came to the door has a bulge under his right shoulder under his jacket that's a little too tight, I think they're armed."

The Judge stopped what he was doing, turned around and grinned at her.

"It's ok Ethel, it's ok, I think I know who they are or what they are, let's go see."

They walked back through the office.

"I'm Judge Mortimer, what can I do for you Sir?"

"I need some identification and your signature and thumb print."

As the Judge pulled his wallet from his back pocket Roger and Ethel stood wondering what the hell was going on.

The Judge gave the man his driver's license, the man scrutinized it carefully and handed the machine he was carrying over to the Judge.

"Put your thumb print right there Sir."

The Judge did as he said and the machine whirred for a moment, the man checked it.

"Put in your password there please."

The Judge wrote on the machine with a strange small pen that was attached to the side of the machine and handed it back. The man pressed some buttons; a slither of paper popped out of the machine and was handed to the Judge.

"Very good Sir, thank you very much indeed, you are confirmed. We are handing this cargo over to you. I trust you know what it is?"

"Yes I do indeed know what it is, thank you very much," the Judge said turning to Ethel "Ethel, can you get the lifter, pick it up and take it behind the building please."

Ethel moved swiftly bringing up the big machine, the four men standing around the truck released the container from the chassis as she lifted it up and even before she had taken it around the back of the building the six men were back in their truck cab and SUV and were driving out the gate.

"What the hell was all that about?" Roger said to the Judge.

"Oh, that's my little secret," the Judge said with a grin on his face "We'll keep it a secret for just a little longer but I think we'd better get that to the camp, make it the next container please."

Roger got his radio out of his pocket and pushed the button.

"Ethel don't drop it behind the building, take it straight over to the lift off pad. The Judge said it'd be best if we got that one to Last Chance as fast as possible."

"Ok you got it," Ethel came back over the radio.

"Ok, Judge, it's on its way," said Roger.

The Judge walked around the corner of the office and called Joshua on his cell phone.

"Hello Judge what can I do for you?"

"Joshua one of the next containers coming to you is a half container, please put it somewhere out of the way since there is nothing in it that will be needed along the way I hope. Just for your information and please keep this confidential, I liquidated all of my portfolios and bought gold bullion, there are a few million dollars worth of gold in that container. I thought that it might be much more valuable in the future than anything else once the world gets sorted out again."

"Whow, that's a lot of gold Judge, I'll have it put somewhere safe, is it safely sealed up?"

"Yup, the men who delivered it here gave me the only key to it. Thank you and we'll just keep this between us for know."

"Ok that we will do, chat with you later" and the phones went dead.

21

Pattern moves to last chance.

Washington.

Two days before the President's speech to the Nation.

Pattern parked his 1984 Porsche on the sloping driveway to his home, he got out of the car, grabbed his briefcase and went up the steps to the front porch. The house was a very large English Tudor just on the outskirts of Washington, he had bought it about five years ago, it had been in very bad repair. When a real estate person had shown him the house he had fallen in love with it immediately and, because it needed so much work, he had been able to purchase it at a very reasonable price. The house had four bedrooms and two bathrooms on the second floor upstairs, on the main floor there were two bathrooms, a formal dining room, a front reception room, a very large kitchen with an eating area, a good size living room and a very nice office situated in a sunroom on the back of the house. On the third floor there was a complete two bedroom apartment that had been the servant's quarters with a separate staircase that went down the back of the house so that the servants did not have to use the owners' main staircase which was in the front of the house. The front yard was not very large but there was a beautiful back garden that backed onto a ravine. There was a full basement, one side was divided into two, a workshop and a laundry room and the other side of the basement was set up as a games room. This was the playroom complete with a pool table, darts and table tennis.

Pattern had remodeled the whole house, he could do his own plumbing and electrical wiring, he could do rough woodworking but was not very good when it came to fine carpentry. He had met a young man called Arnold in a local bar one night who said that he was a carpenter, Pattern had brought him around to the house and he had proved that he could do very fine finishing woodwork. Pattern and Arnold had fallen in love in the three months of working together to rebuild the house and Arnold had moved in and they had been together ever since. They completed renovating the home in just under one year and found that the house was just too large, they never used the servant's apartment on the top floor so Pattern decided to rent it out. They put an advertisement in one of the local gay magazines and one week later they had rented the upstairs to Nan and Molly, a wonderful lesbian couple. Originally it had been intended that Nan and Molly would just stay in the top apartment but as the four of them got to know each other they all came to share the whole house, they had all been together now almost four years. The four of them were like family to each other and Pattern had confided the situation to the other three, as he had no other family, it was decided that the four of them would stay together and all go to Last Chance.

Pattern entered the house through the side door that led directly into the spacious kitchen, everything was very neat and tidy, they had found out that all four of them were neat freaks so nothing was out of place throughout the whole house. Nan sat at the kitchen table, she was a small lady, she was the butch of the lesbian pair and was quite masculine looking but even so she was very beautiful. She looked up from the newspaper that she was reading and said, "well good evening, you're home a little early today. You look worn out and haggard, did you have a bad day?"

"Yes" said Pattern shrugging off his jacket and hanging it on a hook on the back of the door "Things are going from bad to worse, I'm afraid we don't have as much time left before we have to leave for Last Chance as I thought we had. This fucking crystal has spread further and faster than we thought. Are we all packed up and ready to go?"

"Yep," said Nan "I think we have everything packed up except for a few last minute items."

"That's excellent, I've been trying to get through to the President all afternoon but things must be really hectic up on the hill. I've left messages for him to call me here if possible."

"Gotcha, if he calls I'll make sure you get the phone. Molly's upstairs working on the computer and Arnold won't be back home for another hour."

They both heard the telephone ringing; it rang twice before Molly, upstairs, answered it. The next thing they heard was Molly rushing into the room with the phone held out in front of her, "Pattern, Pattern it's for you, it's the President's secretary, the President wants to speak to you."

She put the phone to her ear and said "He'll be with you in just a moment."

Nan and Pattern saw the surprise look on her face as she held out the phone she whispered, "It's him, it's him, I just spoke to the President." Shoving the phone into Pattern's hand.

"Hello Pattern here."

"Hello Pattern" he recognized the President's voice. "I got the message to call you, I apologize I couldn't get back to you sooner, things are pretty rough here at the moment. What can I do for you?"

"Thank you for calling back Mr. President, I just wanted to report that my further investigations have proven that the situation is worse than we thought. It has in fact spread much wider and is affecting more structures much faster than I previously reported. The areas and the amount of damage seem to be increasing exponentially."

"I see," said the President "It is therefore our worse case scenario, this just confirms my decisions. For your ears only, I will be giving a speech to the nation in exactly two days time. I thank you for that information."

"In that case Mr. President, I would hereby like to hand in my resignation effective immediately, if that's all right I will e-mail it to your office?"

"I understand and I reluctantly accept your resignation, I can't thank you enough for what you've done. If there's anything I can do for you please let me know. I hope you have somewhere to go to, if not you would be welcome to join my advisers and myself on one of the aircraft carriers."

"Thank you for the invitation but I do have somewhere to go to. If I could ask one favor of you Sir?"

"Please go ahead."

"I would desperately like to contact Doctor Jack Brown and his wife Doctor Anna Brown who are presently somewhere in the Sudan working for Doctors without Borders and to try and get them to Phoenix safely. Apparently their base camp has lost touch with them for the last twelve or so days. If they could be contacted and, if they want to, be transported to the Phoenix area it would be a great help."

"I will ensure that they are contacted and if they wish I will arrange for them to be brought safely to Phoenix. Is there any message that you'd like them to be given?"

"Thank you Mr. President. I will e-mail a message for them to your secretary immediately. I will also include in that e-mail phone numbers and the call sign of the ham radio that will be in operation at my place of refuge, if I can ever be of any further assistance please call on me."

"I will indeed," said the president "God speed and God help us," and the phone went dead.

Pattern pushed the button on the phone to hang it up and he put it down on the floor beside him. He looked at Nan and Molly, they saw in his face how serious it was, "Well," he said "the shit is about to hit the fan, the President will speak to the nation in forty eight hours, God only knows what will happen after that. We need to be at Last Chance before his speech because I think there'll be instant chaos and anarchy once the public knows what's going on."

The President's phone call had brought home the seriousness of their situation. His mind was now clicking on a dozen different levels of what had to be done, and done quickly.

"If you two will pack up the last of our stuff, I'll make arrangements for us to fly down to the camp."

"Okay," said Nan, "This thing has been hanging over our heads for so long that in a way I'm glad that, at last, it's arrived and to be truthful I'm excited about all the changes. I know it's awful but in a way I'm really looking forward to making a go of it at Last Chance."

"Yes," said Molly "I feel that way too, no more nine to five job and worrying how to pay the mortgage and all the bills. This will be a whole new way of life, out of the rut of everyday living and into something completely new, I find it quite exciting."

"I completely understand," said Pattern. "I've been worried about this for so long it's almost as if a huge weight has just been lifted off my shoulders by the President's phone call, at last the end of the investigations and now we can swing into action for ourselves. Before I do anything else I'd better warn all the others, I'll blow a phone call through to Rob and June and let them know that we only have two days left." He picked up the phone and he dialed Rob's cell phone number.

Later on the four of them were flown down to Phoenix in a hired aircraft that took off and landed on grass runways. Once at Phoenix Pattern leased a helicopter for the next month and piloted them down to the transfer station.

The Judge's cell phone rang; he picked it up off the desk beside him. "Hello, Judge Mortimer here."

"Oh, hello there Judge, this is Pattern."

"It's nice to hear from you Pattern, where are you?"

"We're just coming to your transfer station, we're coming in from the southeast and have you in sight."

The Judge stood up, walked out of the office and looked into the distant sky.

"I can't see you yet," he put his hand over his eyes trying to block the glare of the sun.

"Well we definitely have you in sight, we can see you. Where can we be of assistance, where would you like us to land?"

The Judge stood thinking for a minute.

"We have things here at the station fairly well under control, we're really busy but it's just a matter of taking deliveries and then lifting them over to the camp, I think you'd be more useful over at the camp. There's a helluva a lot to do over there, far more then there is here. I see you, I see you now, I've got you in sight, welcome to the party Pattern."

The Judge watched as the helicopter swooped in, he could see everyone in the helicopter looking out the windows.

"Boy, they've got quite a few containers there," Nan said pointing down at the station.

"I wonder how many they've taken to the camp?" said Molly.

"We'll find out real soon, the Judge says we'll be more use at the camp."

Pattern wiggled the helicopter backward and forward and swung one more loop around the transfer station.

"Ok, the helicopter's pretty full so we'll head straight over to Last Chance, anything we can do before we go over there?"

The Judge shook his head. "No, nothing much you can do here but boy do they need some help down there, I think they're a little swamped, God only knows how many containers we've lifted down to them, it'll take weeks to sort them all out."

"How are you doing with the deliveries?"

"Well, thank God for Roger, I don't know what we'd have done without him, you haven't met him yet, he was in charge of purchasing all the requirements for the entire fleet in San Diego and he had all his computer files available, he's been indispensable, we've had supplies and stock coming in from all over the country, he's had to grease a few palms and pay top dollar but it's all coming in. We're lifting an average of one container per hour so you can imagine how many we've lifted in the last ten or twelve days."

"Rob did inform you that the President's going to make a speech in less than forty-eight hours, didn't he?"

"Yes, Rob told me, we hope to be able to get all this stuff moved before he goes on the air. I don't think we'll have many deliveries, if any, after his speech, I think we'll have got everything air lifted by then and if not we'll probably have to go without."

"I think you're right there Judge, I think everything's going to come to a stand still extremely fast. Has anybody heard from Ghost or Indian?"

"Indian's on his way down, I guess they're coming overland, we haven't heard from them since they left their cabin up in the Pocono's. We know that Ghost was told what we're doing and we know that he was going to head back to Florida as fast as he could but after that we haven't heard anything."

There was silence on the radio for a second and then Pattern said, "Both of them are very capable, they'll turn up like pennies. Ok we're off to Last Chance, see you there."

"Ok, see you there," and the Judge switched off his cell phone watching the helicopter swoop off toward the camp.

Pattern dialed Joshua's number, the phone rang three times.

"Hello, hello, Joshua here."

"Hello, Joshua, Pattern here, how are you doing? You sound a little out of breath."

"A little out of breath," laughed Joshua into the cell phone "You have no idea we're absolutely run ragged down here. Where the hell are you?"

"We're just leaving the transfer station, we didn't land there, the Judge said you could use some help down at the camp, is that right?"

"Need help, no we don't need any help, we've got everything under control." Joshua said bursting into laughter, Pattern could hear a couple of people laughing in the background. "We're not quite sure whether we're coming or going and we're so goddamned tired we can hardly stand up. Yes, we sure could use your help."

"Well, there's four of us coming in on this chopper, don't worry, we'll get everything under control for you," grinned Pattern.

"That would be fantastic."

"We've a helicopter full of personal stuff, we'll be there in a few minutes. Where would you like us to land?"

There was silence for a moment.

"Bring her in on the usual spot, we'll unpack it as fast as we can and then if you could lift her off and park her as far down river on the lower level as you can to keep the chopper out of the way?"

"No problem, it should only take us a few minutes to unload it, the four of us can do that, don't interrupt what you're doing, then I'll take it down to the lower level."

"Excellent, then I'll see you in a few minutes."

It only took them a few minutes before Pattern swooped down into the gorge going up river, all his passengers were looking at the river.

"My God, it's beautiful," said Nan, Molly nodded enthralled at the different colors and different formations in the cliffs and rocks that now towered above them.

"The camp's just around the next bend," said Pattern swinging the chopper into full view of the camp, he held it still over the river so they could get a good look, their first look, at Last Chance.

"It's exactly like you said it would be," said Arnold "it's bigger then I expected, there's a helluva lot of land on that lower level. My God, look at all the containers, it looks like organized chaos!"

Pattern nodded there were containers stacked two high along almost three quarters of the entire length of the outer edge of the granite slab. On the lower level there were numerous containers obviously placed in strategic positions, he could see people opening some of the containers and moving things out with forklifts and a backhoe. He was amazed at the number of animals that seemed to be running wild wherever they pleased.

"Well, it's exactly as I remembered it except there's a helluva lot going on down there, I remember it as a very quiet peaceful haven not any more I fear, I think we're going to be busy folks."

"You know what Pattern, that sounds really good to me," said Nan "we've all been waiting for this and now, at last, we've arrived, now we can get to work starting a new life."

Molly nodded, "Isn't it strange, I've been kind of worried and scared about what was going to happen to all of us for so long but now, seeing the camp, seeing the layout, seeing its isolation, my fears are gone and now I'm excited. This is all new, we can forget the old civilization and start our own, come on Pattern put this baby down, let's get started."

"I'm with you," said Arnold, the others could hear the eagerness in his voice, "Set her down Pattern and let's get on with life."

Pattern grinned happily as he brought the chopper in to gently land on the X marked on the big granite slab.

22

Sylvia and Wayne Dunstan.

Seattle.

Two days before the President's speech to the Nation.

Sylvia Dunstan came up out of the cabin carrying a cup of hot chocolate in each hand, she steadied herself against the rail and then eased down to sit between her husband's legs. She lay back against him and handed him one of the cups and smiled up at him, he lent forward and kissed her, holding onto the wheel to keep the yacht on course. They had met nine months previously at a friend's party, it had been love at first sight, it had been a bit of a whirlwind romance and they had been married just two weeks ago in a very small private ceremony, they had left the night of the wedding, on their honeymoon, aboard Wayne's yacht. He had spent more than three years completely rebuilding the boat; he had bought it in extremely bad condition, very cheaply, after it had been damaged in a hurricane down near New Orleans, he had had it trucked up to Seattle to work on it.

Wayne was an auto mechanic and he had his own very successful business, he had the uncanny knack of being able to repair just about any kind of motor and was extremely good with his hands, a jack of all trades, and could do very fine woodworking, he had the patience of Job. Sylvia was a pharmacist; she had, just over a year ago, opened her own pharmacy, she loved her work and had to spend a great deal of time building up her business. They had both taken two weeks off for their honeymoon and when they had left the harbor they had switched off their phones so that they could not be disturbed.

Wayne put his hand on his wife's shoulder and rubbed her neck gently, "I love you" he said, "I wish this honeymoon didn't have to end so soon, it's been wonderful."

"Yes it has," said Sylvia leaning against him "it couldn't have been any more perfect."

They snuggled together and watched the sunset over the ocean as they came round the headland and headed into the Seattle harbor.

"Well I guess we'd better come back to reality," said Wayne as they coasted into the harbor and came up to their anchorage. "We'd better tie her up, we'll come back and clean up and put everything away tomorrow evening."

Sylvia turned her head and nibbled on his inner thigh laughing before she stood up and ran to the front of the yacht and jumped onto the wooden pier. Wayne cut the motor as the back of the boat drifted in, he too jumped onto the dock and tied up the stern rope. They went back down into the cabin and made sure everything was stowed safely and locked up. Then they went to pick up their van that they had left in the nearby parking lot.

They drove back to their apartment; it was a recently renovated two-bedroom apartment in a huge old Victorian mansion that had been split up into a number of apartments. Wayne had always been fascinated by Victoriana and had been only too thrilled to find out that Sylvia too enjoyed all things from the Victorian era. So they had furnished their apartment with a lot of genuine antiques and some Victorian replicas, it was extremely homely. Wayne gathered up a huge pile of mail that had been stuffed through the mailbox as he closed the heavy oak front door behind them.

"It'll take me a week to get through this lot, I bet half of it's junk mail."

"Some of it's most probably for me," Sylvia said moving their two luggage bags over to the side of the hallway.

"I wonder what name they used for me, it's very strange to be called Mrs. Dunstan." She moved on into the apartment gave him a great big kiss as she passed him. He dropped the mail and grabbed hold of her and passionately kissed her.

"God I love you," he said.

Sylvia ran her nails down his back and pushed away and said laughingly "well Mr. Dunstan, I'd have thought that you'd had enough sex on the boat."

He tried to reach out for her but she moved on into the kitchen slipping through his hands.

"I don't think I could ever make love to you too much, you're one very sexy lady."

He bent down and picked up the mail again and followed her into the kitchen.

"Well," she said pointing to the telephone "before you think of anything else, you dirty old man, I think you'd better check the messages on the phone, that little red light is blinking so fast you must have a dozen of them at least. I'm going into the bedroom and get out of these clothes."

He picked up the phone and dialed in his code and found he had twelve messages. The first message was from A.T. and T., something about his account. The second call surprised him, he heard "Wayne this is Rob from Last Chance. I must speak to you urgently. Do you remember Fishslice? I'm hereby invoking Fishslice, I repeat Fishslice. It's imperative that I speak to you immediately please call me" and Rob had left two phone numbers. Wayne stood there with a surprised look on his face, it was a voice out of the past with a message that worried him. He went through the rest of his messages only to find that nine out of the twelve were from Rob always saying basically the same message. Sylvia came out of the bedroom wearing a big white robe, she looked over at him and saw the worried look on his face.

"Honey what's the matter, you look worried."

"Do you remember me telling you about Last Chance and the young men I grew up with?"

"Yes of course, so who was that on the phone?"

"Would you believe that nine out of the twelve messages were from one of those young men, they were from Rob. While at the camp we'd setup an emergency word, if anybody said that particular word it meant that everyone had to stop and listen to him or her, or there was an emergency and we had to react or do something immediately. That word was Fishslice and in each of Rob's messages he's been repeating the word Fishslice and saying that he has to speak to me immediately, I don't quite understand what it's all about, it worries me a little."

"Well my love," said Sylvia moving over close to him "it's really very simple, if he left you a phone number call him back."

Wayne looked at her quizzically for a moment, nodded and then dialed one of the numbers that Rob had left on the answering machine.

Rob's cell phone rang twice.

"Hello Rob here what can I do for you?"

"Well hello Rob," said Wayne recognizing the voice on the other end of the line "Wayne here, just got back from a trip and found your messages, what's up? "

"Well hello Wayne, yes, boy! Have I been trying to get hold of you. Hope everything is okay with you, how're you doing? I really need to talk to you about something really urgently."

"Everything up here is just fine, I just got married and we just got back from our honeymoon. What's up?"

"Well congratulations," said Rob "listen, is your wife around, can she get on the phone too, it would probably be best if I spoke to both of you at once."

"Sure, hang on a second." Wayne looked at his wife. "Honey Rob would like to speak to both of us together, can you grab that other phone in the living room please."

It only took a couple of seconds for Sylvia to pick up the phone and push the button.

"Hello" she said, "Okay I'm on the line."

"Rob this is my wife Sylvia."

"Hello Sylvia, nice to meet you and congratulations to both of you." Rob said "Wayne I have a report from Pattern, you remember Pattern, he's now working directly for the President of the United States. You must read this report, I can't discuss it on the phone and it's extremely urgent that you see it immediately. Do you have a fax?"

"Yes we have a fax but what's it all about, why's everything so urgent and mysterious?" Said Wayne.

"Once you've read the report you'll understand," said Rob "I'll fax it to you immediately, please read it and call me back the second that you've finished. What's your fax number?"

Wayne gave him the fax number and immediately Rob hung up.

"What the hell's all that about?" Said Wayne to his wife as she came back into the kitchen "why's it so damn mysterious?"

"Well hang on a second, we'll find out just as soon as we've read the report, he sounds quite desperate."

They only had to wait a couple of minutes before the fax machine rang and they went over and waited until the complete report had been printed out. Wayne took it into the kitchen and sat down at the table and Sylvia lent over his shoulder and they read it slowly. When they'd finished it Sylvia slowly walked around the table and sat down opposite her husband, there was silence and then Sylvia reached across the table and held Wayne's hand.

"Is it possible that this is correct? Could this just be a big hoax?" She said, her voice quivering a little bit.

Wayne sat there staring at the report and then he looked up "I doubt very much if it's a hoax, if it is it's a very elaborate one. Do you realize what this means if it's correct, our lives, everybody's lives, are about to be changed, there'll be panic in the streets. If it's true what are we going to do?"

Sylvia squeezed his hand, "let's see what Rob has to say, perhaps he has some answers."

Wayne nodded his head.

"You want to get on the other phone so we can both hear what he has to say?"

He dialed Rob's number as Sylvia went into the living room and picked up the phone.

"Hello again," came Rob's voice "I take it that you've read the report? "

"Yes," said Wayne "Sylvia and I have both read it, she's on the other phone listening in, and it's very disturbing."

"Well let me just say that everything in the report is true, in fact everything in the report has been checked over and over again and has proven to be correct, believe me when I say I wish to God it wasn't but it is true and the consequences are already beginning to happen. Do you understand the full impact that this will have on all of us?"

"It's horrendous," said Sylvia "are you sure that there's no way that it could be incorrect?"

"Trust me when I say it's all correct, that report was prepared and has been presented to the President and I've just received a phone call from Pattern; the President is going to make a major speech about this report to the nation in two days time. When the people hear what's going to happen there'll be chaos in the streets, we were just most fortunate that we had some forewarning."

"My God," said Wayne "this is horrific, what the hell are we going to do?"

"Let me tell you what we're setting up, do you remember Judge Mortimer?"

"Of course I remember the Judge, he was the one that sent us to Last Chance."

"Well it turns out that he is an extremely wealthy gentlemen and he is the person who's provided all the funds to maintain Last Chance and who's paid for all of our educations. Pattern showed us this report at a meeting at Last Chance and we agreed, that is Joshua, Bella, my wife, myself, the Judge and Pattern, that we would try to prepare Last Chance as a secure haven that we could all, if we wished, move to and stay there until the worst of the chaos has passed. The Judge has agreed to finance everything that we need, so far we've set in motion the purchase and delivery of everything that we can think of that we might need to see us through for the next five years. I've been in touch with Indian and he's on his way here as we speak. We have a friend of the Judge who was a quartermaster and, thank God, he still has all his contacts and has bought everything that we think we'll need. The only area where we're having trouble is with pharmaceuticals, apparently you must be a pharmacist to purchase the pharmaceuticals that we think we might need. The question is would you and Sylvia like to come down and join us at Last Chance?"

"This is one hell of a shock," said Sylvia "what you're telling us is that our lives are about to completely change, that we have to give up our work, our jobs, everything that is normal day-to-day living and just move to this Last Chance. What you're asking is a hell of a lot."

"I'm not asking you to do anything Sylvia," said Rob quietly "I'm just trying to relate the facts to you, to give you some warning about what's about to happen in two days time and to offer you, possibly, a safe place to go."

There was silence on the phone for a moment and then Wayne asked, "How long do you think we have to get down to Last Chance safely?"

"As I've said, the President will inform the people in two days time. We're estimating that within a few hours of that speech there will be chaos; a lot of people will be trying to move out of the cities and towns and find somewhere to live in the country. We know that this crystal, throughout the country, has infected random cement structures and it's had time to break down that cement. There are going to be more and more incidents of cement breaking down with some catastrophic results. The deterioration already started and things are speeding up. So far we have managed to truck in all of our supplies to a transfer station up on the plateau and from there we've been airlifting them to Last Chance. I fear that within a week or two most of the country's infrastructures won't be safe or passable and there'll be a lot of problems with our services, such as electrical, gas, water and sewerage."

"That doesn't give us a hell of a lot of time to make up our minds and get down to Last Chance, if that's what we decide to do" said Wayne.

"Rob, you say that you have, or are getting, everything that you can foresee that will be needed at Last Chance except for the pharmaceuticals, is that correct?" said Sylvia.

"Yes that's correct."

"Well it just so happens that I'm a pharmacist, I have my own business up here in Seattle, I should be able to get any pharmaceuticals that you need."

"My God that's fantastic, we've been having one hell of a time trying to get anything. My wife is a surgeon and we've purchased a complete mobile emergency field surgery unit but are having a real problem trying to get the pharmaceuticals that she might need. How long would take to get stuff in if you had to order it?"

"Well I have a great deal of supplies already at my shop but I also act as a supplier to one of the local hospitals, I have all their requirements on my computer. Unlike other supplies pharmaceuticals are normally delivered within twenty-four hours, if I placed an order the first thing tomorrow morning they would certainly be delivered that evening or at the latest the following morning."

"That would be marvelous," said Rob, "we need everything, you as a pharmacist would know more of what we need than we would. We estimate that we'll be living at Last Chance for at least five years and are trying to provide for up to fifty people for those five years. Even if you don't decide to come down, is there anyway that you could get us these supplies?"

There was a moment's silence and then Wayne said "Sylvia Honey if this report is true and I think that we have to accept that it is true and accurate and if the President is going to tell the people what's going to happen in two days, I can't think of a safer place for us to be than at Last Chance. I know this is a major decision, I realize that it changes our lives forever but I don't think that we really have much choice, I think we should plan on going down to Last Chance. What do you think Honey?"

Again there was silence on the phone and then Sylvia said, "I have to agree with you it certainly won't be safe to stay here. I hate making such major snap decisions but we really don't have any time or choices, I say let's head down there immediately."

"I agree," said Wayne "alright Rob we're with you, we'll leave here as fast as possible."

"That's wonderful to hear, you won't be sorry I promise you. Now the question is how do you get down here and how do we get the pharmaceuticals, somehow you have to leave Seattle before the President's speech otherwise it may be impossible for you to drive here and even now it's not really safe to drive and I certainly wouldn't recommend flying even if you could make the arrangements at this short notice."

"I've an idea," said Sylvia "I can order and get all the supplies in before the speech, Wayne can we put all of the supplies in the yacht and sail down the coast?"

"Yes," said Wayne "that's an excellent idea, there won't be much room left for us but I'm sure we could do it. That way we wouldn't have to drive down and we wouldn't have any problems on the way."

"You have a yacht?" Asked Rob.

"Yes we have a thirty five footer, that's where we've been for the last two weeks on our honeymoon, that's why you haven't been able to contact us, it's down in the harbor."

"Well that sounds like the best idea. Sylvia can you please make sure that you have all the supplies that we would need for the surgical unit?" Asked Rob.

"I can do that, the only problem I have is that it will be extremely expensive to purchase all these supplies and I certainly don't have the money on hand and the suppliers will want to be paid up front."

"That's no problem," said Rob "the Judge is paying for everything, if your suppliers will take a charge card, they can clear the funds before your orders are delivered, then I can give you the details of a card that has been set up with funds already paid into it. Would you're suppliers take a charge card?"

"I don't see any problem with that," replied Sylvia "just as long as they can clear the charges before deliveries, hang on for a minute." She dashed into the back room and got a pencil and paper. "Okay give me those details."

Rob gave her all the pertinent information for the credit card.

"The only problem that I can foresee," said Wayne "is at the other end, there's no way that I want to sail into Mexican waters with a boat full of drugs. Where can we put ashore down your way and how do we get them moved from the coast to Last Chance?"

"Hmmm let me think about that one, I'll work out the details and let you know. We don't know how much longer the cell phones will be working, do you have a G. P. S. phone on board?"

"Yes we do, if you have one we can stay in touch that way if necessary."

"That's excellent we're all planning to stay in touch by G. P. S. You realize that you must be out at sea before the President's speech, God only knows what's going to happen afterwards."

"We'll be at sea before he begins his speech," said Wayne.

"Yes we will," said Sylvia "What supplies haven't arrived by then will just have to be left behind but I can't foresee anything not being delivered on time."

"Wayne can you bring down all the supplies that you'll need as a mechanic, we'll have all sorts of equipment and machines that at some time in the future will need to be repaired. Bring down anything that you think that you'll need."

"Sure no problem there, I can get everything I need locally and if I need to I can use the same charge card can't I?"

"Sure you can, both of you can spend as much as you like, I know for certain there's at least one million dollars that's been prepaid onto that charge card. You have no idea how much we're spending, I've spent one million dollars just buying prefab cabins for everybody."

"Wow" said Sylvia "that's a hell of a lot of money, thank God someone has that sort of money to spend."

There was silence on the phones for a moment.

"Well then," said Rob "I guess that's it, thank goodness we were able to get hold of you. I'll talk to you when you're at sea and let you know the arrangements to get you from the coast to the camp."

"Okay thanks, we'll be in touch shortly," said Wayne.

"Yes good bye for now," said Sylvia and the phones were hung up.

Sylvia moved into the kitchen and moved into Wayne's waiting arms, they hung onto each other in silence.

They were up early the next morning, Wayne took his wife's old Honda Odyssey van to his garage where he packed up everything that he thought he might need. It only took him a couple of hours and then he went to Sears and purchased all the tools and equipment that he thought he might need much to the delight of the salesman. He then took everything down and loaded it onto the yacht. In the meantime Sylvia went to her pharmacy and, much to the disgust of her three employees, she closed the business until further notice citing personal problems. Her three employees left as Sylvia put up notices on both entrances to the shop that it was closed till further notice, the three ladies were somewhat placated after being promised two months of separation pay.

Sylvia immediately got on the phone and placed rush orders for all the supplies that she thought she would need at Last Chance, she paid the premium price to have them all delivered later on that afternoon. Luckily she always kept plenty of empty cardboard boxes that her stock had been delivered in in the basement. She started to pack everything up, the prescription medications first and by the time that Wayne arrived just before twelve she was packing up the stock off the shelves in the front of the shop. She was very careful to label what was in each box and had the packed up boxes stacked by the back door. Wayne turned up driving a large rental U-Haul truck, he backed it up as close as possible to the back door, pulled out the walk up ramp and after he and his wife had eaten their MacDonald's hamburgers and french fries which he had bought, he started loading the packed up boxes into the truck.

By six o'clock that evening all of the supplies that Sylvia had ordered had been delivered and they along with everything else in the shop that Sylvia deemed necessary had been loaded into the truck. Sylvia locked up the building and wistfully, with tears in her eyes, she said her good bye thinking of all the work and love and studying that had gone into her opening this, her own business.

They stopped and had a good supper at their favorite restaurant, the Taiwanese buffet, and then went down to the docks and loaded everything into the yacht. The boxes took up all of the bedrooms and cabins except for the galley that had an armchair that went down into a single bed and the sitting bench behind the table, which folded out into a double bed. Luckily the head was at the back of the boat so that it was still usable.

It was about eleven o'clock by the time they were finished, they returned the U-Haul truck and then went back to their apartment where they packed up all of their personal belongings in suitcases and then snuggled into bed. There had been very little conversation all evening, they had both been concentrating on getting everything loaded and trying hard not to think about why they were doing it but once in bed Sylvia broke down crying in her husband's arms. They lay holding each other and talking until the wee hours of the morning. They only got about four hours of sleep before they got up, a little bleary eyed, had a big breakfast with two or three cups of coffee to wake them up and then they loaded their belongings into the van. Locking up their apartment for the last time was almost overwhelming but by nine o'clock they were casting off the ropes and were chugging out of the harbor.

The yacht was a little sluggish with all the cargo stowed in her and she sat a lot lower in the water. They sat and held onto each other as they rounded the point and then they ran up the sails on the two masts and as they filled up with the wind coming out of the North Wayne cut off the motor and they both seemed to breath a sigh of relief as they headed out and down the coast. Sylvia snuggled down between Wayne's legs and he lent over and kissed her gently, it was at this point that they truly realize that they had made a complete break with their old lives and were now free to face a new beginning, they could feel the excitement welling up inside them both.

They made excellent time with a strong wind blowing them down the coast. Sylvia made them a light lunch and just afterwards the weather station on the radio announced that there was a storm coming in off of the Pacific Ocean.

Wayne checked over his maps, "Well Honey we'd better find shelter from the storm, there's a nice little harbor at Charleston in Coos Bay, I visited it once before I met you, it's well protected from the ocean, we should be able to make it well before the storm hits us."

"Sounds like a good idea to me," said Sylvia "I could do with stretching my legs and I prefer sleeping safe and sound in a harbor than trying to sail through a storm."

They were safely tied up to a cement jetty two hours later in Coos Bay and sat on deck watching the lightning as the storm came inland. With the first few rain drops they went down into the cabins and battened down the hatches and made themselves comfortable.

Later they sat glued to the radio listening to the President's address to the nation; they hung on every word in silence. As the President finished his speech Sylvia reached across the table and held her husband's hands.

"My God," said Sylvia in a husky voice "Rob was right, everything in Pattern's reported was true, down deep I had my doubts but now having heard the President's report my worries and doubts are gone."

"I know what you mean," Wayne said looking lovingly at his wife "I had my doubts too but not anymore, now the shit will really hit the fan, thank God we made the right decision, all hell will break loose now."

Sylvia got up and Wayne folded down the table, they pulled out the bed and Sylvia threw on the sheets, blankets and pillows, they lay down holding onto each other listening to the reporters on the radio trying to make conclusions from the President's speech and trying to figure out just what it all ment. Later they gently made love to the sounds of the rain beating on the top of the cabin, illuminated every now and then by the flash of lightning through the portholes and then they fell asleep.

The early morning sunshine coming through the portholes woke Sylvia up, she looked over at her sleeping husband and watched him as he lay there. They had been exhausted when they went to bed last night and both of them had slept like logs but she knew they should get a fairly early start this morning. The water was calm; there was no sign of the storms that had gone through the night before. She moved over closer to her husband and hugged him, kissing him gently on the cheek feeling him coming awake. He sighed as he came through his half sleep, he rolled over to cuddle her in his arms and whispered in her ear "I love you, I really love you."

They held each other close for a few minutes and then she said "We'd better get an early start this morning, we need to clear the harbor as soon as possible. I'll put a quick breakfast together while you get dressed."

She climbed over him, gave him a quick kiss full on the top of his head and moved away as he tried to grab her naked body knowing full well what he liked to do in the morning.

They had a quick breakfast of coffee and bagels and then went topside, it was a beautiful morning with just a nice breeze coming out of the North. They had moored against a long cement pier, which had a commercial building running right down the center of it around which was a walk way about twelve feet wide. Wayne looked around as they both jumped onto the pier; it was very clean except for a large pile of what looked like cardboard boxes that lay against the side of the building directly across from where they were moored, he was surprised to see four young men walking down the pier towards them. He stood and stretched and looked around enjoying the morning sun, he moved to the front of the yacht to undo the rope as Sylvia moved to do the same at the stern. As he bent down one of the four young men, who were now fairly close, called out to him "Good morning to you, isn't it a beautiful morning?"

Wayne stood up, "Good morning to you to gentlemen, yes it is a beautiful morning."

"Are you leaving?" Asked the young man who was closest to him, Wayne noticed that the other three were moving round behind him, the one who had spoken was obviously the leader of the group, they were all dressed in jeans and had light fall zipper jackets on.

"Yes we're leaving, we only pulled in for the night to escape the storm. We'll be out of here in a couple of minutes."

"No I don't think you will," said the young man and much to Wayne's shock and amazement he reached into his jacket and Wayne found himself facing a pistol.

"What the hell, what is it, what do you want? Put that damn thing away."

All of the young men laughed, "Well it just so happens that we would like your boat so I don't think that you and your lovely lady will be leaving in it any time soon. Hey you lady," the leading man called to Sylvia "come on up here beside your husband, come on move it, we don't have all day."

Silvia was visibly shaken, she'd gone quite white as she walked up behind her husband. "What do you mean you need our boat, it's ours, you can't just take it."

"This pistol in my hand tells me that I can just take it and in fact it's now mine."

The other three boys just stood with grins on their faces.

"Now listen here," said Wayne taking a step towards the young man "you can't just take someone's boat, you'll get caught, the police will get you."

"There aren't any police here anymore, didn't you hear the President's speech last night?"

Both Wayne and Sylvia nodded their heads.

"Well everyone is trying to get out of town, including all the police, the roads are blocked you can't go anywhere there's panic and chaos so we figured we'd take your boat and that way we can get out of town safely and have something safe to live on, so it sucks to be you but you've just lost your boat."

Wayne had taken a couple more steps towards him, he realized that he had to do something, all of a sudden he rushed towards the young man who at the very last second stepped aside and brought the pistol down on the side of Wayne's head, by the time Wayne hit the cement he was unconscious.

Sylvia screamed and made to rush towards her husband but the look on the young man's face made her freeze.

"Well that was a silly thing to do wasn't it," he said "It saves us from having to shoot him any way, now my pretty little thing I guess perhaps you can come with us on my new boat."

The other three young men began to leer at her and move towards her, she backed away, until she found herself at the edge of the pier, she was so scared she began to shake.

"Now come on, sweetie pie, no need to be so frightened, we're going to take good care of you," said the young man to her left taking a step towards her.

Suddenly all heads turned toward the building at the sound of the pile of cardboard boxes moving, they made a slight rustling noise and the outer layer made a wet sloping sound as they fell away from the building wall. They all stood stock still staring as, at first, a hand came out and pushed the last of the boxes away and a grubby lady stood up, dressed in shabby brown pants and a well worn leather jacket. She straightened up and shook herself and ran her hands through her long brown dirty hair, pushing it away from her face, she took a step forward as she picked bits of wet cardboard off the sleeve of the jacket. Sylvia could see that she wasn't as old as she looked.

"Well good morning, if it isn't the dirty smelly Amber, so this is where you sleep at night, God you look awful, you'd better move on up the pier if you know what's good for you."

Amber looked a little bewildered, she took two or three steps forward and seemed to wobble on her feet.

"Good morning, good morning," she mumbled still trying to brush her dirty hair to one side "what you all doing down here at this time of the morning? What's going on?"

"It's none of your business," said the young man nearest to her, he took a step towards her and shoved her so that she stumbled and came to a stop almost falling onto the young man with the gun who swung his arm around and pointed the gun at her.

"Whoa, whoa you've got a big gun, what you doing with that thing? Point it somewhere else, please."

The leader roared with laughter, followed by the other three.

"You filthy dirty useless hag get out of here, you're not worth wasting a bullet on," and he waved the pistol pointing back down the pier.

Sylvia watched all this in a sort of daze, slowly she was beginning to get herself back together, she realized that she was really in trouble. Then there was a sudden blur of movement, Sylvia had to blink, she couldn't quite understand what her eyes saw; Amber had suddenly moved, one second the leader of the men was waving his pistol back down towards the shore and the next moment he suddenly flew up in the air crashing down on the cement on his back screaming in pain as the arm that had been carrying the gun was twisted viciously and Sylvia heard the snap of one of his bones. Amber suddenly seemed to have the pistol appear in her hand. It happened so fast that Sylvia wasn't sure she'd really seen it, the screams of the man lying on the pier brought her back to reality.

Amber straighten up as the three young men stepped backwards, white with shock. She put her foot across the throat of the young man lying crying on the pier, "Shut up you rotten piece of meat" she said, putting more pressure on his throat causing him to fight for breath.

"Come over here you three," she said.

The other three young men hesitated for a moment and then moved towards her. She stepped away and said, "Get him on his feet, come on all of you get him on his feet."

The three hesitated for a moment and then rushed forward and stood the young man up, he screamed as one of them got hold of his broken arm.

"Now get out of here," Amber commanded, "get out of here, get off the pier and don't come back." She stepped back to allow the three young men, who almost had to carry their leader, to move down the pier towards the shore.

Amber tucked the pistol into the top of her dirty brown pants and turned towards Sylvia.

"Are you okay?"

"Yes" said Sylvia dashing over and kneeling beside her husband, she was relieved to see that he was breathing quite steadily. She lifted his head slightly, there was a trickle of blood running down from a small scratch behind his right ear, gently she felt with her fingers around the break in the skin, she couldn't feel any damage to the skull, she breathed a sigh relief. Amber knelt down beside Sylvia to look to the wound, "It doesn't look too bad, I've seen a lot of these things, I've had a lot of experience with injuries, he'll be just fine, he'll have a stinking headache for a few days on and off but he should be fine. Listen we've got to get you on that boat and get you out into the open sea, those fucking idiots will be coming back and this time they'll be fully armed. You've got to get out to sea."

"Yes your right," Sylvia said "please would you give me a hand to get him on deck."

Amber nodded and between the two of them they gently picked up Wayne and carried him onto the boat and made him comfortable on the cushioned seating in the cockpit so that Sylvia could keep an eye on him while she sailed the boat. Amber jumped up onto the pier and said, "You'd better get going" and went to cast off the bowline.

"Wait a minute," called out Sylvia "I can't sail this damn thing by myself, I've only helped my husband, it takes two to sail her, I've never done it by myself, what am I supposed to do?"

Amber could hear the panic rising in her voice, she looked around thinking.

"Listen I have to get out of here before these idiots get back, are you sure you can't sail this by yourself?"

"Yes I'm absolutely certain, it takes at least two people. What are you going to do, where could you go? Why don't you come with me, you can help me sail this thing and we can both get safely away."

Amber thought for a moment, she knew that the panic that had set in after the President's speech the day before was only going to get worse, she really did not have anywhere to go so, what the hell, she might as well go for a sail on the boat.

"Well I guess I've got nowhere else to go in a hurry, I might as well come with you." She undid the bowline, throwing the rope onto the boat, ran to the back and cast off the stern line and jumped onto the boat as Sylvia started the motor.

"Better get this heap moving," said Amber looking back up the pier "I can see some movement up by the shore I'd bet it's those fucking idiots coming back again. Can you speed this thing up?"

Sylvia pushed the throttle forward and the boat slowly, very slowly, shuddered and picked up speed. She came about and they headed out towards the exit of the harbor. They both turned around and watched, they could clearly see a bunch of young men starting to run down the pier. They had almost got to the exit of the harbor when the men reached the end of the pier yelling and screaming at them. Two or three of them started firing weapons at the boat, Sylvia and Amber crouched down low in the cockpit, they could hear the whistle of bullets flying by, a couple of them actually hit the boat, one taking a chip off the mast another taking a chip off the railing and then they were heading around the spit into open water and could no longer see the pier behind them.

"Thank God we're safe. Have you done any sailing, do you know how to run up the sails?" Asked Sylvia shakily.

Amber did not answer she just bounded forward and raised the sails, Sylvia could see that she knew just what she was doing. The boat shuddered as the sails filled and leapt forward, Sylvia shut down the motor and in next to no time they was speeding away from the land under full sail.

Amber came back and smiled, "Yes I've had quite a lot of experience sailing all kinds of boats, how you doing?"

"I'm OK now, thank God we got away, thank you for coming with me I would never have been able to do this without you. I suppose we'd better introduce ourselves, I'm Sylvia and this" she pointed to her husband unconscious beside her "is my husband Wayne, we're out from Seattle heading down the coast." She held out a hand.

Amber grasped her hand, Sylvia was surprised at the strength in that grubby hand, "I'm Amber, I'm sorry for my disgusting condition but I haven't been able to find anywhere to have a shower or a wash up for the last two or three days, I'm usually not this dirty and grubby."

"That's fine, I'm just glad you were here, I don't know what I would have done without you. You sure took care of those boys."

"Oh that was nothing, I've had a little military training, besides, they were just punks, now if it's okay with you, I'll have a closer look at your husband's head and just make sure he's OK."

Amber moved over and gently moved Wayne's head and felt around the cut.

"It's just like we said, he's going to have a hell of a headache, I don't think he's going to have a concussion but he'll be out for little while yet. Do you have a safety kit on board, I'll clean him up" she said looking round at Sylvia.

"Yes we have a safety kit on board" said Sylvia with a silly grin on her face, the grin spread into a smile and then Sylvia began to laugh and laugh and laugh. She was roaring with laughter, all the worry and panic came out and she cried and roared with laughter hysterically. Amber just stood and watched wondering what was so funny. Sylvia slowly she got control of herself, "I'm sorry," she said "Please just go below decks and you'll see what's so funny, while you're down there, if you want to, you can use the shower. Help yourself to any of the clothes down there, there must be something there that'll fit you and then if you want to come up here and relieve me I'll put on a cup of coffee and get us something to eat."

"Thank you, I think I'll do just that, I really really need a shower," said Amber pinching her nose as she disappeared below only to suddenly reappeared with a great big grin on her face. "I see what was so funny, you've got enough damn pharmaceuticals down there, I'm surprised the boat can float. None of my business but I'd sure be interested to find out why you got this boat packed with all those drugs. I'm going to have a shower, see you in a few minutes."

After Amber came back onto the deck all nice and clean in some of Sylvia's clothes, she very gently cleaned the back of Wayne's head then she took over the wheel from Sylvia who turned her attention to her husband. She made him as comfortable as possible and a little more than an hour later he moaned and opened his eyes.

Sylvia bent down and gently kissed him on his fore head, "It's okay my love, it's okay we're safe, just lay still, welcome back. Everything is okay, how are you feeling?"

He rolled his eyes and moaned again and put his hand up and gently rubbed the side of his head, "Oh my God my head hurts, what the hell happened, where are we?"

He tried to sit up and grabbed his head, Sylvia held onto his shoulders and gently pushed him back down, "Honey you'd better just lay still for a while, you took a nasty bang on the head, we're okay and under full sail down the coast."

Wayne rested his head back on the pillow rubbing his temples trying hard to remember what happened.

"Now I remember, we were on the dock and those men attacked us, one of them had a gun, I don't remember anymore" he said with a quizzical look on his face.

"Yes that's right my love, the man with the gun knocked you unconscious with it, gave you quite a belt, they were going to steal the boat and take me out with it but thanks to the lady that's now sailing the boat," and she looked up and smiled at Amber, who was looking down on them, "Thanks to her we're safe and sound and running down the coastline. I don't know if you noticed a pile of cardboard boxes that were lying up against the wall on the dock right where we were standing when the men attacked us, well Amber was sleeping underneath the cardboard and she came to our rescue and somehow, I still don't know how, she took the gun away from them and sent the men packing, she seemed to do it so easily. The two of us got you on board as fast as we could and then we sailed out of the harbor, thank God Amber knows how to sail this thing, we were just in time because the men came back down the pier yelling and shooting at us but we're safe. You're going to have a headache for quite a bit I think."

Wayne looked up at Amber and smiled nodding his head gently, "Thanks I guess we're in your debt."

Amber nodded back to him, "No problem, I've had a wonderful shower and I've got clean clothes and I'm sailing before the breeze, your wife has paid me back in full and she's given me something to do and a place to go, what more could a lady want?" and she smiled.

Wayne reached back with his hand gently and grimaced as he felt the large lump that had formed on the side of his head.

"How much does she know, have you told her what we're doing or where we're going?"

"Relax honey, she's seen all the supplies down below when she went to have a shower but I haven't said anything about why we have them or where we're going. She heard the President's speech last night and after she'd rescued us she decided to come with us because I desperately needed help in sailing the boat, you know I couldn't possibly sail this thing by myself and besides she didn't have anywhere else to go and she knew that the men would be coming back. We've been getting a few bits and pieces from the radio, all hell has broken loose across the country, people are going crazy trying to get out of the cities and the towns, there doesn't appear to be any more law and order, it seems to be every one for themselves, thank God we have the boat and are out to sea. When you feel a bit better and can sit up and have had something to drink you can tell her anything that you want, it will be fine with me, but she has truly saved our lives."

Wayne seemed to relax and put his hands down by his side, "Talking about sitting up, help me to get into an upright position would you please honey, let's see if this headache gets any worse, besides I'd like to look around." He began to push himself up, his wife helped him and as he did so he hung his head down moaning a little.

"Is it really that bad?" asked his wife sitting down beside him.

"It's pretty bad," he said as he lifted his head up, Sylvia noticed that he looked a little white.

"Take it easy, I'll give you some pain meds, they may take the edge off it but I fear you're going to have a nasty headache for quite a while."

Wayne sat upright and looked around, he could feel the breeze blowing across the boat and smiled. "You're right honey, it'll take a while to get rid of this headache but oh that breeze feels so good." He felt the sunshine on his face, saw the sea was calm and the sky was blue with only with a few clouds and that they were making good time down the coast.

"I think you'd better get some fluid down you," said Sylvia pouring him a cold glass of lucozade from a thermos "and you'd better take these pain meds," she said as she handed him two percosets, "they may make you a little woozy but they'll help with the pain. You haven't eaten for a long while, let me know as soon as you feel like eating something."

Wayne swallowed the pills with the drink and sat back and relaxed, everything seemed to be under control. They sat holding each other enjoying the movement of the boat for about twenty minutes.

"Those pills are kicking in, the pain is subsiding, let's see if I can stand up, I need to move around a bit."

With his wife's help he stood up, he was a little woozy for a minute or two and then he felt steady on his feet and nodded to his worried wife.

"I'm fine honey," he said "really, honestly I feel much better I can handle the pain." His wife's saw that he looked much better and he could see the relief in her face. He walked over to Amber who was happily sailing the boat.

"Hello Amber, we haven't been officially introduced, I'm Wayne and I thank you for helping us."

Amber shook his hand, he felt the strength in her grip and was a little surprised.

"I'm pleased to meet you Wayne I'm Amber," she said with a grin "it was no trouble I assure you and I thank you for letting me sail this beautiful boat, it's been a long while since I did any sailing and it brings back some wonderful memories. At the least we're safe for now, but I hope you have some idea of where we're going and what we can do because as your wife said it seems that the world has gone to hell and I have absolutely no idea where we could go to be safe."

Wayne let go of her hand and realized that he liked her, there seemed to be an enormous amount of inner-self control. Wayne looked over at his wife, "I guess we'd better let her know what our plans are and see if it's okay with her."

Wayne looked back to Amber, "I'll make you a deal," he said "if you'll tell us all about yourself then we'll tell you all about ourselves and what we're doing, do we have a deal?"

Amber smiled, she liked this man, "We have a deal."

Sylvia moved up so she could hear everything, Amber said "Now where should I begin, I was born and raised in Detroit, we lived in a fairly rough neighborhood so I learnt at a very early age to look after myself. After I'd finished high school I joined the Marines, I loved it, I loved the life, I loved everything about it and I was very good as a Marine. I was asked to join a special forces group doing some special work for the government, going into places before the rest of the Marines went in, needless to say we had some very specialized training, including," and she grinned at them both, "learning to sail just about every kind of boat available. I saw and did some terrible things in places all around the world, I was very comfortable with this because I knew that it was the right thing to do at the right time. Then our group was sent into Iraq, we were just to do reconnaissance and to do some evaluation before fucking President Bush ordered in all of the god damned United States forces. Two of us were cornered and had to hide in one of President Hussein's "guest houses", we had to sit and watch what his men did to some of his own people, to men, women and children and we couldn't do anything to help." Sylvia saw the expression on her face and saw that her knuckles were white as she gripped the wheel. Amber was silent for a minute and Sylvia and her husband could feel the tension in her, she shook herself, "We couldn't do anything to help them, we just had to sit and watch," she whispered "we managed to get away but I couldn't shake the visions of what I'd seen. I was sent back to the States and shortly there after my tour of duty was finished and I chose not to reenlist. Since then I've been back and forth across this wondrous land of ours all by myself, trying, I guess, to find peace of mind, I've managed to put it all behind me thanks to the mountains, national parks, the sea and the wind and some of the wonderful people that I've met along the way. I'm back to where I want to start making something of myself, it's funny that we met when we did because if this mess that the President has just announced hadn't happened, I was going to head back to my home in Detroit and find myself a job or go to college. But there you were and you needed help and so here I am" she looked at him and said, "that's just about all about me, will that suffice?"

"That's quite a story," said Wayne "I'm glad that you managed to find yourself, do you have any family?"

"No, no brothers or sisters and my parents died a while ago."

"Our story is nowhere near as exciting as yours, I'm a mechanic, a very good one if I may say so," he said grinning at his wife who was nodding enthusiastically, "my wife is a pharmacist, that's how come we have all that stock down below," he grinned "I was a very bad and quite a nasty young person......" and he went on to explain all about Last Chance and why they were sailing down the coast in a boat jam packed with pharmaceuticals.

"I guess you've been caught up in our plans, now the question is what would you like to do?" he looked over at his wife who understood his silent query; she nodded back to him firmly. "If you don't have any other plans we'd be thrilled if you'd join us and the rest of them at Last Chance."

Amber stared silently ahead for a minute or two and then smiled. "I guess nobody's making me any better offers," she said "I would love to join you, it sounds quite an adventure and I'd love to see what we can make of this camp of yours."

They sat and talked and then Wayne took over the yacht while the two ladies, still chattering away, went down and made supper, Wayne could feel his headache going away slowly.

After they'd finished eating dinner and the ladies had cleaned up the dishes, Wayne handed over the boat, Sylvia was still chatting away with Amber as if they'd been friends all their lives and as he went below decks he said. "I guess I'd better see if I can contact Last Chance and see what plans they have for us and how we're going to get all this cargo over to the camp, I certainly don't fancy trying to sail up through Mexican waters with all that's going, I sure hope they have a better idea."

He sat down and pulled out the radio equipment. "Last Chance, Last Chance, Wayne here, Wayne here, do you read me? Over."

The radio crackled. There was no answer.

"Last Chance, Last Chance, Wayne here, Wayne here, does anybody read me?"

The radio crackled some more and then "Last Chance to Wayne we read you loud and clear, real glad to hear from you. Are you safe?"

"Hello, yes we're safe and sound and on the high seas. We have a full cargo, who am I talking to?"

"Glad to hear that you're safe Wayne, this is Joshua. Long time no see or hear."

"Hi Joshua, yes it's been a long time. What's happening and are there any plans to get us and our cargo over to Last Chance? I don't fancy trying to sail this boat through the Mexican waters."

"Well that's good news, we were beginning to worry a little about you since we hadn't heard from you. Well everything here is a bit chaotic, there's piles and piles of stock and food and building materials and livestock, anything you can possibly think of has been dropped down into the camp and we're trying right now to sort it all out. It's quite a chore," laughed Joshua "you wouldn't even recognize the place, there are containers everywhere and animals running wild. There seems to be people everywhere, they're all sleeping in the cave, I guess it's what you might call organized chaos but there's still plenty of room for you."

"Well that's wonderful to hear, by the way there are now three of us, I hope that it's okay, it's a long story and I'll tell it to you when we get there."

"That will be just fine, no worry, now we need to make plans to get you over here."

"Yes, as I've said before, I really don't want to take this boat into Mexican waters but that's the only way that I can see us getting to you."

"Okay now I'm going to put Bert on, you don't know him, he came down with the Judge, he's going to let you know how we're going to get you over here." The radio went dead for a minute.

"Hello Wayne, Bert here, nice to meet you. Now I need to know some information about your boat, how long is it from end to end and how many masts do you have?"

"She's thirty five feet from stem to stern and we have two masts which can, of course, be taken down."

"Excellent, now do you know where your hoist points are for lifting it out of the water and putting into dry dock for storage?"

"Yes they're clearly marked, when I rebuilt her I made sure that they were well marked, I planned to have her pulled out each winter and put into storage."

"That's excellent, now listen, we're going to meet you at these coordinates do you have a pencil and paper?"

Wayne pulled out a pencil and paper from a cubbyhole in his desk. "Yes I'm ready." Bert gave him the exact coordinates and Wayne read them back to make sure he'd got them accurately.

"Okay now can you get down to those coordinates this evening? "

"Yes we can be there easily."

"Good. Sunrise is at six forty five tomorrow morning so we'll meet you at those coordinates tomorrow between seven and seven thirty a.m., can't be any more accurate than that but be ready."

Wayne had pulled out a map and saw that the coordinates he had been given were approximately ten miles off the coast of Baja.

"I need you to make sure that everything is tied down tight, batten down the hatches and lower your masts and tie them down. Is that okay?"

"I guess so, we'll be there and waiting for you between seven and seven thirty tomorrow morning, can't wait to see what you have in mind."

"Okay we'll see you then."

The radio just crackled as Wayne broke the connection.

Wayne went topside and told the ladies what was going to happen, they showed their surprise.

"I guess they must have some helicopter or seaplane or something and are going to ferry us bit by bit to the camp, we're just going to have to wait and see, we'll have no problem getting down to the coordinates, we should have time to have a good night's sleep. I guess we'd better keep a watch all night, we never know what's going to happen. I'll take the first watch since I've slept most of the day," he said with a grin "and then I'll pass it on to one or both of you. Is that okay?"

Both the ladies nodded.

Seven o'clock the next morning found them sitting at the exact coordinates. Everything that had been loose on the deck had been safely stowed below, the masts had been lowered and tied off and the three of them were standing in the steering well anxious to see what was going to happen.

The radio suddenly squawked making all three of them jump in the stillness of the morning. "Last Chance, Last Chance to Wayne come in old buddy, do you hear me?"

Wayne grabbed the microphone, "Wayne here, good morning, we're here waiting for you, all ready and waiting for you. What's the plan?"

There was silence for a moment then "Okay Wayne, we're coming in from the coast, we have you on visual, you should see us and hear us any moment now. Let us know when you see us."

All three of them turned to look towards the coastline, "There, there, I see a black dot," said Sylvia pointing and almost at the same time they heard the distant roar of a helicopter.

"We see you," said Wayne into the microphone "my God, by the sound of it you're flying a very big helicopter."

As the black dot got bigger, "Holy mackerel," said Amber "That's a got damn monster, you know what it is, it's a Sikorsky, where the heck did they get one of those? You know what, I bet my last bottom dollar they're going to pick up the whole fucking yacht, I don't believe it," she roared with laughter "this is wild; this is just plain fucking wild."

"I think we're in for a rough ride," said Wayne as he reached for the microphone, "we got you, where the heck did you get one of those things from?"

The radio roared with laughter, "That's a long story, we'll tell you all about it later. We'll be right above you in just a couple of minutes and then we'll get going, hang on a second."

The three of them watched as the huge helicopter came in and hovered directly above them, the noise from the mighty engines was almost unbearable.

Wayne switched up the volume of the radio "Do you get what the plan is?" It roared.

"Yes, you're going to pick up the whole fucking boat, am I correct?"

"You've got it baby."

"We're going to lower you down two chain slings, one will go over to the bow lifting point the other will go down on the stern lifting point. You'll find two other chains attached to the front sling, when you have the lifting chains in place take these two chains from the front sling to the back sling, these should stop the slings from sliding outward and you'll find two more chains attached to the rear chains, take each one of these across the boat from side to side as low down as possible, this should make a very secure hammock, did you get all that?"

They saw the slings coming down.

"We get you," said Wayne.

"Make sure one of you stays by the radio and keeps us informed of what's going on."

Sylvia stepped forward next to her husband. "Let me work the radio," she said, "I think Amber will be better at this than I am."

The husband looked at Amber and they both nodded. "Okay honey, you got it but remember you're going to have to really yell loudly over all that damned noise."

Sylvia nodded and took the microphone.

It was amazing, the slings slid into place easily on the first try, they hooked the four chains between the slings and Wayne yelled to his wife "We're ready honey tell them that we're ready."

Sylvia nodded and waved a hand "Everything's in place, we're ready for you, take it gently, please take it gently," she yelled into the microphone.

"You've got it, here we go."

The chains were pulled up slowly and suddenly the boat shook and shuddered and the noise from the helicopter engines increased. Wayne and Amber rushed back to the cabin and all three of them hung onto the boat. The chains creaked and the boat seemed to moan slightly and then very slowly the whole yacht was lifted out of the water. Suddenly the boat jerked and tipped slightly to the starboard, Amber and Wayne slid down and bumped into Sylvia, the boat was now at a very slight angle. Everything seemed to hold.

"Are you okay down there?" roared the radio.

Wayne grabbed the microphone. "Yes everything's fine we've tipped at a very slight angle but everything seems to be okay."

"Okay then, we're going a bit higher and then we'll head to the coast, it might be best if you three could tie yourselves individually to one of the chains, that way if anything were to happen and we lost the boat at least you three would be safe, do you have any ropes?"

"We sure have, we'll put on the lifejackets and tie them to the ropes and then we'll stay in the outside cockpit just in case anything happens, we can stay in touch with you from there. We'll let you know if anything goes wrong," said Wayne as he gathered up three ropes. They each put on a life jacket, made sure they were good and tight and then attached a rope to each of the lifejackets and then Wayne tied them off on one of the chains supporting the boat, they settle down in the comfortable seats in the cockpit. .

"Okay," said Wayne "we're battened down and ready to go, this is absolutely wild, I never thought I'd be in a flying boat. Let's go, how long will the flight take?"

"Barring any incidents we should be home in about two hours. Hold tight here we go."

The three of them held on as the boat began to sway and swing as the helicopter turned around and lifting slowly started roaring towards the coastline. It was a wild flight, every time a puff of wind came from one side or the other the boat swayed drastically, the three of them hunkered down and held on tight. Just over two hours later they dropped down into the River Valley heading upstream towards Last Chance, the helicopter slowed down and there was very little breeze between the Canyon walls but the sound of the helicopter engines echoed from wall-to-wall and they put pillows over their ears. The radio crackled, it was impossible to understand what was being said and then they stopped going forward and swayed like a rocking chair in the breeze. They felt the boat going down and could hear the sounds of the chains being lowered from the helicopter. As the boat finally stopped rocking they put their hands over their ears and moved to the side, they realized that they were being lowered into the water just a few feet away from the end of the dock and people were rushing down to meet them. The boat slid into the water very smoothly and as soon as the chains went slack the three of them rushed out and released them, and pushed the two swings from the front and the back of the boat and at last the helicopter rose up higher and the noise from the engines faded. They had a ringing in their ears but could hear the people shouting and yelling from the dock. Wayne threw a rope which was taken up and they were pulled to the edge of the dock with a slight bump, the boat was tied at the stern and the front and before they could get off the boat people were running and jumping onto it yelling and screaming happily, they had made it to Last Chance safely.

23

Mary and Roger Reed.

In the Amazon jungle.

Two days before the President's speech to the Nation.

Mary and Roger Reed stood on the bank of one of the tributaries that flowed down into the Amazon River, they were surrounded by a very noisy group of natives from a tribe that lived way back in the Amazon Forest. Mary and Roger stood head and shoulders above all the tribes' people who were each taking their turn to run up and give each of them a hug goodbye. Roger worked for an international pharmaceutical company, he was one of the best known pharmaceutical research chemists in the world, he and his wife had been coming down to this part of the Amazon for two months out of each year for the previous five years. They were in fact two of the very few people that were accepted by this particular tribe of natives who had accepted them and made them one of their own.

This year Roger had been quite successful in his research while his wife, who was an expert in animal husbandry had been studying the local farming practices. They had spent the last two months in the jungle, spending time with three different tribes. Wayne had been collecting samples of the various potions and poisons that each of the tribes were using to kill or paralyze the game that they hunted or for healing their sick. He had collected a dozen fairly large gourds of noxious substances that he was going to take back to his laboratories. They brought nothing of the modern world with them, when they traveled they left modern civilization and society behind them and would, as much as possible, go native and live as the natives did. This was their goodbyes, they were leaving but would, they hoped, be back somewhere in this neighborhood the following year. Roger, his wife thought, was a magnificent sight, he stood six feet two inches tall and his skin was jet black, blacker than blue black, he was dressed in nothing but a loincloth and he was extremely fit.

As each of the men of the tribe came forward and gave Roger a hug they said, in their native tongue, "Goodbye Ghost, may we see you yet again." They called Roger 'The Ghost' because he was even a darker color than the members of the tribe and when he closed his mouth and made slits of his eyes he would disappear into the darkness of the night. It was very strange because 'Ghost' had been the nickname they had given him when he was at Last Chance. Roger had learned to go hunting with the men of the tribes and was extremely proficient in the use of their two weapons, the blowpipe and the bow and arrow. He had learned their tribal crafts for making poisons to tip their arrows and darts.

Mary herself stood five feet eleven inches, she too made a beautiful sight dressed only in a loincloth, her beautiful shining skin was almost as dark as her husband's. Although she was not allowed to go hunting with the men, she was quite proficient with the blowpipe and the bow and arrow as Roger had taken her out and taught her how to hunt. She had learned how to prepare and cook as the women of the tribes did. She loved to get away from the modern world and looked forward to coming back again each year.

The tribe's people gave them gifts, mainly functional gifts such as a bow and arrows and a blowpipe and darts to each of them, special gourds full of poisons, medications, potions and good luck charms. Roger carried a full backpack, the only modern convenience that they allowed themselves, filled with both of their notes and some of the samples that he wanted to take back to the laboratories. As soon as they had said their goodbyes the tribe turned and disappeared into the jungle, Mary and Roger climbed down into the dugout canoe, loaded up the gourds and paddled away down the tributary. It would take them all day to get back to the base camp on the first bend just after they entered the main Amazon River. It was nothing but a cluster of huts used as a trading post by various jungle tribes and was operated by a half crazy Australian gentleman who had exiled himself to this lonely post many years ago.

They enjoyed the trip down the tributary and as they arrived at the dock of the trading post, Buster, the Australian, grabbed the rope that they threw him and tied up the canoe and helped them unload their goods.

"Well gooday to you both and I must say you both look extremely well, especially you Mary," he said leering at Mary as she got out of the canoe wearing only the very briefest of loincloths. Mary was used to this and wiggled her almost bare butt at the lurid old gentleman.

"Well" said Mary "If I didn't know you better Buster, I would have said that you were just a very dirty old man." She loved to tease him and ran over to him and threw her arms around him giving him a great big hug and kiss much to his delight and embarrassment, he blushed from head to toe.

"You err umm err, and welcome back" was all that he managed to stammer as she released him and bent over to pick up the gourds and then walked down the dock wiggling her behind suggestively at him.

"Wow, that's quite some young lady you have there," he said turning to Roger grinning from ear to ear, "How was the trip? Did everything go okay? Welcome back, it doesn't seem two months since you went away."

"Hello there you old bugger, you look just fine. Yes everything went very well, we've accomplished a great deal," said Roger pointing to the numerous gourds that Mary was carrying and those that he was just picking up from the dock. "Time flies really fast in the jungle, it seems like only yesterday that we were leaving here, anything exciting happen while we were away?"

"No just the same old same old" said Buster "All your stuff is safely in your hut. Oh by the way someone has been calling you and calling you for the last eight to ten days on the GPS phone. Every time he calls I tell him that you're not here and he leaves the same ridiculous message for me to give to you as soon as I see you."

"That's strange, the only people that can get through to that phone is my company. What's the message?"

"I've got it written down on a piece of paper in my office but it went something like this 'Tell Ghost that this is Rob, Fishslice,

Fishslice, Fishslice, he must call me immediately' and he left a phone number. Bloody strange I'd say, wouldn't you?"

Roger stopped dead in his tracks as he was bending down to pick up his knapsack, he stood up and looked at Buster. "That's extremely strange, I haven't heard that word for many years, I wonder what on earth he wants. I guess I'd better phone him as soon as I get cleaned up." He picked up his knapsack and the two of them strolled back down the dock.

Roger met Mary back at their hut, it was just a small two-room thatched building, one room was large enough for the two of them to sleep on a rolled out blanket on the ground, the other room just housed a rickety table and two chairs and their bag of clothes and the special metal canisters that could be sealed tight that they had brought with them to transfer their precious samples for transport home.

"Honey," said Roger putting his arms around his wife and pulling her to him "Buster tells me that I've had several phone calls from one of the old boys at Last Chance, I've no idea how he got that phone number but it seems that he wants me to call him as soon as possible."

His wife moved in close to him and ran her hands through his long black hair, "That's most unusual, if it's so urgent you'd better call him and find out what he wants," she said pushing him away "But I think before we do anything we'd better have a shower, we both really really need one."

Roger kissed her as she wrinkled up her nose, "Yes I suppose we do, come on, I'll make sure that you're clean all over in the shower hut."

They ran over to the shower hut laughing, it wasn't really a hut, it was just four walls open at the bottom and top with a big showerhead overhead. This was the first shower they had had since they left the camp two months ago, they'd been washing in streams and out of large gourds of water while living with the tribes. They took a long luxurious shower enjoying the hot water that they had missed while up river.

Wrapped in towels they went over to Buster's office, he had built himself a small one bedroom thatched hut, he'd made it very comfortable for himself and had a generator to supply the power that he needed.

"Okay then Buster" said Roger "Let's have that phone number, let's find out what this is all about."

Roger and his wife sat down in two very rickety chairs opposite Buster's desk, he handed them a grimy piece of paper and the telephone. Roger dialed the number, it only rang once and a voice said "Hello Rob here."

"Hello Rob, Ghost here, I see you've been trying to get hold of me. How on earth did you get this number?"

"Oh thank God I've got hold of you at last, I've been trying to contact you for the last ten days. Where the hell are you?"

"Well Mary and I are many miles up the Amazon River at the last outpost of civilization. This is a GPS phone, now how did you get this number?"

"Oh you really are way out, you remember Pattern, he now works directly for the President of the United States, he gave me this number, he has ways of getting just about any information that he wants. Do you have a fax or any way that I can send you a copy of a report?"

Roger looked over at Buster, "is there any way that he can send me a written report?"

"Of course, you think that we're not civilized here?" Said Buster with a big grin on his face "I have to have a fax so that I can take in special orders."

Roger hated to think what sort of special orders Buster took.

"Yes we have a fax, the number is" and he read off the number from a piece of paper that Buster pushed across the desk to him "Now what's all this about?"

"Let me send you this fax, it's a report that was made by Pattern that he has now presented to the President. Let me just assure you that everything in it has been checked and double-checked and proven to be correct, everything has been verified and the predictions are already proven to be true. I just got a phone call from Pattern telling me that he's been in touch with the President who's going to make a major speech to the nation in a little less than forty-eight hours. Time here is of the essence because I could not get hold of you you have very little time to decide what you want to do before the President's speech.

Enough said, please read the report and then call me back immediately."

"Okay, I don't pretend to understand but I'll read your report and get back to you ASAP. Talk to you in a little while" and he hung up the phone

They only had to wait a few minutes before the fax machine spat out the report and much to Buster's disgust they picked up the report and sat on a log down by the dock. They each read the report and then Mary reached across and held Roger's hand.

"This is terrible" she said, "it's unbelievable, I just can't believe that this could be happening."

"Neither can I," said Roger "but if what Rob said was correct then we have to believe that everything in this report is accurate. Where does that leave us?"

"Well" Mary said with a smirk on her face "I guess we could just stay here and live in the jungle, I don't think any of the catastrophes would really affect us down here."

"That's true but do you really want to live here?"

"No, of course not " she said squeezing his hand "What alternatives do we have? If we head back home to Miami I don't think it would be safe, by the sounds of this report the cities are going to collapse, our apartment complex will almost certainly collapse. What are we going to do?"

"You're right," he said standing up "we have to make a major decision, we have to find somewhere safe to go to, people will be going crazy in the streets, chaos will rule and the guns will come out. Let's see what Rob has to say."

They went back to the office and phoned Rob, he told them all the things that he had told Sylvia and Wayne and invited them to join them at Last Chance. They had a lot of questions but by the time they had finished on the phone they knew that they had decided, somehow, to make their way back to Last Chance.

"Well that's decided" said Mary after the phone was hung up "Now what do we do?"

"Well I suggest we head down to Belem, we can be there in a few hours if we pay Buster to run us down in his powerboat. We're supposed to be picked up there in two day's time; it will mean that we'll be going early, from Belem we know that we can get a seaplane to fly us to Miami, because that's how we came down, we should be able, for a fee, get them to fly us to the Texas coast somewhere and from there we'll have to make it overland to Last Chance. The extra flight will cost us a lot of money but we know that the company in Belem will take my company's charge card because that's how we usually pay them. Let's face it the charge card won't to be worth anything in a few days. We should be able, providing the seaplane is available, to make it to Texas about the time that the President will be giving his speech, from there we'll just have to wing it. How does that sound my love?"

"Sounds like an excellent plan to me, we'd better get going as soon as possible. Let's go up and see if we can get Buster to run us down river, you know he's going to want an exorbitant amount of money because we want to leave in such a rush."

"Yes I know, I brought cash because we know that Buster doesn't take charge cards." Roger laughed as they got up and headed back to the office.

The next day Buster took them down river in his half million-dollar cigar boat, it was his pride and joy and it cost them most of their petty cash. They had never found out why Buster was living in the jungle, what ever businesses he had going on the side were extremely lucrative since he had once told Roger that he had bought the cigar boat for cash. Immediately upon arriving at the very small port of Belem they went directly to the seaplane company. Here they ran into some problems, no seaplane was available until the following morning and furthermore they could not or would not fly them anywhere else but back up to Miami, after much bickering back and forth Roger and Mary were unable to get them to change their minds so they had to wait till morning. They booked into one of the small hotels and enjoyed a marvelous dinner at one of the local restaurants and then spent the evening making love on the first bed that they had slept in for over two months.

Very early the next morning they were on their way back to Miami packed into two very small seats in a seaplane that was used for carrying cargo. It was a long and miserable journey. They arrived at the port in Miami some six hours later, they had no difficulty getting through customs and excise because they knew everybody there and then they got a taxi back to their apartment in a high-rise that overlooked the ocean.

Roger called into work to let them know that he would be taking a further two weeks leave of absence because of a personal emergency while Mary packed up what few belongings they would need for the trip to Last Chance. They locked up the apartment and went down into the underground parking facilities. They had decided, because they wouldn't know what state some of the roads would be in, that they would take Roger's big Harley Davidson motorcycle. They packed everything including most of the samples that they'd taken from the Amazon into the side containers built onto the motorbike and into the utility trailer that they towed behind it. By four o'clock in the afternoon they were saying goodbye to Miami and heading out onto the freeway heading north west wanting to get as far as possible before the President's speech that evening.

At five p.m. they listened to the President's speech over the earphones built into their crash hats as they were approaching Lake City. They listened in silence hardly believing what they heard. As soon as the President was finished they pulled into a diner for supper and listened to all the people discussing the news. It was very obvious to them by the time that they had finished their meals that people were really beginning to get spooked.

"Hey mister is that your bike out there, looks like someone's playing with it."

Roger jumped up and looked out the window, three youths were by his bike, two of them were trying to open the lid of the trailer and the other one was sitting on the bike trying to start it. He and Mary ran out of the restaurant, Roger ran to within a few feet of the three men and Mary hung back about ten paces.

"Can I help you three?" asked Roger as he slipped his right hand into a fanny pack that was round his waist, "that happens to be my bike."

The three of them turned round stopping what they were doing, the one that got off the bike, a bedraggled looking young man who could not have been any more than twenty years old with a big mop of unruly hair and wearing an old pair of blue jeans with his shirt undone flying in the breeze, the other two were dressed similarly but he was obviously the leader of the group, he reached behind him and his hand came out with a six-inch knife that glinted in the evening sun.

"If this is your bike give me the keys," the youth said, nodding his head at the other two who moved slightly away and each of them reached behind and produced a knife, one had it in his right hand and the other held at in his left.

"Yes give us the keys," said the one furthest to the right.

Roger just stood there looking at them.

"Let me tell you a short story, there's a tribe of Indians living up the Amazon. To become a hunter in the tribe, each young man is sent out on his own to live in the jungle by himself and can only return when he brings back some part of an animal or reptile that could have killed him. Some come back with claws, some come back with the fangs out of poisonous snakes, some come back with a vicious tooth. I too was sent out by this tribe to pass this test though I was much older than the young men that they usually sent out." Slowly he pulled his right hand out from his fanny pack and in it he held a vicious looking curved black knife, from his hand to the tip it had to be a foot long, on one side was a sharp edge, on the other side were lots of little knobs. "This is what I came back with, in the jungle they have wild boars, the male boar is the most vicious animal and will attack anything it sees. It has two front tusks, one on either side of its snout and they are extremely sharp. It runs at or under an animal and the tusks will slice the animal open from end to end, I brought this tusk back to prove that I would be a really good hunter," his left hand slid in to his pouch and came out holding an identical tusk, "I brought this one home too, the chief of the tribe was so pleased he had them made into knives for me. How close would you like to see this pair?"

As he finished speaking the leader of the three boys saw Roger's facial expression change, his eyes hardened and his muscles tightened as he moved his feet to balance his extremely agile body, it sent shivers down the young man's spine and he felt the hairs on the back of his neck rise, he could see that this man was not going to back down.

"Errrr um I guess we just wanted to see your bike mister" he said looking sheepishly at the other two, he slid his knife back into his pants behind him, "No problem man, we was just looking."

The other two looked at him with relief on their faces. The three of them backed away and started walking down the street, Roger relaxed and a smile came to his face as he slid the two boar's tusks into the sheaths in his pouch, he turned grinning to Mary,

"You're terrible Roger," said Mary slipping what looked like a short black piece of bamboo back into her fanny pack. "I think we'd better get out of here and get going as fast as possible, the roads are going to get very bad very fast."

Roger nodded as she came up to him he grabbed her around the waist spun her around and kissed her. They jumped on the motorcycle and headed west as fast as they could, they stopped at the first gas station that was open and filled up the bike's gas tank as well as four five gallon containers that were packed away in the trailer.

They made excellent time till around about midnight when the roads started to get really busy.

"Honey," Roger heard in his headphones, "what do you think, it's getting busy should we try to find a place to camp or keep going."

"I think we'd better just keep going, this traffic is just going to get worse and worse and worse, we need to make as much time up as possible. What do you think?"

"I agree with you, in a few hours these roads will just about be impossible, let's just keep going and see what happens."

"Okay."

Gradually the road became more and more packed with cars, at times they had to take to the gravel shoulder but at least the traffic was moving. By four o'clock in the morning the traffic had come to a complete stop with vehicles everywhere, numerous small fender benders and people were out of their cars yelling and screaming at each other. Roger had to take the motorbike off road quite often just to get by vehicles that had been trying to pass on the hard shoulder and had blocked it completely. By the time the sun came up the roadway was a complete disaster, it was impossible for any vehicle to maneuver, it was a gridlock so they took off across country.

They had been riding off-road parallel to the road itself but the trailer made that difficult. He spotted a small bunch of trees a couple of fields away from the road and headed over there pulling well into the trees so they could not be seen from the road. They got off and stretched their legs.

"We made pretty good time, the whole trip from Miami to Phoenix normally would take about thirty five hours driving time. We've got in a good fourteen hours and I think we're about a third of the way there, that's not bad going under the circumstances," said Mary as she stood and stretched her hands above my head and bent down trying to release aching muscles.

"You're right but from now on it's going to be a lot more difficult and much slower. We're going to have to stay off road and I fear that the trailer's going to have to go."

"Yep you're right, let's get us some breakfast and have something to eat and drink and then we can unpack it. We'll have to travel light, I packed all the essentials up in two knapsacks before we left home so it should be easy to get what we want, we can just leave the trailer here and stay on the bike. One thing that we're going to need more than anything else is the bolt cutter, I'll keep that handy because I think we'll be cutting our way through a few fences."

"Excellent, well let's make a smokeless fire and have some breakfast and maybe we could make some strong black coffee I think we're both going to need something to keep us going," said Roger with a grin "The adventure has really started and we're on our way."

While he went and gathered dried twigs Mary unpacked the trailer, took out the two essential knapsacks and put them on the bike and by the time Roger had finished getting the fire started Mary had the food out and the coffee pot on. While she was getting everything onto the fire Roger took out of the trailer one of the gas cans and filled the motorbike which was just about out of gas. When the tank was full he put the empty gas can back into the trailer and took out a second gas can and attached it to the small rack on the back of the motorbike covering it with a canvas bag and tying it down tight, he unhitched the trailer and pushed it into the trees.

"That's the last of the gas, I have the siphoner handy, we may have to get some from one of the abandoned vehicles."

Camping and "going native" was something that they really enjoyed, they both knew they were perfectly capable of supplying all their needs which, when you got right down to it, were few.

"Well we should have enough gas to keep us going for at least another ten to twelve hours," he said as he settled down beside the fire and his wife served him a big plate of scrambled eggs and chunks of bread and butter and a big cup of strong hot black coffee. An hour later they rode out of the trees and back on their journey running as parallel as possible to the roadway. Luckily it had been a dry season and they had very little trouble running across country stopping every now and then to cut their way through a wire fence. The wind was blowing from the direction of the road and every few minutes they could hear some one yelling or screaming and the sound of gunfire, chaos had started and so had the law of the gun.

Some four hours later they were traveling close enough to be able to see the road that disappeared around a hill. There were people everywhere yelling and screaming, as they pulled up to the top of the hill they could see that the road wound slightly to the right and then over to the left up an embankment to a bridge. The land dropped off sharply to a river flowing a good three hundred feet below the bridge in a narrow gorge, the road on the other side was clear for a good quarter of a mile before it disappeared around another hill.

"The bridge is gone honey," Mary said "these people are going nowhere, what are we going to do?"

Roger pulled a map out of a leather pouch on the side of his gas tank and opened it.

"We're here," he pointed to a spot on the map "There's no other bridge across the gorge for miles in either direction, it's really going to put us behind. We've got to try and follow around the side of the gorge till we find another bridge and who knows what condition that will be in, even if it's still standing it may be blocked solid so that we can't cross it. I don't know what we can do." He put away the map and pulled out a small pair of very powerful army binoculars and surveyed the bridge.

"The metal structure of the bridge seems to be intact, there are two massive metal girders still going across the gorge which the concrete surface used to rest on before it collapsed. The pillars supporting the girders have metal through the center, some of the cement has come off but the metal supports still looked quite solid. The only problem is that at the far end there's a slight gap between the end of the metal girder and the rest of the cement bridge. I wonder if we could go across on one of the metal girders, they still look quite solid?"

"You've got to be crazy," said Mary, her voice ringing in his ear a little too loud "Who knows if it'll take the weight of the bike and how are you going to get across that little gap at the far end, how big is the gap?"

"It's only," Roger brought it into better focus and stared at it through his binoculars, "It's only about a foot or so but who knows what sort of condition the cement on the other side is in. It looks as if the cement has been covered by a layer of asphalt at some time, it's quite a thick layer but maybe you're right, it's really not worth while taking a risk. Perhaps we'd better head down south and see what the next bridge is like."

As he finished, they heard a lot of yelling and the revving of a powerful motor coming from behind them. They turned around to watch as an open jeep bounced over the edge of the road and down the slope and then started climbing up the hill towards them. The jeep pulled up beside them, in the front were a young couple, they both stood up and looked over the windshield, the driver was a young man in his early twenties, a wild mop of curly blond hair on top of his very handsome face which smiled at them.

"What a fucking mess, this is just absolutely impossible, everyone down there is going nuts, some of them wanted to take our jeep because it has four wheel drive," said the young man shielding his eyes from the sun with his right hand."

"What the hell are we going to do now?" asked the young girl beside him as she leant forward over the windshield.

The driver looked over at Roger.

"What are you going to do? This is one hell of a mess, we'll never get across that bridge, God knows where to go from here, what are ...." He never finished speaking, the top of his head seemed to explode and he was thrown forward so that he came to lie across the top of the windshield, there was blood and bits of bone and brains splattered right across the hood of the car. The young girl screamed as they heard a sound of the gun that had shot the young man from down the hill. Roger whipped his head around to see three men coming up the hill, each of them with rifles; one of them was crouching down taking aim up the hill. There was a whine and Roger's helmet suddenly jerked as a bullet bounced off it followed by the sound of the rifle behind them.

"Oh shit," Roger yelled, "they're after the vehicles, hang on tight honey."

He felt her hands tight around his waist and he opened the throttle, the big bike leapt forward cresting the hill and roaring down towards the bridge, behind them the young girl was thrown forward right out of the jeep with blood pouring out of her chest.

"Just hang on tight," he yelled at his wife "we have to get out of here," as the big bike picked up speed going down the hill towards the bridge.

"What the fuck" Mary screamed into her helmet mike, Roger opened the throttle as the bike hit the bottom of the hill and started up the incline to the road right at the beginning of the bridge. The bike flew over the top of the embankment to the road, they were airborne for split-second, the bike came down and bounced off the roof of a van, then the wheels came down on the metal girder across the gorge. Roger heard his wife scream and her head came down onto his back as her arms tried to hold him even tighter.

"Don't look down, just don't look down."

Of course Mary looked down: There was nothing between them and the raging river way below in the gorge, the big girder was approximately two feet across and seemed to be as solid as a rock. Roger held the bike steady in a straight line along the girder until they reached the gap at the end. He dropped one gear and opened the throttle wide, the front wheel of the bike came off the ground about a foot, it was just enough so that when they flew off the end of the girder the bike bounced onto the asphalt, chunks of cement fell down into the gorge. The back wheel grabbed onto the asphalt and they leapt forward, Roger kept the throttle wide open as the rear tire spun for a second and then grabbed again and they roared off the bridge, big chunks of the bridge were falling into the water below. Roger kept the bike screaming down the road until they got out of sight of the bridge around a small hill, he slowed down and stopped.

"Are you okay honey?" he whispered to his wife.

"All right, all right, I'm fine but I think I just shit my pants," she said as she got off the bike tugging at the back of her pants.

Roger got off the bike and pulled his wife close to him. "It was no problem the girder was at least two feet wide."

"It was when I opened my eyes and looked down, there was nothing but open air between us and that raging river down in the bottom of the gorge."

"I told you not to look down honey."

"Yes I know you did but I still looked down."

"I had to get us out of there as fast as possible, those were high-powered rifles they were using, if we'd tried to go along the edge of the gorge they could have picked us off when they got to the top of the hill, we're safe now though."

They hugged each other for a moment and then Roger said "Come on we'd better get out of here."

The road was clear for about a mile and then they hit a massive traffic jam again so they took off across the countryside running parallel to the road stopping only to cut their way through wire fences.

24

Indian returns to the US.

Aden

Indian had to stay in his bed for another eight days before they got so fed up with his demands to let him out of the hospital that the doctors let him up. They took x-rays, took off his "halo" and put him in a fiberglass-walking cast that started just below his knee and then wrapped around his ankle and his foot. Metal bars ran down both sides and under his ankle so that when he walked he was actually walking on the metal under his heel. They kept him in the hospital for a further twenty-four hours so that he could do some physical therapy and to make sure that everything was all right for him to leave the hospital using a walking cane. By now he was chomping at the bit to get going home.

He got a lift down the mountain in a Land Rover to his small apartment that was over a restaurant in little Aden overlooking the open-air market. He was constantly bombarded by the smells of the meat and fish half baked in the hot sun and the smell of numerous different kinds of fruit and spices, there was a constant barrage of voices as the market vendors called out to the passing people to come and buy their wares during the day and then at night he could lay in bed and hear the buzz of swarms of flies as they came in to clear up the bits of food that were left laying around in the open air. It had taken him two or three days to get used to all this, it was the smells that wafted up and seemed to penetrate the very walls that took the most getting used to, he had, after all, spent quite a lot of time in various parts of the middle and far east.

His apartment was at the corner of the building and he had windows on both sides that he kept open so that he could catch what little breeze there was. The temperature during the day was around one hundred degrees and even now in the evening before the sun went down it was ninety two degrees, the only saving grace was a very large overhead ceiling fan that made a whamp, whamp, whamp sound as it went round and round and kept the air moving. Now he did not even notice these things as he packed up what few belongings he had and took a taxi to the airport. He had the taxi drop him off at the far end of the civilian airport at an unmarked hanger where he knew that the British Air Force had a small contingency housed. Since the British forces had moved out of South Yemen there was no love lost between England and the new Yemen government but every now and then they would allow the Royal Air Force to use this hanger as a staging point. There were only three civilian flights in and out of the airport to Cypress each day and these were always booked well in advance, there would be no hope of him getting a flight out on a civil aircraft today or tomorrow.

He entered the hanger and stepped into a small office. Behind a desk sat a rotund Air Force Sergeant who was busy sweating over a pile of papers, he looked up annoyed that someone should come in and disturb him but when he saw who it was a big smile came over his face and as he lent back in his chair he said, "Well look who it isn't, hello there Indian, haven't seen you in a while, to what do we owe this pleasure?"

"Hello Sergeant" said Indian striding forward and reaching out to shake the Sergeant's hand, "I'm very well except as you see," he raised his leg up to show the Sergeant his cast, "I've been slowed down a little."

"My word, I bet that really does slow you down, what happened?"

"Well you see I was jumped by twenty four Arabs in a dark alley, they managed to break my leg before I killed the last of them, I was the only one to walk away" Indian said with a big grin.

"Oh yes, you're full of shit, now what really happened?"

"Had a slight accident in my hummer, I was in the hospital for a while but now my leg is almost as good as new."

"Well you haven't come here just to chat, what can I do for you?"

Indian had met the Sergeant on many occasions in various parts of the world. The Royal Air Force contingency that was here in Aden at the moment was a small advance unit that was sent into different countries mainly for search and rescue missions, though Indian knew that they had many other special functions.

"I'm in a bit of a quandary, I've been called back to New York in an extreme emergency. I know it'll be impossible to get a civilian flight out of here for at least forty-eight hours so I was kind of hoping that, may be, you'd have a flight that I could hitch a ride on."

The Sergeant sat up roaring with laughter, "We don't have any flights going that far," he said.

"I know that," said Indian leaning on the desk "I was hoping you had a flight going back to the UK or somewhere in that direction."

"What's the matter Indian, no money? Are you broke?" Said the Sergeant.

"Well you're probably right, if I had your money and your pay I'd be wealthy" shot back Indian.

The Sergeant just sat there grinning at him.

"Well now, if you go out through that door," the Sergeant pointed to a door to his left "in the hanger you'll find Lieutenant Jamison, you can't miss him, he stands about eight feet tall and is as skinny as a rat, he's in charge of all the flights coming in and going out. But I'd better warn you he's a miserable old bastard, he's very strict and goes by the book, he's the only one that can get you on a plane but I wouldn't hold my breath if I were you. I wish you the best of luck."

"Well thank you," said Indian going towards the door "I owe you one."

The door led into the hanger, it was huge and there were a number of people doing various things to a number of aircraft. He looked around and just as the Sergeant had said, he could not miss Lieutenant Jamison, he stood a head and shoulders above everybody else, he had his back to him and as Indian approached he said, "Excuse me Lieutenant Jamison?"

The Lieutenant turned around slowly and peered down at Indian over his long hawkish nose, a scowl on his face. "Yes I'm Lieutenant

Jamison and who may you be and what is a civilian doing in my hanger?"

"Lieutenant my name is Indian and I was told to come and see you about possibly hitching a ride back to the UK," said Indian doubting very much if he could get anything from this Lieutenant.

The Lieutenant took a step backwards and gazed at Indian as if he was an article that he was about to buy in one of the local markets. Indian stood there expecting to be escorted out of the hanger.

"Well," said the Lieutenant in a very deep husky voice with a frown on his face, "so you're the infamous Indian, I've heard a great deal about you."

Indian thought, "Oh shit there goes my ride, what the hell have I done that he knows about."

But slowly a great big smile came over the Lieutenant's face, he stepped forward and put out his hand, "well well well, I'm very happy to meet you at last, I believe I'm in your debt."

Indian shook the Lieutenant's hand, his grip was far stronger than expected.

"You have the advantage of me Lieutenant, I don't quite understand, I'm sure we've never met so how can you be in my debt?"

The Lieutenant shook his hand vigorously "I believe, or so I've been led to believe, that a little over two years ago you came to the rescue of a British patrol unit in Niger. You managed to rescue all four men and smuggled them safely out of the country, the Captain in charge happened to be my brother and I've waited, hoping that one day I might shake your hand and thank you."

Indian managed to let go of his hand and stood there blushing, he hated any acknowledgments or complements. "Oh yes I remember, it really wasn't anything, I just gave them a helping hand, they would've got out safely by themselves."

"Well that's not quite how I heard it," said the Lieutenant "I heard a much different account and I thank you, now what can I do for you?"

"Well now," said Indian still a little surprised, "I have an emergency and I need to get back to the States as fast as possible, it's impossible for me to get a seat on a civil air flight for at least twenty four to forty eight hours, I was hoping that possibly you might have a flight going back to England that I could hop a ride on."

The Lieutenant stood and looked at him for moment thinking.

"We have a flight leaving in the next half hour, it's a cargo plane, it has to go down in Cyprus to pick up some cargo and then it'll be flying on. Now let me think, we can't have a civilian flying on a military aircraft." He looked at a sheath of papers that he was holding in his left hand, he pulled out a pen, flicked through the papers and then wrote something down as he said "You are now Warrant Officer R. Indian attached to the Royal Air Force Intelligence Service returning from a special investigative mission if anyone questions you. How does that sound?"

"Well that sounds just fine though I'm not sure that I'm all that intelligent." Indian said with a smile.

"Well then welcome to the Royal Air Force" said the Lieutenant smiling "Do you have all your things with you or do you have to go and get anything?"

"Well thank you Lieutenant, I have all my bags in your office, I'm ready whenever you want the plane to leave."

"Good," grinned the Lieutenant as he turned around and pointed to a plane sitting just outside the front of the hanger "There" he said "take this piece of paper and show it to the Corporal who's in charge of loading and give him your bags. You'd better be quick, we like to keep everything strictly on time."

"I thank you very much Lieutenant," said Indian once again shaking the Lieutenant's hand, "You don't know how much this means to me."

"Then perhaps in some small way I have repaid you, I hope you get back to the States in time to look after your emergency. Better get going" the Lieutenant said and Indian turned to get his bags, "By the way, there's no service on this flight, you'd better get yourself something to eat and drink, just across the road from the airport is a small but excellent Arab bakery, you just have time to get yourself something."

"Thanks again" said Indian and he rushed back and got his two bags from the front office and took them over to the Corporal who was loading the plane. He handed him the piece of paper that the Lieutenant had given him, the Corporal read it and looked up at Indian with a grin on his face. "Welcome to my flight Warrant Officer Indian," he said with more than a little sarcasm in his voice, "Let me load your bags, we'll be leaving in exactly one-half hour."

"Thank you very much Corporal I'm just going to go across the street and get myself something to eat since I've heard that you don't serve meals on this flight."

The Corporal just looked at him quizzically and said, "Oh no Sir we don't serve anything."

Indian rushed out of the front of the airport and was immediately surrounded by three young boys pulling at his pant legs begging him to let them be his guide while he is in Aden thinking that he was a tourist. Indian spoke to them in fluent Arabic, much to their surprise and explained that he did not needed a guide but he thanked them very much and gave them each two American dollars, they happily rushed off down the street. He went into the little Arab bakery, there were wonderful smells, a little wizened old gentleman looked at him expectantly.

"I would like three rooties please." Indian said in Arabic.

The little old man looked really surprised "Welcome to my bakery, it's a pleasure to serve someone that speaks my language. What would you like in your rooties." He said as he pulled out three foot long rolls, crusty on the outside and soft on the inside, freshly baked and cut each one open and scooped out some of the fresh steaming bread from the tops and the bottoms, "we have chicken, boiled fish, beef, lamb and goat" pointing to some pots boiling on an old stove behind him.

Indian knew better than to try the beef that they had here, it was always extremely tough and tasteless. "I would like two with goat and one with lamb please."

The old man put a scoop from the pots into each rooty, the wonderful smells made Indian's mouth water. The old man wrapped each rooty up separately in old newspaper and put them in a brown bag.

"If you have any Coca-Cola I'd like three cans please."

The old man went over to the ice bucket on the floor and pulled out three wet cold cans of Coca-Cola, wrapped them up in newspaper and put them in another brown bag.

As Indian was paying him he asked, "Are you having a party?"

"No I'm taking a flight."

"I see," said the old man with a big grin on his face "the last time I went on a flight all I got was a bag of peanuts." He burst out into a fit of laughter and waved goodbye to Indian who was smiling as he left the bakery and went to catch his plane.

The plane took off on time, Indian's seat was not very comfortable but it was not long before he fell asleep. The stop in Cyprus was very short; Indian just had time to make a phone call to Quiet Sunshine to say that he hoped to be in New York within the next twenty-four to forty-eight hours and then the plane left onward to England. By the time they landed at R. A. F. Grandey in England it was seven a.m. their time.

As he got off the plane a Land rover pulled up and the driver stood up and said. "Excuse me Sir"

Indian looked around; there wasn't anybody else to be seen. "You mean me?"

"Yes you Sir, Warrant Officer Indian," the driver said striding forward and taking Indian's bags and putting them in the back of the Land rover, "I'm Corporal Roberts, we got a phone call from Aden, we've been told to give you the royal treatment. Lieutenant Jamison has given us strict orders to drive you anywhere you want to go if that's all right with you?"

"Boy that's some service, I'd better remember Lieutenant Jamison." Indian thought to himself.

"Yes that would be fine, thank you very much indeed, don't I have to go through customs or anything?"

The Corporal picked up the two bags in the back of the Land Rover, shook them gently and said "Sir, you've just been through customs, that's all taking care of. Where would you like to go?"

"If you could take me to the nearest car rental agency it would be wonderful."

"The closest one is an Enterprise dealership about two miles away, will that do you?"

"Sure that's excellent," said Indian as he jumped into the land rover.

As they pulled up at the barrier at the exit to the camp a military police officer marched over to them very smartly. "What do we have here Corporal?"

"This is Warrant Officer Indian," said the Corporal indicating Indian sitting beside him, "just returning from a special mission in Arabia, I believe you have his clearances, you should have got a phone call from Aden."

The police officer thought for a moment then looked at Indian and said. "That's correct Corporal thank you very much indeed." He strode over and lifted the barrier and they were on their way.

Indian thanked the Corporal and watched him leave before he limped into the Enterprise office, he stepped up to the desk and looked at the two young ladies to see which one would look after him, a dark haired lady came forward and said. "Good morning Sir, how may we help you?"

"Good morning," said Indian "I'd like to rent a car please for one day."

"Certainly Sir, what size car would you like?"

"I would like a fast car," said Indian, he liked to indulge himself when he got the opportunity, "It must be an automatic," he said as an afterthought. He preferred to drive stick shift when in Europe but with his leg in a cast he would not be able to operate the clutch.

"Well let me see Sir," said the young lady clicking away at the computer. "We have a jaguar sedan available, at the moment it's being cleaned, it should be ready in a few minutes, is that acceptable?"

"Yes that would be quite acceptable," said Indian "let's write it up, please put it on this credit card," he handed the young lady one of the credit cards out of his wallet. "I'll take the extra insurance please."

The young lady typed into the computer and then went and retrieved the documents from the printer, she ran through them with him and he signed in all the appropriate places. They had just got finished as the jaguar was pulled to the front. The young lady came out and went around the car inspecting it with him to make sure there were not any scratches or dents.

"It's almost brand new, are you satisfied with it Sir?"

"Yes indeed thank you very much," said Indian as he threw his two bags into the trunk and took the keys. "Now if you could just give me directions to get down to Heathrow airport I'll be on my way."

The young lady went back into the office and came out with a map, she marked the route for him and then he was on his way. He had no difficulty finding the motorway. He enjoyed driving a fast car; he accelerated up to a hundred miles per hour and enjoyed the feeling, he knew he was speeding but nobody in England seemed to stick to the speed limits even though he was going a hundred miles per hour there were still vehicles going past him. It only took about three hours and fifteen minutes before he pulled up in the "Taxi only" parking spot in front of the international departure lounge at Heathrow airport. He jumped out of the car, pulled his bags out just as a policeman came and said, "Sir you can't park here, you must move your vehicle or it will be towed."

Indian looked at him for a moment and thought to himself "by the time I get any tickets or fines it'll be too late."

"Officer, I'm in a great deal of a hurry, please have the vehicle towed" and he threw the keys to the car to the officer who stood there with a very surprised look on his face as he caught the keys. Indian didn't wait to hear anything more, he just picked up his bags and hurried into the airport.

He saw a young man with a luggage cart and signaled for him to come over. "Please take these two bags and follow me to the British Airways counter just over there," he said as he slipped the young man a ten-pound note.

"Yes Sir," said the porter smiling and putting the ten pounds in his pocket "I'll follow you anywhere in the airport for that Sir."

Indian hurried over to the British Airways counter, a young gentleman was standing there and Indian said to him "Excuse me I need to get to New York as fast as possible."

The young man looked up, "Yes Sir, do you have a ticket?"

"No I don't have a ticket," said Indian "What seats do you have available?"

"Sir, you have to book up the seats in advance, let me see what's available," and the young man clicked away on his computer. Indian stood and waited impatiently.

"We have a vacancy on the flight leaving here tomorrow morning Sir I can book that up for you if you wish."

"No," said Indian "that's way too long, I need to get to New York now. What flights do you have leaving in the next two or three hours?"

The young man looked at him and then clicked away on his computer. "Sir we have a plane leaving here in exactly one hour."

"And do you have any vacant seats on that plane?"

"Sir it would be extremely expensive even if we had a seat vacant," the young man said bringing more information up on his computer. Indian waited and then the young man said "the only seat that's vacant in that flight is in first-class, if you were to book that seat at this time it would be extremely expensive."

"And what do you mean by extremely expensive?"

The young man punched in some more information, "that ticket the will cost you one thousand six hundred pounds," the young man said.

Indian thought for a moment and then pulled out his wallet and slid the young man his Visa card. "That'll be fine," he said to a now slightly shocked young man, "Please hurry it up I don't have much time to catch that plane."

The young man's mouth dropped open as he hurriedly prepared the ticket. Indian put one of his bags on the scale and said "I'll just be checking that one bag, the other will be coming on the plane with me."

The young man just nodded "Your passport please Sir."

Indian handed him his passport and a couple of minutes later the young man handed him his tickets, pointed to his right and said "Your plane leaves in less than one hour, you'll have to hurry."

"Thank you," said Indian looking around at the young porter, "Come on young man we have to hurry" and they rushed to go through security.

The flight across the Atlantic was uneventful, he read and dozed off a few times, when they landed at LaGuardia airport, he got a porter to give him a hand with his bags, he had no problem going through customs since he was traveling on an American passport. He tipped the porter and caught a taxi back to the Dojo.

When he was in the building he called Quiet Sunshine on the cell phone and told her that he was safe and sound and that he would probably be staying in New York until tomorrow and would then head out and meet her at the cabin. Quiet Sunshine said that everything was all right out there and that she would talk to him when he arrived. After he had hung up the phone he realized that Quiet Sunshine's voice had been agitated as if something was wrong or something was bothering her, he worried about it for a minute or two and then decided that if anything was really wrong she would have told him.

He went around the Dojo checking to see if Quiet Sunshine had forgotten anything, he knew he would not find much because she was extremely efficient. He repacked his belongings in the side bags of his motorcycle and checked the package that Quiet Sunshine had left under it, he found his throwing knives, a pistol and ammunition, his multi pulley short hunting bow and a sheath of arrows and secured everything to the motorcycle. He tucked the pistol into his waist belt and put the ammunition into his coat pocket. He ordered in some Chinese food from his favorite Chinese restaurant and when it arrived he sat back and switched on the television, he was just in time to catch the very beginning of the President's speech to the nation, he grabbed his crash hat, put it on and plugged it into the radio on the motorcycle and tuned in so he could listen to the President's speech. He pushed a button and the garage door went up, he drove off, pausing only to close the garage door behind him. He roared out of town as fast as he could and was just hitting the highway when the President finished speaking. He opened the throttle and flew down the highway ignoring the speed limits, he knew he had to get to the cabin before the panic began, he relaxed and enjoyed the wind whistling past him and the throb of the roaring engine between his legs. He got to the cabin in half the time it usually took him. The traffic on the main roads was just beginning to get heavy as he turned into the driveway to the cabin.

25

Steam power.

At the transfer station.

The Judge came into the office to find Cassey on the computer.

"Well good morning Cassey, you're up bright and early this morning."

"Good morning Judge." Cassey looked up from some notes that she was making on a pad in front of her "Judge, could you take a couple of hours off this morning I'd like to show you something."

The Judge saw a smirk behind those beautiful eyes as Cassey walked out from behind the desk.

"Sure, what can I do for you? The others can look after everything for a couple of hours."

"Well, I don't want to be mysterious but I'd like to take you somewhere and show you something and see what you think."

The Judge smiled, Cassey loved drama. "Ok, what'll we do? Where are we going?"

"It's only about twenty minutes from here, we can take one of the vans and then you can decide what you want to do about it." There was a playful look in her eyes.

"Ok, let's go."

They went out of the office and moved over towards one of the vans just as Brad was getting out of it.

"Good morning you two, looks like a beautiful day again, I see we've had some containers delivered overnight, I guess we'd better get working and get these over to the camp."

"Brad I'm going to take the Judge out for a short drive, can we use the van?"

"Well sure, where are you both off to?"

The Judge grinned and leaned over and whispered in Brad's ear, "It's a secret, Cassey has a secret."

Brad looked at the expression on the Judge's face and both started to laugh.

"If Cassey gets a secret and she wants to be dramatic she sure can do it."

Cassey slapped Brad on the shoulder.

"Now that's not true, I'm never dramatic but I did want the Judge to tell me what to do about this problem that I have." Brad knew better than to push.

"Ok, well we'll see you two when you get back, the rest of us have got plenty to do around here."

The two of them jumped into the van, Cassey had a map she had downloaded from the internet, the Judge navigated her down into one of the villages and onto a side road where, twenty five minutes later, they turned left into a long driveway. This went through a field and around a hill and then they saw a one floor ranch nestled in a small valley. To the left of the house was a massive metal barn.

"The gentleman here is quite elderly," said Cassey with a wicked grin on her face, "I met him once a number of years ago at a convention and I only just remembered that he was in this area. He used to have this place open to the public but closed it down about five years ago when his wife died and it became too much work for him. I hope he still has his collection because if so you may find it very interesting, he can be a bit cantankerous.

"Collection of what?" asked the Judge only to be answered with that same wicked grin. They pulled up in front of the house, got out and Cassey knocked on the front door. There was no answer so Cassey knocked a little harder, they heard a dog barking inside the house.

"It doesn't look like anybody's home," said the Judge "we should have phoned before we came down here."

"As far as I know the gentleman doesn't have a phone, after his wife died he virtually became a recluse. I hope he's still alive because I had no way of checking."

Then they heard a gruff voice behind the door telling the dog to be quiet, the door opened a crack and Cassey could see an eye looking out at them.

"What d'you want? What're you doing here? I don't like visitors," came a voice through the crack of the door.

"Good morning Jake McGurdy, I don't suppose you remember me, we met at a convention a number of years ago and you and I sat and had lunch, we talked about your collection and I always said that one day I'd love to see it but never got around to it until today. I'm really sorry to disturb you but could we talk to you and maybe you could show us your collection, I presume you still have everything?"

There was silence for a second and the door opened a little wider. The Judge could see an older gentleman, he had to be up in his late eighties or early nineties, a bit of a disheveled figure with a beard, mottled gray and black and a mop of half gray hair tousled and uncombed.

"What's your name, missy, what's your name?"

"You just know me as Cassey, I don't think I ever gave you my last name but just in case I gave it to you and you remember it, my last name is Chads, Cassey Chads, we both share a love of the same equipment."

The door opened a little more and the old man stood there in a scruffy T-shirt and a pair of jogging pants, wearing flip-flops. By his knee there was the brown muzzle of a dog sniffing at them.

The Judge could see the old man trying to recollect who Cassey was and then a light came on behind the old eyes.

"I remember you, we had dinner and shared a bottle of champagne because I'd just won the competition, I remember," and the door went open and he opened the screen door and said, "Come in young Cassey, come in, I don't usually see visitors but come on in."

The Judge let his breath out relieved that the old man had recognized her. They went into the front room of the ranch, it was nicely furnished but the furniture was old and it obviously had not been cleaned in a while. A German shepherd nuzzled and sniffed at them, even the dog looked old.

"Well, you know I don't do any conventions anymore, I don't even let anyone from the public come in anymore, not since mother died." Cassey could see the sorrow behind the wrinkled façade. "Everything's just got too much for me. Couldn't handle it all alone by myself so I just shut the doors up. Me and Bonnie here…" he reached down and ruffled the hair on the top of the dog's head who nuzzled up close to him and sat down at his feet, "we just live quietly. Don't know quite what to do with the place, we try to keep the outside neat and tidy but it's getting too much to look after now, we never had any children and I'm loath to sell it. Can't afford to go into a home."

"Well, Jake," said Cassey giving the old man a big hug, "maybe we can help you a little bit, this is my friend Judge Mortimer."

Jake hesitated for a moment and then shook hands with the Judge, "A Judge heh, nice to meet you."

"Could we see your collection? You still have it all, don't you?" asked Cassey

The old man's eyes opened wide. "Aye, I still have the collection, it's all out there in the barn," he said "I don't know who's going to get it when I pass on, someone will have to look after it. It sure would be a shame to let it just go to waste after all the years of love and tender care I've put into it."

The Judge's interest was peaked, he just stood there itching to blurt out, "What the hell is all this about, Cassey? What's this collection?" But he could see that Cassey was handling this very gently and kept himself in check.

"Well, we didn't want to disturb you too much," said Cassey "Do you think you could show us your collection then maybe I could tell you what we have in mind."

The old man looked at her quizzically. "I guess so, I haven't been in there for some months," he said, "I just keep it locked up, let me fetch the key." He went out to the kitchen, the Judge could see him looking through an old tin. He leaned over to Cassey and whispered in her ear, "What the hell's all this about, Cassey? What's this damn collection? Come on, tell me, I'm itching to know." Cassey looked at him with an "I gotcha" twinkle in her eyes.

"You'll have to hang on just one more minute," she whispered into his ear, obviously enjoying his anticipation. The old man came back in waving a key.

The Judge took a deep breath holding his curiosity in check.

"I got it, this is the key, c'mon I'll show you my whole collection."

The Judge could see the pride in the old man's eyes and he seemed to straighten up a little bit.

"You stay there Bonnie, you stay there and guard the house." The old dog sat down and watched as they walked over to the barn. It took a couple of tries to get the key into the lock and turn it and then the old man opened the door and they all stepped in. As the Judge stepped through the door he saw that the barn was even much bigger on the inside than it looked on the outside and it took him a moment or two to realize that he was looking at a collection of steam-powered machines, there were these huge machines all lined up and down both sides of the barn, they all looked brand spanking new, it looked like they had just been delivered by the manufacturer but even the Judge knew that these must be many years old. The old man stood back pleased at the expression on the Judge's face.

"Wow!" said Cassey walking slowly down the center aisle "When you said you had a big collection you meant it didn't you, they are beautiful!" She stopped and put her hand gently on the front wheel of a steam-powered tractor, rubbing it lovingly. "They're beautiful, did you do all the work yourself?"

It was as if the years had fallen away from the old man, he looked younger. "Yes, everything that's been done to them I did myself all through the years, my wife, God bless her, helped, she had a love for these, too. Now what do I do with them?"

Cassey looked over at the Judge and saw the surprised expression on his face and watched as he realized the possibilities of what Cassey was offering him.

"Are they all steam-powered Sir?"

The old man seemed to shake himself back from the past. "Yes young man, they're all steam-powered and they're all in perfect working condition, I didn't collect or keep anything that couldn't be put back into running order. You can start any one of these up and it'll run like a dream."

"What exactly do you have?"

"Well there's two tractors, they're both about the same age and then there's a thrasher," and the old man led them down the aisle losing himself in memories, his steps a little more spry, stopping every now and then to gently rub a loving hand on a particular piece of machinery, "And then we have the chipper, the bailer, the cross saw," and he went down naming them all one by one. By the time they got to the far end the Judge realized that here was a collection that, if you put them on a farm, you could operate it completely by steam.

Cassey saw the wonderment in the Judge's eyes as he looked at her and she winked.

"Jake," said Cassey gently taking hold of his arm and looking over at the Judge who nodded back at her enthusiastically, "Jake, we have a proposition for you."

By the time they left, one hour later, the Judge had purchased the entire collection along with all the old man's equipment, his tools and his spare parts for a very favorable cash settlement which left Jake very well off and with the knowledge that his collection was going to be loved and cherished just as he had loved and cherished them all through the years. They made an arrangement to return the following day with the cash and move all the equipment out to be picked up on flatbed trailers, the old man was extremely happy. He believed that now he could stay in his ranch for as long as he liked and afford to move to a retirement home when he was ready. As they drove out of the gate, the Judge looked over at Cassey.

"Oh, that was sneaky! That was a wonderful idea! Fantastic! I've never ever even thought of steam, we'll get everybody on it tomorrow, I'll get the cash, it's exactly what we need and nobody ever thought about it. Well done Cassey it's just a crying shame that the old man may not have quite as much time left as he thinks he has."

Cassey drove on with a pleased expression and a smile on her face.

26

Rats.

Consequences

The Hoover Dam the day of the President's speech to the Nation.

Deep within the bowels of the Hoover Dam, some six hundred and fifty feet below the ramparts in one of the cement vents sat King rat. He was a very large creature and he prided himself in the length of his tail as he sat up on his hind legs preening himself. He had lived down here in the holes, nooks, crannies and conduits of this massive cement dam all his life. He could find his way from top to bottom and from side to side passing through any of the walkways or working facilities without ever being seen. He had a very large extended family, of whom he was the King, they all lived throughout the dam. A few months ago while going up one of the vents which ran from the base of the dam right up to the very top with branches going off in all directions every few feet, he had been infuriated to find himself covered from the top of his head to the tip of his tail in a white sparkling powder. He had tried to clean himself off but for days afterwards every time he made a sudden move or went through a very small fissure he left behind him some white sparkling crystals. Much to his surprise he had found out, when the family all got together one evening, that most of the other rats had had a similar contact with a white powder. Since that first encounter he had learned to avoid the areas in question, but to his dismay and to that of the rest of his family there were more and even larger areas of the white crystal. Sometimes it made it quite difficult for him to go from one place to another.

Now he sat preening himself thinking about going up and going out into the cool night air to see what was going on outside his massive home. He heard the steps of one of the maintenance men a few feet above him and he smiled to himself knowing full well that no man could ever find him way down here in the dam.

The man above him was Will Towers, he was a maintenance man who had worked and looked after the dam for the past thirty two years, he had taken the job on as soon as he'd finished his school education and had been there ever since. He really enjoyed his work; he was a very quiet individual who preferred to be on his own rather than mixing with others, he stood five feet eight inches tall with thin brown hair balding on the top. Just last year he had had to wear his first pair of eyeglasses. He was overweight; he weighed in at two hundred and eighty pounds, which at times proved to be a problem moving around in the bowels of the dam. Today was the day of his monthly inspections, he had done them so many times before that all he really had to do was walk up and down and through the various passageways and structures, this day he was thinking about treating himself to a trip to the gay men's bathhouse, something he only allowed himself once a month, he would not allow himself to admit that he was gay but he really did not enjoy women and in his dreams he always made love to some young man.

He ambled through the concrete corridors making sure that he switched off all the lighting as he went from one zone to another, leaving the areas he had inspected lit with only the dull light of the red emergency lighting.

King rat suddenly stopped cleaning himself, his whiskers twitched, something had changed, something was different. He dropped down onto all fours and his coat stood up on end, he could feel a vibration, no not so much of a vibration but of some kind of movement in the cement. He turned and peered down the passageway; in the dull red light he could see at least six other rats frozen in the same pose. His very keen eyesight spotted a slight movement way down at the far end of the passageway, a slight sparkly powdery movement. He let out a warning squeal that was immediately picked up and repeated by the other rats, he could hear the squeals of alarm being spread throughout this lower level. He turned and started running up the corridor as fast as he could, the rats behind him caught up with him and as they past each passageway junction more rats joined them. He led them up the corridors moving as fast as they could knowing by instinct that they had to get out or at least get as far away as possible from this area of the dam.

"Hello George, hello George, do you read me?" Will said into his headpiece microphone. They had had so many problems trying to maintain contact between the people down in the dam and those up in the control center, which was to the very west side of the dam up against the canyon wall. That they had just had this new radio system put in with various relay points set up throughout the miles of corridors that perforated the massive cement structure in all directions. This latest communications system seemed to work quite well but there were still areas where it failed.

"Hello there Will, I read you loud and clear, everything is OK I presume?" Will heard George's voice in his earpiece.

"Yes everything's OK as usual, hang on a second, I hear something." Will stopped moving, he could hear a slight scratching noise coming from one of the other corridors, he moved forward and went down towards his right. The sounds got louder, something was coming up the corridor towards him.

"George, what the hell is this, there's something coming up the corridor, I can't see what it is." George could hear the fear in Will's voice.

"Calm down, calm down Will. Now what is it?"

Will stood terrified against the side of the corridor, he could not see anything moving down the corridor, which was illuminated only by the emergency lighting but he could hear this squeaking scratching sound that seemed to be rushing up towards him.

"George, George I don't see anything but I can hear it, though my God....." and George heard Will's scream, a scream of sheer terror.

Will pushed himself against the cement wall wanting to disappear into it, the one thing that he hated most in life was rushing down the corridor. There must have been ten dozen rats led by this great big brute. They made a moving carpet along the corridor floor their claws making a scratching noise on the cement and they were all squeaking madly. Will watched in sheer terror as they came past him, some actually ran over his feet but they did not seem to even notice him, then the moving carpet suddenly turned up the corridor on the left going up to the next upper level. Will sank down onto the floor sobbing hysterically.

George stood in the control room looking out of the massive observation window through which he could see the entire upper length of the dam and see to the base some seven hundred feet below him.

"Will, Will calm down, what's going on down there?"

Will slowly pulled himself together, calmed his breathing down and managed to stutter, "Rats George, fucking rats, hundreds of the fucking things came tearing up the corridor from lower down and disappeared going up towards the east. If there's one fucking thing that I'm scared of, that's rats. I almost shit my pants; some of them actually ran over my feet. I think I'm OK now."

Will put his hands flat against the corridor wall to push himself up and he felt a vibration in the cement, he stopped moving holding still as the vibration got worse.

"George something's wrong, I can feel a vibration in the cement, I've never felt this before, oh dear God George," Will's voice rose to a scream, "George the dam, the fucking dam...."

Will's voice was screaming in George's earpiece, it turned from a scream into a massive coughing fit, it was so bad and so loud that George had to pull the earpiece out of his ear and hold it in his hand. He stared out of the window, he blinked his eyes and grabbed his pair of binoculars he could have sworn that he had seen two small puffs of smoke come out of the air vents towards the center of the Dam, he felt panic beginning to rise up inside him, he pushed it back down trying hard to stay calm. He could hear Will coughing horribly and choking over the airwaves as he focused his binoculars on the glistening clouds of white dust rising above the parapet of the dam. He swung the binoculars down towards the base, for a second he thought he saw a slight movement in the cement right at the bottom; he lowered his binoculars and shook his head. He stood in sheer horror as he saw, as if in slow motion, right in the center of the dam, a section of the cement from almost the bottom of the dam right up to the top parapets seemed to very gently drop down a few inches as a massive cloud of beautiful white glistening powder came out of the base of the dam.

George stood petrified as the whole central section exploded out of the face of the dam, he heard a massive roaring sound as a wall of water seven hundred feet high came crashing through the center, washing away what remained of the dam on both sides. George managed to slam his hand down on the emergency warning button and the shrill scream of the alarm klaxons reverberated out across the canyon only to have their warning sounds disappear into the deafening roar as the wall of water raced down the narrow canyon following the riverbed. George just stood there frozen, he did not even realize that the coughing in his earpiece had stopped; he stood frozen to the spot as tears started to form in his eyes.

Nobody saw King rat and his followers tumble head over heels as they were washed away down the canyon by the wall of water that had been Lake Mead.

27

The President's speech.

Ruth Goldston slammed the phone down and jumped out of her chair, she stormed out of her office and into one of the main control rooms for C. N. N. in Atlanta.

"What the fuck's going on? Would someone please tell me, what the fuck's going on?" She yelled to the room in general. All heads jumped up and looked at her, Ruth was normally very self controlled and very seldom, if ever, swore and if she did she certainly never used the 'F' word.

"What's the matter?" Asked Fred, her executive assistant, coming out of his office next to her's. "What's the matter Ruth? What's going on?"

"I've just received a phone call," said Ruth calming down a little bit, "I've just been officially informed that the President of the United States is going to make a major speech tonight at five p.m. He has respectfully requested that every radio and television station throughout the United States carry his message live. I say again, and I repeat, he has respectfully requested, which means folks that it is an order. He has asked all major networks and stations to share with their affiliates and with other smaller stations their availability to carry his speech. Furthermore he has again asked that on every hour and every half-hour starting at," she looked at her watch, "five a.m., that's in three-quarters of an hour from now, that every station and network broadcast the following statement and I quote.

"'The President of the United States will make an extremely important speech to the Nation this evening at five p.m. It is imperative that all residents of the United States and all Americans overseas hear this speech.' Now folks something extremely important is coming down the pipe, this has never been done before; it's the first time that any President has ever commandeered the whole of the communication network throughout the country. What's going on? Has anybody heard anything? Are there any leaks? Do we have any inkling what's going to be said this evening?" and she peered around the room. There was complete silence, everybody looked around at everybody else to see if anybody knew anything.

"Well isn't that just wonderful," Ruth said glaring across the room "Here we are, supposed to be the biggest and best news company in the world and we don't have a clue what's going on in the White House. All right everybody start pulling in your favors, get in touch with all possible contacts, find out what the hell's going on. Somebody somewhere must be willing to leak the story. Do I make myself perfectly clear? I want answers fast, get off your arses and get to work folks." And she turned round and stormed back into her office leaving mouths gaping open.

For a few seconds there was silence and no movement and then everybody seemed to leap into action all at once.

While, it seemed, that every reporter in the country tried to find out what was going to be in the President's speech, the whole nation heard every half hour, the short message that at five p.m. that evening the President would make a speech of unparalleled importance. It soon became the most popular thing for discussion and no one wanted to miss the speech. Employers allowed their employees to listen at five. All of the news media was disappointed, there were no leaks, there was not even a hint of what was going to be said. They too had to wait until five and much to Ruth Goldston's disgust she had to wait like everyone else.

At exactly five p.m. the President, accompanied by the Secretary of Homeland Security, entered the press office and faced an overcrowded room of reporters, cameras and microphones. The reporters noticed the President was dressed in a dark charcoal gray suit with a dark gray tie and white shirt and he looked haggard and worried.

"My fellow Americans, good evening" began the President "I have taken this unprecedented step of requesting all stations and networks to broadcast this speech live because what I have to say to you will affect every one in the United States and indeed the world. I have been in contact with the heads of State of most of the other nations in the world and very shortly, they too will be making a similar address to their people. Let me say at this point that everything that I'm about to say has been checked, rechecked, verified and reverified, there are no mistakes, what I'm about to say are true proven facts. Some of you may recall a train wreck in the mountains in northern Oregon some weeks ago; you may also remember the catastrophic plane crash at Chicago O'Hara airport about a week later. I instructed a team of specialists to investigate these two incidents and report back to me, they did so, having read their report I contacted the Secretary of Homeland Security and we dispatched teams of specialists to investigate their findings. These teams have also reported back and verified the facts. As near as we can tell, sometime ago the cement abutment holding up one of the vertical supports at one end of the bridge that collapsed was damaged by a minute meteor, this meteor introduced into the cement a completely new substance, a pure white crystal. This crystal chemically combines with the elements in any and all concrete, cement or mortar and as it combines it replicates itself. It breaks down the tensile strength of the cement. When the bridge abutment collapsed it introduced a cloud of this new white crystal into the air, the crystal is extremely light and can be carried in the wind or by an animal or even an insect. The cause of the plane crash in Chicago was the breakdown of the cement runway caused by this same crystal. As the plane landed a huge cloud of this white crystal was released again into the air. Our teams of specialists have found traces of this new crystal in every major airport throughout the United States. I can assure you, through my discussions with the heads of State of other countries, that they have now found pockets of this infection in all of their major airports and many other structures.

It has spread throughout the United States, we've even found pockets of it in the cement of the White House. No scientific studies thus far have come up with any way to stop or slow down these infestations. The crystals have been spread everywhere by our transportation systems and by animals and insects that have carried them into our basic infrastructure. We have every available team of scientists working on a solution to this major problem, we have to date found no way of foretelling the speed of the deterioration of the cement that is infected.

I am hereby declaring a State of Emergency for the whole country, I have ordered all nuclear power plants be shut down immediately. I have ordered that all nuclear warheads be dismantled and made safe. As of today's date we will be trying to maintain one runway open at all major airports, we can only maintain these open for the next seventy-two hours after which time all airports throughout the country will be closed and all air traffic will cease in the United States except for light aircraft that can take off and land on grass or water, helicopters or vertical takeoff aircraft. I am hereby giving orders for all U.S. military and diplomatic personnel to be brought home immediately. I would recommend that all U.S. citizens overseas come back home. The Secretary of Homeland security will be working with the airlines to provide transportation, free of charge, to all U.S. citizens who wish to come home from overseas within the next seventy-two hours. The indications are, and I must make myself explicitly clear, that there will be, over a reasonably short period of time, a complete and absolute breakdown of all cement structures throughout the world. My fellow Americans this means that there will be no road transportation systems, virtually no rail transportation systems, there will be a breakdown of all electrical power supply systems, most of our waste systems will cease to function, there will be no water supply, any buildings relying on cement foundations will collapse and at this time there is nothing that we can do to prevent these catastrophes from occurring. The only safe way of traveling will be by water but even then any docking facilities made of cement will eventually collapse. I have ordered all military personnel and equipment to be made available to assist the public whenever and wherever possible. I am hereby ordering that the government be moved to a safe and secure location yet to be determined. The only recommendation that I can make to you at this time is to make an orderly move out of the cities and establish communities out in the country. As I have said scientists throughout the world are trying to come up with a solution to this horrendous situation and as soon as they find one we will instigate it and I will report back to you."

The President looked over to his right as a young man came in and handed a sheet of paper to the Secretary of Homeland security who read it and looked over at the President. There was absolute silence in the room as the Secretary gave the sheet of paper to the

President who read it. Some of the reporters noticed that his already gaunt face went even whiter as he read the note a second time.

"My fellow Americans I have just been informed that the Hoover Dam has collapsed and has been washed away, it appears that the towns and cities below the Dam have been destroyed. I don't have any information on the number of people that have been hurt or who have died, this is a very preliminary report. Our hearts go out to everyone who has been affected by this horrendous incident. I thank you for listening to me in this hour of dire need and I ask you all to have patience and keep calm. Thank you very much and may God be with us."

The President and the Secretary of Homeland security immediately left the room that had become completely and absolutely silent.

28

Immediately after the President's speech.

Atlanta.

In C.N.N. headquarters in Atlanta there was complete silence at the end of the President's speech, indeed there seemed to be a complete silence over the whole country as the President's devastating report was being absorbed by the people. Ruth Goldston sat in her office staring at the television, not quite believing what she had just heard although she knew that it must be true. The silence was shattered by two or three phones that seemed to suddenly scream into the silence, Ruth picked up a phone and her face went white as she got her first report on the collapse of the Hoover Dam. She went outside into the general office and looked into the shocked faces of the news crews.

"All right, all right everybody, this is news folks and that's what we're here to report. Let's find out exactly what's happening. Bruce, you pull together whatever you can find on the President's speech, check the background, pull up the stories that can be linked to it, find out about this white crystal, come on let's get on this folks. Anna you take the Hoover Dam project contact the local people down there find out what's going on, the people expect us to report, this is the biggest news story the world has ever seen let's go folks."

People just sat there staring, nobody moved.

"Come on everybody let's jump on this."

Bruce stood up, he had worked for C.N.N. for twenty two years and was one of the senior reporting staff, "I'm sorry Ruth, I have a wife and three children living in a high-rise apartment ten blocks away, if what the President said is true and I have absolutely no reason not to believe him, then my family is in immediate danger. In fact even here it may be dangerous, I'm going home to get my family out of the city, God help us, there's going to be chaos and anarchy and I must try and get my family to safety. I'm sorry Ruth I'm out a here." He grabbed his jacket from the back of the chair and rushed to the elevators.

All of a sudden the office was filled with noise as everybody started talking at once, chairs were knocked over, papers were knocked flying as people grabbed their coats and personal belongings and made a dash for the elevator and the stairs.

Ruth looked on as the huge office complex emptied, in a couple of minutes she was alone. "Oh my God," she whispered to herself. She stood staring across the empty desks and was surprised by a noise behind her; she spun around as Fred, her executive assistant, said, "What the hell do we do now?"

"Holy mackerel you scared the living shit out of me, how come you haven't left with the rest of them?"

"I'm the same as you Ruth, I don't have anyone to rush home to try to save, there's only me and I know that you're in the same boat. So what do we do now?"

"If what just happened here is any indication of what must be happening right across the country the shit has really hit the fan. My God there'll be instant panic everywhere, I think I'll stay up here and do what I've always done, give the people the news for as long as I can. Do you want to help, can we put out the news, just the two of us?"

Fred was silent for a moment.

"I guess I've nowhere to go and nothing to do so let's try and get the news out for as long as possible."

"Okay," said Ruth.

It was as if the President's speech had pulled the stopper out on a bottle of champagne that had been shaken up, there was instant panic and chaos in every city and town across the country. Phones started ringing all over the place, news flashes started coming into the CNN office, everything was going crazy. With the collapse of the Hoover Dam towns and cities further down the river were literally washed away. The hydroelectric generating station and the people on duty at the time were washed away and huge areas across Arizona and Nevada were plunged into darkness.

It was less than an one hour since the end of the president speech, there was a very eerie silence throughout the main control room at CNN headquarters. Fred looked over to Ruth and said, "Well what are our plans Ruth?"

Ruth shook her head, "I guess that the first thing to do is to find out if there's anybody else in the building, I would think that there are others like ourselves, not everyone would have left surely."

Fred nodded and moved over to one of the control panels, he pushed one of the buttons and picked up a microphone.

"Attention, attention, if anybody remains in the building if you are in the building please call extension six four six immediately. This is an emergency check-in, I repeat anyone left in the building, anywhere at all in the building please call extension six four six immediately."

"What now?" He said looking over at Ruth as he put down the microphone.

"I don't know, I really don't know, we're in a very precarious position up here, if things are going to get as bad as they say then we can't stay up here, it just won't be safe. Just what are we going to do?"

Fred just stood there and shook his head and shrugged.

They were both startled when the silence was suddenly broken by one of the speakers on the desk. "Helo-base, Helo-base, Helo-one here, does anybody read me?"

They both leapt forward to push the button on the intercom, Ruth's finger made at first.

"Helo-one, Helo-one, base here."

"Hello base, to whom am I speaking? This is Jack Reuben here."

"Jack, Jack, this is Ruth, it's good to hear your voice, where are you, everybody here has left the building."

Fred looked at Ruth and sat down grinning.

"I'm flying back to base," the speaker said "Ruth it's a total disaster out here, panic is rampant, people are going crazy, it's as if everybody's gone nuts. Nobody can go anywhere there's so much traffic everything has been brought to a standstill, everything is bogged down, we're almost down to gridlock. Even the side streets are blocked. I've seen two over passes that have collapsed with vehicles on them. This white crystal must be damaging everything much faster than they thought. I've seen two building façades, one from a high-rise and one down by the main train station that have collapsed on top of people in their cars, it's absolutely terrible, it's horrific, the worst part is that there's nobody to help and even if somebody wanted to help it would be impossible for them to get through the traffic."

There was silence in the control room for a moment.

"Jack what are your plans when you get here, as far as we know there are only two of us left in the building, I guess it's not safe to stay here."

There was silence for a moment.

"Ruth I have no idea what I'm going to do, I don't have any family here, I live alone, I guess I'll have to try and find somewhere safe to go to, at least I have the Helo. What do you plan to do?"

"Fred and I are like you, we have no one to rush to, we've decided that we're going to try to put out the news for as long as possible and we'll try to keep people informed of the situations. How long would it take you to get back here?"

"I should be landing in about five to ten minutes, I'll come down, where are you, are you in the control room?"

"Yep we'll wait for you here, we'll have to form some sort of a plan but God knows what," said Ruth.

"I'll see you in a few minutes."

And again there was silence in the control room. Suddenly one of the phones shrieked out into the silence, Freddy reached over and grabbed it, "Hello, hello who's this?"

"This is Albert down in the servicing department, you asked anybody to give you a phone call if they're still in the building, well here I am and I don't see anybody else around. What's going on?"

"Hi Albert, this is Fred up in the control room." Fred knew Albert, they had both worked for CNN for many years, Fred was the gentleman who always came up and repaired the equipment.

"Albert why don't you come on up here to the control room it looks like you, I and Ruth are the only ones left in the building, nobody else has phoned in. We need to form some sort of plan of what we are going to do, that is if you're not in any rush to leave the building."

"I've got nowhere to go," said Albert gruffly in the phone, "I'll be up there in a few minutes."

In twenty minutes all four of them were sitting in the control room.

"All right it's agreed that we'll try and put out the news for as long as possible. My worry is what to do if the electricity goes out and how long will the building be safe? It's not just the structural integrity of our building that we have to be worried about, it's all the high-rises around us too, if one of them collapses towards us it could make a terrible mess of this office building."

Jack looked up from the desk, "I don't see any alternative, we have to move out of here, there's just no way to know how long we'll be able to stay and work safely."

Albert had not said a word since the start of the meeting, he had been scribbling on a pad of paper in front of him. "Humph," he said, "Now you know that I was just coming up to retirement in six months, I've worked for this corporation for the last thirty years and what do you know, now I won't even get to see my pension."

The others all looked at him and then Jack began to snicker, Fred burst into laughter and after a few seconds all four of them were roaring with laughter, they sat around the table laughing their heads off. It took a few minutes for them all to recover.

"Well Albert, if you've worked that long for the corporation you should know all the skeletons in the closet, what can we do?"

Albert sat there thinking and then said "Do any of you know about the emergency evacuation procedures that were put in place in President John Kennedy's reign?"

The other three looked really surprised.

"What the hell are you talking about?" asked Ruth.

"Back in the days of the cold war with Russia, it was decreed that in the event of our country being attacked by some nuclear force, there had to be an emergency measures procedure put in place to maintain communications. At enormous cost there was an emergency broadcasting bunker built in the top of one of the hills about sixty miles from here, apparently there were quite a few built all over the country, it's a self-sufficient unit. Every six months since it was completed, it has been inspected and upgraded to ensure that it's readily available and in full working order with the most modern equipment. I only know about it because on numerous occasions I've had to go up there and assist them in sorting out problems they had putting in new equipment. The idiots didn't know what they were doing. Its location was a closely guarded secret by the government and only a few people knew about it. Somewhere up in the director's office is the full emergency procedures measures plan, the exact location of the unit and all the necessary information to gain entry. I believe he keeps it in his private file cabinet."

The other three sat there with dumb founded expressions on their faces.

"Well I've never heard of it, I know nothing about it," said Fred.

"Nor have I," said Ruth looking over at Jack who just shook his head.

"Well I assure you that it exists, it's a completely self-contained unit with quite a large broadcasting section and four or five bedrooms and bathrooms. There's a natural well supplying water and a generator for the electricity should the main supply be cut. There's sufficient dry tack and canned foods etc to last twenty people for approximately one year. It's very sparsely furnished but it is fully functional, perhaps we should consider moving up there. It's a natural cave that has been sealed off at the opening with very thick cement security doors, even if the cement were to crumble at least we would be safe inside a cave I would imagine," said Albert. "We could always replace the cement entrance with wood."

"I think that's a fantastic idea," said Ruth with a grin, "If it's as secret as you say then there shouldn't be anything around it or anything that could attract attention to it, we should be fairly safe for a while."

"I agree," said Fred "Let's go up to the director's office and see if we can find these emergency procedures."

Jack just nodded and got up and they followed him to the elevators, the director's office was four floors up, Fred pushed the button and they could hear the noise of the elevator as it came up.

"Excuse me folks," said Albert "do you think it's safe for us to ride the elevator, especially all of us in one elevator."

"My God, you're right," said Ruth pulling away from the elevator "if we lost the power we would lose the elevator, we could all be stuck in there forever."

The other three moved back away from the elevators as if it was the devil itself.

"Well," said Jack "guess it's the stairs, we'll get our exercise today."

They all moved over to the staircase and started up.

It didn't take long to find the brown manila envelope in the bottom of the director's private filing cabinet, it had been locked but Albert popped it open with a screwdriver that he had in his pocket. They spread the contents of the envelope out on the director's desk and each one of them began reading bits and pieces of it.

"Well," said Ruth pointing to a piece of paper, "looks like you're right Albert, it's all here just as you said it would be, it even says that the generator can be used intermittently for up to twelve months and you're right about the water and it's fully stocked with dry rations, boy I hate the thought of eating dry rations. Looks like it might be the best idea for us."

"I'm looking at the schematics, it looks as if, should the cement frontage collapse we would still be safe in the cave and here are the card keys to get in," said Albert holding up a set of card keys and two very weird looking keys.

""Well I guess that seals it, I vote we move there as fast as possible."

They all nodded their heads in agreement.

"Well, you know we're not going to make it by road, we'll have to go in the helicopter, thank God we've got one," said Jack.

"I just had a thought," said Ruth "we've got that cafeteria downstairs with every possible food imaginable, it services every body in the building for coffee breaks and lunches and sometimes for dinners. We should pack up all the non-perishable goods or at least as much as we can carry and take them with us. I hate the thought of eating dry tack for the next six to eight months."

"I agree," said Jack "we'll have to make two or three trips in the copter to move everything but we can do it. I suggest we get going, let's get down to the cafeteria and start packing everything up and taking it up to the roof."

"Oh my God, up and down to the roof by the stairs carrying all that stuff, I'm not sure I'll be able to do too many trips," said Fred.

"Listen, I have an idea, let's go down and pack everything up and put it beside the elevator, we can send the goods up and down in the elevator with nobody in the elevator with it. Two of us can go to the top and take it off and two of us can stay down on the bottom to load the elevator. If the electricity goes off the only thing that we'll lose is a load of food. We may be able to get all of it into one elevator load and only have to take one chance."

"That's an excellent idea," said Fred and they all moved off down the stairs to the cafeteria.

"I'm going to make a slight foray on my way down and get a few special tools from the service department that I think we may need, I'll meet you in the cafeteria, it'll only take me a minute or two."

"Okay," said Ruth, they were feeling a bit better now they had a plan of action. "I'll just be a minute or two and will meet you down there."

While the others were going down and starting to pack up everything useful they could find in the cafeteria Ruth set up a recorded loop that went out over and over again across all the broadcast bands, both television and radio, anybody tuning in would hear, "We apologize for any inconvenience this may cause but CNN is suspending all television and radio broadcasting for a few hours while we regroup. As you can imagine this very volatile situation has caused us to make some major changes in our location and transmissions. Please keep tuned in. We'll be back on the air within a few hours. We will be broadcasting on all radio bands starting with the ham radio bandwidths. Again we apologize for the inconvenience but hope to be back on the air as soon as possible."

They had no problems with the elevators but it took them most of the night to pack up everything and move it to the roof. By the time they got it up to there they were all very tired and were finishing their third large flask of strong coffee.

"Well that's it," said Albert with relief in his voice "I think we got every damn thing except the kitchen sink. Ok, how're we going to get this across to the cave?"

"Well, in the first load I think Jack had better take you, Albert, with him since you're the only one who knows where this place is. Do you think you can find it from the air?"

"Sure, no problem, that's how we always got there, flew in by helicopter. There really aren't any roads going to it, they were very careful to hide this place."

"Ok then, let's load this helicopter up and then Albert and I will take it over and unload. If it's as well hidden as you say it is and if there's nobody around, we can check that when we fly in, we can just unload this stuff and leave it by the front door. How does that sound?"

"Sounds good to me," said Fred picking up a box and handing it up to Jack who was in the helicopter "That'll give us two people at this end to load and two people at your end to unload. Let's get this thing done."

It took them half an hour to get as much into the helicopter as possible. By the time it was loaded they estimated that it would take five flights to take everything and everybody to the cave.

"Well," Albert heard over his headphones "where the hell is it? I don't see anything that even looks like a cave."

Albert was searching the ground below them.

"You see that slight hill over there on the right hand side, the one with the big group of evergreens on top, that's it."

"Are you sure? I can't see anything that resembles a cave."

As the helicopter swooped in lower Albert said, "There, you see that bunch of shrubbery just at the base of that little cliff face, that's it, the entrance is in amongst the bushes there."

Jack scrutinized the little cliff face and the bushes as they came down and landed on a flat grassy spot within thirty feet of the bushes.

"Are you sure you're right, I still don't see anything."

"I'm sure, I told you it was hidden, this was meant to stay completely unknown to anybody except in a case of an emergency, after all these years it's finally going to be used."

They waited until the rotors had stopped and then jumped out. Albert moved over to the bushes, there was no pathway, no walkway and no footprints, nothing that would indicate what was behind the greenery. Albert moved between the bushes with Jack right on his shoulder and as they moved away the last of the branches Jack was amazed to see a patch of cement. It was about nine feet tall in a semicircle and about twelve feet across at the bottom and in the middle was a large metal door with a small plaque attached that read EBS 48. There was no other identification anywhere that Jack could see. Albert moved forward with the set of special keys he had obtained from the boss's office, he inserted the keys and a small door slid down exposing a keypad. Jack looked down at a piece of paper in his hand and tapped out the numeric code. They heard a loud click and the door cracked open about three inches, Albert slipped his finger around the edge and the door opened smoothly without a sound and they stepped into the cave. Much to Jack's amazement the lights came on automatically and they found themselves in a very large room stacked full of broadcasting equipment and workstations.

"My God, you were right! Well done, old boy, well done," Jack said patting Albert on the shoulder "This is amazing, nobody would ever have known it was here, some body did a good job at disguising this. Ok, what do we do next?"

"Well, let's lock her back up again and we'll just unload all these boxes back here in amongst the bushes just to keep them out of sight and then we'll go back and move the rest. Question for you, Jack, how much fuel do you have in the copter?"

"Don't worry about it, there's a filling station on top of the CNN building and I know of at least five other rooftop filling stations that are set up across the city for various enterprises with helicopters, we should be just fine. I may have to stop a couple of times to top her off."

"That's wonderful I was beginning to worry about it a little bit," Albert said as he moved back and started to unload.

Their estimate was almost correct, it took them six loads to get everything over to the cave. Ruth and Fred went with the last load.

As they took off Ruth looked down ruefully at the rooftop, "God, the years I've spent in that building, I always thought that I would retire going out the main door into the street, I never thought I would be fleeing off of the roof. How life changes when you least expect it."

There was silence for a moment then, "You and I both," said Fred "I was really looking forward to retirement but Lord only knows what the future has in store for us now."

There was silence in that final flight, each of them keeping their thoughts to themselves. Both Ruth and Fred were equally amazed as they came in for a landing not being able to see the slightest markings to indicate that there was a broadcasting station anywhere nearby except for the marks in the grass where Jack and Albert had moved back and forth with the piles of boxes that now were bursting out of the bushes.

Albert came forward and called, "How do, how do, welcome to my motel, hope you'll be very comfortable here, we have a bedroom and a bathroom for everyone. This motel is self-contained, all you need is a change of clothes, we do have valet parking and a steward will be down to pick up your bags. Please step forward to the main lobby and sign in, we accept MasterCard, VISA and any other damn charge card, all entertainment is included, this is an all-inclusive resort, as long as you do it all yourself," he laughed. They all started to giggle and ended up roaring with laughter.

They were amazed at the inside structures within the hill, they found a number of bedrooms and bathrooms and a very large kitchen and eating area and a recreation room with exercise equipment, television, radios, comfortable couches, books, most of which were classics and a store room full of clothing, everything from underwear to overalls. Then Albert took them on a tour behind the control room showing them the generator system, the power system and the inside well pumps, it was indeed a self-contained unit.

"I believe that is supposed to be a blast-proof door at the front, funny isn't it, it's made to withstand man's attempts to open it and yet we know that sometime in the very near future it will just crumble before our eyes. We're going to have to replace it with a wooden structure fairly soon."

"Well, if you folks don't mind, I think we should get back up on the air again as soon as possible and we need to hide that helicopter somewhere or somehow or move it away from the building. Jack, if it's alright with you, do you mind flying around to see what's going on out there after you've had a rest?"

Jack nodded.

"Ok then, let's get this place up and running and then we'll unpack and put stuff away, it looks like we're going to be here for a while folks."

"Albert, you know this equipment, I presume that we're on the electrical grid as well as on the generator."

"We sure are, the generator will kick in if the main lines break down. Let's go and get it all running."

It was amazing, everything clicked on smoothly as if the place had been used regularly everyday. Fred and Ruth were astonished as things came on line.

"Ok," said Jack as Albert handed the microphone to Ruth, "that's it, you're up and running, ready to broadcast."

They were all exhausted but Fred went over and checked the router's international reports coming in and other recording devices from all over the country, there were still some that were in operation. He handed Ruth a stack of reports as the printer spat them out.

"There you go, Ruth, you take first watch, I'll get a nap for a couple of hours or for as long as you can stay awake then I'll relieve you and then Albert can relieve me."

They saw the shocked expression on Albert's face.

"No, no, no, no, I'm in maintenance, I look after the equipment, I don't go on the air, never have been, never will be, I'm not a reporter."

The three others burst out laughing at Fred's terrified expression.

"No sweat," said Ruth trying hard not to roar with laughter at poor Albert. "It's not difficult, all you have to do is sit here and read from these papers, there are stacks of them. These reports, of course, will be dwindling pretty fast I would imagine, you've just got to read them into the microphone, that's all you have to do."

"That's all, that's all, you expect me to read to millions and millions of people. They're all out there listening. I can't do it, I just can't do it, I mean, I can maintain the equipment but I can't read to thousands of people."

"Don't worry," said Fred "we'll show you how to do it. Maybe we'll break you in slowly by letting you read a report here and there and let you get used to it but if everything's running, what else have you got to do?"

There was something of a long silence and then Albert said, "Well, ok if we do it a little bit at a time I'll try it but if I make a big mess I'm not going to do it."

"You'll be fine," said Jack stifling his laughter "you'll be just fine, don't worry, you can do it."

"I guess, Jack, once you can't fly anymore you can give us a hand on the microphone to," said Ruth.

Jack stopped dead in his tracks, swallowed his last laugh and looked a little bit shocked. They all watched him and then he said, "Um, um, I don't know if I could do that, I'm used to speaking into the microphone of a helicopter but not reporting directly."

"You can do it," said Albert "No problem, man if I can do it, you can do it." They all burst out laughing and let the nervous energy escape until Ruth began to cry with laugher. Ruth turned around and sat down at the console, there was a click as she turned the microphone on and the others moved away from her.

"Hello everyone, hello, then she realized that they hadn't switched off the loop being broadcast from C.N.N. headquarters. Ruth looked at Albert who raced over, threw some switches and then nodded at Ruth.

"Hello everybody," she looked over at Albert who nodded at her smiling and indicated for her to carry on, she was now live. "This is C.N.N., your news center, coming back up on the air, we apologize for not being able to broadcast for the last few hours but, as you can imagine, we have been extremely busy regrouping and sorting out just what we can and what we cannot do. We are unable, because of the lack of personnel, to do any television broadcasting whatsoever, you will not receive any pictures but you will still be able to pick up the sound. We are broadcasting on as many radio frequencies as possible, you may have to do a little bit of searching to find us. We are also broadcasting on the ham radio bandwidths and again you may have to do some searching to find us. As you can imagine, we are extremely short of personnel, nearly everyone went home immediately after the President's speech to look after their families, friends and loved ones. We will continue to monitor all incoming reports as long as our routers and information centers are in operation. If you have anything you would like to report to us we would be much appreciative. Again, as you can imagine, we do not have anybody at all in the field, we are relying on our incoming information channels and hopefully reports from you. Our phone number here is," and she gave out the phone number, "again, we may have only one or two people to answer phones so if you get a busy signal, please keep trying. We are also monitoring the ham radio frequencies so you can report in that way to, all right, that's it. We can catch up on some of the reports of what's been happening around the country and around the world while we've been off the air. I have a large stack of reports here, we don't have anyone here to edit, check, or verify any of these reports so I'll be reading them verbatim, please bare with us."

Ruth smiled, relaxing into her chair, it had been a number of years since she herself had broadcast live, it brought back some sweet memories and she realized that she was extremely tired but was actually doing the fundamental core duties that she had started off with many years ago when she had been talked into going into broadcasting by a friend of her professor at the university. She picked up the first sheet of paper, glanced over it, turned back to the microphone and began to read the news. Reports came in and the flow seemed to speed up, the Bluewater Bridge at Port Huron collapsed, the tunnel under the

Detroit river caved in. Overpasses on numerous roads broke up blocking other roads below. Airport buildings collapsed, huge pieces of high-rise buildings fell off blocking streets, the tunnels to New York City flooded all within three days of the President's speech.

29

Hope Valley Ranch.

Idaho

The evening of the President's speech to the nation.

"What the fuck are we doing here?"

"Shut up Mike," said his wife.

"Why does the old man want us to be here for this goddamn speech, we could've been at home and who wants to listen to the goddamned President's speech anyway, it's just gonna be another bullshit speech. Why do we have to do as the old man wants all the time?" Mike spat out at his wife as he pulled the Cadillac esplanade into a parking spot in front of the huge family home.

The Shelby family had been living in the valley since 1850; the homestead had passed from one generation to the next. It was a huge parcel of land, over ten thousand acres, that encompassed the whole of the Kilowatt Valley. In the early years it had been developed into a huge farm to support the large family and it had been easy to defend, when necessary, since the only entrance to the valley was through a narrow gorge between two very steep hills. Before you actually got from the road into the gorge there was a deep cut in the valley floor from the Eupachala river that had worn its way down leaving vertical sides that dropped approximately ninety feet to the now gently meandering water below. The ancestors had built a wooden bridge across the river that had eventually been replaced with a modern day cement structure and as you turned off the main road onto the cement driveway leading to the bridge great big brick pillars had been erected with a metal arch crossing the top from one to the other and, in large wrought iron letters, it read 'Hope Valley Ranch'. After you passed over the bridge you came out of the gorge between the two hills and the valley spread out before you, it was excellent land for cultivating, a river ran gently through it, eventually flowing across the front of the property. The original Shelby family had started out cultivating only a small area around a small farmhouse but as the years passed and the family grew the farmhouse was enlarged and enlarged, it now had ten bathrooms, ten bedrooms, a living room, a recreation room, two sunrooms and the pride of the household was what they called the great room. This was the center of the house from which all the other rooms led. It had a ceiling that was forty-five feet at the peak, at one end there was a hot tub, and the rest was a sitting room, recreation and games room. Grandpa, General Shelby to his close friends and Grandpa to all his relatives, owned the whole valley, he had spent thirty-five years in the military and had retired ten years ago from active service but had acted as an advisor to the President on certain special projects. Since retirement he had spent his life happily at the family ranch reading military histories and replaying famous battles and maneuvers with his miniature armies. He spent many hours in one of the sunroom making the molds, casting the figures, filing them down and painting them, he had, perhaps, one of the best collections of military miniatures in the United States and possibly even in the world.

"Ok, let's go and see what the old bugger wants. This is gonna be dead boring," said Mike as they got out of the vehicle and headed for the massive oak door entrance.

"Now you behave yourself Mike, you know that Grandpa's been really good to you, he let you build that house down at the front of the valley and he even let you put in those massive storage tanks for your business."

Mike was in the heating fuel business and supplied diesel to the various farms in the area, it had taken a lot of wrangling and even some bribery to get permission to put in the huge underground tanks on the private property in the valley so that he could deliver oil and diesel around the countryside.

"I didn't really need the old bugger's permission, he only gave it to us because I was willing to pay rent to him. Shit! You're his granddaughter, why should we have to pay him any money at all, one of these days this place will belong to you and your brothers anyway."

"You'd better behave yourself, you know what Grandpa's like."

They went through the oak doors, down a most impressive corridor completely encased in beautiful carved oak and into the grand room, off to the right in the living room area they could see the group of family members sitting around.

"There's the old bastard, look, sitting on his throne like Lord Muck." He was referring to a great big magnificent Victorian armchair; pierced back, pierced wooden arms, upholstered in fine purple fabric and there, seated in it, was Grandpa who was now in his late eighties with a mop of shocking white hair, white goatee and white sideburns. He sat lounged in this, his most favorite comfortable chair smoking his corncob pipe watching the smoke waft upward to be caught in the fans that were gently turning in the high ceiling. He hardly seemed to see them as Mike and his wife sat down with the rest of the family.

Dad, Grandpa's only son, stood up, "Well, I think the whole family's here now, Mike, you and Jody are the last two. Thank you all for coming, Grandpa thought that we should, as a family, be together to hear this speech."

Grandpa looked around the room and nodded then went back to staring at the smoke rising from his pipe.

"Grandpa seems to feel that this may be a very important speech, after the speech is over Mother has made some refreshments." He sat down and put his arm around his wife's shoulders, she was a large very attractive woman with a mane of unruly reddish-brown hair, she had looked after the farm and raised their six children, five boys and Jody, she had seen the family through good times and bad. She had lost one son in the Viet Nam War who was buried in the family graveyard on the top of one of the hills overlooking the entire length of the valley. This was her spot to go to when things got to be too much; this was where she had her quiet time. She loved to have all the family around her and her main joy was to cook for the whole family.

Immediately to her right was the oldest son Paul who was holding the hand of his wife, a very beautiful young woman ten years his junior, Juliana, at their feet sat their two teenage daughters fidgeting and pinching one another, they never seemed to get along. To her right was the second oldest son Dennis, Dennis had lost his wife in a car accident ten years ago and had never remarried, he was a very big man standing six foot six inches tall with no fat on him at all, he ran a building company and a house moving business, Grandpa had given him permission to set his business up in the valley and much to everyone's surprise it had proven to be very lucrative. To Dennis's right sat the next oldest son Frank, snuggled in between his legs was his wife, Joyce, they ran a veterinarian business from the valley, they had both wanted children but had been unable to do so, so they spent a lot of time spoiling their nieces and nephews. To their right sat the fourth oldest son Daniel with his wife Matilda, they had been married the longest and had five children all of whom were laying around on the floor on great big pillows whispering and giggling together, they had three boys and two girls, the oldest boy was now eighteen, he was just finishing high school and preparing to go to college to be a lawyer. Then to their right sat Mike and Jody making themselves comfortable or as comfortable as Mike ever seemed to get wiggling and complaining in his chair.

Dad pushed a button and a huge high definition television was lowered down above the fireplace.

"Mike, you just made it in time, the President's due on any minute now," he said pushing another button and the television came to life.

"Ladies and gentlemen, the President of the United States of America," boomed out from the hidden speakers giving them a surround sound effect.

"Ok, let's see the silly old bastard," Mike mumbled showing his dislike.

Grandpa stopped puffing on his pipe in the middle of a draw, brought his eyes down from the ceiling fan and glared at Mike whose wife nudged him hard in the ribs, he looked at her and cast his eyes down unable to meet Grandpa's.

All the family lived in the valley, there was the veterinary clinic attached to which was a nice one-story home, there was the fuel distribution business that had an office and a nice residence, two of the boys had homes built behind the main house and those sons worked the farm, Mom and Dad kept an eye on everything. Dad's pride and joy were his fifteen Clydesdale horses, he had built them up over the years as show and work horses and he could spend every moment of his waking days looking after them, mucking out their stalls, keeping them clean and showing them off at local fairs and events, his horses were renowned throughout the country. Through the years the amount of land that was being worked had grown exponentially, Dad and both of the sons that were now working the farm had moved the family business into areas such as greenhouses as well as the fields of corn, oats, soy beans and around the river as it meandered slowly and majestically through the valley they had sheep, cattle, horses and even some llamas. Mom loved to work the land, every year she herself worked up ten acres and supplied the whole family with every possible vegetable you could imagine, she grew so much that she used to set up a small stand beside the main entrance at the road and now the grandchildren made themselves pocket money by picking the excess food and fruit and selling it on the weekends to passersby.

They sat in complete silence as they listened to the President's speech. Grandpa cast his eyes around, watching the expressions on the faces, even the great-grand children quieted down, he saw all kinds of expressions pass through his family as they slowly realized what the President was saying.

As the President signed off there was complete and absolute silence in the room, you could hear the squeak, squeak, squeak of one of the ceiling fans at the far end of the huge hall.

"I've been meaning to fix that damned squeak for months," thought Dad to himself as he pushed the button and the television went black and disappeared into its hidden alcove on the enormous stone chimney. The silence continued for a couple of minutes and then Mike moved in his seat.

"What does that stupid old fart know about anything anyway, he's gotten everything wrong since he was put into office. He's gotten this wrong, too, you watch, we'll all be laughing about this in a few weeks."

All the adults in the family threw dirty looks at him and they all started talking at once; questions, answers, heated voices, two of the young women were crying, even the great-grandsons and great-granddaughters were talking and arguing. Grandpa sat in his chair watching the smoke from his corncob pipe rise up into the ceiling fan. The arguing and discussion and questions carried on for ten minutes and then Grandpa cleared his throat, it was as if someone had switched off the television, there was almost instant silence and all faces turned to the old man who sat there, pipe in hand, watching the smoke from his pipe rise up into the ceiling fan.

"Has anybody got one of those new fangled goddamned cell radio phone things?" Grandpa asked in his thick deep gruff voice, a voice used to commanding men, a voice that demanded people's attention, a voice that Grandpa very seldom used, a voice that had basically retired when he had retired from the army. He had got tired of issuing orders, delivering lectures, heading up meetings, talking, talking and more talking so in his retirement he enjoyed watching and listening to people and only spoke when he thought it was really necessary so his question really surprised his family.

Joyce fumbled in her purse and passed a cell phone down to Dad.

"Dial this number please," Grandpa said to his son, he dialed the number, pressed the send button and handed the phone to Grandpa. There was silence in the room, every one was wondering why the hell Grandpa was using a phone, he never used a phone.

"Pattern here," Grandpa heard over the cell phone.

"Good evening, Pattern, thank goodness I got through to you, General Shelby here."

"Well, good heavens, hello General Shelby, haven't heard from you in a few years, how are you doing in your retirement?"

"I'm wonderful. Pattern, I've just listened to the President's speech, I know your position, we've worked together three or four times on different projects for the President, what's your take on all this?"

There was silence for a moment and Pattern's voice got serious.

"General it's all true, I've been working on this project since the very beginning and, believe me when I say to you, that it's worse than what the President has presented. I believe he's about a week too late in his announcement but that, of course, was his decision, the inevitable effects of the crystal are, as we speak, multiplying horribly."

Grandpa sat quiet for a moment. "May I ask you what you propose to do and do you have any recommendations for me?"

"Sir, I along with some very close friends, have just finished a move to a very isolated camp. In short, and I'll be as brief as possible because God knows the cell phones are so busy we may lose the connection at any moment, I recommend to you complete and absolute isolation, self-sufficiency and self-protection. We are preparing for a minimum of five years away from civilization, if I may be so blunt General, you've just embarked on another war, you're at war with everybody else in the United States for your own survival. Make a move, move as fast as you possibly can to protect you and yours, give no quarter, take no prisoners and prepare for the very worst."

Grandpa sat listening to the phone, watching the smoke rise up and swirl around in the fan above him.

"Thank you Pattern, I appreciate your directness, I thought it had to be that bad when I heard the President's speech. I hope that you're safe and I'll act upon your recommendations immediately."

"General I can't emphasize how fast you need to move, even as we speak I believe the world is going to pieces. Fantasize your very worst scenarios and believe me when I say they're going to come to pass exceedingly quickly. We have a ham radio here," and he gave the General his call sign and wavelength, "if you can get your hands on a ham radio you could stay in touch. I wish you the very best, the most important thing is immediate isolation and protection."

"Understood, we'll be in touch by ham radio, thanks again. I wish you and yours well." Grandpa said and handed the cell phone back to Dad who hit the 'call end' button. Grandpa sat back and watching the smoke from his pipe rise up into the ceiling fan, there was absolute silence in the room.

Grandpa's eyes came down from the smoke and he looked around his family.

"It's worse than what the President has said, we need to take immediate action." He straightened up, his eyes twinkling, his son noticed that he looked like ten years had just dropped off him. "Does anybody have any dynamite?"

Everyone's faces showed the shock they were feeling.

"What the hell do you want dynamite for?" said Mike glaring at Grandpa.

"I have some, I use it very occasionally when we have to move houses and put in basements."

"How much do you have?" asked Grandpa getting up from his chair holding his corncob pipe in his left hand and slowly walking around behind the chairs his family were sitting in.

"I've got sufficient to maybe blow half of one of those mountains out of existence, it's all locked up quite securely in a special shed away from everything else. I'm the only one with keys to it."

The General stood up and walked slowly behind his family.

Mike turned to his wife and whispered, "What the hell does that old fart want dynamite for now, he's gonna do something stupid."

Almost before he'd finished his sentence his head was jerked around as Grandpa grabbed his hair and literally lifted him out of his seat, turning him to face him. Mike found his face only inches away from the old man's face, pain screaming in his head.

"Listen you revolting little man, this old fart has seen more, done more and killed more people than you can possibly imagine. I've seen wars on over five continents, I've seen men die horribly; I've issued orders that meant that hundreds of young men who deserved to live more than you do have had to die. I've put up with you since you married my granddaughter, I've put up with your stupidity, your self-indulgence, your rudeness and your ill treatment of my granddaughter, it ends here and now. If I have to correct you one more time you will be sent out of this valley; sent out of this valley to find out what's going on in the world, to live by yourself, to be self-sufficient and I hope to God that you manage to live long enough to realize that you should have listened to this old fart."

Mike was dropped unceremoniously back into his chair, face bright red, anger seething through him, shocked and amazed at the strength and power the old man had, not just in his hands but also in his voice, he sat there trying to gulp for air. Grandpa took a puff from his corncob pipe, watched the smoke rise up in front of him completely calm gathering his thoughts.

"Alright family the situation, as I said, is much worse, we have to act immediately, people will be fleeing and I mean fleeing from the towns and the cities into the country. As of right now there is no law and order, no emergency services, no medical aid or hospitals, everyone will be going to look after his or her families, the people who have the most fire power and who are willing to do anything are the ones that will survive, we have to look after ourselves. Daniel, you and Frank, take the dynamite and blow up the front pillars, take the backhoe and make it look like there was nothing ever there and then, blow up the bridge, drop it down into the gorge."

There was one collective gasp from them all.

"Dad, what do you mean blow up the bridge?" Grandpa's son asked the question they all wanted to ask.

"There'll be hundreds and thousands of people flooding into the countryside trying to find somewhere to live, somewhere to be safe, this valley will be a prime target, half the surrounding people in the countryside know of our existence, they must be stopped from flooding in here, we have to become completely self-sufficient and I mean immediately. If somebody moves before we do then you may get hundreds of people driving into the valley any moment now, make the exit from the road look as natural as possible, tear up the driveway so people who don't know where we are won't be able to recognize that there is, or ever has been, a driveway into the valley. We need to do this as of ten minutes ago."

"I'll come give you a hand," said his oldest grandson "Grandpa's right, if the roads collapse, the bridges collapse and the buildings in the towns and cities start to collapse all those people won't have anywhere to go, we can't support them all, God help us, they can't come and live in our valley."

At that moment his Grandpa was proud of him. "You and you," he pointed at Jody and one of other grandsons, "you two, you're excellent shots, get two rifles from out of the gun cabinet, take the ammunition and go with those two, set yourselves up so you can cover them from inside the gorge. Now listen, if necessary, you will stop anyone who gets in their way, I don't care who it is."

Grandpa saw the faces of some of his family members go white.

"Now listen Grandpa," said Samantha, one of his grandchildren, "what about school, what about my friends, I'm supposed to be going to a concert this weekend, you can't blow up the bridge I won't be able to get out."

Grandpa could hear the panic in her voice, he moved over slowly and sat down in his chair, taking a deep puff of his pipe, watching the smoke rise up into the ceiling fan once again,

"Listen, you're all my family," he began slowly, "you all know what I've been through and how I've lived all my life in the military, you're just going to have to trust me on this. Imagine a world where the buildings are falling down into the streets, in the country the houses are collapsing as the basements and the foundations disintegrate. Imagine a world where there's no running water, where the electrical pylons have collapsed and there's no electricity. Imagine a world where there's no communications because the towers have collapsed and when the electricity went out you could no longer recharge your batteries. Imagine a world where there's no sewage system, where the roads were impassible because bridges had collapsed and because the roads themselves have broken up into pieces. Imagine a world where there were no jails and there were no law enforcement officers. Imagine a world where there were no emergency services, no fire departments, no police, no hospitals, no doctors available anywhere. Imagine a world gone crazy where the people who had the guns got what they wanted and people without the guns did as they were told or they died. Imagine a world where there's no supply of food, no supply of water, no supply of goods, no supply of transportation, a world gone completely crazy. A world where there are no concerts. A world where you can't get a hold of your friends because they'd moved fast and furious into the country trying to find a safe haven. This is the world that is now in place. People, this very instant, are coming to grips with the fact that they have to look after their own to find them places to live safely, places where they can protect the ones they love. That world that you are imagining is the world that we are now living in. You are now living in that world and, trust me, the only people who survive are those who move extremely fast to protect their own. Now, does anyone have any objection to us isolating the valley by blowing up the bridge?"

He watched them and saw the understanding creep across most of their faces, he was genuinely surprised because it was the young people who seemed to grasp this news before some of the adults. Nobody said anything, there was silence in the room.

His oldest grandson stood up, "You're right Grandpa, let's go." Daniel and Frank jumped up, nodding at each other, Jody got out of her chair and Michael stood up and grabbed her arm, she looked at him, a look that would've shriveled up a bull elephant.

"Don't say a word, Mike, not one word, just do as you're told."

Mike let go of her arm as if he'd got an electrical shock, he just stood there staring at her, she'd always done just what he wanted, done as she was told, he'd never seen this side of her in all the four years they'd been married, he sat down dumbfounded.

"Here baby, catch," said her father tossing Jody a batch of keys, "You know where the gun room is, take whatever you need, just be careful, all of you, please be careful, keep cool heads but move fast. I understand what Grandpa's saying."

The five of them rushed out of the room.

"Dennis get started on putting support beams under all of the buildings, take down some trees to use as beams if necessary, just make sure that when the foundations start to break up the building will be safe."

Dennis nodded and got up to see what supplies he had and to work out what he would need.

Grandpa sat in his chair puffing on his corncob pipe, watching the smoke rise up to the fan hanging from the ceiling, "Isn't life funny, you never know what to expect or what will happen next," he thought to himself taking a mental inventory of everything in the valley and planning what to do to keep his family safe.

30

Consequences.

The Zoo.

Two days after the President's speech to the nation.

Frank watched his wife as he walked across the plush brown carpet of the bedroom towards the open glass sliding door that led out to the broad balcony, they had built the house on the hill overlooking the vast zoo that spread out in the valley below, the massive bedroom ran from one side of the house to the other with a balcony on each side, so that they could sit out and watch the sun rise from one side or the sun set from the other.

Trish, his wife, stood leaning against the railing looking out at a magnificent sunrise, it was going to be a beautiful morning. The air was still and the sun was just creeping up over the hills in the distance and you could hear the sounds of the animals waking up in the zoo below making their morning calls. Frank stopped at the sliding door; he could hear the roar of a waking lion in the distance and smiled to himself, the sun seemed to reflect off his wife's long auburn hair. "Oh God how I love her, she's still so beautiful," he smiled to himself as he looked down at her slender legs and her trim waist clad only in a very thin, silk nightgown that moved very slightly in the early morning breeze.

For some reason his mind flashed back to when he'd first met her forty years ago, yes, forty years ago next week. He'd seen her during his first year at university; he was doing a degree in 'Animal Husbandry' hoping to eventually take over the family farm, she'd been in his class and he was immensely attracted to her by her giddy laughter and sense of humor. He found out later, when he joined the gymnasium, that she worked out every morning. He was a very shy young man having been the only child brought up on a farm in Montana miles away from anywhere. At first he was very timid, he'd never really had any dates, he'd always been a loner but eventually he got up the courage to ask her to have a coffee, from there it led to a couple of dates. He loved her company, he loved to talk to her, to hear her tinkling laughter.

By the time they finished university they were married. His parents had died and the farm had been sold and just before they graduated her parents had been killed in a car accident so they moved together to her home. Her father had been an intense advocate of rescuing injured animals, animals of all kinds and had built up a small zoo to which visitors were now beginning to come and they had taken over those responsibilities.

He walked out onto the porch, slid his hands around the slim waist of his now sixty one year old wife, kissing her gently on the back of her neck and looked out over the two thousand acres of one of the most unique private zoo in the United States. It was a drive through zoo to which the public flocked in winter and summer and which had proven, through the years, to be extremely profitable, all the money had been put back into the zoo to rescue animals. They had gone out and brought back animals that needed to be bred in captivity to save them from extinction and so the zoo had grown.

"I love you," he whispered in her ear as she leaned back against him teasing him by wriggling her bottom against his crotch. They stood close together enjoying the moment as the sun rose two days after the President's speech, she squirmed around to face him and looked him in the eyes.

"Baby, what are we going to do?" and her eyes swept round indicating what were they going to do with the zoo.

"I think I've come up with an idea," he said "we can't just walk away, we can't just let these animals starve to death yet we don't have the staff to look after them and besides if what the President says is going to happen, and I believe him, it will be impossible to keep the animals enclosed, I propose that we open the enclosures and let them out to fend for themselves. Some will make it, some won't, they'll have to stand on their own, we'll just have to let nature take its course."

He saw a look of relief come over her face. "That's what I was thinking, we can just open the gates and give them their freedom but we'll have to be careful, we can't let them out the front gate," she whispered.

"What I thought we could do is lay a trail of food, various foods, out to the back commercial entrance that opens up onto the fields behind us and then we could let them out in the order of the food chain, we'd have to keep the carnivores until last and let everybody have a chance to get out. We could do it in two days, we have all the mechanized equipment to do it ourselves, what do you think?"

She hugged him tighter, "Yes, yes let's do that, let them fend for themselves and then what will we do?"

"I think we should carry on with what we started out doing all those years ago," he said "we can get on the all terrain vehicles, take all the hunting and camping gear and we can head across country releasing any domestic animals we come across and go from zoo to zoo as fast as we can to let all the animals out. That's about the only hope that some of the animals will have."

She relaxed against him, smiled at him, "That's wonderful, that's a plan, we love to camp, we love to hunt and we love to save the animals. Let's do it, let's start, let's go right now." She started to turn him around, he held her tight and hugged her and kissed her as they walked back into the bedroom.

"Do you think," she saw the little evil wicked grin on his face, "do you think we could just pause and take a little time out on the bed first?"

31

They give up the motorcycle.

On route to Last Chance.

Two days after the President's speech to the nation.

Ghost and his wife sat on the motorcycle on a bluff overlooking the wide river running down below them early in the morning. Last night they had made camp in some woods a few miles back, they had made a smokeless fire and had cooked a couple of squirrels that Ghost had brought down from the surrounding trees. They had buried the hearts, a kind of ritual taught to them by an Amazon tribe, a way of giving back to the earth that had provided them with the nourishment they needed. They never killed anything that they did not need.

They had made excellent time, well, excellent time compared to those who were restricted to the road, every now and again they would come to a point where they could look out over a road as they traveled across country, traffic jams were everywhere; clusters of people were huddled together beside the road not knowing what to do or where to go. The chaos seemed to be getting worse and worse faster and faster. Some of the bridges and overpasses had collapsed with the weight of the vehicles on the weakened cement, in other places the actual road itself had broken down in huge massive holes here and there along the surface, every now and again they heard the sound of gunfire and saw bodies lying in and about various vehicles. They saw wheel marks in the dirt where people had tried to go off road only to find that their two-wheel drive vehicles got stuck in the soft dirt and had to be abandoned. Four-wheel drive vehicles obviously were better and they had seen a few driving across country but they made sure they stayed well away from them. Now, early in the morning, they sat overlooking the river below them, for almost an hour they had been following the river studying the water. Both Ghost and his wife had been trained by the natives to read flowing water, in the Amazon it was very often a matter of life and death.

"Well honey," said his wife "that looks like the most promising spot we've seen, down there," as she pointed down to a small beach beside the river.

"I agree, that looks about the best spot we've seen. I guess it's the end of the bike we'll never get it across, we'll have to go on on foot," he said as they started down the incline to the little beach. They got off the bike and studied the water.

"I think we'll be fine here," said Ghost "Let's get the stuff off the bike and pack it up in the waterproof bags and then we'll head across."

Without another word they both set about the task of taking their stuff out and putting what they really needed into the waterproof bags. The last things to go into the bags were the clothes they were wearing.

"Ok," said Ghost "Let's tie ourselves together and go for a swim."

They waded into the water, it was quite cold and it took a moment or two for them to get used to it. Ghost went first securely tied by a rope around his waist to his wife's waist with some twenty feet of rope loose between them. Behind his wife floated four bags sealed and watertight with all their necessities tied onto the end of the rope. They shivered a little bit as they started wading across, then his wife smiled and said, "Boy that feels good, it's nice to be able to get naked" as she held onto his hand with one hand and let the twenty feet of rope between them float away from them down river.

Carefully they picked their way across the water, as it got deeper Ghost let go of her hand and moved out away from her, she played out the rope to him in case of an emergency. Ghost moved into the river till the rope got tight, he made sure of his footing and carefully pulled the rope and his wife to him, thus they cautiously made their way across the river. At one point they both had to swim but they were strong swimmers and the current was no challenge for them. As they waded ashore, their bodies shining in the morning sun Ghost pulled his wife to him and hugged her and kissed her.

"We'll just let ourselves dry off before we put any clothes back on but boy it sure feels good to be naked and you feel good."

"I agree, you feel good," she whispered as she slid her hands down and held onto his buttocks "hmmmm, you're beginning to feel really good," she said wiggling herself against him, feeling him getting excited.

Ghost kissed his wife and held onto her, sliding his hands up and down her wet back, feeling the pure pleasure of her soft skin, feeling her react to his touch, hearing the changes in her breathing and feeling her nipples getting hard against his chest. She pulled away slightly with a wicked grin on her face and said, "Hmmm, I think we'd better do some exercise to dry ourselves off."

"Well that sounds like an excellent idea," said her husband as he reached around her and lifted her up into his arms and carried her, still dragging the bags behind them, over to a patch of grass between the bushes as she laid her head on his shoulder and whispered in his ear, "God I love you."

They lay there and made love drying off as the sun warmed them.

32

The attack on the family.

The evening after they had crossed the river.

The sun was just sinking down behind them, the sunset had gone from flaming red with the clouds looking like they were on fire, through the various pinks to the dark mauves of the evening and the last of the sun was now sinking beneath the trees, darkness was enveloping the forest.

Ghost and Mary walked side by side quietly through the forest, they knew that they were walking parallel to the main road some one mile away. The road was packed with people, traffic had come to a standstill, people were out of their cars yelling and screaming, tempers were flaring and every now and then, when the wind blew from the right direction, they could hear the noise of the people leaning on their horns. They were accomplishing nothing, no one could go anywhere.

"I think we'd better find a place to camp for the night," said Mary reaching over to grasp her husband's hand.

He squeezed her hand, "Yes I guess we'd better, this is pretty hilly country let's go up over the next rise over there and we'll camp just on the other side."

"Okay sounds like a good idea to me we can start up a smokeless fire and get ourselves some supper."

"We could heat up some of that fried bacon and a couple of eggs for supper, I'm pretty hungry," he said "Do we have any bread left?"

"Yes," said Mary "we do."

"Good, we have enough for supper for tonight so I guess we don't have to go hunting. Tomorrow we'll have to do some hunting."

Mary grinned, they both enjoyed the hunt, it wasn't as if they hunted for deer or anything large but there were plenty of squirrels, muskrats and such that they could hunt down. They enjoyed tracking down small game, cleaning it and having fresh meat.

They were moving to the top of the hillock when they saw lights coming from just in front of them. There was a large open meadow spread out before them surrounded on three sides by forest, it had been recently mowed. There were a series of electric fences that divided up the space into grazing pastures, in the one closest to them grazed a big brown horse, one slightly smaller painted one and an even smaller one all nonchalantly chewing on the grass and ignoring them completely. At the furthest part of the meadow, over the top of some small hillocks, they could see a house, it looked, from their vantage point, like it had been built into the hill, it was a long one-floor home with windows along the side facing towards them. The roofing had been done in, what looked like, metal sheets and there were skylights almost the whole length of the roof, on the grass beside the house a huge bonfire was roaring. To the left of the house two very large pickups were parked, the headlights shone across the bonfire and the grass. To the left of the pickups the land dropped off quite sharply, there was an aboveground swimming pool that had been dug slightly into the hill, on the side closest to the house there was a deck, held up by four by four posts, which rose up to form railings around the deck. To the left of the pool a white hammock was slung between a tree and a huge six by six pole set in the ground, beyond that was a metal barn and down in the lowest part of the meadow to the left of the barn was an old horse carriage which looked like it had not been used for years, it looked very rusted. Everything looked very strange in the flickering light of the bonfire, it was obvious that there was no electricity working on the property. The meadow, after the land dropped off from the house, was in darkness. They could see people moving around the fire with men and women laughing and heard the clink of bottles and glasses.

Mary nudged her husband and whispered in his ear, "Look at the swimming pool there are people tied to the posts."

Ghost turned his gaze over there and sure enough he could make out four bodies tied to the uprights that held up the deck.

There was a lot of shouting and yelling from the people around the fire, one of them picked up a lantern and walked down to the people tied up to the pool jeering at them. Ghost could see by the light of the lantern that there were two young girls and a younger boy and someone that looked like their mother tied up, all of them were naked and tied so tightly to the posts that even in the light of the lantern they could see that the ropes were cutting into their flesh.

"Well," the man with the lantern yelled, "are you ready to perform yet or do we have to go and look after your husband and father again."

They could hear the children crying and they could hear the mother whining and begging, "I'll do anything you say, I'll do anything you say, please just leave my husband alone."

The man laughed and said, "Let's just make sure of that shall we." He turned round and yelled "Hey Joan just show them what's going to happen to their daddy if they don't cooperate."

A woman dressed in dirty jeans and top and thick scraggly hair moved away from the fire, they could see the glint of a knife in her hand, she moved over to the post that held up the hammock. Mary and Ghost suddenly realized that there was a naked man tied to it, the woman just walked up to him, looked him over from top to bottom and very slowly she pushed the knife into the outer flesh of his right thigh, the man screamed and screamed and begged her to stop. She wiggled the knife and the night was filled with agonizing screams. The man's family tied to the posts yelled for them to the stop, begging them not to hurt him anymore, they would do anything that they asked.

The woman with the knife roared with laughter and the men by the fire yelled and jeered. One of them yelled out "Bring up the youngest daughter I want her first, she's one sexy little bitch."

The woman pulled the knife out of the man's thigh and his head went down and he hung there crying and moaning with blood running down his leg. He disappeared into the darkness as the woman moved back up the hill. The man with the lantern untied the young girl, she couldn't be any more than fourteen years old and dragged her, fighting and kicking, up the hill to the fire taking the lantern with him. As they got close to the fire they saw him grab her hair, he untied her hands as she fell to her knees begging for mercy. The mother, still tied to the post, was screaming at the people, " Take me, please take me, I'll do anything, just leave my baby, please leave my baby alone."

There was a picnic table between the bonfire and the house, two of the men picked up the young girl and threw her down onto the table on her back, she was begging and crying and whining, the mother and the other children had quieted down into sobs and moans. The man hung the lantern up on the umbrella over the picnic table so they could see what was going on and what was being done to the girl.

"Hold the bitch down, open your legs bitch let's have a look at your pretty little cunt," one of the women said forcing the young girls legs apart, two of the men grabbed hold of her arms and pulled her down across the table.

"No, please don't, oh God don't do it please, don't hurt me please, oh please don't do this to me please." They could hear the young girl moan and cry as her legs were forced open.

A man reached down, picked up some rope and threw it to the two men holding her arms; they lashed her down to the table. One of the men pulled her head up roughly by her hair and unzipped his jeans, "I got a present for you, want to see my present?" He pulled down his jeans, he was already excited.

"Oh no, oh no don't do this please, I'll do anything, anything you want, please don't do this to me please," cried out the young girl.

"Now that's what I call a good position," another man said pulling down his jeans and underwear, "you take her head and I'll take her down here."

The young girl had stopped talking and was just sobbing.

Mary reached over and grabbed her husband's hand and squeezed twice, he looked at her in the darkness, it was now so dark that they could hardly see one another, Ghost nodded, "let's do it."

Mary just nodded, she knew what he meant.

They looked back to the scene in front of the house across the meadow, the man between the young girl's legs grabbed her butt and in one swift vicious movement entered her. The night was cut by the most horrendous scream that seemed to echo through the forest, the screams were followed by the jeers and laughter of the men and women watching.

"You make too much noise," said the other man who had his jeans down around his ankles. He grabbed her hair and moved in close.

"Open your mouth bitch," there was a sound of a loud slap as the man slapped the young girl's face "open your mouth bitch, now that's better here comes daddy." The women were laughing and jeering.

Ghost put his lips close to his wife's ear, "I see one person on guard," he whispered "to the right of the house on top of that hill, the idiot's just lit a cigarette. I'll go to the right you go to the left look after the family let them know we're here, I don't think any prisoners are necessary."

Mary just nodded," we'll signal when in position."

Ghost nodded and she felt him taking off his clothes. He reached into his knapsack and pulled out a jet-black loincloth and slipped it round his thighs, Mary looked at him and when he closed his eyes he literally disappeared into the darkness. She slipped off her clothes; standing there in just in her black bra and panties she too disappeared into the darkness. They retrieved some other articles from their backpacks and clipped a large black fanny pack around each of their waists, he gave her hand a squeeze and disappeared moving along the ridge towards the edge of the forest. She slipped off to the left moving down the meadow silently, around the horses who just looked at her as her shadow moved down the pasture. Mary made her way along the edge of the meadow down low around the old horse carriage and came up the hill directly behind the swimming pool creeping along on her hands and knees. She moved to the edge of the swimming pool closest to where the man was tied to the post. She peered around the side of it as one of the men up on the hills said "Come on one of you two it's my turn now." He took off his clothes and moved around the picnic table and stood beside the fire playing with himself, "Come on, come on, my turn, hurry up."

The man who was between the young girl's legs said "Wait your turn George, there's no big rush."

They all began to laugh and George just looked frustrated and continued to play with himself.

One of the women stepped forward and slapped the young girl viciously on one side of her butt; the other woman stepped to the other side and slapped the other side laughing, the noise of the slaps rang out across the meadow.

Mary turned her gaze to the wood line running on the far side of the house up the hill, she could make out a small speck of light as the man on guard duty sucked on his cigarette, she waited watching silently. The guard must have been anxious to see what was going on below him, he moved slightly forward out of the shadows a couple of feet, he was still hard to see, he was obviously anxious to get down and enjoy the play with the rest of them. As she watched the night seemed to move, a dark black line moved around the guard's neck and face, the cigarette disappeared and a piece of the night seemed to envelope him then he was gone into the darkness. Mary smiled to herself, now she knew where her husband was, now it was a little safer for her to move.

The man between the young girl's legs gave one last moan and collapsed over her, his butt still twitching slightly, a couple of moments later the he got off her saying, "She's all yours George she's all yours."

"About fucking time, get out my way, I don't think this is gonna take too long." And he stepped up between the girl's open legs.

"I'm next, I'm next," said a small man moving up from around the fire as he started to take off his clothes.

The two women just leered and jeered at the men.

A big man who had been leaning against a lounge chair stood up and said, "I want to have a go at the young boy, he's about the right age, he's got to be about nine years old and you all know how I like young boys."

The two ladies laughed as one of the men said, "You dirty old pedophile."

The big man just laughed.

"You want me to go down and get him?" asked one of the women.

There was silence for a moment.

"No," said the big men "let's do them one at a time, let's wait till they've finished taking the girl and then we'll bring up the young boy, we're not in any rush."

Mary watched for a moment looking around carefully, knowing that there had been five men, and now there were just four men and two women, "No competition," she thought smiling to herself.

She waited until one of the men moved across between her and the fire casting a long shadow down the hill and then, on her tummy, she moved silently across the grass and rose up without a sound behind the wooden post that the man was tied to, his head hung down and he was crying and weeping. She put her hand around and grabbed his mouth pulling his head back hard on to the post, his whole body went rigid and tried to struggle.

"Be still," she whispered into his ear "be still, I'm here to help you, don't make a sound. If you understand what I say nod your head forward twice." She slackened the pressure slightly off the man's mouth as his head nodded twice.

"I'm going to take my hand away, don't say anything or move just hang your head back down like you had it before." And slowly she removed her hand, the young man's head lent forward to the same position that he'd been in before she touched him.

"Please help my family, please, please help my family," the man whispered very quietly without moving his head.

"That's what we're here for," said Mary "I just wanted you to know that there's somebody here to help, I'm going to leave you tied to the post, I'm going to go over and take care of your family."

The man nodded his head and she felt his body relax and slumped down a little bit more. She dropped to the ground and even though the man was listening for her he did not hear a sound as she moved back to behind the swimming pool.

She moved around the swimming pool, there was enough room under the deck for her to go underneath it between the supports, she moved silently till she was between the three people tied to the posts. She realized that she could not whisper to each separately they were tied so closely together that they were bound to hear her even at a whisper. She just had to take the chance and speak just a little louder so that they could all her at once, there was really no fear that anyone up around the fire would hear her there was too much noise from the crackle of the fire and the jeering noise of the people.

"Don't be frightened, I'm here to help you."

All three bodies suddenly jerked trying to look around behind them, they stopped moaning and groaning.

"Don't try and turn round, hang your heads down like you were before, don't stop moaning and groaning, I don't want anybody out there to be able to see any difference in your posture. I just want you to know that we're to help you, if you understand me don't say a word just nod your heads."

One by one all three heads nodded.

"I've already been over and told your father that we're here, you just have to wait, be very patient and keep moaning and groaning as if there was nobody here to help you. I'll be back to cut you loose in just a little while."

Three bodies seemed to slump a little bit and they started to moan. She moved to the edge of the deck where she could see up to the house, she reached behind her and, out of the black leather bag that was strapped around her waist, she removed what looked like two dead straight wooden sticks stained pitch black, they were in fact hollow tubes. She screwed the end of one tube into the end of the other one making a four foot long blowpipe. She pulled out a small packet, opened it took out and inserted into one end of the pipe a small black dart; she got into a comfortable position and waited. If anyone from around the fire looked down towards the swimming pool they would see the other members of the family tied firmly to the posts with their heads down and moaning, no one would notice that at one end of the deck the shadows were slightly longer than they had been before.

She watched the timberline on the far side of the house where the man had been on guard, she thought she saw, with her trained eyes, a very slight movement in the darkness where the house was built into the hillside. Then she heard the song of a bird, just a few notes, sing out across the meadow coming from the far end of the house. She tilted her head back slightly waited a couple of seconds then the same bird song could be heard coming up from somewhere around the swimming pool. They both knew they were now in position.

Ghost watched from the little niche where the house met the hill, in his hands he had a blowpipe, just a little bit longer than the one his wife had. He watched as the man who was at the head of the young girl on the picnic table let out one big moan and collapsed over the girl's body still twitching slightly. Ghost brought the blowpipe up to his mouth and there was the slightest puff that could not possibly be heard unless somebody was really listening hard for it. The man lying across the young girl slapped at his neck with his hand, his head turned as if trying to see where he had been bitten or stung by some insect, he started to get up but it looked like his legs did not have enough strength in them and he just laid across the young girl completely still.

The tiny little dart the Ghost had used was one that they used down in the Amazon forests, it had been soaked in a poison that could only be taken from a certain poisonous frog, the poison was lethal and extremely fast acting. Ghost slipped another dart into his blowpipe.

"Come on get off the bitch," said the little man who was next in line "come on, don't just lay there, get off, it's my turn." He moved over and pushed the man who was lying on the young girl, the man did not move except he appeared to slide down to the right of the little girl, over the edge of the picnic table and slowly down onto the ground. "Stop pissing around, come on, get up I'm as horny as hell."

The man did not get up, he did not move, the laughter seemed to die down and, as Ghost watched, the man between the young girls legs slapped at the side of his neck and his knees seem to buckle and he slipped sideways and collapsed on the ground without making a sound.

Suddenly there was silence; all Ghost could hear was the moaning and crying of the family tied up down the slope.

"What the hell," said the largest of the two women bending down and shaking the man on the ground "Get up, stop playing around, what the hell's going on."

The man didn't move.

The big man moved back against the house and grabbed a shotgun that was leaning against the brickwork.

"What the hell's going on?" Asked the other woman.

"Something's wrong," hissed the big man "I think they're dead."

The man who was naked standing in front of the young girl suddenly grabbed his throat as Ghost took the pipe from his lips and slipped in another small dart. The man looked around wildly for a second took one step back and slipped to the ground.

The big man brought up his shotgun waving it around staring into the night. "Better get against the house girls," he said, "What the hell's going on?"

The two women moved towards the house, one of them made it, the smaller one seemed to just fall forward onto her face and lay on the ground.

"Show yourself, come on show yourself, get out of the darkness, be a man come on face me," screamed the big man into the night moving away from the house waving his shotgun wildly around.

Mary put her blowpipe to her mouth and without hesitation killed the big man watching him fall, the shotgun tumbling out of his fingers, he was dead before he hit the ground. The woman standing against the house ran forward and picked up the shotgun, she had not even got it in both hands before she fell face down into the grass, she seemed to twitch once and then lay still.

The family had been watching the drama unfold before them, they became silent and the night was so quiet and still that you could hear a cricket somewhere down by the barn.

They watched as the night seemed to move from the far side of the house, the darkness took on the form of a large tall black man dressed only in a black loincloth who moved forward into the light of the fire. The dark shadow of the man bent down and touched each of the bodies around the picnic table as the young girl tied down to the picnic table started to moan.

The man moved across and gently stroked the blonde hair of the young girl, putting his head down to her he whispered, "It's all right, it's all right, they're all gone we're here to help you."

He stood up "Mary", he called into the night "it's safe you can release the family."

He watched as the shadow at the end of the pool turned into his wife. She took a knife from around her waist and cut the bonds off the young boy who fell forward onto his knees and then cut loose the young girl who stood rubbing her hands and her legs and then she released the mother who moved swiftly and grabbed hold of her children.

Mary went over to the hammock and cut the father loose, he staggered forward and turned, "Thank you, oh dear God thank you, who ever you are I thank you, I must go up and see my daughter." He held onto his leg that was still bleeding slightly and moved up hurriedly to the picnic table where Ghost had cut the young girl loose. Her father gathered her up in his arms and sat on the edge of the picnic table crying and whispering in her ear.

Mary followed the rest of the family as they hobbled up the hill into the firelight and gathered round the father and his child on the picnic table, all of them were crying and weeping and holding each other.

Mary slipped over and hugged her husband.

"Any problems honey?"

"Nope, no problems and no regrets."

"You look after the family, I'll gather our darts and have a quick look around, I'm sure there's nobody else but I'd better check the house." He bent over and quickly kissed his wife who moved over to help console the family.

33

Boston

The Best Retirement Home

Three days after the President's speech to the nation.

Ethel Jean came out of her a small apartment that was part of the Best Retirement Home, she had bought the home thirty-five years ago, she was now seventy years old. She was in good health but knew that she couldn't keep up working the hours that she presently spent working in the Home. She had no family and the Home was her whole life. She was an R. N. There were forty retirees living in the Home all of whom needed a great deal of care, most of them were unable to get out of bed. The Home employed eighty people, it was without a doubt the best retirement home in the Boston area.

Within a few hours of the President's address to the nation all the employees had left, since then Ethel Jean had managed to feed all the retirees but she was unable to provide the care that they needed. She had tried to contact any relatives of those living in the home to no avail and had spent yesterday and last night trying to contact any authority that could help but none of the phone calls were answered.

After three days without any employees reporting in to work the retirees were now in desperate need of attention, attention that could no longer be provided to them.

Ethel Jean went down and unlocked the medical room, unlocked the medical supplies cabinet and with tears in her eyes prepared forty syringes. One by one she went to each of the retirees trying very hard to be pleasant and smiling and saying that breakfast would be a little late coming today, she gave each one an injection. Each one of them fell asleep never to wake again.

Ethel Jean went back and checked each one of them making sure that there were no heartbeats. She then went back to the medical room and prepared yet another syringe, she went back into her small apartment put on her favorite music and put herself to sleep.

34

Jack and Anna Brown.

The Sudan.

Four days after the President's speech to the nation.

In the Sudan Doctors Jack and Anna Brown sat on a pile of sand covered with an old cardboard box beside the tent and relaxed as the sun went down over the dessert.

"Well, I guess that's it for the evening," said Jack taking his wife's hand in his and giving it a little squeeze. "We could've got more done if those damned rebels hadn't taken the generators."

Anna turned to her husband squeezing his hand, "Just maybe, maybe, it wasn't such a bad thing that they took the generators, it forces us to stop seeing any patients after dark, we just don't have enough light to do the job properly. We were working such long hours that we were driving ourselves too hard, now we have to stop each evening and we can get some rest."

She moved over closer to her husband so that she could snuggle against him as he put his arm around her.

"Boy! The sun really goes down fast, it's hard to believe that just half a mile away over those dunes all those hundreds of people are living in makeshift tents. We can't look after them all, we can only work around the edges and sometime soon, hopefully, a lot more doctors and people will come out to look after them. Luckily the rebels are leaving them alone for now, God help us if they attack those poor people and drive them out of the oasis, where the hell would they go?"

"I don't know," said his wife putting her head on his shoulder "This whole damned mess is just unbelievable I really don't think that anybody knows what they're fighting for any more. Why can't people just live and let live?"

"Well I" started Jack when he stopped and cocked his head to one side listening, "Do you hear that honey?"

Anna sat up, "Yes I hear it, engines coming from the distance God I hope it isn't those damned government troops coming this way, they always stir up the shit. I think I hear two helicopters."

They sat still for a minute, "Yes it's two helicopters coming down from the north."

They sat still as the noise of the whirring motors came closer, then, over the top of the dunes, they saw the two helicopters flying low, kicking up dust as they came across the sand. One climbed up a bit and then held steady almost over the top of the other one which swooped in low and made a smooth landing on the sand some one hundred yards away from the tent. Jack and Anna stood up protecting their eyes from the flying sand, they could see that these were American helicopters.

"What the hell's going on, what are they doing here?" yelled Jack to his wife over the noise of the engines. She gave him a quick look and a shrug as they watched two men jump out of the helicopter, one stood with a rifle in his hand, the other flipped up his visor and looked around, saw them standing by the tent and immediately started towards them, it only took a few seconds for him to step right up in front of them.

"Doctor Jack and Doctor Anna Brown?" a young man's face said from inside a large helmet.

"Yes that's us, what can we do for you?"

"I'm Lieutenant Gibson, I've been instructed to come and pick the two of you up and take you back to base. Needless to say we're way out of our jurisdiction and don't want to be seen or found in this airspace so please will both of you come with me immediately." He pointed towards the helicopter.

"What the hell do you mean?" said Jack holding his wife close to him "We don't want to go anywhere, we're working here, I know we've been out of touch for the last few days but we're perfectly all right, we need to continue our work."

"I'm sorry Sir but there have been some drastic changes in the world in the last few days and we've been instructed directly by the President of the United States to pick you up and fly you back to the aircraft carrier. Please hurry we can't stay here any longer than is absolutely necessary."

Anna looked at the officer, "What the heck are you talking about, changes in the world, what kind of changes and why the hell send a helicopter to pick us up?" she said to the Lieutenant "We can't leave just like that, we have all our gear and surgical units and equipment to be packed up, it'll take us at least four or five hours to get it all ready to be moved."

"I'm sorry Ma'am I didn't quite make myself clear, you, both of you, have got to get into the helicopter immediately, we won't be transporting any of your gear or equipment or medical supplies they'll be left here."

"If we leave them here they'll disappear, how the hell are we going to do our work if we haven't any instruments or medical supplies. When are you going to bring us back, even if we just leave them here for two or three hours without somebody watching them they'll all disappear."

"Sir you won't be coming back here, please, we have to get out of this area, just get into the helicopter and I'll try to explain things to you, please get in."

Anna looked at Jack and shrugged, "Something drastic must've happened for us to have to abandon all this equipment I guess we'd better do as he says."

"Guess you're right honey." Jack said to his wife nodding to the Lieutenant he said. "Okay we'll come as we are but this better be good, God knows it costs enough to get the equipment and supplies out here in the first place, just to leave them is just not acceptable."

The Lieutenant turned away from them and headed back to the helicopter, Anna held onto Jack's hand as they ran after him. The man standing guard stood still as the three of them were helped into the helicopter by another airman, he then jumped in and even before they had time to put on their seat belts the helicopter was up and flying off and they could see the second one off to their right joining in formation. They sat there quietly for a moment, their ears ringing with the noise from the motors and the wind. The man, who'd been in the helicopter, handed them each a helmet which they put on with some difficulty and then were surprised by a very clear voice saying, "Thank you for coming so fast." Jack could see Lieutenant Gibson's mouth moving but was hearing it through the earphones in his helmet.

"Let me just explain very briefly, the President has ordered all American citizens back to the United States as fast as possible, he made that order four days ago. We, that is the aircraft carrier and other ships of the fleet, are steaming round the world back to the States picking up the last of the American citizens that want to go home. All forces and diplomatic personnel have been recalled from all over the world, apparently there's some sort of a bug that's causing havoc throughout the entire world. All air travel has been cancelled." The Lieutenant saw the shock and surprise on both of their faces. "Yes there are no civil planes flying other than those that can land on grass strips or water. There are a few, a very few, military landing strips still being kept open for emergencies and to ensure the safe return of military personnel and equipment but these won't be in operation much longer, it's becoming too difficult to ensure the integrity of the landing strips. We've been given direct orders from the President to find you two and to take you back to the aircraft carrier, it took us awhile to find you since you didn't have any radios."

"No the radio and a lot of our equipment including the generators were taken by the rebels about two weeks ago, they rode into camp on camels, the leader's son had been wounded quite badly and, though we aren't medical surgeons, just a dental surgeon and an eye surgeon, they made us operate on him and luckily it went very well. They moved us, lock stock and barrel, from the place where we had been originally to where we are now so that we would be closer to them if they needed us again. Thus we lost contact with our base unit not having any radio equipment. Now what's all this about a bug causing chaos?" asked Anna realizing that she didn't have to yell because there was a microphone in her helmet.

The Lieutenant proceeded to tell them all about the crystal and the President's speech, he went on to tell them that within a few hours all the heads of state of nearly every country in the world had delivered a similar message to their people. As far as he knew all major airports were now closed and there were no more civil aircraft flying. As many Americans as possible who had been overseas at the time of the President's speech had been taken home. The carrier that they were heading to was the last U.S. naval ship in this part of the world, they were heading down around Africa and then up the other coast and eventually going home picking up any American stragglers that they could find or that could find them. It had only taken a few hours after the world population became aware of what was happening and had come to realize what the future held for them that there was chaos. In the States law and order had broken down immediately as members of the various law enforcement departments had gone to look after their families. C.N.N., after a brief break, had recommenced broadcasting the news and were now the only ones doing so. The incidences of structures collapsing had increased swiftly, the population had immediately made, or tried to make, a mass exodus from the towns and cities only to find that the only form of transport that was possible was in private vehicles. Very soon there was gridlock on the roads and people had had to abandon their vehicles and had taken to going on foot.

By the time the Lieutenant had finished answering their questions, he pointed out a black dot in the distance.

"My God," said Anna staring out the open door "That tiny little dot down there is where we're going to land?"

"Yes that's it, don't worry it's much bigger than it looks from up here."

There was silence as they watched the black dot get bigger and bigger and at last they were able to distinguish the details of the carrier but even as they got closer it looked very small compared to the vast ocean surrounding it. The helicopter pilot swooped in swiftly and expertly and landed on the markings as a man stood by waving a pair of paddles at them. The motor was switched off and then it went quiet. Jack and Anna breathed a sigh of relief as they removed their helmets and realized that they could talk without using their microphones and earpieces.

"Here comes a Captain," said the Lieutenant pointing to a man coming across the deck towards him, "I'll hand you over to him, my duty is done, you're safely here on the carrier."

"Thank you Lieutenant," said Jack shaking his hand "Thank you for the information, do you know what's going to happen to us next?"

"No Sir I don't, perhaps the Captain can fill you in."

Jack and Anna walked towards the Captain, he was slightly older than the Lieutenant, he had that very military bearing in his walk and posture, he smiled and said, "Hello Doctors I hope you had a good flight, this must be a shock to you, I apologize but we couldn't contact you by radio."

"No Captain," said Anna "our radio was taken from us, we've been out of touch for a few days."

"Well at least your safe and sound, now did the Lieutenant tell you what was happening?"

"Yes," said Jack "he told us what was happening with this crystal and everything, it sounds impossible but I guess it must be true because here we are. Are we going to be staying here on board until you get back home?"

"No Sir, we have been instructed by the President to get you back to the Phoenix area as soon as possible if that's Ok with you."

"Why would the President give specific orders about us and why on earth would we want to go to Phoenix?" Asked Anna with a worried look on her face.

"I have a message here that might help to explain everything," said the Captain pulling a piece of paper out of his top breast pocket and handing it to Jack.

Mary moved over to Jack so they could both read the note, it read "Fishslice, Fishslice, Fishslice. Jack we have established a safe haven at Last Chance. All old boys are returning. Camp has all the supplies it needs for us to survive. If you're reading this message you and your wife are of course invited to join us. If you can get to these coordinates," and the coordinates were written down, "you can contact us by the GPS radio hidden beneath the floorboards in the office under the front window and we will pick you up. Hope to see you soon," and it was signed Pattern.

Jack and Anna stood staring at the note for a few moments.

"Last Chance, that's where you spent all those years isn't it, I remember you telling me about somebody called Pattern but what's this Fishslice thing?"

Jack looked up, "Fishslice was a word that was set up for anybody to use if there was an emergency or they wanted someone to listen or do something that was very important." He looked over at the Captain, "Why would the President issue special orders regarding us?"

"I have no idea," said the Captain. "I only know that it was explicitly ordered that we should find you and take you where ever you want to go to, be it Phoenix or somewhere else."

Anna looked at Jack, "Honey what are we going to do, if all this about chaos and breakdown of law and order is true, which it obviously is, what the hell are we going to do?"

"Baby I don't think there's anything else we can do, we'll just have to go to Last Chance, it sounds like they have things organized. There's no sense in going home, it'll be impossible to live in a city or a town." He turned back to the Captain, "How on earth are you going to get us back to Phoenix?"

The Captain turned around and pointed down the deck, right down at the far end they could see some jet aircrafts being raised up from down below coming up to the main flight deck.

"We have a fleet of six Hawker Siddeley Harrier jump jets that have been ordered back to San Diego immediately because they can take off vertically, they're a few of the remaining fighter planes that can still fly. The six will fly directly from here to an aircraft carrier in San Diego, they'll be refueled in flight, if you wish to go back they can drop you off at the coordinates in your message, there's room for one passenger in each of the planes. You must make up your mind soon, they'll be taking off within the next thirty minutes, that flight can't be delayed they're wanted back home urgently."

Jack turned to Anna and pulled her close to him, "Well this doesn't give us much time to make up our minds does it?"

"No honey it doesn't but I really don't think that we have to decide anything, we only have one choice and that's to go to Last Chance and just hope that we can contact them when we land at this place wherever it may be."

"I love you," Jack gave her a squeeze and kissed her "Okay the decision is made." He held her close to him as he turned to the Captain.

"Okay Captain we'll go with them, what do we have to do?"

"Excellent Sir, follow me and we'll get you into some flight gear and then I'll introduce you to the two pilots who will be traveling with you. Have either of you ever been up in a jet fighter?"

Both Jack and Anna shook their heads.

"Well it'll be quite an experience for you, I hope you enjoy it," and the three of them walked across the flight deck and into a room which had flight suits hanging all around the walls.

"Sergeant," the Captain said to a man sitting at the desk "please put both of these into flight gear immediately they'll be taking off with the Harriers."

The Sergeant jumped up and looked over at Anna and walked over to the wall and pulled down a set of flight gear, "Ma'am I believe you should take a small, these should fit you," and he proceeded to help her into a suit, at first it was a little awkward but soon she was standing in full flight gear with her helmet under her right arm.

"My! My! Quite a sight," said her husband "Perhaps you missed your calling, you should've been a pilot." He grinned and smiled at her.

"Sir how tall are you?"

"Five feet eleven"."

The sergeant moved over and pulled down another suit, "Try this on, it should fit."

In just a very short time both he and Anna looked like they'd been flying all their lives.

"Thank you Sergeant I think that'll do, come on we'll get you into the planes. Sorry this is such a rush but time is of the essence," said the Captain as he went out the door onto the flight deck.

"Captain Williams and you, Captain Smith, we have those two passengers that we spoke about earlier for you. Doctor Jack Reed this is Captain Williams, Captain Williams, Doctor Jack Reed."

Captain Williams stepped forward and put out his hand, he was a big man, not so much in height but he was very broad in the shoulders, slim in the waist and looking extremely fit, Jack put out his hand and it was gripped with a great deal of strength. Jack looked into his deep blue eyes set in his black skin, he oozed self-confidence. "Pleasure to meet you Captain I hope you don't mind us hitching a ride with you?"

"Not at all, not at all, I hope it's you that doesn't mind hitching a ride with us, I don't suppose you've ever been up in a fighter plane before, this will be quite an experience for you." A wicked grin lit up the Captain's face.

"You're right, this will be a first, a brand-new experience, please just call me Jack and I hope you'll be very gentle with us," Jack said looking across at his wife.

"Captain Smith, Doctor Anna Read she will be your charge for the trip."

Captain Smith was a little shorter than Captain Williams but it was obvious that he was equally fit, Anna's hand was gripped in a strong self-assured grasp.

"Doctor a pleasure to meet you, I believe this will be a wonderful adventure for you, I'll take good care of you," said Captain Smith.

"I put myself entirely in your hands, this is going to be a very exciting adventure for me," she let go of the Captain's hand and their conversation was interrupted with the sound of jet engines starting up.

The Captain that had brought them over and introduce them stepped back and said, "Gentlemen I leave these two doctors in your capable hands please make sure they get to the coordinates that Doctor Jack gives you. I believe they're supposed to find a GPS phone at the location where you're going to drop them off, however, in the note, there's a ham radio call sign and it may be possible, when you get closer to Phoenix, for you to get a message to that ham radio or on that GPS phone when you're going to drop them off just in case the hidden GPS phone isn't there or it doesn't work."

"Yes James thank you we'll take good care of them, I'll get the coordinates and the communication information from Doctor Jack when we're up in the air."

"Thank you Captain," said Jack as he and Anna stepped forward and shook the Captain's hand. He immediately turned round and marched across the flight deck to disappear in a door below the conning tower. Jack and Anna turned back to their pilots.

"Okay let's get you two aboard and set up, it looks like the squadron is ready to go. Doctor Jack you come with me," said Captain William.

"And you Doctor Anna come with me," said Captain Jones.

Anna gave her husband a quick hug as best they could in their flight gear and a kiss and said, "Well I guess were off on another adventure my love I'll see you when we get there, will we be able to talk to each other in the air?"

"Sure can, no problem," said Captain Jones as the two doctors were lead off to their respective aircraft.

It took a little bit to get them both settled in to their seats behind their pilots, it seemed to Jack that it was a very tight fit. He looked at all the instruments and was amazed and wondered how anybody could ever make sense of them all. A Sergeant helped him on with his helmet and he looked over to see them closing the cockpit of the plane where his wife was. Captain Williams just seemed to slide into the plane, he made it look so smooth and easy. The cockpit was closed.

"Doctor Jack we're not going to take off vertically from the carrier, vertical flight takes up a lot more fuel and we'll need as much as we can get to get us home. We're going to be taking off by catapult, this is a steam-operated catapult and there will be a vicious acceleration. Please don't get me wrong but I'm going to switch off our intercom until we're up in the air because I believe you're going to be making a lot of noise."

"I understand," said Jack "I've seen pictures of planes taking off from aircraft carriers, I should be okay I don't think I'll make any noise."

The pilot just grinned to himself as they taxied into position. Jack could feel something being attached onto the bottom of the aircraft, someone was waving paddles around off to their right.

"We're going to be the first to take off, hold onto your hat here we go."

Jack heard a click as the pilot switched off his intercom and suddenly the plane leapt forward, the acceleration was incredible, Jack was forced back into his seat. The skin on his face was pulled back and he felt like his eyes were going to disappear into the back of his head there was only a split second from standstill till Jack saw the end of the aircraft carrier suddenly fly at them. Jack screamed as he never screamed before, there was no way the plane could ever take off with just that shorter runway, as the plane came to the end of the ship it dropped a couple of feet and if it was possible to shout any louder Jack screamed louder. The engines roared and the plane leapt forward up into the air climbing into the clouds, slowly the gravitational force eased and Jack found that his throat was a little hoarse and his hands were shaking.

There was a click in his helmet, "Are you okay Doctor Jack?"

It took a few seconds for Jack to gather himself together. "Oh my God, I don't believe it, is it like that every time you take off?"

"Like what, that was just a normal takeoff, of course you didn't make any noise, but I swear I heard something even above the noise of the engines but I guess it must've been my imagination."

Jack blushed from top to bottom, he was glad that nobody could see him.

"Well I did make a little noise, that was the most exciting, exhilarating and scariest thing I've ever done in my life, once is enough, I hope to God we never have to do it again."

The pilot roared with laughter, "Yes it's very scary the first time, trust me, we all go through that same feeling. Here comes your wife, look to your right their coming up into formation."

Jack looked over to his right and saw another aircraft come up and settle in almost directly beside them, he saw his wife looking over towards him giving him a thumbs up, he did the same thing.

"Jack, Jack can you hear me?" he heard his wife's excited voice in his ear.

"Yes honey I hear you, my God that was something wasn't it?"

"Jack that was fantastic, it was absolutely amazing, I loved it, can we do it again?"

Jack thought to himself "Not a hope in hell," but he said to his wife "Yes it was quite good wasn't it um ah um um I don't think we'll be doing it again though."

"Wow, did you see the end of that flight deck coming at us, I never thought we were going to get off in time and the acceleration, it pressed me right back into the seat, it's better than any roller coaster I've ever been on, I loved it."

"I'm proud of your wife Doctor Jack," said the voice of the pilot in Anna's plane, "she's a real trooper she didn't make a sound."

"Doctor Jack did very well too," his pilot said and Jack could swear he heard the grin behind the voice.

"Thank you Captain Williams," said Jack.

"All right we'll remain in formation straight across to San Diego, Captain Jones and myself will be dropping you two off at those coordinates if you have them Doctor Jack and then we'll be joining the rest of the squadron which will be flying on to San Diego. If you can let me have the communication detail and the coordinates we can then sit back and relax, we'll have to refuel somewhere in midair, you'll find that interesting."

Jack pulled out the piece of paper and read him off the coordinates, the ham radio call sign and the GPS details and then settled back to enjoy the ride.

For the first couple of hours Jack and his pilot chatted on and off discussing what had happened in the last couple of weeks, Jack was brought up to date on the President's speech and the speeches of the various heads of state and about some of the chaos that had ensued. There had been a drastic nuclear accident in North Russia, not too much of it was known because the Russians had kept it very quiet. In Britain people had been horrified to watch on television, immediately after the Prime Minister's speech to the Nation, as the whole face of big Ben crashed down into the streets. In France one of the supports of the Eiffel Tower had collapsed and it was now leaning over threatening to fall. Throughout the world these incidents were increasing rapidly. Most of Americans living abroad returned to the United States before all the major airport runways and airports had been closed, the remaining few were being picked up by naval ships all of which were now headed back home. Within a couple of days of the President speech all television and radio stations had ceased to broadcast. CNN in Atlanta was still broadcasting but only over the radio bands. Huge areas in different parts of the world had lost their electric power and were now in darkness at night. Most people had moved out of the cities trying to find places in the country, this had given rise to fights and deaths, nobody had a count of the huge numbers that had died.

Eventually the two of them dropped into a comfortable silence. Jack was amazed as he sat in the cockpit that there was very little feeling of just how fast the plane was traveling, they were well above the clouds and a beautiful blue sky surrounded them, it seemed to go on and on forever. If it was not for the sound of the air rushing past Jack could almost imagine that they were standing still. He sat and thought about what was to come and what was going to happen to him and his wife.

"Harrier one, Harrier, one, this is tanker one, do you read me?" Suddenly jolted Jack back from his reveries as it came across his earphones.

"Tanker one, tanker one this is Harrier one, we read you loud and clear." Jack's pilot responded.

"We have you on radar Harrier one, we should be within visual range in approximately ten minutes, do you have us on radar?"

"Roger, I have you on radar, am changing course to meet you."

"Squadron, does everybody have the tanker on radar?"

One by one each of the pilots responded to the affirmative and on Jack's pilot's command the whole squadron turned a few degrees to the north. Almost exactly ten minutes later Jack could see a tiny black dot in the distance.

"Tanker one we have you on visual, will be ready to connect in approximately four minutes."

"Roger on that, lowering the stinger, we have you on visual, awaiting your directions."

Jack was amazed at the speed that the little black dot turned out to be a massive plane which, at the back, was trailing what looked to Jack, to be a miniscule thread at the end of which, from his point of view was what looked like an umbrella viewed from the underside.

On his pilot's command the whole squadrons slowed down to equal the speed of the tanker.

"Harrier one," said his pilot to the rest of the squadron, "breaking formation for refueling."

Jack was slightly dizzy as the plane swung out of formation.

"Dr. Jack," said his pilot "this is something to see."

Jack sat there amazed as the jet fighter eased into position behind the trailing umbrella and his pilot very gently eased the nose of his plane into it. It happened so easily Jack was amazed, the umbrella just got closer and closer and as the nose of the plane connected with the short pipe that came out from under the umbrella there was a slight click, not heard but more felt, a slight shudder throughout the plane.

"Tanker one, Harrier one connected ready for refueling."

"Refueling on my mark." There was silence for a moment "mark."

Jack swore that he could actually feel the fuel being rushed into the plane, it only took a matter of minutes before his pilot said, "Tanker one, Harrier one, refueling complete."

"Harrier one break connection on my mark," again there was silence for a moment "mark."

Again Jack felt the click as his plane dropped away from the umbrella and moved off to the right away from the tanker and the rest of the squadron. Jack watched mesmerized as each one of the Harrier jets easily slid in and connected and was refueled and then moved back into formation on his plane. The whole squadron was refueled in a matter of thirty or so minutes and got back in formation. Jack watched as the refueling pipe began to be pulled back into the tanker.

"Tanker one, this is Harrier one, all refueling completed. We thank you very much and have a safe trip home."

"Harrier one same to you, you'll be home before we are," and Jack felt the acceleration as the squadron returned to their cruising speed.

"That was absolutely amazing, everyone made it look so easy, how many times have you done it?"

"Too numerous to mention," laughed his pilot "it's not as difficult as it looks, once you've done it once it gets easier and easier every time. We now have sufficient fuel to get us back home, in a little while we'll try to raise your friends on the GPS phone, if that fails will try the ham radio."

They relaxed and sat back in silence, Jack was wondering what they were going to find.

"Okay let's see if we can get anybody on the GPS phone," said the pilot "we're about one hour from those coordinates you gave me."

"Okay, how's this going to work?"

"I'll get through and once we get a response it's all yours."

Jack heard clicking in his headset and then it sounded just like a normal phone. "Last Chance here, who's this?"

"It's all yours," said the pilot.

Jack spoke into the microphone in his helmet, "hello Last Chance, Jack Brown here, who am I speaking to?"

"Jack, Jack is that really you, this is Joshua, we'd almost given up hope, where the hell are you?"

"It's a long story but right now I'm in a jet fighter flying into San Diego, my wife and I got your very cryptic message and decided to take you up on your offer to have us come and join you. Captain can you put this through so that my wife can hear?"

"Sure can," there was a couple of clicks on the line and then "honey can you hear me?" said Anna

"Sure can honey, we have Last Chance, Joshua, on the phone, Joshua my wife Anna."

"Hello and nice to hear from you, I hope we all meet soon. Now what's happening Jack?"

"We should be at the coordinates that you gave us in your message in approximately one hour, we're in a Harrier jump jet. The pilot assures me that we can land vertically at those coordinates, is there a space for us to land?"

"Sure is, it's a truck container transfer station, lots of open flat land. If you give us fifteen minutes warning we'll be in the air and check it out before you arrive. Things are pretty unstable out there but there shouldn't be any body in the facility."

"Okay, we'll do that, we'll see you in a little while."

"Okay see you then." And the Captain disconnected the phone.

It only took them about thirty five minutes before Jack's and Anna's planes left the squadron who carried straight on to San Diego without them. The two planes slowed down as the pilot called Last Chance again and informed them that they would be landing in approximately fifteen minutes.

A couple of minutes before they arrived at the transfer station someone in a helicopter informed them that there was nobody around that area and that it was safe to land. It was a fantastic and very strange feeling as the jet fighter slowed down and eventually stopped in mid air coming down to land at the transfer station vertically like an elevator coming down the chute. What was even more amazing was watching Anna's aircraft come down and land a few feet away from them.

"Well I guess Dr. Jack we'll be leaving you here," said his pilot "you might as well keep the flight suit and helmet, can you get out and climb down on your own?"

"I sure can, thank you for a wonderful trip, this is the most amazing plane I've ever been in. Thank you for everything."

"You're very welcome," said the pilot as the cockpit slid open, "I hope you find everything safe and sound, good hunting."

Jack disconnected himself and climbed out of the plane dropping down to the ground.

"Thank you for everything and be safe."

He turned round and watched his wife climb down safely from the plane, they ran over to each other, Anna gave him a hug and both of them ran out of the way for the planes to take off. There was a tremendous roar as the jet engines lifted both planes up vertically, they seemed to shudder slightly as they started their forward motion and then they roared off into the distance. They took off their flight helmets and watched as a helicopter flew down to land a little way away from them, they waited until the blades had slowed down and watched as Joshua got out of the plane and ran to greet them.

"God it's good to see you, we'd almost given up hope but you're safe and sound. You must be Anna, it's good to meet you at last, come on let's get you into the helicopter, it's not safe to hang around anywhere up here for any length of time, all hell's broken loose.

"It sure is good to see you," said Anna "okay let's get out of here."

The three of them ran across to the helicopter and jumped in, before they even got their safety harnesses fastened it took off flying them to Last Chance.

35

Lions.

On route to Last Chance.

Ghost and Mary both saw the ponies at the same time, they were just coming out of the wooded lot where they'd camped for the night. The sun was coming up, it was a beautiful morning and there were just a few flecks of clouds in the sky and a slight breeze that rustled the leaves gently. Ghost signaled to his wife who moved off to their right dropping down into the tall grass, he disappeared toward the left, both of them moving off in a slight circle toward the ponies. Ten minutes later the two of them rose to their feet having encircled the ponies completely.

"Well," said Ghost turning to his wife "I don't see anybody, I don't hear anybody, all I found were the ponies' tracks coming down that little lane type thing over there."

"I agree, no sign of people, it looks like they've come by themselves, they could be a blessing to us they still have bridles and saddles, I wondered what happened to their riders?"

"Well let's see if we can get hold of them," and they both moved slowly, but obviously, toward the ponies. They were two beautifully painted horses, it was obvious to both of them that they were riding and work horses, short and thick in stature, well muscled and very well looked after. The two ponies did not bat an eyelid as they approached and gently spoke to them, Mary took hold of the reins of the black and brown one while her husband got hold of the other bridle speaking to the pale white and yellow pony in a soft mellow voice. They led them both round in a small circle and the ponies seemed quite happy to be controlled again.

"I think we'd better back track these for a little ways and see what happened to their riders."

"Ok, fine with me," said his wife leaping up into the saddle, they were both very competent and comfortable riding and looking after horses. Ghost mounted and they followed the tracks back down the little used pathway, all their senses were alert. The tracks led through some long grass, through a small gully and as they were coming out the ponies started getting a little jittery.

"Something's frightening them, I think I can smell something," said Ghost sniffing gently at the breeze "Don't know what it is, it's vaguely familiar but I can't quite place it. How about you?"

"It's, it's something, I don't think it's quite possible," she said. Ghost knew that his wife's sense of smell was even keener than his.

"What is it?"

"It's a big cat smell," Mary was quieting down her pony "I swear, it's big cats but that's impossible."

"Nope, anything's possible these days. I think you're right, we'd better tie the ponies up, I don't think we should take them any further."

They both dismounted, took the ponies back about a hundred yards where they seemed to quiet down and tied them firmly to some trees.

"Ok, let's go, be careful."

They both reached into their packs and took out some short arrows with leather covered tips and pulled forward a short bow no more then three feet from tip to tip. They put one end on the ground, bent the bow, and hooked up a catgut twine.

"The poison on these arrows will stop a big cat in a matter of seconds but we'd better have spares ready," said Ghost checking to be sure that his arrows were free and ready to be pulled out of the pack behind him.

"I'm ready, let's go," said Mary, Ghost could hear the tension in her voice. They both moved off silently through the trees, going slightly to their right following the scent on the breeze.

"I hear them, we're really close," whispered Mary in her husband's ear "They're quiet but I can hear them breathing and licking, they're to our right, we're downwind."

Ghost nodded as they lowered themselves down and crept through the trees coming out into a small field with long grass. They lifted their heads and there, not a hundred yards from them, they could see a pride of lions lying down. There was one great big male sitting on his hindquarters totally unconcerned licking himself and around him were four females, they were all just lying around, Mary could see some blood on the lions' paws as they lazily cleaned themselves.

Ghost rose up standing tall, the male lion looked at him unconcerned, one of the females stood up, looked his way, turned around and laid back down again. Mary rose up beside her husband, both had their bow and arrows in their right hand.

"I don't think there's anything to be afraid of, they've obviously eaten and won't want to hunt or kill again until tonight or tomorrow. If you look to the left of them you can see their kill, it's another pony."

They both moved slowly but obviously to their left, only the male followed them with his head. As they came a little closer it was obvious that the lions had killed a pony and they'd all fed well tearing it open.

"That's three ponies and still no riders," said Ghost.

"Perhaps they ran when they saw the lions."

"Let's follow round and see where the ponies and the lions came from."

They moved back to their right, going round in a circle until they picked up the tracks of the pony.

"Here, this is where they first hit him, it was the females, two of them got him from the front and one got him from the back, he must have kept going up to where he fell, where they fed on him. Ok, let's back track him for a bit," said Ghost.

The tracks went through the edge of the field and into a small cops, in the middle of the trees they came across two human bodies, one female and one male, both had obviously been mauled to death by the lions.

"What a mess," said Mary walking over to the female who'd had her stomach ripped open and her head twisted right around. "It looks like they killed these two first, decided they didn't like the taste and went after the pony, these two didn't have a chance."

"We can't leave them like this, they're obviously Native Americans."

"I guest we'd better bury them."

Her husband nodded.

"I believe they're Navajo Indians, they don't have very much with them," Ghost said as he went around the small encampment "they must've been traveling very light, or else they're just out for a day trip from home."

"Well they won't need the ponies anymore, we could sure use them and we'll take some of their bits and pieces with us, we'll just leave their stuff till after we've buried them."

Suddenly they both stopped, they heard a weak crying sound.

"What was that?" said Ghost looking around alert for any danger.

"If I didn't know any better I'd have said that was a baby crying," Mary said answering him and looking around, suddenly a baby started crying loudly, they both stopped dead in their tracks and looked up, the sound was coming from above them.

"Well, bless my soul," said Mary, the surprise showing in her voice "Will you look at that?" and they both looked up into the tree branches above them and saw a papoose hanging above them on a branch, way out from the tree trunk. They both just stood and looked in amazement.

"How the hell did it get up there?"

"About the only way it could get up there is if someone threw it up there. I'll bet one of these two realized the trouble they were in and, as a very last resort, threw the baby up into the tree hoping that it wouldn't fall back down to the ground. They obviously saved the baby's life."

"The question now is how are we going to get it down?" Mary said grinning at her husband.

"I guess one of us is going to have to go up the tree and see if we can shake it loose, the branches are too flimsy to climb out onto, we'll never reach it before they break off. The other one will have to stay below and be the catcher."

"Well now, who said that they were a monkey back down in the Amazon and who used to show off climbing through the trees while they hunted without the women," Mary mocked her husband.

"Ok, ok, I get it, you catch, I climb," Ghost said as he started to hoist himself up the trunk of the tree.

"You be careful," laughed Mary taking her place below the papoose "I don't want to have to try and carry you to Last Chance."

It only took a couple of minutes for Ghost to climb the tree up to the branch that went out to where the baby was, gingerly he climbed out, lying along the bow. He felt the bow bending, he inched a little closer and then stopped, it was obvious that he did not dare go any further out on the branch.

"That's about as far as you dare go," Mary called out seeing her husband bending the branch down toward the ground.

"I'm gonna start shaking it, get ready to catch it, it only looks like it's caught on a small branch, it might bounce in any direction. Are you ready?"

"Yup, ready and waiting, it's time to deliver the baby," his wife laughed.

"This is one helluva a way to get a baby, here we go," Ghost started to wiggle the branch up and down, the papoose just went up and down and the baby started to cry. It was obvious that he or she was now wide-awake and was not enjoying the ride provided by the movement of the branch.

Ghost continued moving the branch up and down for the next few minutes but the papoose just would not let go.

"You're not very good at delivering babies, I don't think you're going to get it off like that, try swinging side to side."

Ghost found it much more difficult to swing the branch from side to side and it took a few tries to get the movement right but suddenly the papoose fell, the branch did not break, the papoose just came loose and down it fell baby and all. It bounced off one of the lower branches and Mary had to do a running dive but she caught it before it hit the ground, the baby was screaming and crying as Mary cuddled it to her chest.

"Is it ok?" called down her husband.

"Yes, it's fine just a little scared," his wife said as she undid the papoose that had held the baby in tightly. Easing the baby out, she held it and rocked it and slowly the baby settled down.

"You can come down now, you did very well indeed, for a man of your age," she grinned up at her husband who was inching his way slowly backward until he got to the trunk and then he came down quickly.

He stood looking down at the baby. "Is it a boy or a girl?

"I don't have the faintest idea you nut, we'll have to look and see, I think it most likely needs its diaper changed. See if you can find some baby milk or formula and clean diapers, they'll most probably be over there in that colorful bag."

Ghost went over and brought the whole bag back to Mary. Hunting through it they found half a dozen baby bottles filled with milk or formula and some disposable diapers and some clean baby clothes.

Mary laid the baby down, undid the suit and changed the baby's diaper. "Pew! Sure does need changing," she said "Give me one of those diapers, is there any baby powder in there?"

Ghost felt down to the bottom of the bag and came up with some Johnson's Baby Powder.

"Well, it's a boy," said Ghost peering down at the naked child "Now what are we going to do with him?"

"We'll just have to take him with us," said Mary as she finished changing the diaper.

"Well you said you were thinking that maybe we should have a baby, now you've got one."

"That was just a little fast, I was saying we should think about it when we got to Last Chance but you're right, instant family," Mary grinned happily as she fed the baby a bottle and watched him gurgle in her arms.

They dug one grave and lowered both the bodies into it, the baby watched them, propped up on one of the blankets.

It took them almost three hours to finish the burial and when they were done Ghost went back and brought up the ponies. They loaded one of them with all the belongings of the two who had died and then they went on their way with Mary happily holding a drooling baby in her arms.

They had been riding side by side for some hours in a comfortable silence since the baby had fallen asleep, it was almost dusk.

"You know we're being trailed," Mary said.

"Yes, they've been with us for about the last half an hour. We have at least two people further back on your side and one or two people closer up on my side, they're not doing very well at hiding."

"I wonder who they are, they haven't attempted anything yet which they could have done very easily as we passed through that gully, I guess they're not too unfriendly."

"I think we'd better stop and let them know that we know they're there, stay ready and keep the blow pipes handy," Ghost said as he put his hand behind him into his knapsack and put a small dart into his two-foot blowpipe putting it on his lap and hanging the container of darts on the pummel of his saddle, Mary did the same. They reined in the ponies and sat there, both of them putting their hands up on their heads showing that they were unarmed. They only had to sit there for a couple of minutes when two men on horses moved out of a bunch of bushes and stopped some distance from them to their right. Ghost looked over his shoulder and sure enough, two more riders came up on the other side and stopped about the same distance from them. They all sat there silently and then from a rocky outcrop in front of them another man rode out and slowly came toward them.

"They're Navajo," whispered Mary and Ghost nodded. The man eased his horse forward holding a rifle in both hands and stopped twenty feet in front of them.

"Where did you get the ponies?"

"We found them some hours ago, their owners had been killed by some big cats."

"You're telling me that they were killed by wild animals?"

"Yes, lions to be exact."

"Lions my foot, a very likely story, I think you killed them and stole the ponies."

"That's ridiculous," said Mary as she held up the baby "We found the baby up in a tree, at least he's safe."

The man made a gesture and the other four riders moved in close, they all had rifles at the ready.

"I don't think I believe you but we will see, follow me." He didn't wait for a response but spun his horse around and started off. Mary looked at Ghost who nodded to her, they put down their hands and followed him with the other four bringing up the rear.

About three quarters of an hour later they rode down a slope to a small river where they could see an Indian camp laid out on a small plain beside the running water, it looked like something out of a cowboy movie. There were twenty or thirty teepees set up and men, women and children stopped what they were doing watching them come into the camp, there were dogs yapping and a bunch of ponies tethered in the tree line off to the right. They rode into the encampment silently, all the people lined up to watch them as they passed through the camp. The leading man stopped in front of one of the teepees, jumped off his horse and disappeared inside. A couple of minutes later he came out with an old man dressed in full Indian clothing.

"He looks magnificent," thought Mary.

The man stepped out and looked at them.

"I'm the Chief of this group," the man said running his hand around as if to show off the encampment "Who are you and what have you done with Snake in the Grass and his wife?"

"They call me Ghost and this is my wife Mary, we found your friend's camp, he and his wife had been killed by a pride of lions that also killed one of their ponies and ate it for lunch."

The Chief paused for a moment. "Get down off your ponies and give the baby to her," he said pointing to a young woman who came forward. Mary bent down and handed the baby over reluctantly. They both dismounted sliding their blowpipes into their knapsacks as they did. Two of the men on the horses behind them moved forward, gathered up their ponies' reins and moved off, the other men still covered them with their rifles.

"What do you intend to do with us?" asked Mary.

There was silence for a moment. "We'll have to check out your story before I decide what is to become of you," the Chief said nodding at the man who had led them in. He leapt agilely back onto his horse, spun it around and rode off followed by the two other men.

"Until then you are our guests," said the Chief indicating to them to enter his teepee. Mary looked at her husband who nodded and they followed the Chief into his abode. They were amazed at how comfortable it seemed inside, there was a very small fire, barely embers, in the center, whatever smoke there was rose up and exited through the opening at the top of the teepee. There were blankets all around one side and folding chairs that seemed oddly out of place on the other side. The Chief signaled for them to sit in two of the chairs while he made himself comfortable on the pile of blankets.

"Now tell me exactly what happened."

Mary and Ghost proceeded to tell him, in great detail, of what they had found and what they had done, he listened intently, at times he almost seemed like he was asleep.

"That's quite a tale," the Chief said as both Mary and Ghost stopped talking. "What you're telling me is that we have a pride of lions on the loose. I guess it may be true but it's not very likely. We'll have to wait, in the meantime can I offer you some food and refreshments?

Mary nodded enthusiastically as Ghost realized they had missed a meal and he was really hungry.

"Thank you, that would be wonderful and I thank you for your hospitality," Ghost said.

"Don't mistake my hospitality for softness, if it turns out that there are no lions and that you killed my people, trust me, there will be very swift consequences."

"Your men will find everything just as we said. It's fantastic to see how you've managed to realign your lives."

"We were fortunate, there was a gathering of the tribes the night of the President's speech and we had set up our wigwams and teepees with some of the other tribes, there must've been over a thousand natives. As soon as we heard what the President had to say this, my tribe, went back home which isn't too far from here and gathered all our belongings and came down here and made camp. This is the area where we used to camp, where we used to live so we have almost reverted naturally back to our old ways, of course, we still have some of the modern conveniences. We do have radios and generators and ham radio facilities, we are trying to follow what's going on but here we don't have to worry about that little white crystal. I guess we're just going to have to live like this until everything's settled down. Our greatest fear is of intruders such as you, needless to say, we are well guarded in all directions."

The Chief went out of the teepee and returned followed by two young women carrying two glasses of lemonade one for each of them and the Chief settled back down again sipping on a glass of something. In what seemed like only a few minutes later two plates of food appeared and Mary and Ghost dined slowly while making small talk with the Chief.

It was in the wee hours of the morning when they heard a commotion outside, the Chief led them out into the cool night air and much to Ghost and Mary's surprise, it looked like the whole camp was still up. The encampment was lit by a large number of fires, each one surrounded by people sitting and talking, they watched as the three riders came in from the far end of the encampment, leading a couple of horses behind them over which two bodies lay. The Chief waited for them as they came through the camp and through the crowds of people who had left their fires and were crowding in to find out what was going on. The three horsemen pulled up in front of the Chief, Ghost and Mary and dismounted, the young man, who was obviously the leader of the three, approached them.

"What did you find?" asked the Chief.

"They have spoken the truth, everything was as they said it would be."

"We found the remains of the pony, we dug up Snake in the Grass and his wife, they had been mauled to death, we brought them home for a tribal burial. If it hadn't been for these two the baby would have died. Snake in the Grass must've been on his way back and taken a short cut, one that we don't usually use, I don't believe any of us would have found them in time to save the baby."

"Well done. Did everybody hear that?" the Chief asked to the crowd "Are there any questions?"

The crowd stood still and silent.

"Then I find these two exonerated and we must welcome them as friends and thank them for saving the baby."

He turned back and shook hands with both Ghost and Mary. "I apologize for keeping you under suspicion but you must understand that we needed to know."

Ghost and his wife relaxed for the first time.

"That's ok Chief, we understand completely," said Ghost as Mary nodded her head vigorously "We would have done the same thing if we were in your shoes. In this very strange, chaotic and unstable world in which we now find ourselves you can't be too careful. You've done extremely well in placing your tribe in a position to be fairly safe and secure, any stranger must be treated with suspicion or you may bring a terrible end to all of you."

"Thank you," said the Chief turning to his people he called out, "Ok, ok, all you nosy people, you may all go to bed we have work to do tomorrow so don't expect to lay in too long."

The crown moved away with murmurs as pent up nervousness and energy was released.

"Please would you two accept my hospitality and sleep in my home, later on we will talk and see what has to be done." The Chief turned to the three young Indians.

"Thank you, please place the bodies over in the storage tent, we will have the women look after them later, they must receive their last rights before the sun goes down today."

The men nodded and led their horses off to the right of the encampment.

Ghost and his wife had slept remarkably well, though only for a very few hours, on a pile of very soft blankets in the Chief's tent, were woken up with breakfast of hot strong tea and fruit and, much to their surprise, the Chief was already up and gone. They ate and then washed at the river followed by a crowd of young children asking all sorts of questions about the lions. After they returned they sat before the Chief in the center of the village.

"What are your plans?"

'We're heading toward our sanctuary, it's not too far from here, down in the valley of the river, we hope to find safety there amongst friends," said Mary.

"I see, there're only two places down in that steep canyon river, the place that rents out motorboats and rubber rafts to tourists and further down the place that they call Last Chance, which of the two are you going to?"

This caught both Mary and Ghost off guard, not too many people knew of Last Chance.

"You know of Last Chance?" said Ghost surprised.

"Yes, we know of Last Chance and I know Joshua and Bella well, through the years we have met on several occasions. The caves behind their cabin were once used by members of our tribe and still hold some religious meaning to us. Thanks to Joshua we have, on a couple of occasions, visited our ancestral caves and sat and eaten at Bella's table."

"Good heavens," said Ghost with a big grin on his face "I was one of the young men that grew up at Last Chance, now that you mention it, I remember a group of natives coming and holding some ceremony on the granite plateau, was that you, or at least were you one of them?"

The Chief grinned with surprise, "Yes, the medicine man held a ceremony there, now I remember you, you were the only black boy there, you were the one we caught hiding in the rocks inside the cave after we had explicitly told everyone that they couldn't watch the ceremony. I remember, you were most angry when we made you leave."

"That's right, that's right, that was me, good heavens all those years ago, it just doesn't seem possible. Well, all the boys that were at the camp at that time are coming back to try and be safe from the horrors and the dangers going on in the rest of the country. We hope we'll be safe there but you know as well as I do that no one will really be safe, there are too many bastards and mad idiots out there, we've seen some horrific sights."

They sat silently for a minute all deep in their own thoughts.

"Well I wish you well, again, I cannot thank you enough for rescuing the baby. Is there anything that you could use that we can help you with on the last leg of your journey?"

Mary and Ghost thought for a moment. "If we could have a couple of ponies it would certainly speed up the trip, I realize that they're a very important commodity but if you have a couple you could spare it would certainly help us."

"Done, no problem, we have quite a few, there's a herd just over the other side of the stream past that hill. It was the very first thing that we did when we heard the President's speech, our tribe was pretty well off because of the casinos and we have always kept plenty of ponies on hand, you are welcome to two of them. Anything else?"

"No Chief," said Ghost gratefully "just those two will be wonderful we are completely self sufficient."

"Good, when would you like to leave?"

About two hours later Mary and Ghost rode out of the encampment, it seemed like the whole tribe turned out to say goodbye and, just as they were about to leave, a young woman ran up beside Mary's pony and handed her the baby that they had rescued. Mary held him tightly for a moment, kissed him on the forehead and handed him back.

They rode out quietly and Ghost saw a tear running down Mary's cheek.

They made excellent time on the ponies and, just as the sun started to go down, they came to the canyon rim and looked down at the river, way down below them.

"It's beautiful," said Mary "You've often talked to me about this place but I've never seen it, you're right, it is truly awesome."

They followed the canyon rim down river until they came to a spot where the canyon walls were not quite so steep, the walls sloped down with just the slightest angle that had allowed shrubbery and trees to actually grow on the cliff face.

"This is it, we're now directly above Last Chance, as you can see, from this side of the canyon it's invisible, from the other side, of course, it can be seen quite clearly across the river canyon."

"How the hell are we going to get down to it?"

"We're going down through those trees and shrubs," grinned Ghost seeing his wife become quite uncomfortable at the thought.

"What the hell do you mean, we can't go down there it's way too steep."

"Years ago Indian and I found a way to go up and down, we used to have a lot of fun disappearing from the camp and letting the others try to find us. I won't lie to you, it's fairly dangerous but I'm sure we can make it."

"What about the ponies?"

"These are Indian horses, they're sure footed and they have four feet compared to our two, they'll be much more comfortable going down than we are. In fact, we may just be able to follow them once they get the idea."

Mary just stood there, mouth open.

Ghost led the way down, the most frightening part of the experience was stepping down from the edge of the canyon rim into the bushes. Ghost was right, the ponies seemed to have no problem, in fact, they watched with interest as the two humans, slipping and sliding and grabbing hold of bushes and trees and twigs made their way down the canyon wall. By the time they all got close to the bottom the last rays of the sun were disappearing. Ghost motioned to Mary to be still and pointed off to his left where she saw a man sitting on an outcrop of rock, obviously a look out.

Ghost whispered in his wife's ear, "I think I recognize him, I haven't seen him for many years but I think that's Joshua, stay here with the horses I think I'll give him the surprise of his life." His wife nodded as Ghost silently moved through the shrubs coming up behind Joshua.

Joshua sat comfortably on some rocks on top of a couple of folded blankets, he was deep in thought watching the river as it flowed by. There was a sentry on the other end of the granite slab probably doing the same thing. In his lap he had a pair of powerful binoculars and propped against the rock beside him was a rifle with a telescopic sight, laid out on the rock to his left was his radio, he had a couple of hours left of his shift.

Suddenly his hair stood up on the back of his neck and his head whipped around this way and that as he heard a whisper in the darkness.

"Hello Joshua." His eyes searched the rocks around him, he grabbed his rifle and picked up his radio.

"Hello Joshua." The voice got louder and Joshua could here the amusement in the dulcet tones, "don't be alarmed Joshua this is Ghost."

Joshua stood up and turned around, all he saw behind him were bushes and shrubs and darkness.

"Ghost? You've gotta be kidding me, where the hell are you?"

A patch of darkness moved out from behind the shrubbery and there before him stood Ghost.

"Aw shit! You scared the daylights out of me! How the hell did you get down here? My God Ghost I almost had a heart attack."

Ghost roared with laughter and stepped up close to Joshua and swooped and grabbed him and held him tight.

"God it's wonderful to see you, we're here at last"

Joshua relaxed and hugged him back.

"Are you alone?"

"Mary, Mary, it's ok, come on down." Joshua heard some rustling in the trees and then Mary came out followed by two ponies.

"How the hell did you get down here, how did you get the horses down here? My God, it's good to see you," he ran forward and hugged Mary "Thank God you're safe, we've been worried about you, are you both ok?"

"Yes we're fine," said Mary "It was a little scary coming down that cliff face but we're here. We didn't have a radio so we couldn't call you, cell phones of course are dead but we're here, safe and sound. It's wonderful to meet you at last."

"It's wonderful to meet you too," said Joshua hugging her and giving her a kiss on the cheek "My God we were so worried, this means everyone's here except Indian, we haven't heard from him in days. Come on down, come down and meet everybody, I just can't believe that you've made it."

Joshua led them down along the granite slab where they were greeted enthusiastically with open arms and dozens and dozens of questions.

"Thank God, just one more group to come in and we'll all be here," thought the Judge to himself.

36

Prisoners.

On route from Indian's cabin.

The first day Quiet Sunshine, Indian and the kids made excellent time, for the first few hours they had tried to stay on the side roads but even these soon became so busy they had to take off across country to get anywhere. They quickly learned to stay away from people, there were crowds along the roadways blocking everything up so that no one could go anywhere and anger and tempers flared. There were fights and arguments going on everywhere. They were all desperate to find somewhere to live or to find somewhere safe and some had taken off across the fields, there were tracks every where, some showed where some had made it, other tracks just led to abandoned vehicles at various distances from the road. On numerous occasions people tried to take the Hummer and the horses away from them either by threats of force or by begging for help. Quiet Sunshine and Indian were well armed, and with a show of armaments, they had managed to keep moving without actually having to resort to fire power even though Diane wanted to help everybody, it was very obvious that they had to stand on their own two feet and they had had to recognize that they could not assist others if they wanted to survive.

By the evening of the second day they had made good time going across country but were still wasting some time trying to get across the blocked roads that they kept running into. On the roads where the traffic was jammed bumper-to-bumper and was at a complete stand still, many of the vehicles had been abandoned. It was impossible to just drive across the road, so they had to attach the front winch onto one of the cars on the road and pull it out of the way to make themselves a big enough gap to get their vehicle across safely. This all took a lot of time and left them open to being approached by people, if there were any, which meant that they had to handle them too.

The second night they made camp in a wooded area and as the young folk were looking after the horses Quiet Sunshine turned to her husband.

"Honey, I think it's time to abandon the Hummer, we're losing time trying to get it through the traffic on the roads we may make better time on the horses. What do you think?"

Indian nodded, he had been thinking the same thing.

"You're right Sunshine it's time, we've had two good days, if we can keep up on the horses we should take about another five to seven days to get down there, I think we'll make better time without the Hummer. It's getting dark right now, let's have a good night's rest and in the morning we'll head out on the horses."

"What about all those people along the roadways, what's going to happen to them?"

It was a rhetorical question, there was, of course, no answer but Indian said. "They'll have to fend and fight for themselves or they won't survive, you've seen what happens to the weak, only the strong will survive."

He was referring to the bodies that they'd seen here and there and reading the signs it was obvious that people had commandeered vehicles from their owners and set off across country leaving bodies lying beside the roadway. It was amazing, at first the young ones had been really upset at the sight of the dead bodies but already they seemed to just accept it, it hardly seemed to bother them any more, Indian wasn't sure if this was a good or a bad thing.

Quiet Sunshine moved over and wrapped her arms around her husband from the back and kissed him gently on the back of the neck. "I love you, I think the kids are ready and prepared for a trek on horseback. Diane's going to be the problem; she's such a softhearted one, all this death and destruction will hit her hard later on when she has time for it all to bubble back up to the surface."

"You're right but deep down she'll be the one to accept it all given time. Paula, on the other hand, eventually it'll hit her and she'll go to pieces, you'll see, once we're safe you'd better keep a close watch on her. Lord only knows what Kerry's going to be like, he's been through hell already this is just piling more on top of more, we'll just have to wait and see with him but I think they'll all hold up until we get to Last Chance."

He twisted around in her arms, held her close and kissed her tenderly on the ear, then whispered, "We'll make it, we'll be safe, just stay on guard."

Quiet Sunshine held onto him nodding her head gently against his shoulder.

The next morning, much to the disgust of the young folk, they packed up everything that they needed from the Hummer and the horse trailer, they set up two Indian travois's, one on each of two of the horses, these consisted of two poles, one on either side of the animal harnessed to its chest, shoulders and back with crossbars keeping the poles apart and spreading them wider as they left the flanks of the horses. The poles were quite long and their ends just dragged along on the ground. These were covered with canvas and then were loaded with the things that they wanted to take with them.

Quiet Sunshine went through everything as the young folk unpacked it and then repacked it and loaded everything up. They put on the saddlebags, making sure all the riders had weapons readily available and, after having a hearty breakfast, they set off, each one quiet in their own thoughts, each one glancing back to see the Hummer slowly disappearing behind them. Iggy was the happiest one of the group, he was jubilant to be free of the Hummer, he was out and about, running here and there, sniffing at everything, disappearing every now and then only to reappear suddenly to check on them.

By noon they had settled in to a good steady pace, staying out of sight of roads. At first they were quiet and then slowly they started talking and there was even an occasional laugh. Quiet Sunshine knew that they were now ready for this last trek to Last Chance.

Later that day they came out of a wooded area to see yet another road jam of abandoned vehicles. It was now easier with just the horses to cross the roads, all they had to do was find a gap big enough to go through but as they approached this road Indian raised his hand and they stopped quickly, Quiet Sunshine brought her horse up beside his.

"Something's wrong, it just doesn't feel right, look, you can see bullet holes in the sides of the cars and there's a body hanging out here and there. I don't like it, we've seen the occasional fight and a few bodies but this looks like it goes right down the line of cars. I think we'd better check this out before we ride up there."

Quiet Sunshine nodded and they turned their horses back and led the group into a wood.

"What's wrong, Indian?" said Paula.

"I don't quite know, it just looks… well, it just doesn't feel good." Said Sunshine "You three stay here with the horses, keep Iggy with you, Indian and I are going to go and have a look. You know the bird songs, if you hear all safe you can come out and join us, if you hear anything else, stay put unless you hear the call for help signal. If you get the help signal you tie the horses down and you come in carefully, staying apart, use Iggy, you all know his signals."

Since they had left the cottage Indian and Quiet Sunshine had been teaching them some of the birdcalls and how to use them in case they ran into a circumstance such as this.

"You sure you don't want one of us with you?"

"No Kerry, Sunshine and I'll go, you stay here we may need you three to back us up."

Quiet Sunshine and Indian dismounted, took off their backpacks, told Iggy to stand guard and moved quietly toward the road. As they came up to the side of the roadway Indian pointed down at the ground.

"There's been a couple of four-wheel drive vehicles in this dirt, going down the side of the road, every vehicle on the road has been shot with a high velocity machine gun then someone's come along and executed anyone that was still alive," he said as he examined the body of an old man that lay beside a car. Inside the car was an old lady with white hair, probably his wife. She had obviously been killed in the hail of gunfire presumably from the four-wheel drive vehicles, her husband had taken a bullet through the arm and had then been shot through the back of his head outside the vehicle.

"God this is awful," said Quiet Sunshine moving from vehicle to vehicle, "they're all dead."

They moved slowly down the line of vehicles noting that it was nearly always the front drivers and passengers sections that were riddled by gunfire. They came to the front of the line to find that an overpass had collapsed onto the roadway blocking it completely. Some vehicles had apparently tried to take off and go around the base of the overpass; some had even tried to go up the grassy slope but got stuck before they reached the top, some had disappeared across the fields, others had been bogged down in the dirt but there was nobody alive. They crossed to the other side of the road and walked back slowly and carefully, all the cars on that side had been riddled with gunfire too, there had to be forty or fifty cars lined up, two abreast. As they were passing a transport truck Quiet Sunshine hesitated for just a second and looked at her husband, seeing his hand move down to the butt of his pistol on his waist.

Indian just nodded, he had heard something from under the transport truck.

"Honey I'm going to cross over here and check those vehicles on the other side of this transport, I don't think anyone's left alive."

"Ok but do you notice that there are hardly any young people here, just a few who have been killed in the crossfire, the gunfire seems to have been aimed almost exclusively at the drivers and front passengers."

Again, Indian nodded. "By the looks of these marks in the mud it appears they've taken some people with them, must be the younger ones," he called to her as he moved around to the back of the truck and came towards the cab. In one very smooth motion he threw himself down prostrate on the ground, the gun in his hand pointing up under the rear wheels of the transport.

"Don't shoot, don't shoot, please don't shoot, oh God, please don't shoot."

Indian saw a teenage girl hiding right up above the rear axle, almost invisible.

"Alright, come out slowly, don't make any sudden moves, we're here to help you, we're not here to kill you or hurt you. You understand?"

Quiet Sunshine appeared on the other side of the truck, lying down on the roadway, her gun covering her husband and the area where the voice came from, from where she was she could not see anybody. Slowly a pair of grubby jeans and white runners climbed down onto the road underneath the truck followed by a white blouse and big mop of red hair, both hands held forward as she knelt on the road.

"You're not with them are you? You're not with them? Please, don't hurt me."

"We're here to help you," said Quiet Sunshine, hearing a female voice the young lady's head whipped around. "You're safe, c'mon out, be careful."

The young lady began to crawl out toward Quiet Sunshine, Indian stood up, walked around the truck and gave her a hand, as she stood up she had to lean on the side of the truck for a minute.

"Thank you, thank you, I thought I was a goner, they killed everybody, all the older people, they took the young ones, they even took my younger brother," said the young lady as she burst into tears and slid down to sit on the road. Quiet Sunshine sat down beside her and pulled her close.

Paula, Diane, and Kerry heard the all-clear birdcall and came out cautiously keeping apart as they had been taught; Iggy suddenly appeared from a tall clump of grass and began investigating every thing. At first they could not see anybody and then Indian appeared on the top of one of one of the cars waving his hands, they moved down the line of cars until they found a gap wide enough for the horses to walk between, they dismounted as the young lady from under the truck looked up.

"Kerry, Paula take guard one on one side of the road, one on the other, Diane up on top of the truck, keep your eyes open." The three of them moved swiftly, dismounting, tying the horses up to the car doors and taking up their positions without a word.

Quiet Sunshine looked at her husband with a slight smile on her face and he nodded back, they were learning and they were learning fast. Quiet Sunshine squatted down. "Can you tell us what happened?"

The young lady wiped away her tears and held onto Quiet Sunshine tightly. "My name is Muirlene, Muirlene Jacobson. We were all stuck in this terrible traffic jam, we heard gunfire from behind us, mother and father were in the front seat and my brother, Thomas and I were in the back. Father started screaming, 'Get out, get out, c'mon get out and hide.' I managed to open the back door and fell out as the gunfire got closer and closer I saw my mother trying to open the door and my brother frantically trying to undo his safety belt and get across the back seat to get out and then I watched from under the car as a vehicle drove up slowly shooting as they came up along side the parked vehicles," she began to cry and weep. She paused for a bit and then carried on, "they were shooting everybody in the front of the vehicles. Anybody who got out and tried to make a run for it they just mowed down. They were laughing and jeering and calling people names. There were vehicles doing the same thing on either side of the road, I could hear them, it all seemed to happen so fast. They came from the back and from the front of the line up, they swooped down and met somewhere in the middle and then these men and women walked up and down the line on foot shooting people. They forced all the young people to the sides of the road, some of them tried to make a break for it and they just shot them. It was as if they were just playing a game. Slowly all the young people just stood, I saw my chance to get up underneath the transport truck, I curled up as far as I could underneath the chassis above the back wheels where you found me. Suddenly it was all over, there was a horrible silence, just the occasional shot but then I could hear the young people crying as they were herded towards the back of the line up. I heard some one shouting telling everyone to get into a school bus and then they all disappeared, they just drove off and there was just me and all these dead people and silence." She buried her head into Quiet Sunshine's neck, her body racked with sobs.

"Can you tell me how long ago this happened? It couldn't have been that long ago."

"They left," the young lady looked at the watch on her wrist, "an hour ago. Oh God, they've got my brother."

Quiet Sunshine helped her to her feet as Indian called his group together. "Ok everybody, let's head over to that wooded lot over there, we need to talk."

They moved their horses into the trees and let them graze.

"I checked the signs they left, they took off down the road, they left here about an hour ago according to Muirlene," Indian said nodding his head toward the young lady. "These bastards have taken the young people captive with them, apparently in a school bus. There were four four-wheel drive vehicles, two came from the front and two came from the back and they just mowed everybody down in the front seats of the various vehicles."

There was silence for a moment. "The bastards! The rotten, stinking bastards!" said Paula.

"What are we gonna do?" said Diane, forever the logical one.

Indian looked over at Sunshine who read his face and nodded back.

"Normally we should just head out and keep going, we can't worry about everybody but these are evil people and they've taken the young people, God only knows what they plan to do with them. I think we should at least have a quick look and see what's going on but this time we're going to put it up for a vote. Who's for just carrying on and walking away?" No hands went up. "I take it then that we're all in agreement to at least go and have a look?" All the hands went up. "Ok, let's follow them for awhile, just keep your wits about you and be ready for anything."

They helped Muirlene up on the horse behind Kerry, she clung tightly to his waist, Indian led them down the road keeping parallel to it, him on one side with Paula and Quiet Sunshine with the others on the other side, everyone was on alert and watching for any signs of the bus and vehicles.

A short time later Quiet Sunshine called from her side of the road, "Hey honey, they turned off here, there's a well used driveway and all the tracks point that way." She pointed to a gravel driveway that went around a small hill.

"Ok," said Indian guiding his horse across the road, "now let's spread out, keep a good distance between us, Sunshine and I'll go first, leave a good fifty feet then you Diane and Paula second, leave another fifty feet, and then Kerry and Muirlene you'll follow up behind. Keep your eyes and ears open, these people are dangerous, we don't want any surprises."

Indian looked around, everybody nodded. Quiet Sunshine took her side of the driveway and Indian took his position on the right side as they moved down the drive, senses alert. They slowly went around a small hill, the track went up around a wooded area where it forked but there were mud marks where the vehicles had taken the right fork.

Indian signaled to Iggy to stay at the back with Kerry.

They moved slowly through the wooded area and as they came to the last row of trees Indian reined in his horse. He looked over at his wife who nodded at him.

"Do you smell that?" He whispered.

His wife nodded, "that's a Havana cigar, they must have lookouts."

He turned in his saddle and gave a sign to the others who moved just as slowly and quietly grouping together in the thick of the wooded area. He and Quiet Sunshine tied their horses to one of the trees, motioned to the others to stay there and, keeping Iggy with them, moved quietly and carefully through the shrubbery sniffing the air as the wind blew toward them. It only took them a couple of minutes to spot a very bored lookout on a slight hillock to their left at the edge of the wood lot leaning against a big old oak tree smoking a huge Havana cigar. A machine gun and what looked like a rocket launcher lay on the ground beside him. Quiet Sunshine sank down low nodding at her husband. There was no noise, Indian moved silently through the underbrush, the guard never even knew that he had died, there was the slightest crack carried on the wind as Indian rose up behind him and in one swift motion broke his neck. Quiet Sunshine moved up to him and together they searched the guards clothing and found a radio.

Indian pushed the send button, heard it click a couple of times and then a gruff voice came back 'That you Charlie?'

"Yeah, yeah," grunted Indian into the microphone.

"You ok? Everything ok?"

"Yeah," grunted Indian into the microphone clicking the send button on and of quickly. "…. Fucking …..radios……."

" Yeah, fucking pieces of shit, those fucking cigars are gonna be the death of you. Keep your eyes open." The radio went quiet.

The two of them moved quietly through the wooded lot, a small single story bungalow came into view, built actually into the side of a grass-covered knoll, the driveway went right up to the house and parked out front were two all terrain vehicles. There was no sign of a school bus or the four-wheel drive vehicles they had been following. On either side of the bungalow were two large barns, the sliding doors were open and they could see a backhoe and an assortment of farm equipment sitting inside them.

"To the right," whispered Quiet Sunshine.

"Yes, I see him on top of the barn, you take care of him, something's horribly wrong, where is everybody?"

"Well they're not in the barns, they must be in the house but the house doesn't look big enough, there's no basement, it doesn't look very big unless it's built way back into the hill."

"We're just going to have to take a look." Indian nodded to his wife who immediately disappeared into the brush. He followed her movement through some tall grass, watching the very slightest of movement as the blades of grass moved and swayed in the breeze. Then he heard the slightest whisper of sound and the guard fell off the side of the barn and disappeared. Very quietly, very carefully he moved through the grass toward the bungalow, Quiet Sunshine appeared at the right hand corner of the building and he heard a birdcall, it was all clear from her point of view. Indian raised himself up and peaked through the bottom of the big bay window, he could see four men sitting playing cards, empty cans of beer were strewn around and they were laughing. He signaled to his wife who slid up beside him.

"There're four in this room," he whispered in her ear "You want to check the other windows? I'll keep an eye on them."

Quiet Sunshine nodded and moved from window to window; at each one signing to him that all was clear, it was obvious that no one expected any company real soon. Quiet Sunshine moved next to him underneath the bay window.

"You take the two on the right, I'll take the two on the left," she nodded.

Indian nodded his head three times.

There was a look of shock on the faces of the four men as they suddenly saw two figures rise up within ten feet of them outside the bay window, one of them reached for a gun on the chair beside him but his hand never reached it. The glass in the window shattered and all four men were dead before they hit the floor, there was an eerie kind of silence, the only noise had been the fot-fot-fot-fot as the silenced pistols went off in the well-trained hands of the two intruders outside the window. Quiet Sunshine and Indian dropped back down, stayed still for a time listening for the sounds of others but none came, there was silence. They moved to the front door, found it unlocked and slipped into the bungalow, Quiet Sunshine moved to the left, Indian to the right and they met back in the hallway.

"There's nobody else here, the place is empty," said Quiet Sunshine with a quizzical look on her face.

"We're missing something," said Indian carefully looking around.

Quiet Sunshine moved to the back of the hallway where there was a big bookcase, something looked slightly askew, she touched it and the bookcase moved. She pulled it towards her and it opened easily on well-oiled casters, behind it there was a tunnel going into the hill, Indian smiled at her and nodded, together they moved into the well-lit corridor. A short way in on the left hand side there was a door slightly open, they moved in silently, it was a large dormitory with twenty sleeping areas all very neatly laid out. They moved back into the corridor and tried a door on the right finding a similar dormitory but this one was very messy and obviously being used. They continued down the main corridor, to the left was another dormitory and to the right was a living room area with empty beer bottles and cans, dirty plates, food everywhere but no people. The next door they came to was a kitchen and eating area in a disgusting state and over the door they got their first clue, above the kitchen door was a sign that read 'Arian Nations'.

"God damn it, now it makes sense" said Indian "This is one of those crazy supremacy groups that want to overturn the government and take control, they must have been preparing this place for years, this crystal has played right into their hands, now they are free to do as they want. We've run into a hornet's nest."

His wife smiled at him, "Let's see if we can find the young people."

They moved down the corridor, found a set of steps going down and followed them, they could hear people whispering and whining. The corridor turned to the right and they paused, Quiet Sunshine nodded twice and they stepped around the corner, guns at the ready but there was just more empty corridor. The voices came from a room to the left, they carefully and quietly moved up to it only to find that the door was locked tight with a barred window in it. Quiet Sunshine cautiously looked in and looked back at Indian, she put her mouth close to his ear, "There's got to be ten or twelve adults in there, they're all naked and they're chained. Should we look for any others before we free them?"

Indian looked down at the lock, a heavy-duty padlock, he nodded and the two of them moved on down the corridor. To the right was an open door, they carefully stepped in and stood there amazed.

"This must be the armory," whispered Quiet Sunshine staring at the vast array of armaments that lay on racks all around the room. Rocket launchers were laid out on the table, hand grenades were in boxes against the far wall, too many, too much to take in, Indian signaled to go back into the corridor. They found another locked door on the left, peaking in through the small barred window Indian saw fifteen or twenty young females all naked.

They moved silently on down the corridor and came to another locked door with a small window in it, Indian carefully peeked in.

"Young men, there's got to be ten or fifteen of them, just like the ladies all stark naked and chained."

He stepped away from the door and they moved on, the next room on their right was a huge store room with shelves all the way around on the walls, stacked full with what looked like nonperishable food stuffs, boxes and boxes stacked in the center, nobody was in the room. They moved on to the next room on the left, again another huge store room full of all sorts of household goods.

"They're very well supplied, they must have enough basic necessities to keep everyone for at least three or four months," Sunshine said quietly.

Indian nodded and moved on, they found themselves in what looked like a clothing store, a military clothing store, there were racks of army fatigues and uniforms. In the middle of the room was a pile of civilian clothes.

"That looks like the clothing from the people in the lock ups," said Indian.

Sunshine nodded and they moved on. There were three more rooms before the corridor came to a dead end, all storage rooms.

"Ok, what's our plan of attack?" asked Sunshine.

"First of all we'll free all the prisoners, hopefully some of them will have had some military or armament training. I don't suppose it'll be too long before the others in the vehicles return since there aren't any vehicles here, we need to set up some sort of a trap for them. We'll get somebody up on the top of the barn where your sentry was, we'll put him or her in his clothes. It looks like they've had trouble with the walkie-talkie system so we can use that in our favor. There are rocket launchers galore in the armory, if you, with somebody else, want to take up a position on the opposite bluff from where the first sentry was, someone will take up a position where we found that first sentry and put on his hat, hopefully we'll be able to find somebody capable to accompany me. We'll set up two more positions a little bit further back down the driveway. We know that they're using four vehicles as attack vehicles and then there's the bus, we'll take out the four gun ships with rocket fire and then we'll finish them off with the sniper rifles. We'll just have to see what happens with those people who are on the bus if there are any. It doesn't appear, from everything that we've seen and heard, that these bastards are too well trained, hopefully the driver and any guards in the bus won't panic and start killing any prisoners if there are any and we can take them out without any prisoners getting hurt. How does that sound for a plan?"

Sunshine nodded in agreement, "Sounds good to me. If you're going to free these prisoners, I'll head up to the bungalow, check and make sure everything's all right, then I'll call in our group. I'll feel much better if they're here inside."

"Ok, let's do it."

Sunshine moved quickly up the corridor and disappeared around the bend as he came to the first locked door, she heard the fot of her husband's gun as he shot the lock off the first door. He stepped in, there was a look of fear, hatred and horror on the faces of the young men chained up in the room.

"It's ok, it's ok, settle down, we're here to help, I'm going to set you free, we're gonna get you out of here."

There was silence for a minute and then smiles appeared on their faces, a couple of them started to cry with relief.

"Who are you?" said a big burly youth who could not be any more than fourteen years old.

"People just call me Indian, you can call me Indian too. We came across the shot up vehicles over on the highway and followed the tracks here. My wife is upstairs watching to see if anybody else comes back. Is anybody in here hurt?"

There was silence for a minute and then the same young man said, "Nobody in here's hurt, anyone who was hurt they shot. Can you get us out of these chains?"

Indian studied the chains, there was a leg iron attached around the left ankle of each young man, one continuous chain ran through them and through some eye bolts that were set into the cement around the room, one padlock held that main chain in place. He went over and shot the padlock off, the young men pulled the chain through till they were all free.

"Alright gentlemen, we'll get rid of those ankle irons as soon we find some keys. Listen, do exactly as I tell you, we've only killed six people, does anybody know how many there were in the group?"

A teenager who couldn't be any more then twelve years old stepped forward. "I counted four people in each of the gun vehicles, usually there were two men and two women. Two were handling the guns and ammo, one was in the passenger seat and one was driving, there were four gun ships then there were two people inside the school bus and one driver." Indian could see the hatred in his eyes.

"Well done, that makes nineteen men and women not accounted for."

"They were talking about going to make one more run, they said something about needing more young women, they said they didn't need any more young men."

"That's right," said a young blonde boy "They said that they needed at least another ten young women for breeding purposes and they needed another ten adults to work in the fields."

"Yep," said yet another young man "They're planning to set this farm back in motion, they were going to use slave power, the rotten bastards. You got any spare weapons?"

"All in good time, all in good time."

They moved into the corridor. Indian freed the young ladies, nobody seemed to be upset to see all the young men and women milling around naked, some were obviously brothers and sisters and were hugging and crying. There were lots more questions but Indian indicated for them to be quiet as he stole down the corridor and blew off the lock where the adults were, again, he freed them from the main chain. There were questions; everybody wanted to ask questions.

"Everybody be quiet, there's only a few of us here to rescue you. I know you must have dozens of question and I don't have all the answers but we need to make sure that everybody's safe, these idiots may be back at any moment. Now, this is going to be hard but I want you young people to go up, after you find some clothes and settle yourselves down into the dormitories, don't go into the front house. Have any of you had any experience with weapons?"

Four of the young men and two of the young women stepped forward, no one in the room could be over thirty years old.

"Ok, you six come with me, the rest of you, please, look after the young people, get them settled down in the dormitories. Please keep quiet, we have to prepare for them to come back. Is that clear?"

The adults nodded and they went in search of some clothing, all beginning to get a little embarrassed at their nakedness.

Indian let the six of them go and put on some clothing and then took them into the armory, they looked around surprised at the variety and number of weapons available to them.

"We don't have much time, Lord only knows when these bastards are going to come back. Names, what are your names?"

"Mine's Jocelyn," said the young woman with short brown hair, Indian could see that she was fit and moved lightly.

"What experience have you had with weapons?" he asked.

"Ex Marine Sir," she looked around the room. "I can handle just about every one of these."

"Excellent, pick yourself a rifle, something for up close and a rocket launcher. Your name miss?" he said turning to the red head who looked extremely young at first glance but Indian realized that she was much older than she looked.

"I'm Danielle, police force in Philadelphia, I can handle rifles and am an excellent shot with a hand gun."

"Get whatever you think you're comfortable with. What about you men?"

Three of the men seemed eager but the fourth man, a very handsome young man who appeared to be in his twenties with unruly blondish-brown hair flopping down over his shoulder was looking around the room at the weapons with an intense gleam in his eye. He stood there quietly, hands behind his back, not looking at anybody, just eyeing the weaponry.

"I'm Nathaniel," said one of men, slightly overweight and standing about six foot two inches tall with broad shoulders and enormous hands. "Ex Navy, I don't see much in this room that I can't handle, I think, most probably, my favorite would be the rocket launchers and pistols, never was really much good with a rifle Sir."

"Good enough," said Indian "Take what you're comfortable with."

"Everyone calls me YoHo," said the second young man, he was lean and, stood about six feet tall, Indian could see the muscles rippling under his skin, he was obviously extremely fit and his eyes gleamed. "I'm pretty good with a rifle, I've shot the rocket launchers a few times and I'm excellent with a hand gun."

"Excellent and you?" Indian asked to the third young man who was feverishly running his hands over the rifles.

"Me?" he turned and Indian could see the fury and anger in the young man's eyes "I'm a Marine, you give me anyone of these and I'll show you how to use them."

Indian turned to the quiet young man who was still eyeing the weapons, Indian could see his mind working as he recognized each weapon, analyzed it and looked for appropriate ammunition for that piece. He was obviously very analytical. He had not really looked at any of the other people in the room, Indian could feel a kinship with him, it was almost as if he could see his mind working.

"The name's Abraham, you're going to have to make one fell swoop on this convoy coming in, do you know what you're doing? How do you handle weaponry?

"Well, well," said a surprised Indian "just so you all know, I'm an ex Marine, served in special forces and I've made my living for the last few years training people in many different countries all about war and weapons. I understand what you mean Abraham, we're only going to get one chance to surprise them, what do you suggest?"

The young man was silent for a moment.

"Well, we have the weaponry and it seems like we have some experienced people, if we set it up right, we should be able to take them out as they come up that driveway, around that last bend where they had sentries posted. If we hit the four gun ships all at once with rocket fire, a couple of snipers up on the hill can take out anybody who gets out through the rockets. Then, if we have two or three people hidden in close they'll have to take out anybody who's in the bus before they start taking out any of the prisoners. We'll have to presume that they'll have prisoners in the bus and their safety has to be our highest priority."

Indian was pleased, here was someone who had a lot of training, on his way in he'd made mental notes of where sentries were and where positions of cover and advantage were, he was very impressed with this quiet young man.

"I agree with you Abraham, I think that will be the plan that we put in place, I presume that you're familiar with all the weaponry?"

Abraham moved from the table to the shelves, his hands lightly touching a weapon here and a weapon there, the other young people stood and watched. Eventually he picked up a sniper rifle, his hands went through dismantling it, checking it, reassembling it and attaching the scope almost without thinking, he was obviously very familiar with the weapon and Indian saw that he could do it blind folded if he had to.

"Yes Indian, I'm very familiar with the weapons, this particular one would be my favorite." Abraham turned, still holding the sniper rifle and met Indian's eyes for the first time, Indian felt his blood run cold. He had seen those eyes on numerous men, men who were used to killing, men who were used to war, men who were willing to die for what they believed in.

"Mosad trained," said Indian quietly "by the way you handled that rifle."

Abraham nodded.

The other young people knew that something had passed between the two of them but could not recognize it; Indian knew this young man was extremely capable and not just in weaponry. The Israeli Mosad trained specialists not just to kill but also to analyze, to recognize patterns, to take charge of men, to be willing to die if necessary, this young man was an extremely capable and very dangerous young man.

Indian watched as each of them retrieved weapons and ammunition and then they all moved up into the ranch.

"There's people coming up the driveway," Danielle said pointing out the kitchen window.

Indian turned and looked out. "They're with me, that's the rest of my party."

Abraham looked out of the window and looked back at Indian giving him a nod and a slightly raised right eyebrow, Indian knew what he was saying, he was saying, "Is that it? Is that your whole party? Some of them look too young."

"The lady is my wife, her name is Quiet Sunshine, trust me when I say she is very capable and very well trained, almost as well as I am," he said with a smile "Just don't tell her I said that."

For the first time the young people were smiling, everyone except for Abraham.

They waited until the group came in the door, the first one in was Iggy who came in obviously on alert, looking around and seeing his master he lumbered over to him eagerly while the young people looked at him in surprise, he really was a large shaggy beast. He went around the room and sniffed each one, got to know them and then went over to Abraham. Iggy sat in front of Abraham and looked at him, Abraham squatted down and just looked into the eyes of that big furry head. Normally someone gently puts out a hand when first meeting any dog but Abraham just squatted and looked and Iggy looked straight back. Abraham stood up, Iggy moved around behind him, moved into position on his right hand, and laid down looking at his master.

"Yes Iggy, I agree, he is something special, I'm glad you approve."

He introduced his group to the young people and then Diane, Paula, and Kerry went out through the back into the tunnels, they were going to stay with the others. They had orders to make sure that they were armed just in case something went wrong and one of the bastards got through to the cabin. Indian and the rest of them went outside.

"Let's do it this way, Sunshine, you take up a position where the guard was on the barn, take your sniper's rifle. You," he pointed to one of the young men who'd said he was good with a rifle, "take a position on the hill on the other side where the other sentry was, take your sniper's rifle. The rest of us will take positions down beside the driveway. Abraham and the others take rocket launchers. As the bastards come around the bend they'll probably make contact with the sentries, when they do just sort of click the microphone on and off, grunt deeply a couple of times, don't try to say anything, it's obvious they've had trouble with the radios before and they'll just think it's a problem with their communications. As they come up level with those of us hidden beside the driveway we'll take out the gun ships with the rocket launchers and the two snipers will take out anybody who's not killed in the first attack. We're not taking any prisoners, there's nowhere to keep them and we're not letting anybody go, so shoot to kill. Abraham, you and I will be on opposite sides, we'll take out the people on the bus. If any one finds a shot, take it." He looked at Abraham who nodded, still caressing his sniper rifle. "Any questions?"

Everybody looked around but nobody said anything.

"Ok, let's go. Arm yourselves and get into position."

They all moved out down the driveway taking up their assigned positions, they were all well hidden in the rocks and shrubs from anybody coming up the driveway, they waited silently.

About thirty minutes had gone by when they heard vehicles coming toward them, Indian raised his hand and wiggled it, other hands popped up here and there and waved, they were all ready. He picked up his rocket launcher and waited. They could hear the sound of people yelling and laughing as the convoy came into sight. The radio clicked on, "Jerome, Jerome or Charlie, you there? Come in Jerome. Come in Charlie."

There were clicking noises and some sort of a grunt.

"Is that you Jerome? Jerome? Come in Jerome."

Again the radios clicked and there was static as the mike switch was keyed and a couple of noises that could be recognized as someone trying to speak.

"Fucking radios! Fucking useless shit!" came over the radios. "Listen, if you can hear me, Jerome, click the mic three times."

There was silence for a second then there were three clicks.

"God damn it, we're gonna have to get some new radios, it's us, we're coming in. We'll see you in a couple of seconds."

The radios went dead. Indian smiled.

As they came down the driveway toward them there were three of the gun ships in the front, then the bus and the last gun ship was bringing up the rear, they were all laughing, some of them were standing up in the vehicles. The guns that were mounted on the back of the pickups were pointing down and were not manned, not ready to use in case of an emergency, Indian realized that these people were not very well trained. He waited patiently as they came down the driveway, the three front gun ships moved just past him, he took aim at the one behind the bus and pulled the trigger. The rocket launcher kicked back at him and instantly he heard the noise of the other launchers going off, almost simultaneously there were three massive explosions in front of the bus. As he watched the gun ship behind the bus explode, he pulled out the sniper rifle beside him and concentrated on the bus, people in the bus were yelling and screaming. He heard the snipers shooting from up on the hill, he knew they were taking out anyone who had survived the rocket attacks. The people on the bus had dropped out of sight. The gunfire ceased. There was just the noise of the burning vehicles and the roar of the bus engine. The motor on the bus roared higher and it started to move backward, he still could not see the driver, almost the same time as he shot out the rear tires on his side he heard Abraham's rifle take out the tires on the other side, the bus tires flopped backward as they tried to back it up, Indian shot out the front tire. The bus moved a couple of yards and then stopped. He focused on the driver's window.

"C'mon you bastard, lift your head, c'mon, let me see you for a second." Suddenly the top of a head appeared as someone was trying to look out of the window, he took the shot and the head flew backward.

"Ok, ok, we're coming out, we're coming out, don't shoot, don't shoot, we're coming out."

The door on the bus opened on Abraham's side, Indian eased himself up carefully watching everything, he watched as the others came out of hiding very carefully. Abraham stood up, his pistol in his hand.

"We're coming out, we're not armed," and two middle-aged men with big floppy stomachs, both of them going bald, stepped out of the bus.

Indian watched as if in slow motion as Abraham stepped up close to them and, without any hesitation, shot them both in the head. Indian nodded "God help anyone who messes with that man," he thought to himself as everybody came up onto the driveway. Those who had seen Abraham execute the men stared at him but nobody said a word.

Everybody stood silently, taking in the victory and then Abraham moved into the bus, everybody in there was safe, nobody had been hurt in the assault and they were all thrilled to see him.

Later on, as the sun got low on the horizon, Indian and Abraham sat on a rock watching the last wisps of smoke rise up from the burned out hull of the bus. The group had gathered up the bodies, including those in the house, and all the bits of bodies they could find and put them in the bus, they had then driven it off the road, poured gasoline over the inside of it and set it on fire; a funeral pyre. This was the fastest and easiest way of getting rid of the bodies. Indian had sent Sunshine back to the ranch to make sure that nobody else came down the driveway, it was not necessary for all those young people to see the carnage.

"Well, Abraham, what are your plans now?"

Abraham sat staring at the smoke rising up into a windless sky.

"I really don't know, I'd planned to get to Los Angeles, that's where I was heading. I'd gotten a lift in a friend's vehicle when those bastards surprised us. I really don't have any family here in the states."

"Well, how the hell did you end up over here any way?"

"I'd spent a number of years in the Mosad, I'd been used in a number of under cover exercises in Pakistan, Iran and Iraq, all the way through the Middle East and I was quite severely injured while under cover just over the border in Palestine. I decided that I needed to get away and get back on my feet so I was on leave over here when the shit hit the fan. By the time I'd come out of the drunken stupor that I had been keeping myself in the President had made his speech and I was too late to get a flight back to Israel, not that I particularly wanted to go back there anyway. My whole family was wiped out a few years ago by a Palestinian rocket attack so I really have nobody. I was going to bum my way around to have a look at this great country but I guess that's been cut short," he started laughing, "or should I say it's been cut long, I guess I'm here for the duration."

Indian liked this young man, he saw a lot of himself in Abraham.

"So what do you plan to do now?" he asked.

"As I said, I don't have the faintest idea. The people here will have to decide what they're going to do individually, this might not be such a bad place to make a stand. Those bastards" and he pointed to the smoking bus "had a nice little set up here. The ranch is completely self-contained, there's a fresh water well and, you haven't seen it yet, but just over the top of the hill there's a windmill that generates enough electricity to run the place, the septic system is tank and tiles, it really is self-sufficient. There's enough weaponry here to protect against any attacks, they picked a good spot because you can defend the driveway from either side as we did and there's open land for what seems like miles around here. I only had a brief glimpse in the barns but I'd say there was sufficient machinery to run the farm and behind that second barn over there," he pointed to the barn to the left of the ranch, "there are two massive storage tanks; one filled with gasoline and the other filled with diesel, sufficient I would guess to keep the place running for a couple of years if you were careful. We would need some more animals I'm sure they wouldn't be too hard to find."

Indian raised his eyebrow in surprise. "How the hell do you know all this?"

Abraham looked at him and smiled. "I listened, I listened to what they were saying, the people in the bus who brought us here were showing off, telling us what they were going to do with us how we were going to run the farm, we were going to be their slaves. So I guess this wouldn't be a bad place to stay.'

They sat there silently watching the smoke rise and enjoying the quiet of the evening.

"My party's got to be moving on, we have a place we need to get to. I think the best bet would be to have a meeting with everybody and let them decide individually what they want to do, there's not much hope in traveling too far unless they go on foot. We just have to see what they say, if they decide to stay they're going to need someone to lead them." Indian looked at Abraham with a quizzical expression on his face.

Abraham scratched his head, closed his eyes and raised his face up, he could feel the last warmth of the sun on his neck. He sat deep in thought for a few minutes.

"I guess I could stay on here, at least long enough to get them organized, they'll need some training in the weapons. I know quite a bit about farming I was brought up on a kibbutz but it would all have to be done democratically; I won't take a leadership role unless everyone is happy with it."

"I understand," said Indian and they sat there watching the sunset.

Meantime Sunshine had got the ladies organized and she came out of the ranch and rang a big bell that hung beside the front door. "Dinner is served, c'mon everybody, come on in." She raised her voice even louder, "Indian, I see you over there, come on, we've got food for everybody."

The few who were outside the ranch went in to eat, Abraham and Indian followed.

The ladies had put on a buffet dinner, down in the kitchen they had set out a variety of foods from the storage room and people were chatting as they lined up, took what they wanted and moved into the dining area to find seats. Indian and Abraham were the last in line. As Indian passed his wife who was helping to set out more food on the buffet he reached over and kissed her gently, "After this we need to be moving on."

"Are you sure you don't want to stay here for the night?"

"I don't think so, I think the sooner we move away from this group the better, they have a lot of decisions to make and we really don't need to be a part of it. I think I'll call a meeting while we're eating, put a couple of ideas out there and then leave it up to them."

"Fine with me," said his wife putting a slice of canned corned beef on his plate.

Indian waited until everyone was seated and the ladies that were helping in the kitchen came out to join them, he noticed that the mood was a bit lighter. He stood up.

"May I have your attention, please?" The babble of voices calmed down a little. "May I have your attention, please?"

The room fell silent, all eyes looking at him.

"I and my party will be moving on as soon as we've finished this meal we have somewhere to go to and we need to be on our way. I don't know all your stories, I don't know who you are, what you do, or where you were going before your journey was so terribly interrupted but let me tell you this, we, that is my party and I, have been on the road for a couple of days and we've seen some terrible sights and, as you most probably have already realized, it's impossible to travel anywhere by road, rail or plane. We are fortunate we have the horses. If any of you people want to keep going on you'll either need to find yourself a four-wheel drive vehicle and go across country or you'll have to go by foot. As you've found out, there are bands of individuals doing horrific things. I think you should recognize what you have here," he waived his hand around, "here at the ranch. The group of idiots and murderers that owned this place must have had it for a number of years, they were members of the Arian Nations, Nazis and white supremacists, living outside civilization hoping to over throw the government. This farm is completely independent, it has a windmill that provides electricity, there's a fresh-water well with endless clean water. It's on a septic tank system and behind one of the barns you have sufficient diesel and gasoline to keep the machinery going for perhaps a couple of years. I haven't had a chance to explore the barns and storage rooms behind them but I would guess that they are well stocked with seeds, etc., for planting. The only things that seem to be missing are animals but I have no doubt whatsoever that when you explore the rest of the local farms around here you'll find livestock. You have sufficient weaponry here to fight off a small army and you are all young people, I would recommend that you make this your home, set up your own community, run your own lives and try to weather out the next two, three, four, or five years. It is, of course, entirely up to you but let me say something, you have one man here" and he pointed to Abraham who looked at him and nodded, "you have here a man who has been trained by the Mosad, that is the Israeli Secret Service. He was trained to be a leader, trained to be an independent thinker, an expert in all forms of weaponry, He was brought up on a Kibbutz in Israel and is willing to stay and help you all. The most important part of setting up a community, especially in the very first stages, is to have someone capable in charge, Abraham has said that he is willing to step up to the plate and help you create a community but he wants you all to take a vote on his leadership. If you all agree and accept his help on these terms he will guarantee to remain until you are fully organized and ready to run your own show. I would suggest, and again I can only suggest because we won't be here, that you take him up on this offer and you all seriously consider staying put. As you've found out, your lives depend on being able to defend and provide for yourselves. I don't want to call for a vote, you all need to discuss this amongst yourselves and the decisions you have to make are individual decisions. Those who choose to stay and make this their home, I honestly believe, will be the ones who have the best chance of survival, I leave it in your hands." He sat down.

There was silence, you could hear a pin drop, the deafening silence was so intense you could cut it with a knife but it only lasted for a couple of minutes and then everybody started talking at once.

When they had finished eating Indian and his group stood up and wandered outside.

"Are these people going to be ok?" asked Diane.

"We don't know, they have to make their own decisions but I think Indian was right, this is most probably the best chance they have, to fortify the ranch and get it running. They've been through some terrible times that surely must have brought it home to them that there is no safety or much hope in going anywhere else," Sunshine said.

"Do we have to leave this evening?" asked Kerry.

"It's best that we're out of here, we have to get on our own journey and if we stay overnight we'll lose time in the morning answering questions and dealing with people who want to come with us. It's better just to move on and make camp somewhere," said Indian checking the horses.

"I think you're right," said Paula "these people have a chance to make a go of it here but I know a couple of them who've already said that they wanted to move on, they wanted to go through to Phoenix and they were questioning us where we were going."

"Yep, I got a couple of inquiries too," said Indian "we have to think of ourselves. We don't have horses for anybody else and if we have to wait for someone to come with us on foot we'll lose a tremendous amount time, the sooner we get to Last Chance the better. C'mon, I think we're all packed up, time to leave these folks to themselves."

They all got up on their horses as Abraham came out the front door, he stepped over beside Indian's horse looking up at him.

"Thank you Indian, there aren't too many people who would have bothered to try to come and find us after they found that mess on the road. I understand what it meant to you and yours. Listening to the people talk it seems like most of them are deciding to stay on, looks like I have a home here in the United States and by God no one, but no one will take it away from me."

Indian stared into the young man's eyes and a chill went up his spine as he saw that this young man would stand for no nonsense. "God help anyone who comes up against him," Indian thought.

"Abraham you're welcome, it has been my pleasure to know you. I wish you well."

"Good-bye then, stay alert."

Indian nodded and looked around as Abraham stepped away from his horse, he turned his horse around and the party set off down the driveway, he breathed a sigh of relief as the ranch disappeared behind them.

Once again he was only responsible for his little group.

37

River rescue.

Last Chance.

Kyle sat on a comfortable chair at the up river end of the granite slab, he'd been on sentry duty now for almost two hours. Everyone was taking turns, four-hour shifts, with one sentry on the up river end and one sentry on the lower river end. He and Alex had flipped a coin to see who would be sitting where and he'd won the toss and had chosen to sit up river. Beside him was a rifle, on his lap was a radio and hanging around his neck was a pair of high-powered binoculars. He yawned, scratched the back of his knee and tried to count the number of chickens he could see running in and out of the underbrush below him when he spotted something floating around the bend in the center of the river. He grabbed the binoculars, it took him a moment or two to focus them then he grabbed his radio, "Base, base, upper sentry here, anybody there?"

There was a moment's silence and then a voice came on. "Hi Kyle, what's going on?"

Kyle recognized Joshua's voice. "Joshua, there's something in the river, it looks like it's two metal drums tied together and there are three people hanging on to them."

"What? Are you sure?"

Kyle readjusted his binoculars.

"Joshua, it looks like there are three young women and it doesn't look like they're hanging on, it looks like they're tied onto the drums, I'm not sure if they're alive or dead they're just bobbing along."

"Ok, ok, I've got it. Watch them carefully, report anything you see."

"You'd better get Doc June, better be quick about it."

It only took three minutes to get the doctor, Joshua and two of the boys got into a boat at the dock and they rowed off. The barrels were only a few hundred feet away from the dock now as they floated downstream.

"Be careful, be careful," said the doctor as Joshua maneuvered the boat closer to the three young women tied around the barrels. Jay reached out and managed to grab one of the pieces of rope that was trailing from the barrels and gingerly pulled it very slowly and carefully into the side of the boat. The girls in the water just bobbed, their heads flopping from side to side as the barrels hit the side of the boat. The doctor reached over and felt for a pulse in the neck of the young woman closest to her.

"I've got a pulse, this one's alive."

Before anyone could stop her she slipped over the side of the boat and worked her way around to the next young woman in the water.

"I think this one's gone, we're too late for this one."

She moved around in the water to the third young lady. "This one's alive but she's bleeding pretty badly from the shoulder, we've got to get them to shore as fast as possible."

"We'll tow them in just as they are, it'll be much faster to get them off those barrels at the dock. Grab that rope."

"I'll stay in the water," said the doctor.

"Be careful."

By the time they'd towed them into the end of the dock a crowd had gathered and people were jumping into the water, knives in hand. Very carefully they cut the girls loose and lifted them up onto the dock.

"Get them up to the hospital unit as fast as you can," said the doctor as she was lifted out of the water onto the dock. Eight of them picked up the three young women as their lifeless bodies flopped around and rushed them up to the first cave where they'd set up the emergency surgical unit. Each one of the young women was placed on a gurney and the doctor moved swiftly to the first girl.

"This one is past help, I'm afraid she's dead," she said as she covered her with a white sheet and moved on to the next one. She checked her over, all three were naked.

"This one's losing blood, it looks like she's been shot through the shoulder on the right side." She grabbed some sterile bandages and pads. "Bella apply pressure on these pads, hold them down tight, stop the bleeding."

Bella grabbed the pads as the doctor moved to one side and with her hands pushed down hard. The doctor moved on to the third one.

"This one's been shot too, it hit her in the lower left side of her chest, there's an entry wound and an exit wound and I think there's internal bleeding, this one's the most critical. I'm going to have to get in there and see what's going on," she said almost as if to herself. "Anna put some pressure on here while I scrub up. Everybody out, everybody except Bella and Doctor Anna out." Everyone moved out and the door closed. Doctor June scrubbed up and returned, taking over Anna's position.

"We're going to need some blood, we don't have time to do any cross matching, see if anyone is O negative." Said June.

"Ok," and Doctor Anna went out to swiftly come back with Slade.

"Are you sure you are O negative?" Questioned June.

"Yep, I had to be tested just last year when I cut myself really badly."

"Good. Prep him please Anna."

"I'll scrub up and join you," said Anna, "looks like we're going to be busy for a while."

"Yep, you ok over there, Bella?"

"Yep, I'll just stay here and hold onto this until you tell me not to, I always did want to watch an operation and now I'll see one up close."

Outside everyone was asking questions, wondering what on earth had happened and who they were. The Judge came out and told those who had not gone into the surgery unit, "Two of them are alive, they've all been shot. One's been shot through the right shoulder, which doesn't seem too bad, the other one's been hit in the left side of her abdomen and they're operating on her now. The third one didn't make it, she's been shot in the head."

There was a look of shock and amazement and people started talking all at once, this was the first violence that many of them had seen up close, they had all heard of the turmoil that had been going on since the President's speech but it had never been really brought home to them, it really stunned them, they quieted down and slowly drifted back to work.

Five hours later Doctor June came out.

"How are they doing?" questioned Pattern.

"The young lady who was shot in the shoulder is doing fine, she should be ok, she's lost quite a bit of blood but it appears that we got to her in time. She's resting and should be coming around in a couple of hours. The other one took a bullet that entered just below her left ribs and went down and out through the lower abdomen. I had to remove her spleen but there doesn't seem to be any other major damage, she's lost a lot of blood, we'll have to wait and see. It'll be a while before she can talk to us."

"How long do you estimate before we can find out what happened to them?"

"I think the one with the shoulder wound should be able to talk, maybe in the next couple of hours, we can find out what's going on then. I think we should remove the third one, we need to get her buried. That's one thing we never thought of, where are we going to have a graveyard? After this I think we had better set up a blood bank and type everyone for future emergencies, Doctor Anna and I had better start training a couple of people who are interested in becoming lab technicians."

Two hours later June called for the Judge over the radio and met him in the treatment room, the emergency field hospital that they had set up in the first cave consisted of three rooms, the first, as you entered, was a treatment room used for anything that did not require surgery, the second room was a wash up room, laboratory and storage area, the third room, the back section, was the complete surgical unit.

"First of all, let me give you an update on their conditions, the young woman with the abdomen wound is stable but it'll be a little while before she can talk to you. The young woman with the shoulder wound is going to be fine, there was really no internal damage done at all, she came out of the anesthetic about an hour and a half ago and I sat down and had a long talk with her."

The Judge nodded.

"Her name is Joanna, Joanna Hawkins, apparently there were fifteen boys and girls, all aged between fifteen and nineteen from a school in Toronto, Canada, they'd all flown down here to spend two weeks at a place called Canuck upstream from here."

"Yes," said the Judge "it's approximately fifteen to twenty miles up river. It's run by the Hodge family, it's been in their family for a couple of generations, it's one of the few places that you can drive down into the ravine to a camping and beach area. They set up a family business there many years ago and they still rent canoes and other various small watercrafts, they portage kids further up river above the rapids. The rapids are gentle compared to some but it seems to be quite a thrill to ride the canoes or boats or dinghies back down to the camp where they have a variety of small cabins and a tenting area, it's totally self-contained. Everyone who camps there has to mess in doing the cooking and cleaning, it's designed specifically toward young people, those wanting a little bit of excitement on the river."

"Yes, that's exactly what Joanna said, anyway, I guess they pulled into the camp a couple of days before the President's speech. They spent a couple of days going up river and then coming down riding the rapids and then they heard the President's speech. They had immediately tried to make arrangements to fly back to Toronto but that proved to be impossible, basically they were stuck at the camp. They contacted their parents and told them they were safe and their parents were trying to make arrangements to get them back home. Three days after the President's speech they were woken up in the morning by ten armed men and women who'd come down the slope while everybody was asleep and had taken over the camp. Nobody had even thought about putting out a look out. To prove that they were in total command they'd tied up the two older Hodges and burned them alive, this had assured the cooperation of the sixteen young people including the Hodge's grandson, Gregory, who was twenty-one years old and had been there to work during his vacation from university. Well, you don't need me to try to describe what happened then. Apparently there were seven young men and eight young women in the group from Toronto, plus the Hodge's grandson and having watched what had been done to the adults they were petrified and were very cooperative. They were chained and brutally abused. Joanna, Rachel, and Maryann, the three who were tied to the barrels, tried to escape, they were caught and, to ensure the remaining thirteen wouldn't try the same thing, they were tied to the barrels, set afloat and were then used as target practice as they floated out and downstream. Maryann is the one with the abdomen wound, the other young woman, Rachel, died. So what we're left with is a situation, there are ten maniacs who are now in control of thirteen young people, using and abusing them. We're going to have to do something about that aren't we?"

The Judge sat quietly.

"We all knew that brutality and guns would become a part of living as people tried to survive, we all assumed that being here in Last Chance we would be immune. We've all sat and listened to the tales of horror that Ghost and his wife have related of their journey here but we all thought that these things couldn't possibly touch us. Now they have and this situation is too close to us to be comfortable, our own safety may be threatened and we have the means to rescue these kids. Decisions have to be made, they won't be easy ones but I believe that everyone should have their say. I'll call a meeting immediately and let everybody know what's going on. Can you attend?"

Doctor June shook her head. "I'd better stay with the patients, they need constant attention for a few more hours, until they're completely back from their anesthetic, I'll go along with whatever the majority want. You're right, I think the reality of what's going on in the world is at last being brought home to us in a very personal manner. I don't envy you Judge, you know that you've automatically become the leader of the group, we don't need any votes or discussions on that, everybody's recognized it and everybody, as far as I know is very happy with it. I don't envy you your position. Whatever everyone decides I'll go along with."

The Judge just nodded at her as she turned around and went through the storage/scrub room back to the surgical unit. He sat there for fifteen minutes thinking and planning. He looked at his watch, it was almost seven o'clock in the evening, everyone was back to the work that they were doing before the girls were spotted in the river. Supper was going to be served around seven thirty, they tried to maintain a regular schedule but, of course, sometimes things had to be delayed. He went out of the cave and stood looking down at the river watching everybody doing their work, hearing the noise of the main group putting up a cabin at the very far end of the granite slab down river. Life is a bitch he thought.

"Attention everybody, attention everyone," he said into his radio "the two young ladies have come through surgery just fine. The young lady, Joanna, who had the shoulder wound, is awake and has told us what happened. I believe we should have a meeting. Please will everybody, except the two sentries, come up here to the main cabin we have some things to discuss and some decisions to make."

Much to his surprise, there was no verbal response. He watched as all of them stopped what they were doing and very quietly made their way back towards him. They all gathered in the big room in the cabin, with so many people it was getting a little too crowded but they sat on the floor and on the chairs very strangely quiet.

"I think we're all here, everyone except the doc and the two sentries," the Judge pushed the button on his radio, "sentries one and two, can you hear me?"

Both sentries replied in the affirmative.

"I'm going to leave the radio keyed on so you can hear what's being said, I don't think we should leave the camp unguarded." He saw some eyebrows raised and heard some whispering in the room.

"Ladies and gentlemen this is the first of many general meetings, we haven't made any formal arrangements for decision making or regular meetings so to begin with I think we should set up a couple of guidelines. Since we are such an isolated and small community I believe that everything that affects the running of Last Chance should be discussed, decided and voted upon by everybody. The majority vote will carry the decision. We need to set up an area somewhere where we can all sit fairly comfortably to have these meetings it's just getting a little too crowded in here now. I have asked Jenny to act as secretary for this meeting." He nodded toward Jenny who was sitting beside him at the head of the table taking copious notes, "We'll try to keep notes and records of everything that's said and done here at Last Chance. I propose that we give these general meetings a name to distinguish them from anything else, I suggest that we call them 'Assemblies' and that we hold one each month, any objections or suggestions?"

He looked around, there seemed to be a bit of bewilderment and expectation on the faces around the room but there were no objections.

"Excellent and I think when we get a spare minute," he said with a big smile on his face, and there was some laughter and some caustic remarks made because they were all working so hard to get things set up, "I suggest that we set up an area somewhere on the plateau as a place for Assemblies, we could just cut seats out of some logs, put them in a semi circle and then we can add to them as needed and anyone who wants to speak to the Assembly can stand in the center but we'll look into that later on. Ok we've never taken a vote nor have there ever been any discussions about leadership, who has the decisions on what or why and when or how. For some mysterious reason, so I'm told, you've looked to me for leadership. I don't believe that anyone in this community should have any more decision making powers than anybody else except minor things and in the case of a dire emergency where a decision needs to be made fast and there's no time to have an Assembly. Because of the position that I held in society it came quite naturally to me to step into the leadership role and I never realized that I was doing so. I now submit to you that if there are any suggestions, desires, worries or concerns about who should be leading this group we should deal with them now before we make any decisions that effect all of us. Is there anybody here who would like to take the leadership position?"

Everybody looked around at everybody else, some shrugged their shoulders, eyebrows were raised and then Joshua said, "Judge I think we all agree, it's all yours, you've got it, I don't envy you but you've got it."

"Thank you all for your vote of confidence, I'm not sure that you're doing me a favor" said the Judge with a smile on his face "I'll try to be wise but if I step out of line or anybody has any worries or problems with me, please come and see me. Alright, now to the reason why we're here." He went on to explain to them what the doctor had told him and what Joanna had reported. He watched the various reactions around the room, he saw fear, disgust, annoyance, hatred, frustration, the emotions circulated around the room like a wave.

"What do you propose that we do?" said Brad.

"Yes, what exactly should we do or, maybe just as importantly, what does anybody suggest that we don't do?" said Slade.

There was silence.

Amber stood up. "I know that we're isolated and we've all heard the reports by Ghost and his beloved, we've been horrified at what they've reported but somehow it didn't seem to be our concern. I think this has brought it home in a very brutal way but it has brought it home. We are not completely isolated, those things that are happening outside away from us can, do and will have some kind of effects on us. This camp that you say is just fifteen to twenty miles upstream is close enough that it has intruded on our isolation, I for one don't think that I can just stay here and live on this rock knowing that such a short way away there are atrocities being committed and knowing that I've done nothing to stop them. I would suggest that we form a plan to rescue and liberate those young people before more bodies come floating past our doorstep."

The silence became intense as she sat down and people realized what she was suggesting, now realizing that they could not just sit snug and safe on their isolated granite plateau.

Mary stood up and quietly said, "Thank you Amber for saying what I think most of us had in the back of our minds but perhaps were a little too fearful to voice, I'm in agreement with you. We have the tools to go up and rescue these young people but before we do that lets make sure that we all understand that we are not playing, this is reality, this is real life. Whatever we do, if we decide to go in and rescue them, it's not going to be like a show on the television. There will be death. There are ten maniacs that will have to be dealt with, remember, there is no justice system any longer, we can't call the police and turn them over. We have no prisons here and therefore we cannot allow them to live because if we do then they may become a major threat to Last Chance. If we decide on a course of action it must be recognized that we'll have to kill ten people and some of us that go in to execute the rescue may be injured or even killed so let's not jump into this without thinking everything through and recognizing that there is real danger here. We become the law, the judge and the jury and we can't take prisoners." As she sat down the Judge saw some of the faces go white, heads shaking, people realizing and letting reality sink in.

Ghost stood up. "I agree with everything that my wife has said and what Amber has said, we have to make a decision. Can we live with ourselves if we do nothing and just sit here complacently setting up our camp? On the other hand, can we live with ourselves by becoming the law and issuing the death sentence on ten terrible people? We have the capabilities and we certainly have the weapons." There was a little laughter around the room because everyone had seen the huge container stocked with every possible weapon purchased by the yet to arrive Indian and Quite Sunshine. "Let's recognize that this will probably be the first of many such nasty decisions that we'll have to make," and he sat down.

For the next hour there were questions and answers, people tried to find out how things could be done and what would happen if they did not do anything, bantering backwards and forwards trying to decide in their own heads what each individual could live with. At last the room went quiet.

"If there are no more questions I believe we need to take a vote. Is there anybody who wishes to make a proposal?"

There was silence in the room for a moment.

Ghost stood up, "I propose that we form a posse, make a plan of attack, go up and rescue as many of these young people as we can and that no quarter be given and no prisoners taken." He sat down.

"Does anyone second this motion?"

Pattern stood up, "I second the motion."

"Are there any further questions on the motion?"

There was silence.

"All those in favor?" said the Judge quietly.

There was a moment's hesitation, then every hand in the room went up and two 'yea's' came over the radio.

"Then it's decided. Ghost, you and your wife and Amber have had the most experience in this sort of thing, if you'd take over and decide what and how this should be done I believe it would be the best thing."

"Yes Sir we'll do that," said Ghost as he rose from his chair and saw his wife and Amber nod to him, "we'll do that."

"Then this meeting is closed, please cooperate with Ghost, we need to move as quickly as possible so if you're asked to do something please do it with no arguments or discussions. Everybody in agreement?"

All heads nodded and there was not a whisper as they all left the cabin, each one in their own way realizing that they had just voted for the death penalty for ten people.

The next evening Amber, Mary and Ghost sat on a small rocky outcrop with their feet dangling in the water and a floating log tied up onto the last rock jutting into the river. They sat in silence watching the sides of the canyon appear to move as the sun went down and darkness engulfed them. It never ceased to amaze Mary that once the sun had gone in the floor of the canyon became pitch black. She reached over and gripped her husband's hand.

"Honey I think it's time."

Without a word Ghost stood up, he was naked except for a small black loincloth, he reached over and slung a black knapsack wrapped in plastic over his shoulders and clipped a black waterproof webbing belt with pouches around his waist. He put his hand into a pouch behind him, unzipped it and pulled out a plastic bag checking, for the second time that the silenced pistol and ammunition would be dry, he zipped it up and put it back in his pouch, zipping the waterproof pouch closed tight. Mary did the same, putting on her knapsack and her belt; she wore only a black loincloth and a black halter-top. Amber, seated on a rock to Mary's right, was dressed in a skintight black suit from her ankles to her neck and back down to her wrists, she wore black sneakers over black socks and from her neck right up to her hairline Mary and Ghost had camouflaged her to be as black as they were.

While they were putting on her makeup Amber had joked that it wasn't fair that they didn't need make-up and that they enjoyed torturing her. In the darkness the three of them just disappear as they quietly slid into the water, only the night air seemed to move a little. Amber undid the log and they got into the water underneath the leafy branches and pushed it off, paddling to bring it out into the current, from all appearances it was just a big leafy log that had fallen into the river. About an hour earlier Brad, in the smaller helicopter, had dropped the three of them and their pet log off upstream of the Canuck camp, they had taken a round about route so as not to alert or alarm those at the other camp.

Joanna had been able to give them an excellent layout of the camp and as they floated around a bend they saw lights and the bunkhouses, there were four of them to the left of the camp as you approached it from the water. Closest to the small beach, on the left hand side, was a storage unit where it was obvious that they kept all the boats, rafts, life jackets, etc which were spilling out into the compound, it backed fairly close up to the cliff. To the right, again closest to the beach area, was the main cabin and office area where the owners had lived, it was a large two-story building beyond which were three other buildings for general use. Jutting out into the water was a thirty-foot floating dock with three ladders going down into the water. Moored onto the dock were two powerful motorboats and on the beach were a variety of watercraft. There were lights on in the main house and there was a light on over the entrance to the main storage unit but the end of the pier was in darkness. In the space surrounded by the buildings a big bonfire was burning, its flickering flames playing patterns into the darkness and illuminating the people sitting around it on logs drinking, laughing and jeering.

"I make out one sentry at the end of the dock," whispered Amber.

"I agree, I don't see anybody else that appears to be on sentry duty," whispered Mary.

Very slowly they guided their log towards the end of the dock furthest from the beach. The sentry saw it and grabbed his binoculars, for a couple of moments they could see him staring at them as they watched him through the leaves, he put down his binoculars and went back to lounging in his chair.

"Just as we thought, it doesn't look like he's had any training," whispered Ghost.

As they were coming closer to the dock they saw two naked young women carrying trays of drinks from the main cabin to the seven people sitting around the fire. As they gave out the cans of beer some of the men groped or smacked the naked bottoms, one of the men even pulled one of the girls down and bit her breast. Ghost counted four men and three women sitting around the fire. The women jeered and laughed as they watched the young servers being molested. The two serving women lowered their heads, gathered some empty bottles and cans and went back into the main house. The log moved over very slowly, the sentry looked over at it and got up as the log gently bumped against the very end of the dock, he tried to push it away with his foot and almost lost his balance. He knelt down, went to push the log away with this hand and a look of shock and amazement flashed across his face as a hand suddenly appeared from the leaves grabbing him around the throat, squeezing so hard it broke his larynx. He could not make a sound, he struggled for breath, slowly subsiding to stillness and death. Ghost kept hold of his neck gently easing himself out from the under the leaves, he got a hold of the dock with his other hand, made sure that no one was looking from around the fire and in one very smooth motion stood up, lifting the sentry by his neck keeping the now dead body between him and the flames as he seated him back in his chair, putting his head down so it looked like he was dozing off and then just as quietly and swiftly slid back into the water.

"One down, nine to go," whispered Amber.

"Ok Amber you and Mary go to the left as we planned, you can get fairly close from behind the first storage building, I'll go to the right and check out the main house. I'll signal to you when we're ready to take on that gang by the fire," whispered Ghost.

The two ladies nodded and slipped out from under the log, keeping very close to the floating dock they moved inland. Ghost kicked the log free and back into the current and as it floated by the end of the dock he followed it around to the other side and moved inland against the side of the structure. The beach area was in darkness, a light from the house only cast a few long shadows. He looked across and saw a movement in the darkness against the far canyon wall as the ladies slipped in behind the first building. He silently slid out of the water and moved to the right between the main house and the cliff wall, he took his gun out of the plastic bag, dropped the plastic bag and slipped the gun into his belt in the middle of the small of his back. Very slowly he moved in the darkness to the first window, peeking in he saw what was obviously a shop, there was enough light coming in from an adjacent room for him to see that the shelves were well stocked and in the far right hand corner was the vacant cashiers booth. He squeezed around behind the building, eased himself up by stepping against the canyon wall and the building and found himself looking into a bathroom on the second floor, the window was open, the bathroom door was open, he could see across a hallway into a bedroom where a light was on but he did not see anybody. Silently he took off his knapsack, eased it through the window, lowering it onto the tile floor and followed it just as quietly. He undid the wrapping around the knapsack and pulled out a short blowpipe, slipping in one of little black darts he peered into the corridor, there was nobody. Silently he searched the second level and found nobody, it was amazing that such a big man could move so quietly. At the top of the stairs he could hear voices downstairs, he moved down the staircase. On the landing where the staircase turned to the left he lowered himself down and peered through the banisters. He could see the two young women who had been serving the people around the fire, they stood side by side in front of a counter. From this angle he couldn't see behind the counter but it was obvious from the way that the two were moving that someone was handing them more cans of beer to put on their trays.

"Those pigs out there, they'll drink all the goddamn beer we've got in the place which means we'll have to make another trip to find more booze tomorrow." He heard a woman's voice say.

"As soon as these trays are full you two bitches get back out there, you know that Jacob hates to wait, he's got a nasty temper, especially after he's had a few beers, God knows what he's capable of, I know he wants to have some fun with the two youngest girls in the shed, God help them."

The young woman with the blonde hair said in a whisper, "What, what will they do with them?"

The woman behind the bar laughed, a vicious cackle, "He'll do whatever he wants to do with them and I doubt if there'll be much left after he's finished. What you idiots don't seem to realize is that you're all expendable, you can all be replaced, we just have to take a trip topside, there's prey everywhere, we can pick up what and who we like anytime we wanna do it. Eventually we'll get fed up with all of ya and then we'll go looking for some fresh meat."

Ghost saw a hand reach out across the counter and viciously pinch the blonde's left nipple, the girl flinched backward and gave a small scream.

"Yep, think I'll have some fun with you later on, cheeky little bitch."

Ghost lay down, his head going down the stairs first and like a silent snake he wiggled his way down. The other naked woman suddenly looked in his direction and a look of shock appeared on her face and her mouth flew open, he quickly shook his head and put his finger to his mouth whispering to himself, "For God's sake, pretend I'm not here." The look on the young woman's face quickly changed to understanding and she nodded slightly turning her attention back to the woman behind the counter.

Ghost lay perfectly still, waiting. Another can of beer was put across the counter onto the serving tray. He brought his blowpipe up to his mouth and let his body slide down one more step, now, in this position, he could see the two arms of the woman behind the bar as she put some more beer across the counter. He waited patiently for a couple of minutes, it felt like hours, as the trays were loaded. The woman lent against the backside of the counter putting the last beer onto a tray and rested her arms on the marble top.

"There ya go, take that load out and be quick about it, ya don't wanna get Jacob mad."

Suddenly she slapped her left forearm with her right hand, "What the hell, goddamn bugs!"

She pulled her right hand away and just had time to see the little dart. "What the hell?" was all she managed to say before she slid from the counter, unconscious and close to death before she hit the floor. The poison on the dart was strong enough to stop any animal in its tracks, it worked extremely fast, paralyzing the nervous system, rendering the prey unable to move or make a noise or even blink an eye and then it stopped the muscles in the heart and death came swiftly.

"What the hell was that?" said the blonde startled, leaning over the counter trying to see what had happened. The other young woman just tapped the blonde on the shoulder, pulling her back slightly and pointed toward the stairs. The blonde stood up straight and looked across to where the other was pointing just in time to see a black body slithering down the stairs.

"Oh my God! What the hell?" she opened her mouth and was about to scream, the other girl, realizing what was about to happen, wrapped her hand around the blonde's mouth stopping the scream even as it came to the top of her vocal chords.

"Hush! Shush! Be quiet! Whoever it is is obviously here to help us. Do you understand?"

The blonde stood rigid for a second and then gently nodded her head as the hand was removed from over her mouth.

Ghost slipped down the stairs, staring around to see if everything was clear, as he squatted and started to rise he whispered, "Is there anyone else around?"

Both of the girls shook their heads in unison. The dark haired one whispered, "No, she's the only one," she corrected herself pointing to behind the counter, "She was the only one in the house. Who are you?"

Ghost walked over toward them, slid behind the counter, bent down and made sure that the body was dead and retrieved his dart.

"We're here to help you, Joanna, one of the girls tied to the barrels, told us what was going on. We're here to get you out."

"Joanna, oh my God, are they alive, we saw them shooting at them."

"Two of them, Joanna and another, are both wounded but alive, the other one didn't make it."

Ghost watched the sadness creep across their faces.

"How many of these bastards are there?"

"There's ten, I mean, there was ten, now there's nine," the dark haired woman said with a smile coming to her face "This is fantastic! Oh my God, we're going to be rescued."

"Ok, in actual fact there's now eight, now I counted seven around the fire, three women and four men, do you know where the other one is?"

"There's one on duty at the end of the dock and there's one on sentry duty up at the top of the drive way," said the blonde.

"The one on the dock is dead so we've got to worry about the one at the top of the slope. Ok, what you two have got to do, this is going to be difficult, you've got to take those beers out, you've got to act as if nothing ever happened in here, you've got to take whatever they do until we take care of them, everything must appear normal to them, can you do that, both of you?"

The two stood silent for a moment, looked at each other and then they both nodded.

"Ya know something?" said the dark haired one "I'll almost enjoy doing this, I'll enjoy serving them their beer knowing that it may be their last."

"Whatever you do, don't change your demeanor, don't act as if anything's happened in here, you've got to remain the same beaten down young women as you were before. As soon as you've picked up all the empties move back toward this cabin but as you're coming back move a little toward the river, I don't want anything between me and those at the fire, ok?"

"Ok," said the blonde as they picked up their trays and moved toward the door and as they went through out into the darkness Ghost saw the dark one gently nudge the blonde in the ribs. Ghost made a quick run through the house, it only took him a minute, there was nobody, the house was empty. He went through the kitchen to the right and out of the door at the far end of the building into the darkness carrying his knapsack. He slid down under the wooden deck that stretched across the front of the building; he eased himself out, head first, beside the main steps from where he had a clear path across the compound. He reached into the knapsack and got out another short blowpipe that screwed into the end of the short one that he had used in the house, the new pipe was four feet long. He watched the young women distribute the beer, watched both the men and the women grab them and pinch them, the two young women acted beautifully. He watched as they gathered up empty cans and bottles and two of the women around the fire threw empty cans at them, he watched as they walked away from the fire towards him, carefully their path took them slightly to the right, it wasn't enough to really be noticed but it took them out of the field of aim between him and those sitting around the fire. He put two fingers in his mouth and the night rang out with a piercing birdcall, those around the fire didn't even notice it.

Mary reached out and touched Amber on the shoulder, leaning over she whispered in her ear, "There's possibly trouble up to our left," she had read Ghost's birdcall, "probably some sort of a sentry."

"You ok down here?" Amber whispered, "I'll go and take care of it, ok?"

"Ok, be careful."

Amber moved off behind the buildings.

"She's very good," thought Mary to herself trying hard to follow Amber's movements but failing to see or hear anything as she herself inched forward silently to a small shrub about ten feet in front of the building. She waited giving Amber time to move up the driveway to see what was going on and then she gave her husband a birdcall.

She watched, as one of the men sitting around the fire, the one closest to her husband's position slapped the side of his neck, he seemed to try to stand up but just crouched down and then rolled off the log he was sitting on.

"Gawd you drink too much, you're just nothing but a drunken bum," said the man sitting next to him, kicking what was now, unbeknown to him, a lifeless body beside him, thinking his associate had rolled over drunk.

Mary took a deep breath, put her blow pipe to her lips and let a dart fly and watched as an older woman on her side of the fire sat up straight and said "Fucking mosquitoes" and then slowly rolled over onto the ground.

One after another those around the fire seemed to just collapse, it took a couple of minutes for the others to realize that something was terribly wrong. Five of them were dead or dying before the last ones reacted. One stood up, a stupid mistake, he let out a scream as a dart penetrated his left eye and was still screaming as he died falling forward onto the fire sending red hot ambers flying into the night. The last one had the sense to fall flat on her face in the dirt between her dead compatriots, searching around desperately she kept her head down trying hard to figure out what was going on. She lay there for three or four minutes and, at last, had the presence of mind to reach over and drag a pistol from underneath one of the bodies. She screamed into the night, "What the fuck are you, who are you? Who the hell are you? Where are you? Show yourselves you bastards. C'mon out," she put her head up and shot aimlessly into the night, a bullet passed through the leaves above Mary, she took slow deliberate aim. She could just see the top of the woman's head each time she popped up to take a shot, Mary waited and then, with a big puff of air from her lungs she sent one of her deadly little darts sticking into the top of the woman's scalp. The woman slapped at it, rose up slightly and then slapped at the front of her throat as another dart hit her in the throat, she rolled over and lay still. The silence was eerie; after the shots the silence seemed to eat everything.

Ghost slowly rose up from his position startling the two young ladies who were standing no more than ten feet away from him on the other side of the steps, they had never even seen him, had no idea he was there.

"Stay where you are, don't move you two, let us make sure everything's ok, there's still one of them out there somewhere." He drew his knife from a scabbard around his waist and slowly moved toward the bonfire watching his wife rise up from behind the bush, her blowpipe ready.

The sentry sat on a rock at the top of the sloping driveway leading down from the plateau above the camp. He was thirty-two years old, going slightly bald on top with a mop of unruly brown hair. He was a big man, stood six foot one in his stocking feet, a big beer belly hung over his grubby pants, he had tattoos up and down both arms that disappeared into his t-shirt. He sniffed and wiped his nose on the bottom of his t-shirt, he sat on sentry duty sipping one of the beers that he had managed to take up with him. "If Jacob knew I'd been drinking beer on sentry duty he'd be furious," he thought to himself. He had been on duty for an hour and a half and had another two and a half hours before he was due to be relieved. He sat there, binoculars hanging around his neck and a rifle resting on the log beside him. It was pitch black and his eyes were getting tired, he rested his head back onto a rock and thought to himself, "I want that Michelle tonight," he almost whispered it aloud, "Oh, she's such a sexy little bitch, I've got to get to her before the others do, oh my, the things I'm going to do with that one." His hand went down and he rubbed his crotch.

He thought he heard something, lazily he opened his eyes, looking around and then suddenly something went over his face and held his head still, he felt a sudden sharp pain run across his throat. He reached his hand up, looking at it in the dark, feeling it sticky and warm, he took a breath and the air gurgled in his lungs. "My God," he thought as he realized that something was attacking him, he hazily realized that his throat had been cut from one side to the other and he was dying. He could hear his lungs gurgling as the blood poured down into them and life drained out of him. "What the hell happened?" was his last thought as the hand let go of his head and he died, still leaning against the rock.

Amber moved back in the shadows going down the slope, she heard the gunshots, she counted them; one-, two-, three-, four-, five-, six-. That was it, six in all and then there was silence, complete and utter silence. Slowly, all senses alert, she moved back down the slope, very carefully she looked at the camp. She came around the bottom curve just in time to see Ghost and Mary moving and checking the bodies by the fire.

"Damn," she thought to herself "I'd hate to have to meet them on a dark night and be on the opposite side." She gave a birdcall and watched as Ghost looked round, spotted her in the shadows and waived for her to come in.

The two young women who had been serving moved over to the fireplace, the blonde started kicking one of the bodies viciously. "You bastard, you dirty filthy rotten bastard, you got what you deserved, I wish I could've given it to you but I watched, I watched," she yelled at the still form.

The other one grabbed hold of her, they turned around to face each other and started to cry. Mary went over to them, giving them a hug.

"Are you two ok?"

Both of the young women nodded, moving apart slowly and trying to dry the tears that ran down their faces.

"Where are the others, where are they being kept?"

The blonde pointed to the building next to the one where Mary had been hiding. "They're all in there, they're all locked in. Jacob, that one there," she pointed to the body that had fallen on the fire, the top half of him was roasting in the flames and the smell of burning flesh was beginning to surround them. "That's Jacob, he's the worst, he's the leader, no one dared stand up to him, we actually saw him shoot one of his own because they challenged him, he's got the keys to the building in his pants pocket. He kept them, wouldn't let anybody else have them."

Mary moved over and pulled the body out of the fire by his legs, the clothes on the upper half were still burning and so was the flesh around his face and neck. She quickly ran her hands through his pant's pockets and came up with a set of keys that she held up looking at the two girls.

"That's them," said the brunette "that's them."

"I've got the keys," she said to her husband as Amber joined them by the fire.

"Why don't you two go over, take these two young ladies with you and let the others free. I'm going to retrieve our darts and search these bodies, I think we can just throw them on the fire, I don't think we should waste any time burying them," replied her husband.

Amber and Mary nodded in unison.

"I'll give you a hand if that's ok?" said the brunette to Ghost.

Ghost nodded his approval. They went through Jacob's pockets and then rolled him over onto the fire again knocking the big pile of logs over so that sparks flew everywhere, rising up into the night sky. Then they moved to a woman, the next body closest to them, checking to see if there was anything they should take as Amber, Mary, and the blonde headed for the hut.

It took three tries to find the right key and then the lock came off and the door creaked open and they peered into the darkness.

"Run back and get a burning log will you please, we need some light," Mary said to the blonde who reached around the corner of the door and suddenly the lights went on.

"Silly me, forgot there was electricity," smiled Mary. She looked around at the scared and terrified faces of the young people cowering against the back wall of the building.

"Ok, ok," said Amber very gently "we're here to help you, we're friends, you can come out, all those bastards are dead, you don't have to worry about them anymore. C'mon, anybody hurt? Is everybody ok?"

Very slowly understanding came into their eyes; Mary could see their demeanor alter as they realized that they were being rescued. The first one to her feet was a young woman, Amber thought she could not be anymore than eighteen years old.

"Who are you? How did you get here? Are you sure that everybody's dead and that it's safe?"

The blonde went over and gave her a hug. "Yes, its safe, they've killed them all, all those bastards are dead. Wendy and the man that came with these two are piling the bodies onto the fire right now, come out and you can see them burn."

Amber cringed at the way she said the word "burn".

Slowly they all got up and came out of the hut, only then did they fully realize that they were safe. They were all dressed in skimpy torn clothing and they all slowly moved toward the fire.

"God only knows what they've been through," Mary said quietly to Amber coming out of the hut last having made sure there was nobody left behind. "It's going to take them a while, some of them may never get over it but at least they're safe."

Amber nodded resting her hand on Mary's arm.

"Where did you and your husband learn or get your training?"

"We didn't have any training per se, we learned it from some tribes living up the Amazon."

"Sometime I think I'd like to meet those people," and they both started to laugh, the nervousness coming out in the form of laughter.

Ghost looked up as the young people came towards him and he could hear the laughter behind them. He reached into the back of his belt and pulled out a radio.

"Last Chance, Last Chance, Ghost here."

"Hello Ghost. Are you ok, is everybody ok, what's happening?"

"Everything's ok up here, we took no prisoners. Everyone is safe and nobody's hurt, the prisoners are free, we're going to sort things out here, we'll stay to make sure that we have everything that we can possibly use and to tidy up the mess that we've made, we won't be coming down the river till the day after tomorrow. That will give the young people some time to pull themselves together and to put some sort of closure to their ordeal. There's a couple of power boats, canoes, etc. and we'll bring them home with us but we're all safe now."

"Thank God, we were worried. Ok, we can sleep now, we'll see you the day after tomorrow, be careful, make sure that you're safe."

"We'll set up a sentry post just in case but from what I can tell, other than the prisoners, there's nobody else. We'll give you a call in the morning."

"Ok, well done, we'll see you in the morning."

Ghost then turned to start answering the many questions that were pouring out of the young people. Some sat down and others piled more logs onto the funeral pyre.

38

Indian arrives.

Indian rode around a tall thick line of trees and reined his horse back, he was riding a little ahead of the others, deep in thought. He and Sunshine had discussed how they were going to get the horses to Last Chance. They had decided that the best way would be to go up river to the boat rental place and one of them could go down to Last Chance and get them to come up and pick up the horses up in a boat, or a raft, the horses were too valuable just to let them go loose.

Sunshine pulled up beside him, "What's up honey?"

Indian raised his hand and pointed. "I don't like the look of that," he was pointing at a thick plume of smoke that was rising up ahead of them. "That looks as if it's in the direction where we're heading, there's nothing else around but the Canuck camp, I just don't like the look of it."

"You would've thought that they'd be trying to keep themselves a little more secret, it looks like a helluva big fire, it's just too big to be an ordinary campfire.

They both sat there for a few minutes watching the thick plume of smoke rising in the distance.

"Well, I guess we'll just have to wait and see, as we've discussed, the only way we're going to get the horses down to Last Chance is by boat and it certainly wouldn't be safe to go to the town down river, God only knows what we'd run into there, we've seen enough horrors along the way."

Indian nodded, "we'd better be careful though, who knows what we'll run into, the damn world's gone mad, ordinary people have turned into killers and mass murderers, I'll be so glad to get the girls and Kerry safely stashed away at Last Chance."

Sunshine nodded as the others came up and stopped beside them.

"What'd we stop for?" said Kerry as he stood up in the stirrups and rubbed his butt.

Sunshine just pointed.

"Is that where we're going?" asked Paula brushing her hair out of her face.

"As far as I know the only community in the area is the one that we're going to. It's a camp right down on the river where they rent out canoes, rubber rafts and they have a couple of high-speed boats, it's fairly rough and rugged but it's booked solid most of the year. Mostly young people coming down to ride the rapids just above the camp. It's been there for many years, run by the same family, they've made a few improvements but the accommodations are pretty rugged. They don't normally have any trouble, a few drunks here and there, I suppose these days they might have some trouble with a few people smoking pot, etc. but they kept pretty good control over everybody, I just don't like the look of that smoke, it could spell trouble.

They sat silently for a few minutes then Diane said, "Well, the only way we're gonna find out is to go and have a look, you said we couldn't go down river, it wouldn't be very safe and we all know how important the horses have become, we can't afford to let them go free, so let's go and have a look."

Indian nodded and they moved forward.

Later on that afternoon as they were following a dirt road they came to where the steep driveway went off to the left down to the canoe camp, they were really close to where the smoke was billowing up, it was obvious that the fire was down at camp Canuck, they dismounted and tethered the horses in a group of bushes.

"Sunshine, honey, you take Kerry and Paula and take the right hand side of driveway, I'll take Diane and Iggy and go down the other side, we'll wait until it's dark just in case there's trouble, we can wait in these shrubs, they're pretty good cover, we can have something to eat without building a fire and get some rest and then we'll go down and see what's going on.

His wife nodded and they all settled down, the two girls lay back making themselves as comfortable as possible on the ground, Paula fell asleep immediately while Diane just closed her eyes, the rest of them sat and watched the sun going down, the shadows lengthened and moved and as the darkness came it was so quiet that you could hear the night animals and insects coming out.

"Ok, it's dark enough, let's go," said Indian rousing everyone, "Be very careful, Diane and I will take the point on this side of the driveway, you stay back a little ways on the other side."

They moved off across the road going from cover to cover, Indian kept Iggy close by him with Diane just behind him. The driveway went around a bend in the rocks, it was fairly narrow and Indian realized it was the perfect place for an ambush, he signaled to Diane to stop behind a rocky outcrop as he peered around looking out for any one who might be watching out for them, he could not see anybody and all he could hear was the sound of the wildlife. He whispered something to Iggy who immediately disappeared around the rocks, Indian watched the dog very carefully as he went from cover to cover, his brown fur making him invisible against the brownish rock, Iggy went about two hundred feet and suddenly stopped and took up a point position, crouched low, nose pointing forward, completely still.

"Somebody's in those rocks across the driveway, see how Iggy's pointing? There must be a sentry or a lookout or someone up there, I can't see anybody, they must be very well hidden. I'd better warn Sunshine."

He put his fingers to his mouth and a lovely bird sang in the evening darkness. A couple of seconds later he heard Sunshine's birdcall coming from slightly back from where they were.

"What do we do now?" he thought. Suddenly his head twitched as another birdcall echoed through the night, he knew instantly it was not his wife but the birdcall had said that somebody knew they were there. Somebody was familiar with the birdcalls taught to him in the Special Forces. He knelt down a little shaken, whoever was on guard duty now knew they were there. He sat there for a minute or two collecting his thoughts, he shook his head and then he put his fingers in his mouth and his birdcall rang into the night.

There was silence for a moment and then a bird answered back from the rocks ahead, "Friend or foe?"

Indian shook his head, the tone was familiar to him, everyone had their own peculiar way of making the bird calls, after a little while you could actually identify who was sending out the calls just by the very slight changes and innuendos. The person up there on sentry duty was familiar, he shook his head trying hard to remember who it was.

A birdcall rang out again it meant, "Come forward."

Indian made a decision, he turned to Diane, "Keep me covered, the only way we're going to solve this mystery is to find out who that is up there."

"What the hell are you talking about that's Sunshine, she's just answering you."

"No that's not Sunshine, that's someone else, somebody who knows the birdcalls and knows how to use them, they're over there in the rocks to the right of the driveway where Iggy's pointing and they're very good because I can't spot them. I'm going to go out and see if they'll meet with me, just make sure you don't shoot anyone unless I suddenly raise my right arm above my head and then you don't miss, you shoot to kill. Do you understand?"

Diane nodded and Indian knew that after what they had been through she would do exactly as he asked.

He sent out another birdcall ringing in the evening air, the answer came back immediately, "Come forward."

Indian put down his rifle, stepped out from behind the rocks, held his hands out away from his body and walked into the middle of the driveway. He watched as a dark shadow slid from the top of the rocky bluff and stepped out of the darkness of the shadows and onto the middle of the driveway. The way the person moved and the outline in the darkness was familiar but Indian could not put a name to the figure he was seeing.

"Indian, my old friend, I would recognize your birdcall anywhere, anytime, yet you've failed to recognize mine."

The use of his name shocked Indian, he knew that voice, he had not heard it for a number of years, it took him a couple of seconds but suddenly he put the name to the form that had climbed down from the rocks and started walking towards him.

"Amber? Amber is that you?"

There was a roar of laughter as Amber moved towards him.

"Yes, Indian, it is I, what the hell are you doing coming down this driveway?"

"Well what the hell are you doing hidden up there in those rocks? What are you doing in this part of the world anyway? My God!" He walking toward her, happy to see his old friend, they had been on many missions together but he had lost track of her when she left the forces.

"Iggy, stand down." Iggy relaxed and moved out of the shadows to stand beside his master.

"Oh, so that's how you knew I was there," Amber said looking at Iggy "I didn't even know you were coming until I heard your birdcall. Are you alone?"

"First of all, what are you doing here? Are you friend or foe?"

"I've come up from a camp down the river, we came up to rescue some young people who were being held prisoner down the driveway here at the canoe camp. What are you doing here?"

"You're from Last Chance, how the hell did you find out about Last Chance? How did you get there?" Then he remembered that the rest of his party was still in hiding. "It's ok, Diane, it's ok, you can come out. Sunshine bring everyone forward, it's ok, this is Amber and somehow she's up here from Last Chance. Come and meet her."

Shadowy forms emerged from the rocks and the bushes as they all came forward, eager to meet Amber.

"We're heading to Last Chance, we have horses back in some bush a ways down the road and we figured the only way we could get them down to Last Chance was from the canoe camp. What's all the smoke, you can see it for miles and miles."

"There was a bunch of maniacs mistreating a group of young people, Ghost, his wife and I took out the bad guys and the young people are putting the bodies on a funeral pyre, it seems to help them get some closure on what was being done to them and it seems to be easing their misery a bit. Now who do we have here?" she said shaking hands with Sunshine.

Indian introduced his party to her one by one and then Kerry and Paula went back and brought the horses forward.

"I'll let Ghost know that you're coming down, I'm going to get back on look out duty just in case," she took a walkie-talkie from her belt. "Ghost, Ghost, come in."

"Hello, Amber what is it?"

"We have visitors, it's ok, they're friendly, I believe you know who they are, the leader of the group goes by the name of Indian."

There was silence for a moment. "You've got to be kidding, are you sure it's Indian? What the hell's he doing here? Oh my God, send them down, send them down."

"They're on their way, I'm going back to sentry duty, I've still got a couple of hours before you send someone to relieve me."

"Well done Amber, I just can't believe that Indian has turned up here!"

Amber stepped forward and threw herself into the arms of Indian, hugging him.

"It's been a long time my friend, we've a lot to catch up on, you go on down and we'll talk later" and she moved back and started up the rocky cliff. Sunshine moved over to her husband and took his hand.

"Well that was one big surprise, wasn't it? Who's Amber?"

"She was one of my team members back in the days before I met you, she ran into some terrible mess in Afghanistan and she couldn't get over it. We never knew exactly what happened, she'd been with the team for a number of years and she was extremely good but whatever happened twisted her badly and she left the forces. I never heard from her again, I did get a report from another old friend that she was going wandering around, living on the streets but I don't know if that was true or not. I'm sure glad to see her, she will be a great addition to Last Chance. Let's get down to the camp, Ghost is waiting for us, let's go," he turned to the rest of his group, "this is the last leg of our journey."

They all moved down the steep sloping driveway, around the bottom corner to be eagerly met by Ghost, who introduced them to everyone, it seemed like old home week, Indian and Ghost just kept chatting away trying to catch up on what had happened to each other through the years.

Diane, Paula and Kerry eventually went off and sat talking with the other young people, their arrival seemed to have lightened up the mood somewhat. By the time the last of the bodies had been burned the sun was coming up over the canyon walls. Ghost, Indian and Amber had sat around talking all night bringing each other up to date on what had been happening in their lives before the President's speech and then what had followed in the aftermath. The next morning Ghost informed Joshua at Last Chance that Indian and his group was there, Joshua was shocked and thrilled. Now the problem was to get everybody down river to Last Chance with the horses.

The young people, with Sunshine and Amber, were raiding the camp and packing up everything they thought could be useful.

Indian and Ghost stood and looked out over the river.

"We can take all the people and all the supplies down by the boats, the canoes, and the rubber rafts, there should be plenty of room for everybody. The question is what do we do with the horses, we can't just leave them," said Ghost.

"I don't know, I really don't know but you're right, we really can't just set them loose, they may become invaluable."

A young black man overheard their conversation and walked over to them.

"Excuse me, if I might make a suggestion?"

"Yes Bob go ahead," said Ghost.

"You really don't have a problem, that dock is a floating dock, all you have to do is cut it loose, it's big enough to take all the horses and just about everybody else. You just have to guide it downstream."

Ghost and Indian sat there in silence looking at each other then they both roared with laughter.

"God aren't we stupid! The solution's right in front of our eyes and we didn't even see it, Bob you're wonderful, you're right that's the answer, we just have to cut it loose. Thank you Bob."

Bob just nodded and moved on as Indian turned to Ghost. "Well, there's our answer, let's get this party on the road, or rather, let's get this party on the water."

39

Last Chance.

Joshua stood with his back to a rock that was part of the canyon wall facing out toward the river, around him, in a semi-circle seated on log seats were all the members of the community, off to his right Jenny sat at a desk, paper and pencil ready and her recording devices set up on a desk.

"May I have your attention please" he waited as the chatter subsided. "Your attention please ladies and gentlemen." The chatter slowly died and the quietness of the early evening engulfed them.

"Ladies and gentlemen, I call to order this, the first full Assembly of the community known as Last Chance. This Assembly will be held and controlled by the members of the community so my first order of business is to make a proposal. I propose that Jenny," he looked over toward Jenny who nodded at him, "be appointed the secretary for all the assemblies for a one-year period, will someone second that motion, please?"

Ghost stood up, "I second that motion."

"Are there any questions on the motion?" Everybody looked around at each other and shook their heads.

"There being no questions, we'll take a vote, all those in favor of Jenny being appointed "Secretary of Assemblies" for a one-year period please raise their hand."

Every hand in front of him was raised.

"Excellent," Joshua looked over at Jenny "you are now the official Secretary for a one-year period." He looked back over his audience.

"This is, thankfully, the first full Assembly of this community at last everyone has arrived safely. We do have some unexpected members who have turned up or been collected along the way," there were giggles and laughter and some nudging going on, "everyone is welcome to the community. Now then, for those of you who don't know, everything that we have here and even the very existence of Last Chance has been financially made viable by Judge Mortimer, this included all the tuitions for the original six 'bad boys' right through their professional and university educations. He has financed all the supplies, equipment, livestock and everything that is now part of our existence, I think we owe him an enormous debt of gratitude." He looked over to the Judge who was sitting in the front row in front of him. "Your Honor, we thank you." Everyone stood up and clapped and whistled, trying to show their appreciation for what the Judge had done.

"I have asked the Judge, after consulting with everybody in this Assembly in a one-to-one conversation, I have asked him if he would take over as the "President Elect" of the community to set up and put in place some form of governing body. I've done this because some of us don't know each other well. Even the original young men from the first class of Last Chance have not seen each other for many years, we've grown apart, we've married and we even have one young one on the way. We don't know the young men of the second class, although we are getting to know them very fast and we're even beginning to learn who's a pain in the arse and who isn't." There was a roar of laughter from the young people. "Some of us are strangers who've been thrust into this community and who we all need to get to know. So, because of this, I put another motion on the floor. "I propose that Judge Mortimer be elected the 'President of Last Chance' for a one-year period with the full authority to form some sort of a governing body and to appoint, at his discretion, a body of people into whatever key positions he deems fit. At the end of one year all positions, including that of the President, will be voted on again. Do I have a second to that motion?"

Brad stood up, "I second that motion."

"Are there any questions on the motion?"

"What positions of authority does the Judge expect to create?" Kyle asked.

"At this time," said Joshua addressing his question "I believe we should leave it entirely up to the Judge, he's had many years of experience. This will be a learning process we are an unique community and the Judge will, as will we all, have to find our way by trial and error, lets leave it in his capable hands for now and see how things work out for the first year. At the end of one year the Assembly may change, alter and/or remove, by majority vote, any of the positions, etc. that the Judge has put in place. The one-year period is purely to give us all time to recognize and to learn what our community needs and doesn't need. Obviously, not everyone will agree or be happy with every decision that's made but we have to put some form of order in place to keep running smoothly. Does that answer your question, Kyle?"

Kyle nodded and sat down.

"Are there any other questions?"

There was silence.

"Ok, let's vote on the motion, all those in favor raise their right hand."

Every right hand in front of him was raised.

"So be it, Judge Mortimer, you are now the official 'President of Last Chance'. I yield the chair to you."

Judge Mortimer stood up in front of the assembly as Joshua took his seat.

"First of all, I would like to welcome you all and to say how proud I am of the way that you have handled yourselves and of the way that everyone has mucked in to get all that we have here set up. Being made the President honors me, I really don't like the term President but for now we'll let it stand, it smacks too much of the old governing regime of the country. For the want of better terminologies and on a very preliminary basis, I will immediately appoint six section heads. The first section is Defense, I hereby appoint Quiet Sunshine and Indian to head up that section. The second section will be Agriculture, I appoint Roger and Mary to head up that section. The third section is Animal Husbandry, I appoint Rob. The fourth section is the Medical section and, of course, I appoint Doctor June to be in charge of it. The fifth section will be Housing, I appoint Roger and Jill to head this section. The sixth section is an ombudsman at Large, the function of this particular section is to be in touch with everyone in the community, to listen to suggestions and questions, to gather information and make proposals to me. This position will be my key right hand person and, if for any reason I am incapable of carrying out my duties this person will step in for the rest of my one-year period, this will be Pattern. Are there any questions about my appointments?"

The Judge looked over the assembly, there were some whispers, there were some sighs but nobody stood up.

"So be it. This will be the preliminary governing body of the community for the first year. Everything will be done democratically, everything will be voted on and the majority of votes, even if it's a majority of one, will carry it. It has been suggested by numerous people that we write a new constitution, that we basically adopt the old constitution of the United States but rewrite it, modernize it and address some new concerns and some things that have been left terribly in question. I have already started a rewrite, it is however, a tremendous task and will take a great deal of time and I will continue, to solicit ideas over the next twelve months. Are there any questions about what I've said?"

There were a few questions about the boundaries of the different sections and who was going to be helping or stepping up in place should someone be incapable of fulfilling their duties. The Judge explained that not everything had been decided upon, after all he had only, forty-eight hours earlier, been made aware that he was going to actually be voted into office. He explained that he would have an open-door policy, everyone was welcome to come and discuss anything at any time. Any problems that arose could be discussed, everything was a work-in-progress and personalities would have to be taken into consideration. There was a question about laws and the consequences of illegal actions.

"We will, of course, have to rely quite a lot on the old laws," said the Judge in answer to the question. "We will, however, have to adjust the procedures and the consequences as we go along. As we stand right now I, and I say this fervently, don't believe that there will be an immediate problem or that we will have to face legal action for quite some time. But I can foresee that the ultimate punishment could be the banishment from the community, this, I believe, would be a tremendous deterrent to stop people from doing stupid things."

Many heads nodded in agreement, they realized that to be banished from Last Chance would probably be a death sentence.

"Are there any new motions or new business that we need to attend to?"

There was silence and then the Judge saw a hand raised at the very back row.

"I see a hand in the back row, is that you Nellie? Please stand up."

A small petite young lass, who could not have been any more than fourteen years old stood up, her flaming red hair blew in the breeze and people gasped. Nellie had been one of the young people rescued from the expedition up river, she'd been in a state of shock and had not spoken a word since they rescued her up at the rafting camp. Doctor June had taken a shine to her and had taken her under her wing, she could not find anything medically wrong with her, Nellie had just decided that she had nothing to say. Everybody turned around with a surprised look on his or her face.

"Yes, Nellie what would you like to say?" said the Judge just as surprised as everyone else.

""I errr, I'd like to make a motion," said Nellie, her young voice loud and clear so that everyone could hear her. "I would like to make a motion to change the name of Last Chance."

There was a collective gasp throughout the Assembly, people started to whisper to each other and to look at her in complete surprise.

"Ok, Nellie, you're making a motion to change the name of Last Chance, what would you like to change it to?"

The whispering ceased and all eyes turned to Nellie in expectation while trying to control their emotions.

"I make a motion that we change the name of Last Chance to," Nellie paused, she seemed to be enjoying the attention and the expectation, "change the name to Best Chance."

There was absolute silence, you could have heard a pin drop on the ground as what she was proposing was absorbed, then slowly someone started to clap and then the whole Assembly stood up and started to clap.

"Alright, order, order," said the Judge with a big grin across his face. "Nellie, you have made an excellent motion. Quiet please everybody, come on, quiet," said the Judge waiting for people to sit back down "A motion has been put on the floor to change the name of Last Chance to Best Chance, do we have someone to second it?"

The whole assembly stood as one, hands raised.

"The motion has been seconded, let's say it's been seconded by Joshua. Please be seated, please be seated, are there any questions on the motion?"

Again there was silence.

"In that case let's take a vote, all those in favor of changing the name from Last Chance to Best Chance please raise your right hand."

Every right hand was raised.

"The motion is carried unanimously, henceforth this community will be known as Best Chance.